The Noble Enemy

P9-AEZ-081

The Noble Enemy

A NOVEL

by Charles Fox

DOUBLEDAY & COMPANY, INC.
Garden City, New York
1980

"You Are My Sunshine," Copyright © 1930 by Peer International Corp. Copyright renewed © 1957 by Peer International Corp. Used by permission. All rights reserved.

ISBN: 0-385-14526-8
Library of Congress Catalog Card Number 78-22770

COPYRIGHT © 1980 BY CHARLES FOX
ALL RIGHTS RESERVED
PRINTED IN THE UNITED STATES OF AMERICA
FIRST EDITION

To my mother, Enid Duncan, who lost
a son to America
and to
Diane, for better or for worse

C. 1

Acknowledgment

To my editor, Luther Nichols.

I'd also like to offer Shirley Birdsall, Barouch Feldenkrais, my sister Sue Graham, Sarah Hammond, Yola Jurzykowski, Harri Peccinotti and Tom Quinn, my thanks and my love.

Contents

The Noble Enemy

Part I

THE FIGHT

T HEY SET THE fight for Saturday night at the Okie's place on the slough. Arizo waited until Thursday before he spread the word. He was that cautious because a big fight had been busted only two weeks earlier in the Oakland hills. The crew of a California Highway Patrol helicopter spotted maybe fifty cars parked around a shed in a remote orchard. They ought to have considered that possibility, Arizo thought. It was poor planning. The cops caught them with the ring up, and threw six dogs in the back of a police station wagon. Six fight-ready Pit Bulls. No one ever saw a fight like it. Fresno Wheeler said the cops damn near shot the dogs before they turned the handlers loose to break it up. There was no telling how dumb cops could be. Still, he would do things differently for his fight. To be safe.

When he got home from work Thursday night, Arizo showered and ate dinner, and afterwards, while Ruby was watching the television, made several calls. "It's on for Saturday night," he said. "It's Baby Zeus and Dynamite from Oregon. Top dog in the northwest. We'll pick up. Okay?" To some people he gave a time. But that was about all he said. There wasn't any more to say, and he didn't like the telephone.

Besides the Okie, only four of them knew where the fight would be: he and Eli Gardner, the Oregon dog's handler; Fresno Wheeler, the referee; and Arizo's closest friend, Nick Morrano. Arizo didn't even tell Ruby, the girl he shared his house with.

Morrano was built like Arizo: a dark little handball of a man, shy and always squinting, creasing up a maze of wrinkles about his eyes that stayed pale when the rest of him was burned Sicilian brown. The lines and the sun had put ten years on Morrano. He looked forty, close to Arizo's age, which was thirty-six. Morrano liked his wine. He traveled with a jug, usually Gallo Hearty Burgundy. Morrano had had misgivings about the fight from the start. Now he said so openly. "You sure it's gonna be a good fight, Mike? Saddler says Dynamite's beat the best dogs east to Wyoming." They talked on the back steps of Arizo's house, passing the jug between them. "Saddler says Dynamite can whip your dog."

"What does Saddler know," Arizo said. "Saddler don't know shit. He don't know what I done with Zeus. Anyway, Morrano, you with me or what?"

"Saddler says it'll take a killing to stop the Oregon dog. I don't want Zeus chewed to death," Morrano said. "I like the dog."

"Am I a fool, Morrano? Am I a fool?"

"No," said Morrano. "But you're all wrapped up in that dog. Maybe you can't see it."

Arizo shook his head. "It's going to be a good fight, I tell you. Baby Zeus is gonna surprise a whole bunch of people."

Nick Morrano looked at his friend awhile, making up his mind. Then he closed his eyes and said, "Let me tell you, Mike. You ain't no dummy. But you know what I did?"

"What?"

"I called Saddler myself. Pretended I was smart money. 'What's the tip on this Zeus?' I said. You know what he said? He said, 'It's like I been tellin' everybody. I rolled Baby Zeus three times, an' he's a lousy bottom dog. He's good for maybe twenty minutes.' That's what Saddler said, Mike. Honest to God. He said, 'If that Injun thinks different, he's more full of shit than I thought.' "

Arizo was silent for a moment. He looked straight out across the yard to where the dog lay in the dirt. Then he said, "Is that what he said? Straight up?"

"Straight up."

"Well, fuck him. Goddamn, busted Okie. It's me he don't like."

"Suit yourself," Morrano said and raised the jug to his mouth.

So the smart money was calling Saddler and not him? Well, they weren't so smart after all, Arizo thought. But nonetheless, you didn't argue with Saddler when it came to dogs. No matter what, Saddler had raised and trained and fought Pits longer than anyone alive. He was from Houstonia, Missouri. He advertised in every issue of *Pit Dog Report*: "ACTION. Open to Match. Will Travel." Under that was a picture of his best dog: "Doc's Little Toad out of Hemphill's Geronimo," its Kennel Club number, and then, "Breeder and Shipper of all American (Pit) Bull Terriers. The Kind that Satisfys [*sic*]. The All-Purpose Dog. Satisfied Customers in Every State, Canada & Mexico."

"Then," Morrano went on, "Saddler says Dynamite could fight good anywhere. He'd do good in the south. He'd do good in Texas, even. He's won four money fights. I hate like hell to go 'gainst my own dog. But hell. I gotta be honest with you."

Four fights is a lot. Most dogs aren't ready to fight till they're three. They'll fight before. Pit Bulls will fight and kill anything from the time they're six months. Bitches are usually ready to fight before dogs. But if you fight an animal before it's ready, you'll likely ruin it. So you don't put a dog into a money fight till it's three, and by the time it's six or seven it's usually through. You can lose six months while scars heal if it's a hard fight. Then the dog has to be conditioned again and that can take months, too.

Saddler had rolled Baby Zeus before he sold him to Arizo. There's often a roll before a money fight. Saddler rolled Zeus at sixteen months. He put him in with an experienced fighter twenty pounds heavier. Zeus looked good for fifteen minutes, so Saddler

two-dogged him: threw in another. Soon after that, Saddler reckoned Zeus showed cur: turned away and yelped. Saddler rolled
him a couple more times after that, and it seemed to Saddler Zeus
was definitely cur. So he sold him to the Indian.

Arizo bought Baby Zeus on the telephone for $250, about twice
what he should have paid for a cur. Saddler held back twenty percent to convince Arizo he was buying a winning dog. And now
that Baby Zeus was ready to fight, Saddler didn't care what the
outcome was. He made money either way. He simply bet the Oregon dog.

Considering this, it wasn't smart of Saddler to make light of
Baby Zeus. But Saddler was never a subtle man. If he knew something you didn't, he had to tell you. He was that kind.

When Arizo told Ruby that he was driving to Missouri to buy
a Pit Bull, she was puzzled.

"Is that what you need?" she said dubiously.

Nick Morrano was more probing. He brought over a jug and
they sat on the back step in the Sunday afternoon sun. "It's going
to be a lot of trouble," Morrano said. "You know that?"

"I don't think so. It'll be okay."

Morrano turned and squinted at him. "Whatta you need this
for?"

"Give me something to do."

"You got plenty to do."

"I'll make money with a good dog. I could win a thousand dollars in a good fight."

"You seen what they do to each other. You wanna piece 'a
that?"

"It's natural for them to fight. I'm not doing anything weird.
They fight anyway."

"You're not a cruel man, far as I know," Morrano said. "So it
must be somethin' you want to show off maybe?" He took another
drink from the jug.

"You can't see it, can you Morrano? You can't see a man wanting to make something for himself. Do a job. Build somethin' and
prove it on the line."

"If that's what you want why don't you fight yourself. Get your-

self in shape and fight? Instead of puttin' somethin' else in there
for you. If that's what you want. Put your own ass on the line."

"How the hell can I do that? If I was to do that, I should've
started fifteen years back. You're being a smartass."

"You want a little taste of power. That's what you want. Isn't
it, Mike? You can tell me. You want them sonovabitches to sit up
an' take notice. All them bossmen and gaffers and people you
been workin' for. You wanna little taste yourself. Isn't that so?"
Morrano squinted so hard at his friend, his eyes were just a glimmer. He leaned forward, holding the jug by the neck, and gave
Arizo's knee a shove. "Isn't that so?" he said.

"So what if I do?" Arizo shrugged it off. He took the jug and
drank.

"So get yourself a low-rider like Hansen; carry a pistola like
Weiss."

Arizo spat. "Take Hansen's fuckin' short away and what is he?
Take Weiss' piece and he's a slick-down dude with a ugly old lady
that's got him so pussy-whipped, they mail his paycheck home Friday. Take away his piece, an' Ruby could beat the shit outta
Weiss."

"Take your dog away from you . . ." Morrano began.

"An' I'll take another dog and I'll make *it* a winner."

"An' that'll make *you* a winner?"

"Fuckin' aye," Arizo said hotly. "Because I did it myself. *I* did,
Morrano." He thumped his chest. "That's the difference. Those
others, they're losers. They're all of them workin' for wages and
they're losers."

"Me too," Morrano said.

"Not you."

"I work for wages. I don't do shit."

"But you don't think you're a winner."

"So?"

"So you're not even in the goddamn game."

"Like you?"

"Like me."

Morrano passed him the jug and watched him drink. The air
was golden.

After a while, Morrano said, "You got it all figured out. But I tell you, sometimes I don't think we do a damn thing." He looked down at the foot of the wooden steps. The steps were painted a faded cream that was worn away in the center by passing shoes. "We just like to think we can," Morrano said. His voice was a little thick. He turned to Arizo with a flourish and demanded, "Can you stop yourself from dyin' when it's your time?"

"You're gettin' sloppy drunk," Arizo said.

"No. Seriously. Here." He handed Arizo the jug as though that constituted proof of his sobriety. Then he leaned forward confidentially and said, "It's none of your goddamn business when you die, Mike. Like it's none of your goddamn business when it rains or when the winter comes. There's nothin' you can do about it, nothin'." He ended on a sinister note.

The two men fell silent, staring ahead, struck by the thought. The sun was on the rim of the hills. Neither man noticed the chill in the air. Suddenly Arizo nodded and sighed. "I know," he said. "Don't you think I know?"

Morrano looked at him and gave him a shove.

"You're goddamn gettin' drunk yourself," he said and laughed. Then he said quickly, "Did you tell me everything, Mike?"

The question caught Arizo off guard and he faltered.

"Whatta you mean?"

"About you an' the dog."

"I don't know. Sure. Why?"

"I just wondered is all," Morrano said.

On the way to Missouri, Arizo thought a lot about what he hadn't told Morrano. He took his Ford panel wagon, which had a mattress and blankets in the back. He drove south down Highway 99 through the Central Valley by the San Joaquin, Kern and Kings rivers, through land he had worked and knew like a man knows his own. The valley was broad and flat and dull as the sky. He went through Fresno, Tulare, Merced, and Bakersfield, by the orange trees and the vineyards and the cottonfields and the oil rigs, painted like grasshoppers and praying mantises, pumping on the ground. He felt good in the valley. He didn't hurry. He didn't begin to push the old Ford till he rolled it up the Grape Vine into the Tehachapi Mountains at sunset.

Morrano was talking off-the-shelf power. That's what hot shorts and handguns were about. Arizo had taken Weiss' gun once and gone into the streets of Sacramento. It was heady, walking along with a gun in his waistband under his jacket. It was the weirdest feeling. Take it out, a simple movement, and people walking peacefully would run and scatter or give him whatever he wanted. He went into a grocery store and looked coolly at the clerk, pale and stony-eyed behind the counter, and a moment from death, at Arizo's discretion. He felt brash and completely cynical. It wasn't a good feeling. He was afraid the gun was going to leap out of him and kill somebody. It felt like he and the gun were separate, and he didn't want that. He wanted to be the source of his power.

He knew he couldn't have control. Not because he had no money or education or even because he was a half-caste Portuguese-Indian. Even if it had been otherwise, he knew he couldn't control the course of things.

It was dark now. He was driving through Pomona on the freeway, a chain of headlights blinking through the divider, the heat from the engine making him drowsy. He was ten. Sitting in class at the Davis school, mid-morning in March. Outside it was raining steadily. The principal came in and the children looked in wonder. The principal was bald and smooth-faced. He called to Arizo, beckoned with his hand. Arizo got up and went with him out of the classroom, fearful and bewildered, and all the other children snickering and eyeing him and turning around as he left. The principal put an arm across his shoulders. He had a sharp, clean smell. Arizo had never been so close to him before. The principal took Arizo to his office and opened the door and ushered him in and told him to sit. The principal had a large, shiny desk, and a globe desk lamp, and a wooden penstand with his name carved on it. The president was what Arizo sometimes confused him with now. When he went to say "principal," he said "president."

The principal sat behind his desk and folded his hands together on his green blotter.

"I'm afraid I've got bad news for you, Mike," he said, looking directly at him with large, clear eyes. "Your mother and father have had an accident." Arizo noticed how amazingly clean the principal's fingernails were. How soft and white. "Your aunt is coming to look after you," he said.

In the morning it was on the front page of the *Sacramento Bee*, a short article, he remembered, continued inside. Arizo was waiting for his Aunt Jolene at a neighbor's house and found their copy of the paper. His parents had been killed on an unguarded crossing by the California Zephyr eastbound for Chicago. There were photographs of the wreck and of his parents. It was a very old picture of his parents, taken when they were newlyweds. It had always stood on their dresser in the bedroom, by the window. Arizo sat on the porch of the neighbor's house. It was raining. He watched the water drip from the guttering and wondered how that picture of his parents had got into the newspaper. In the picture of the wreck, passengers were looking out of the windows of the train. The conductor, in his cylindrical hat, was standing beside the track. The paper said the train was delayed half an hour but easily made up the time before it reached Salt Lake City.

His Aunt Jolene came to Davis and took him to the funeral. He didn't cry. He remembered standing, not feeling sad, and a lot of women around him crying. He had never seen adults cry before, except for his mother. She cried sometimes. He stood watching, not saying anything, not feeling much connection with what he saw. After the funeral, he went back to Oakland with his Aunt Jolene, leaving the country for the first time in his life and going to live in a black ghetto.

His Aunt Jolene was a small, wry, wrinkled woman who never weighed more than ninety-five pounds in her life. She chain-smoked, keeping the butt end of her cigarette stuck to her bottom lip so she didn't have to take it out when she talked or did things. It bobbed on her bottom lip as she spoke and burned way down. Arizo was fascinated by it. He remembered her standing in the kitchen, by an ironing board, looking down at him, talking away, blinking her eyes against the smoke that trailed up across her face

from the lighted butt end that bobbed like a fishing cork on her
bottom lip.

She lived in a wood tenement across from the docks at Eighth
and Campbell, next to a laundromat that was a hangout for black
junkies, with Maxwell, her lover. Maxwell was a chef for Matson
Lines, working largely between San Francisco and Honolulu.

For a while Oakland was good. But when he was sixteen, his
aunt ran off and Maxwell got sick soon afterwards and died in a
drawn-out fashion. About that time, Arizo met Mary-Beth. She
was his first love and he was properly grateful for her. She came
from Dimmit, Texas, a willowy girl with dark, shiny chestnut hair
and a fine nose. Her legs were skinny and a little bowed, and she
made love wilder than he could believe. He was half-ashamed to
think about it. One night, approaching the height of her passion,
she choked out, "God, Mike. I'll always do it for you. No matter
what, I'll always do it for you." Whenever her voice came to him,
saying those words, his cock would start to crawl. No matter what
he was doing.

He and Mary-Beth were together about a year when they went
to a party at her brother's house. It was a chicken-coop of a house,
not much more: a bare dirt yard, tarpaper hammered onto a plywood roof, bare wood floors, and bare bulbs hanging from the ceiling. There were bourbon in half-gallon jugs, paper cups, melting
ice, and country music on a cheap record player. Midway through
the evening, there was some shouting in the hall. Arizo was standing in the open doorway. He turned and looked into the hallway.
There was a very muscular blond boy at one end. He had a small
revolver that he was pointing at three men crowded around the
front door at the other end of the hall. The blond boy was waving
the gun and shouting, "Come on, you chickenshit motherfuckers!
Come on! Come on!"

Arizo said, "Hey!" That was all he remembered. He came
around in the hospital. The nurse told him he had been shot in
the abdomen and nearly bled to death. He felt very grateful to her
and said so.

She smiled at him. "You'll be fine," she said. "They took the
bullet out of your stomach. You'll be fine now."

But he wasn't fine. After he got out of the hospital and got together with Mary-Beth, nothing happened. The surgeon told him
it was psychological, the result of extreme trauma. "It's important
not to worry," he said. "It'll come back in a while." But it never
did. When he went back again, the surgeon told him the bullet
must have caused a "vascular lesion."

"It's damaged the blood supply to your penis," the surgeon said
with a passing look of regret. He was young, beefy-looking, a Rob-
ert Redford type. "The penis requires a great deal of blood to become erect."

Arizo whistled and looked down. "You got a cigarette?"

"No," said the surgeon. He obviously didn't approve of smoking. "I'm sorry I haven't. It could also have damaged the nerves.
The bullet," he said.

"Does the nurse out front have a cigarette?"

"My receptionist?"

"Yeah. You mind?"

"I think she may," the surgeon said.

Arizo came back with a cigarette. He felt a little more composed now. "Maybe you cut the nerve when you went in after the
bullet," he said.

The surgeon shook his head and looked steadily at Arizo. "We
know what we're doing." He said it like a politician making a
promise on TV.

"But you don't know what you don't."

"I'm sorry," the surgeon said. Behind him Arizo saw colored
pictures of the surgeon and his family at a ski resort. They were
all very tanned and bright-eyed and golden-haired.

"I wish there was something I could do," the surgeon said. "Believe me."

"There's nothing?"

"It may restore itself in time."

"That's all?"

"I wish I could help you."

Arizo nodded. He could see that the surgeon didn't approve of
people who hung around guns either. He stood up. "Thank you,"
he said. Someday it would come to him, too. Even him. Looking

at the surgeon's robustness, his sparkling teeth and unlined face, it was hard to believe, but Arizo did his best.

This was what he couldn't talk to Morrano about. Not in relation to his getting the dog, not any way. He pulled into a Standard station somewhere on the road to Victorville, into the flat, unaccustomed brightness. The only one who knew was Mary-Beth. He'd never told another soul in the seven years since they had come apart. She must have told later lovers about it because they had had an extraordinary experience together. Sometimes he'd imagined it, as if he were there listening in the bed beside them. He didn't care. She had gone from his circle, and he didn't know the men she told. But he had kept it a secret. In part because he was ashamed, but more because he was afraid of what might happen if he let it out. In the year or so they were still together after it happened, there was only a moment when he thought she had given it away. That was when she left.

He joined the freeway traffic headed north once more, to pick up 66 in Barstow. The traffic was thinning out. It was past midnight, and he had set up a rhythm that he could keep up for hours. A loping gait. She left him cold turkey. He came home from work one night, and her friend Susie opened the door. Immediately he felt some small alarm. He remembered how she had looked at him and hesitated. She had a fragile, neurotic face and freckles. She was chewing gum, but now she stopped.

Mary-Beth had gone back to Texas. "I think she thought she was just holdin' you back from better things," Susie said.

"She was the best thing I had goin'." He heard himself use the past tense. The admission was the beginning of the loneliness. The exact moment. She had kept the secret, so he figured she had left loving him. Otherwise she would have damaged him badly.

It was freezing out. He had forgotten about the winter. Near Topock on the Arizona line, at dawn, he stuffed every hole he found around the firewall, passenger door, and back door with newspaper. Then he got in the back to sleep. He'd been nineteen when Mary-Beth left him. After she went, he left Oakland and went back up into the Sacramento Valley. He lived awhile in Vacaville, Davis, Sacramento. Some summers he went down into

the San Joaquin Valley as far as Bakersfield, but mostly he stayed
in the north, in the Sacramento Valley, just wandering. He
worked in packing sheds, in the beet mills at Crocket and Clarks-
burgh, in the Wrigley's plant at Santa Cruz. He worked in the
fields, drove bobtails, tractors, semis. He pruned, sprayed, irri-
gated, planted. He worked from April to November and drew unemployment through the winter months.

He moved when he got lonely. Moving was a good antidote to
the loneliness which shaped his life; it meant new people, new
work, new places to live. It busied his mind. He did go to bed
with one woman. Quite early on. She was in her twenties with
dark hair she could sit on.

He was in San Francisco, in Breen's Bar at Third and Mission,
and got a little drunk and took her back to his hotel because he
was crazy for her skin, crazy for the touch of her. But she got mad
at him. She sat up in bed with her little breasts standing out and
spat at him. "You knew this?" she yelled. "You knew this? So
what the fuck you doin' in my bed?" After that, he kept to himself.

Saddler's place was out on the edge of Houstonia. A run-down,
swaybacked house with a De Soto and a Studebaker pickup broken down in the front yard. The sky was gray and cold as frozen
fish. Saddler was out back, working a dog on the table. His wife
pointed him out to Arizo from the back door. Saddler looked as
Arizo came across the hard dirt to the table, but he didn't stop
working the dog or say anything. He had a sad expression on a
rubbery face. He wore a beat-up white Stetson and baggy clothes.
The poacher pockets of his jacket were stuffed. The dog was suspended in a chest harness from a beam above the table so that its
rear legs were off the ground, and he was driving incessantly
against the harness using only his forepaws. The dog was powerful, solid looking. When Arizo was by the table, Saddler said,
without looking, "Builds up his shoulders real good. You gotta
table?"

Arizo shook his head. He didn't like Saddler, nor the feel of his
place. "This Baby Zeus?"

"No. This here's Cyclone. Cyclone's won eight bush fights. I only breed good dogs, boy. I'll fetch yer dog. You got money for me?"

Arizo nodded.

"I'd like to count it."

Arizo gave him the money and Saddler counted it on the table, while Cyclone watched. When he had finished, Saddler took out a paper and hunted for a pen. "You got a pen?" Arizo handed him one. "Sign this," he said. "This'll show I get twenty percent of the dog's winnings. You understand that?"

"That's what we agreed."

"Just wanted to be sure, boy."

Saddler fetched Baby Zeus, leading him back on the end of a chain. Baby Zeus was about knee-high, a dusty brindle. He was scrawny, his ribs stuck out, his head hung, and there was no luster in his eye. Saddler saw his disappointment.

"He's just a young 'un yet," Saddler said. "He's not filled out. When he gets filled out, he'll be a helluva dog. Feed him good."

"I know what to do," Arizo said. He was tired. There was light behind his eyeballs.

"If you need advice, you got my number," Saddler said.

It was a long, good run home to Winters. Arizo was triumphant: Baby Zeus lay on the blankets in the back. He made no fuss about leaving. He was amicable and sharp as a whipcrack.

Arizo drove straight through on the wire. He looked over his shoulder at the dog often as he drove. He was no beauty, but it was all he wanted. He didn't want it on a plate, no ready-made champion. That would be like buying a whore. He laughed when he thought of his conversation with Morrano. "Have you told me everything?" He wished he could have shared a joke and told Morrano how he wanted *something* with a bite.

When he got back to Winters, they crowded around the dog. Some people didn't approve, although Arizo said nothing about fighting him. Nick Morrano said the dog looked like him. And there was a resemblance. Arizo was a Shoshoni with Portuguese blood on his mother's side. He was a squat, powerful man, smooth and hairless with a barrel chest that burst out of his shirt like a copper washtub, big, crooked teeth and a nose broad and flat as a shoveler's bill.

Baby Zeus was round and stubby, too. His head was also wedge-shaped with a wide, flat skull and small ears. There was even a similar Oriental caste to the eye. The dog's eyes were flush and protected by a massive zygomatic arch, so that even if he were caught in a raking headhold, his opponent's teeth wouldn't penetrate the eye sockets and blind him. Run-down as he was, his chest was still massive as a bulldog's, with skinny legs that hung from unusually wide shoulders.

"He's you. Even to the colorin'," Morrano swore.

After Mary-Beth, there were years of wandering before he settled in Winters. He took a house on the edge of the town. The back looked out over the valley flatlands to Jon Lindeman's orchard of apricots. Beyond that were the hills forming the western rim. He rented a room to Ruby, a post-urban cowgirl from Daly City. Ruby was twenty-five.

She and Arizo never shared a bed, but they were close. Ruby had her boyfriends. She was halfway between a wife and a sister to him, but he never told her about his problem.

She nearly left the house over Baby Zeus. She had strong ideas. The way Arizo saw it, she took responsibility for all the cruelty in the world.

"That's unnatural," he said to her one night over dinner.

"If you don't do anything about it, it is. If I sit watching you and that dog and don't say nothing, then it would be *my* fault."

"For all the bullfighting, cockfighting, an' dog-eatin' in China, too?"

She nodded. "You do nothing about it, then you're part of it. That's what I see."

"Fighting is what they want," Arizo said. "Stopping them fighting is like stopping women havin' babies."

Unsmiling, she shook her head. "You're encouraging these dogs. If it happens, that's one thing. You're makin' it happen."

"That's what you say," he said.

His case was not helped when Baby Zeus got loose a week later

and Arizo found him in the next garden, standing over his neighbor's half-eaten cat. Or when Baby Zeus mauled the golden Labra-
dor that lived with Floyd Boudreaux up the street. But Arizo was
not put off. He trained the dog daily. He read the training tips in
Pit Dog Report, and every evening, as soon as he came home from
work, he took the dog out training. He was amazed how close
they got. They knew each other's moods, even the subtlest. How
these would affect performance and how to compensate for one
another.

In the beer parlor at the end of Main Street where he sometimes stopped for a beer on his way home after work, they knew
of Arizo's awesome dog. When he walked Baby Zeus on a chain,
people pointed them out. Boys stopped and asked questions; other
dogs crossed the street to get away. They knew a real samurai on
sight. Arizo could even have got women through the dog, if that
had interested him.

There were certain things about the dog he didn't mention
until one night at the bar, after a couple of beers.

"You take an attack-trained Doberman," he said, waving a
hand in the air for emphasis, "or a Shepherd. They have a six-
hundred-pound bite. Per square inch." He looked about him at
the faces of the men at the bar and belched lightly. "S'cuse me.
But Baby Zeus has two thousand! He'll crack your arm like a
chicken bone. He wouldn't crack a *person's* arm," he said quickly.
"Not a *human* arm. They love humans. They'll never attack a
human. Or a child or anything."

The men at the bar looked at one another. Arizo felt uncomfortable. He wished he'd kept his mouth shut.

One man said, "Some people's idea of fun is awful weird."

Arizo fed Baby Zeus table scraps and prepared dogfood until he
filled out to chain weight—that is, his natural weight, which was
sixty-eight pounds. He was then two. When he saw this, Arizo
began the training.

It was May. Arizo was harvesting tomatoes at the Sparks
Ranch. He planned the training as he worked, what they would
do that evening. Arizo thought about Baby Zeus most of the time.

The other men in the packing shed talked about women and
whether they would get laid that night. Arizo thought about Baby
Zeus, while Baby Zeus languished at the end of a chain, waiting
for him to come home.

As the training progressed, Arizo became more and more intense. He did nothing else that wasn't necessary. He saw little of
his friends. The distance between him and Ruby grew, and he did
nothing about it. He was possessed. He didn't stop at the beer
parlor any longer. He drove straight home from work, and Baby
Zeus wagged ecstatically at the sight of the old gray Ford panel
wagon pulling up alongside the house. Arizo would go inside and
fetch a cold beer and then come out and take Baby Zeus off the
chain. The dog would jump up onto the passenger's seat, and together they would drive out of town and turn onto the deserted
levee roads that crisscross the rice fields in the delta.

Nick Morrano came out with them once, in the beginning, but
Arizo found that he was self-conscious around someone else. He
couldn't be himself with the dog, even if it was just Morrano
around. Morrano thought the fierceness with which they did
things was strange. Arizo saw Morrano at a loss, and he didn't
want to explain. He wanted nothing to do with anything or anyone who distracted him. So after that they always trained alone.

When they got out onto the levee roads, Arizo put Baby Zeus
on the end of a twenty-five-foot rope and ran him behind the
Ford in first gear at seven or eight miles an hour, calling to him
out of the window. By the time Arizo was working the apricot
harvest in June, Baby Zeus was running five miles and a couple
of wind-sprints. In July, when they were harvesting peaches and
he was at Tufts Packing, Baby Zeus was up to seven miles and six
wind-sprints; and by the time Arizo was starting in on the al-
monds and walnuts in September, Baby Zeus was running ten
miles with ease and another half-mile of wind-sprints.

After the run, he walked the dog to cool him off and then
rubbed him down before they went home. At the house, Arizo let
Baby Zeus drink cool boiled water until he lifted his head. Then
he took him out again, into the hay field behind the house, on the
end of a one-hundred-foot rope and walked him in the tall grass,

calling to him to make him run and jump. Some days he swam the dog; others he made him pull weights. Every session ended with the rope.

Arizo hung a rope over a beam in the back shed and made the dog jump for the end and lock his jaws like a rattler. He raised the rope end higher and higher to build the dog's speed and kick. He made him hang onto it for fifteen or twenty minutes to build his concentration. He got down on the floor, face-to-face with the dog, and yelled repeatedly, "Shake it Zeus! Shake it, boy!" and the dog would shake the rope end as if he were killing a rat, on and on, until he foamed at the mouth and his veins and muscles stood out in relief.

When they were finished training, Arizo weighed the dog. For every pound the dog shed, Arizo sewed a lead weight into a small leather waistcoat the dog wore. By the time of the fight, Baby Zeus was down to fifty-five pounds and was carrying thirteen. Day and night.

Arizo then watered him again and finally fed him a quarter-pound of half-cooked lean beef, two twelve-minute boiled eggs, two cups of All-Bran, and a can of tomato juice, mixed with vitamins.

Seven days before the fight, Arizo changed this diet to two pounds of meat and two cups of Purina. It was better food than he and Ruby ate. He made around $155 a week with overtime. Ruby told him the dog was costing four dollars a day. Arizo told her it would be worth it.

"We're fighting for a thousand dollars," he said. "And we could make five hundred at the gate."

"*He's* fighting, you mean," said Ruby.

Ruby pointedly went to bed early the night before the fight. Arizo was excited. He wanted to sit up and talk, but Ruby laid out his clothes in silence and then went to bed. Arizo stayed up alone. He went over the fight in his mind, building himself up, envisioning every situation he could imagine, seeing how he would deal with it, to be sure nothing took him by surprise. At eleven o'clock he got up from the kitchen table to go to bed. On his way, he paused and looked out of the window into the darkened yard to see if he could see the dog. He stared out for a while though it was too dark to see anything outside. Then he went to bed.

Saturday morning Arizo woke before dawn. He turned on the light and got straight out of bed. He showered and put on the white polyester Levi's cowboy shirt, fresh pants, and two-tone water-buffalo-skin Tony Lama boots Ruby had laid out. These were his Sunday clothes. Then he went into the kitchen and heated some tacos and drank a can of beer and let himself out of the house. Ruby slept. He carried a black equipment case, like a briefcase, and his Levi's jacket. The morning was mild though the sun was an hour from coming up. The sky was turquoise and the stars had mostly gone. He put his things in the Ford, fetched Baby Zeus, and put him on the seat beside him.

Sitting behind the wheel, Arizo checked his case, pushing the dog gently away. He had pain killer, blood stopper, a broad-spectrum antibiotic, cotton wool, bandages, disposable hypodermics. Even Band-Aids for himself. He shut the case. Some fighters even keep I.V. bottles, blood, and steroids, but Arizo couldn't afford these. Everything else he had bought in a large animal-equipment store in Sacramento, where he was unknown.

"We got everything to take care of you," he said to the dog. Baby Zeus wagged affectionately, laying his ears back on the broad skull, looking intently at Arizo. Arizo rubbed the dog's neck. He pulled out his billfold and counted fifteen new, stiff, $50 bills. He made sure he had the contract. He fingered the bills a moment before he put the billfold back, started up, and slowly drove the truck out onto the highway.

He took the Berryessa road through the orchards south of town. The road was empty. There were still damp patches on the asphalt. The sky was reddening in the east. Arizo was surprised at how relaxed he felt. He sat back in the seat, drumming his fingers on the wheel. Baby Zeus sat beside him, tongue hanging out, staring contentedly into space. When their eyes met, they looked pleased. The dog wriggled on the seat.

The dog looked good, Arizo thought. His brindle coat, no

longer than a boxer's stubble, gleamed rich and oily. He was pure steel—one solid, barrel-chested, wasp-waisted muscle. Arizo grinned with satisfaction.

The road left the valley and climbed through scrub oak and manzanita to the dam of the Berryessa reservoir. At the top he pulled over, turned off the engine, and sat looking out at the lake poised on the brink of day. Beside him Baby Zeus wriggled and stared up expectantly. "You could be a champion," he murmured, stroking the dog's broad, flat skull. It was rare a top dog came out of the far west. They all said that. But Baby Zeus could do it. Arizo had never boasted of it, but he felt sure of himself and Baby Zeus—even in the south. Today they would beat the Oregon dog, and then they would go down and fight in Texas. They would have the money for it after they won.

A heron flew low over the lake. Arizo watched it land languidly on the shore, then started the Ford, put it in gear and moved off.

He picked up Nick Morrano outside the Greyhound bus depot in Napa. Morrano had been setting up the route. He had two braceros from San Luis with him. They rode in the back, Morrano in front holding Baby Zeus. After breakfast at a diner, they went to a Shell station, rented a white Ford Econoline van with cash, parked the Ford, and drove out of Napa headed west, towards the Valley of the Moon.

They picked up two Mendocino woolies and three Chicanos from outside a gas station in Schellville; three chicken farmers, already a little drunk, and a young Mexican couple in fiesta clothes from in front of the pharmacy in El Verano; two straitlaced cattlemen in Petaluma, and a cowboy in white who had flown in from Fort Worth for the fight.

By late afternoon Arizo had covered 200 miles and was headed east with thirty people jammed hip-to-hip, legs intertwined, sweating and jolting in the back. There were slack-faced Okies, bullet-headed ranchers, slick young blacks from East Oakland with platform shoes and combs in their pockets, a suburbanite from Daly City in a crushed velvet suit, chain-smoking Panatelas with plastic mouth pieces and carrying an Instamatic with a flash attachment that made several people nervous. There were a dozen woolies, including two frizzy-haired girls who passed around strong Colombian. The Chicanos had a lot of sweet white wine, the Texan had two large bottles of Courvoisier, and everything was mixed freely. It was a hot afternoon, and you could hardly breathe in the van. But nobody complained. There was conspiracy in the air, adrenaline in the blood. The adrenaline made for fast talk and nervous laughter. From the start there were bets made, mostly on how long it was going to take Baby Zeus to make the Oregon dog howl; how long the fight was going to run; how many scratches there'd be.

An hour before sunset, Arizo stopped the van on the Montezuma Slough near Birds Landing. Everyone spilled out, stretched, pissed and thanked God they were here at last. There were some farm buildings 300 yards away across the flats. Apparently this was where the fight would be. But after thirty minutes Arizo announced, "Okay. This isn't it. Everyone back in the van." Twice more he did this, killing time, waiting for the dusk and making sure they weren't being followed. He reached the Okie's place at sunset.

There was a lot of tension by now. People laughed at anything, and Arizo had a knot in him. Only Baby Zeus was relaxed, tongue lolling out, congenial, eyes following everything that went on. Arizo pulled up in the Okie's farm yard, took the dog and his equipment bag and walked quickly towards the house, threading his way through men waiting around vans and pickups already parked in the yard.

"There's the Indian."

"There's Baby Zeus."

"Look at that, Zeke, will ya?"

"I got fifty dollars to lay on him. Who wants some of this?"

Arizo looked around, but didn't stop. He was anxious to make sure that the Oregon dog had arrived. There was a lot to do. The dogs had to be washed. It is customary before a fight for each trainer to wash the other's dog in cold water, to be certain that neither dog has been rubbed with poison or a tranquilizer. And the rest of the bet had to be posted. Arizo had put up $250 forfeit money when he signed the contract, in case Baby Zeus didn't come in at the right weight or didn't show. Now he had to post the remaining $750. The winner would take the other man's $1,000 plus the gate receipts—less what they had to pay the Okie for using his pit.

As Arizo crossed the yard, he saw the Okie standing waiting for him in the doorway, a disheveled, vacant-looking man with a crippled arm. His wife stood behind him, stooped and withered, with wisps of graying hair floating off her skull like shreds of cloud. Arizo went in, and the Okie closed the door.

The Okie's farm looked like the man; a weathered, run-down place. The yard was dusty and littered with rusting implements. A high, silvered, redwood barn leaned dangerously. Behind it were stock pens with broken fences and beyond these, three long chicken houses, makeshift affairs of corrugated iron.

The only living things in the yard, apart from the hundred and fifty or so people waiting around in groups for the fight to begin, were the Okie's chickens. The Okie was a chicken fighter. Nine fighting cocks were tethered to bushes and stakes around the place, big brilliantly colored birds. They were hobbled with leather jesses and wore two-and-a-half-inch spurs. One of them, a huge, white Silver Spangler, was looking to roost in a tree branch above his head. But his tether was too short and jerked him out of the air each time he jumped. He would pick himself up, stare sideways at the leash on his foot, shake it, and then spring upwards again. The bird had an incredible spring. Fighting cocks are trained to jump. They move with amazing speed. You have to bet fast in cockfighting. The birds often kill one another in seconds.

Two of the men standing around drifted over to watch the white rooster. Once, between jumps, it shit. One of the two men bent down and examined the dropping, pinching it between two fingers. He looked up in disgust. "Look at this," he said. "Even this fuckin' busted Okie's chickens is no good. This bird can't fight in a month. His shit's soft."

The other man bent down and stirred the dropping with a long fingernail. "Jesus!" he said. "When my birds shit, you can roll it like chewing gum."

"Yeah? Well, I like mine so you can crumble it," the first man said. "When they're shittin' pure protein like that, they're ready to fight."

At that moment a new pearl-gray Eldorado pulled into the yard, a dog perched on the seat-back beside the driver's head. Someone said, "It's the Mississippi Hawk." And there were shouts of "Shotgun. Here's Shotgun." A crowd gathered around the car. Shotgun was a brindle Pit Bull, a small, compact, twenty-five-pound bitch, an evil-looking creature, with half an ear missing. She was recovering from her last fight. Her little body was a mass of scar tissue. The crowd pressed around her admiringly. Most of them had been at her last fight. She'd won. The little bitch welcomed the attention. The Mississippi Hawk was the nickname of Maurice Carver, a fat plumbing contractor from Piedmont, with a large diamond ring. He stood beside Shotgun, glowing, perspiring, talking about what a hell of a job his vet had done. "This guy understands these dogs," he was saying. "He don't hold you up on price either."

Someone shouted, "Let's go! They're ready to go," and the crowd began filing through the stock pens into the closest chicken barn.

It was hot inside and smelled of dried-out litter. Overhead lights glared into a crude pit the Okie had fashioned from four quarter-inch plywood boards nailed to corner posts with finishing nails. The pit floor was carpeted in cheap white shag, rows of planks were laid across cinder blocks at ringside, and people sat on them or stood behind. Some were well off, but most were working men: machinists, carpenters, construction workers, pump jocks, and farmhands. There was a loud group of young Mexicans in dark suits and string ties and pointy-toed shoes and their women, beautiful olive-skinned girls in loud printed blouses and tank tops. There were maybe as many woolies, thirty or more, and a lot of joints were going around. The Okie's wife was selling beer at a dollar a can out of an old Kelvinator. The men bought the beer to chase down their hard liquor. It was a wild, noisy crowd, high with anticipation.

Even before the dogs arrived, the betting was fierce. Wages went on the line a week or two at a time. "I gotta C-note here to spread around on the Oregon dog," the shout went. "I got two hundred here says Zeus is gonna do it. Who wants some of this?" The betting was all done by eye contact. A man might make five or six bets across the ring, but none of it was written down. There was a big young Mexican, a good-looking kid obviously on leave from the army. He looked like Ricardo Montalban with a military haircut and was really laying it around. He must have bet a thousand dollars. He seemed to know everyone in the place. The other Mexicans teased him about his hair, but they did it lightly.

The shouting died down when Fresno Wheeler stepped into the ring. Wheeler was a leathery little man in his fifties, with neat, short, silver hair. He looked like the oldest man in the place. Several men in the audience knew him and one of them called out: "Hey, Fresno. Easy on the Injun now. He's cherry, remember."

Wheeler looked around and smiled, enjoying his moment. He hung sheetrock by day and took an hour for lunch like everyone else. But at the fight he was the gaffer, and a good one. He was hoping for a short fight because he had to drive 60 miles to Stockton afterwards to referee another one that same night.

He held up his hands for silence. "You know the rules," he said. "This'll be Cajun style. If we get busted, you guys in front kick down the ring but fast. If there isn't a ring, there isn't a fight. That's the law."

There were shouts and whistles. Wheeler turned away, and the two handlers stepped into the ring. One of them was Nick Morrano. The two men blinked against the glare of the spots. There was more shouting and cries of "Here comes a dog. There's a dog coming up." And hand-over-hand, above the heads of the crowd, Dynamite was passed ringside, followed by his trainer, a serious-looking young man with shoulder length hair, a heavy black Zapata moustache.

"Eli Gardner," the big Mexican shouted, "meaner than his dogs."

The young man from Oregon paid no attention, but elbowed his way anxiously after his dog, although the animal was clearly enjoying being handled. As they passed him, Dynamite licked faces and wriggled and the crowd whistled and yelled at the sight of his scarred and muscled little body.

Baby Zeus followed, equally pleased by all the touching and admiration, tongue lolling out, eyes rolling with delight. Arizo followed, distractedly nodding to his well-wishers, clutching his black equipment case awkwardly, squeezing through the sweat of bodies. When he stepped into the pit, Nick Morrano was waiting for him, holding Baby Zeus. The dog squirmed when it saw Arizo. Arizo went to the corner seeing faces, oddly distinct, beyond the pit wall. He knelt down, holding Baby Zeus in the corner so that he could not see the Oregon dog. He rubbed him down as a trainer rubs a boxer before the bell, to get the blood circulating.

Wheeler had a brass scale, like a butcher's scale. He roped a rafter above the ring and hung the scale, then hooked each dog in turn into a leather harness and weighed him. He called out the weights: "Dynamite, from Portland, Oregon, fifty-six pounds two." And: "Baby Zeus from Winters, California, fifty-five pounds four." And then he took the scales down, while the dogs were held in their corners, backs to each other, and called for silence again. "Okay. Like I said, we're fighting Cajun rules. First dog doesn't make scratch is the loser."

Wheeler turned and checked with each trainer. "Ready?" he asked. Both men nodded in turn. "Face your dogs," he commanded.

Arizo turned Baby Zeus around and the two dogs got their first look at each other, across the dirty white rug. Their eyes locked. Arizo felt Baby Zeus strain in his hands and begin a deep growl, a rumbling, menacing sound that gradually increased until his body vibrated.

There was a thick sexual silence in the barn now. Even the drunks were silent. There was only the growling. Wheeler held the pause like a true showman, but someone burst: "Whoooeee!

Let them dogs go." Wheeler said loudly, "*Release your dogs!*" and
Arizo let go and watched Baby Zeus scramble out to meet the
black dog.

There was no circling, no preliminary shadowboxing. The dogs
hit hard in mid-ring with a grunt and went straight for a front leg,
driving each other into a V, growling continuously with that deep
growl, tails held high in the air. They pushed and butted each
other, testing each other's strength like natural fighters.

For the first few minutes they swapped cheap skin-holds, maul-
ing each other's ears and flanks, fighting fast on their feet. These
dogs instinctively know the best holds, but neither seemed to look
for one early on. After fifteen minutes, a lot of blood had been
spilled, but the pace hadn't slowed. It was impossible to say who
was bleeding most. There were livid splotches all over the white
rug.

And then they began throwing each other. The black dog
started it, driving for a foreleg, pushing Baby Zeus back, and then
suddenly flipping him with a violent twist of his head, throwing
him down on the ground with a *whump* that was greeted with a
roar from the crowd. But as the Oregon dog stood over him and
loosened his bite for an instant, trying to shift his hold higher on
the shoulder, Baby Zeus grabbed a leg hold himself, pushed up,
and in turn threw the black dog. There was another roar, and this
time the black dog struggled back to his feet and again threw
Baby Zeus. They repeated this eight or nine times. It was like a
ritual, as though they were body-punching each other, wearing
each other down.

And then the black dog suddenly changed tactics and went for
Baby Zeus' snout. He locked onto it, and as his trainer yelled encouragement from only inches away, he shook hard. Baby Zeus
seemed to wince. He pulled back. The black dog had him by the
upper jaw and was biting hard, crushing his nasal passages, threat-
ening to cut off his air.

The dogs lay facing each other. Arizo felt shaken. He knelt beside Baby Zeus, telling him, "Take it easy, boy, easy," as calmly as
he could, looking him in the eye. Sometimes Baby Zeus looked at
Arizo for an instant; a flat stare without recognition.

The side bets broke out in the crowd. "I got a ten spot says this is it for Zeus." People who feared they were on the wrong dog began looking to lay off their bets. This was a critical moment. They were thirty minutes into the fight, and Baby Zeus was now bottom dog. He didn't like it. But Arizo could see him thinking. The hold lasted seven minutes, and then Baby Zeus suddenly drove hard and, as the black dog went for a higher hold still, broke free.

Arizo jumped up. "Attaboy!" he yelled. The crowd screamed and howled and whistled, but the black dog was thrown for only a moment and came back hard, snarling, jaws open wide. Baby Zeus ducked as the black dog came on. There were intense shouts of "Turn!" and Wheeler called quickly, "*Turn by* Zeus. *Turn by* Zeus. Pick up your dogs. Zeus to scratch."

The dogs had both taken leg holds, but their trainers pried them apart and carried them back into their corners. Wheeler gave them a moment to sponge out their mouths and then called, "Face your dogs."

Arizo turned Baby Zeus, aware that the betting was going against him again.

"Now get him, boy," he said. "You go get him. You can do it okay, Zeus. Hear me?" Arizo's mouth was dry and he licked his lips and swallowed. "You get him, Zeus," he said, bending to talk into Zeus' ear. "Go get that sonovabitch."

"Your scratch." Fresno Wheeler looked at Arizo. "Let him go!" he ordered. Baby Zeus had to cross the pit and bite his opponent. In the far corner Eli Gardner was still holding Dynamite. Baby Zeus didn't hesitate. He pawed at the rug and sprinted towards the black dog and Gardner let Dynamite go while the black dog had time to build up some momentum himself.

The two dogs met with a thump, growling again, and locked jaws in a grotesque kiss. The grip gradually tightened. The crowd was silent. There was a popping sound and teeth fell to the carpet. It was impossible to tell whose. Neither dog gave any sign of pain. They suddenly relaxed the hold and bit again. The black dog got a shoulder. Baby Zeus was left snapping at air. Turning, twisting, unable to get a hold of his own.

"He's workin' him over. He's workin' out," went the shouts. And it was true, the black dog was definitely in control. His experience was beginning to tell. He drove Baby Zeus slowly back across the pit. Baby Zeus was hot and breathing hard. He was slowing up. He was starting to look like a loser.

They had been fighting an hour when the black dog pinned Baby Zeus with a shoulder hold for almost five minutes, countering every move he made to get up. The Mexicans went wild. There was another feverish rush to lay off bets, but few people were ready to bet against Dynamite at this point.

Finally Baby Zeus turned his head again, as if looking to Arizo for help and Fresno Wheeler immediately blew his whistle. It was Baby Zeus to make scratch a second time. Arizo spoke to his dog as though they were alone together. "Okay, boy," he said. "You got to get him, Zeus. Just one more time." Then he let go. For an instant, Baby Zeus hesitated. The crowd was silent. Then he started slowly across the pit at the black dog, limping badly. A whoop went up. The fight was on.

Arizo pleaded with his dog now, lips pursed, moving his head and shoulders from side to side as if he himself were fighting. The black dog picked up where he'd left off, driving Baby Zeus back, shaking him, growling and picking his holds. Baby Zeus was willing to fight, but he seemed bewildered and off balance.

The Oregon dog kept trying to get under him to flip him on his back and go for the throat. Baby Zeus went over twice. He recovered, but it seemed only a matter of time.

When the change began was hard to say. At first it was a leveling off which the crowd sensed. Perhaps it was the Oregon dog tiring rather than Zeus' second wind. Perhaps it was simply a question of stamina, but gradually the fight turned to Baby Zeus. The dogs were lying on the floor now, both content to let the holds last longer. It was a battle of will, a serious fight. The crowd fell silent and seemed to swallow collectively. Someone cried out a warning: "There's gonna be a killing!" The dogs were laying on, like heavyweights in the final rounds. Now you could see it. Baby Zeus was taking control. Arizo and Eli Gardner were both on their knees, facing each other over the dogs, talking seriously to them, oblivious of each other.

"The black dog's shot his wad," someone yelled.

"He can't finish the job."

"Finish him, Dynamite. Finish the cocksucker."

"Kill that Dynamite. Kill the bastard."

"Kill, Zeus, kill!"

The shouting went back and forth. There was no more betting though. There were no more takers. Now it was Baby Zeus who pinned the black dog with a high shoulder hold, and it was the black dog snapping, arching his neck, eyes bulging, struggling to get a hold in return.

"You got him, Zeus," they shouted. "Finish him. Finish him, boy. Yeah." The black dog shook desperately, trying to throw Baby Zeus off.

But Baby Zeus had four feet anchored in pink shag. He growled at the shake, tightened his hold, then suddenly and fiercely shook in return, as Arizo, on his belly now, eyeball-to-eyeball with him, yelled hoarsely, "Shake him, boy! Shake him! Shake him!" The crowd screamed and Baby Zeus shook harder. The crowd fell silent and the black dog howled, a howl of pain and fear. The crowd went berserk and for a long time Fresno Wheeler couldn't make himself heard. He signaled the two handlers to break the dogs. Dynamite had turned. Wheeler blew his whistle repeatedly. Arizo pried Baby Zeus' jaws open with a breaker bar. The men picked up their dogs and took them to their corners. Baby Zeus was breathing hard. He felt sluggish. The crowd was silent again.

"Hold your dogs. Dynamite to scratch," Wheeler yelled. "Face your dogs." Wheeler looked at Eli Gardner. Gardner was sweating heavily. "When you're ready, Eli," Wheeler called.

Eli Gardner patted his dog and let him go. Dynamite looked out across the ring for a moment, took a step, wobbling unsteadily, looked about him, dazed, bleeding, then turned back, bemused, exhausted, looking for a way out of the pit. Pandemonium broke loose in the chicken shed. Arizo couldn't believe the feeling of tension lifted at last. He looked about. People were leaping up and down, hugging. A fight broke out. People trying to stand on a bench fell onto the people behind. The noise was deafening. Arizo knelt beside Baby Zeus and yelled at him, "You did it, boy. You did it. You did it!" Fresno Wheeler was waving his arms and blowing his whistle again. Arizo let out a shriek and shook a clenched fist at Nick Morrano. Morrano jumped the pit wall and the two men hugged. Baby Zeus sat on his haunches looking stonily ahead across the pit. Fresno Wheeler came over to Arizo's corner. "Hold your dog," he yelled. "He's got to make scratch to finish the fight. Don't let him loose."

Wheeler went back to the center of the pit and when there was silence he called out, "Arizo's dog, Baby Zeus, to scratch. He must be willing to carry on the fight. Cajun rules." There were more yells. Baby Zeus was starting to growl again. Arizo wanted to pat him, but the dog was covered with wounds.

"Release your dog," Wheeler called, looking at Arizo. Baby Zeus was alert now. Arizo felt him trembling a little under his hands and as he released him gave him a jubilant little shove. They were collecting bets already. Baby Zeus wobbled across the pit towards the black dog like a runner with a charley horse. But Fresno Wheeler's whistle was blowing fiercely. Sensing something wrong, the crowd fell silent. Arizo gave Morrano a puzzled look and Morrano shrugged. The crowd was watching Wheeler.

Wheeler called out: "The fight is drawn. Baby Zeus was pushed to make scratch. The fight is drawn."

There was a stunned silence and then somebody shouted, "Whaddya mean a draw? Zeus won it. I was here."

Wheeler looked down and waved his arms in front of him. "The fight is a draw," he repeated. "Baby Zeus was pushed. It's a draw."

A thunderous mixture of boos and whoops filled the chicken barn. Beer cans began hurtling into the pit, fighting broke out in several places and there was a rush for the exit.

Eli Gardner snapped his equipment case shut, scooped up Dynamite, nodded towards Arizo's corner and left. Arizo knelt in his corner, holding Baby Zeus, looking down. Nick Morrano stood over him. Neither man spoke. The noise in the barn was deafening. They were shouting, cursing, falling over benches, pushing to get out. The Okie appeared and started taking down the pit. He avoided looking at Arizo's corner.

Nick bent down and repacked Arizo's case. He shut it and motioned to Arizo that they should go. Arizo's face was crumpled and close to tears. He carried Baby Zeus gently in his arms and walked over to the Ford Econoline. The pickup trucks were pulling out of the yard, headlamp beams swinging back and forth, doors banging, people yelling good-bye. When they reached the Ford, the Mississippi Hawk was leaning against the side, watching them come up, smoking a big cigar.

"He didn't give you boys the break," he said.

Arizo shrugged. "Let me get in there," he said.

"Sure. I got the Caddy. I'll ride you back. That dog needs some quiet now."

Arizo nodded. "Thanks."

Morrano went to find one of his Chicano friends to drive the van back to Napa.

"I got a blanket," the Hawk said. They laid Baby Zeus on the blanket and Arizo shot him with more antibiotic and stopped the bleeding.

"You got steroids?" the Mississippi Hawk asked. Arizo shook his head.

"Pity, I didn't think to bring my case. That dog needs blood, too," the Hawk said.

When they had sponged Baby Zeus, they wrapped him in a blanket and laid him on the back seat of the Cadillac. Morrano rode up front with the Hawk. Arizo was in the back next to Baby Zeus.

It was an hour's drive back to Winters. They didn't talk much at all, though Arizo said, "How could I fuck up? After all he did, how could I fuck up like that?" repeating the question to himself several times as they drove.

Morrano directed the Hawk to Arizo's place. The car rode smooth and silent, and the silence made Arizo's distress all the more palpable. They pulled into the driveway and Morrano got out. He went around and opened Arizo's door.

"I guess you'd better keep him in the house tonight," Morrano said.

Arizo looked towards the house. A blue glow came from Ruby's room. He got out. The Mississippi Hawk stood beside the driver's door. Arizo reached in and lifted the dog in his arms. "He's asleep," he said. He backed out of the car and stood up.

"Let me see him," Morrano said. He flipped back the blanket and looked. After a moment, Morrano said, "He's dead, Mike. He ain't asleep. He's gone."

"Bullshit," Arizo said. "Bullshit!" he said urgently.

The Mississippi Hawk came over and looked close. "Bring him around into the headlights," he said. "Be quick." Arizo did as he said. The Hawk looked. "Hemorrhagic shock," he said. "I was afraid of that."

Arizo laid Baby Zeus down on the ground, feeling the limpness in the dog's body. He uncovered him and looked closely.

"I gotta be going," the Hawk said.

The two men, bent over the lifeless dog, heard the sound of the car door close, and the soft hum of the Cadillac backing out of the driveway. Neither of them looked up.

Ruby switched on the bedside light when Arizo came into the room. He stood inside the door staring blankly at her. She sat up urgently in the bed.

"Bajista," she used their private name for him, "what happened?"

He came around and sat slowly beside her, his back to her. "I cost him the fight," he said. "He's dead."

Ruby clicked her tongue and slipped out of bed. Kneeling before him, she drew off his boots. Then she got back into the bed, opened the front of her nightdress, and pulled him gently down beside her. She covered him. She made little clucking noises and stroked his dark hair as she held his face to her breast. Arizo put his arms about her, and they lay still. Slowly she felt her softness relax him, felt him drifting into sleep.

In the morning she left the bed quietly, before he woke. When he did he called her, she came to him with coffee. He sat up, only briefly meeting her eyes. She put the coffee on the stand beside the bed and sat next to him. At last he asked, "Are you angry?"

She shook her head. "I am quiet for both of you," she said. "That's all. It is a little death for him, but a big death for you." She stroked his cheek, looking at him intently. Then she rose, went to the window, drew back the curtains and stood looking out, her back to him. The light made him blink. He saw that they had returned the Ford.

"I don't know what to say to you," he said softly.

She shrugged without turning. "There's nothing to say. You did your best. You always do your best. Everyone knows it."

"I made mistakes. I didn't think. Is that my best?"

She went to him with quick little steps and he held her, pressing his head against her warm belly.

"I felt so strong," he said. "For a little while I felt so strong. I rose up, above myself. It was a fine feeling, Ruby. Sometimes I felt like this when I was a boy, but never since. I was so full of myself, I forgot and made a mistake and lost it all."

"It will come back to you," she said. "It will come back. It's best when things find you," she said. "Then you're ready."

Arizo wasn't sure what she meant, but he nodded anyway and said, "Yes."

He went east, up through Sacramento and over the Sierra Nevada on Highway 80, by Gold Run, Dutch Flat, and Emigrant Gap to the summit at Donner. He drove the big curves of the four-lane interstate with the window down, wearing his parka against the sharp air. Summer had faded the mountains a down-at-heel olive drab. The rocks were dusty, and the sky was gray, and the dark firs stood flat against the outcroppings. It was a lackluster time for the mountains, he thought, but the first snow would put teeth back into them. The first sparkle of powder would snap them back to life like a cold shower after a long night. The snow was late coming this year, he thought.

He relaxed as he crossed the mountains. He leaned out of the window to breathe the cold wind. The tensions of leaving dis-

solved. The mountains put a stop to what was behind. The downhill road from Donner was rolling him into something new. He
coasted the old Ford through Truckee, headed for the Nevada
line at Boca. He had suffered a loss: loss of a dog he loved, loss of
a friend, loss of prestige, loss of expectations. He thought of Maxwell. Some people lose a quarter and make more of a fuss than
Maxwell did about losing his life, he thought. It's a question of
what you make of anything. That's why he was crossing the
mountains instead of staying in Winters or heading down south
into the San Joaquin. His friends in Winters would want to hold
him to the memory of the fight with commiserations, looks and
murmurs. They would have him feeling sorry for himself and
Baby Zeus in no time, and he'd be stuck back there where he
wasn't comfortable anymore.

So it was best to leave. It wasn't chickenshit, like Morrano said.
It was just best to spend your time with people you could enjoy,
and he couldn't enjoy them in Winters anymore. It wasn't their
fault, but they took too long to forget. So he buried Baby Zeus
and said his other good-byes. He threw his gear and his rifle on
the mattress in the back of the Ford. He gave the house to Ruby.
He took the twenty $50 bills saved from the fight, and left. It took
him three days to pack up his life there and get on his way.

He was going to find Lumpy Weldon in Cope, Idaho. He didn't
know much about Idaho, but Morrano did. Morrano hunted
there. He made a big point of getting out the map he had of the
western states and showing off what he knew. He was glad to be
able to do something for his friend. Arizo saw from the map Morrano spread out on the kitchen table how Idaho rests on the
shoulders of Utah and Nevada, driving a northward wedge 400
miles to the Canadian border that splits Oregon and Washington
from Wyoming and Montana.

"The panhandle here," Morrano said with emphasis and an air
of importance, "is maybe forty miles wide and it cuts right into the
main heart of the Rockies as they slide across here from British
Columbia here, kind of southeast into Montana and Wyoming.
Down here," Arizo could see him under the kitchen light, stabbing the map with his thick forefinger like Ike showing Monty

the plan for D-Day. "Down here the panhandle opens out into
the Salmon River Mountains. That's where we go huntin'. The
Salmons are like a fat spur, see. They curl outta the Bitterroots.
They're like the western wall of the Rockies."

Sandwiched between the Salmon Mountains and the Bitterroots he saw on the map the Big Lost, the Lemhi and the Beaver-
head ranges, running parallel, north and south, to sink into the
broad arc of the Snake River plain.

"This," Morrano said, stabbing the plain, "is where the people
live. Up here in the mountains"—he shifted his finger—"about all
you're gonna meet is white pine, bobcats an' bears an' a lion
maybe. This is some of the wildest country that's left. I tell you.
In the summer the heat'll make your head buzz an' in winter
your piss'll freeze 'fore it hits the snow. Honest to God."

Arizo didn't say anything.

"There was a whole mess of Injuns here." Morrano went on,
"There was Shoshonis, Sheepeaters an' Couer d'Alene [he pronounced it Curdaleen, as if it were all one word] an' more, but
when the miners come they put 'em on reservations. They give
'em all the shit land. Now of course that's where they're findin' all
the uranium an' oil an' everything so now they're tryin' to get it
back from them."

"I heard about that," Arizo said.

"Yeah, well you won't hear too much," Morrano said, "because Injuns don't have it together like we do." He gave Arizo a
nudge and laughed. Then he thought he'd gone too far and
winced.

"They killed all the beaver, they took all the gold, they cut
down 'bout every tree they could an' now they're comin' back for
the *rocks* because the rocks,"—Morrano clapped his hands—"are
filled with uranium."

They found Cope on the map. It was in the central south,
where the Big Lost Mountains and the Big Lost River run out
and sink into the broad plain of the Snake River.

"Well that's gotta be a one-horse town," Morrano said. "You
ain't gonna get work there I guarantee. Those are Mountain boys
up there. They're a tight-assed raggety bunch I'll tell you."

"I know about them," Arizo said.

"Cajounes is all that counts with them."

"Weldon's gotta have cajounes to find work in a little town like that."

Morrano folded up the map and pressed it on him. He had it with him now in the glove locker. It wouldn't be hard to find Weldon if he was still in Cope because Cope was so small and Weldon usually worked as a short order cook or Greyhound mechanic. They'd been friends for six years and more, crossing paths here and there in their wanderings. Weldon had been disappointed when Arizo stuck in Winters, but he kept sending an occasional postcard. The last was from a trailer camp in Cope, in the Big Lost River valley, saying he should come up. The postcards were always an invitation. Weldon had said there was work and good people and big country in Cope.

But that was in the spring, eight months ago. He hadn't heard from him since. Probably he was gone by now and the work, too. The great thing about Weldon was that he never wanted to know what had been happening to you or what your plans were. Weldon picked you up where you came in and let you off where you left. All that counted to him was what went on between those points. That way, Weldon said, he was spared a mess of half-truths, misunderstandings, and bullshit.

Part II

COPE

Rᴵᴄᴋ Cᴏᴜʟᴛᴇʀ woke at 7:35 ᴀ.ᴍ. and remembered it was Saturday and he didn't have to work. He turned to face his wife, Sue-Ellen and studied her nose-to-nose. Women were always more beautiful lying down, he thought. When she didn't have gravity to contend with, it softened the way a woman looked. Coulter liked to gaze upon Sue-Ellen while she slept. "If only you was really like that," he whispered to her, "I swear I'd never have no trouble lovin' you." She had a fine profile: a small straight nose, the softest curve to her upper lip and a pleasing set to her jaw. The rest of her ballooned out under the bedclothes, her head the tip of an iceberg. She weighed a good 200 pounds and reminded him of one of those vast pink Playboy nymphs or a full, round cumulonimbus, rose-tinged by the setting sun.

A spontaneous rush of love for her came over him. He slid a hand beneath the bedclothes. She stirred and turned towards him, reaching for him. But he rolled her back and slid upon her, gently as a Polynesian upon a basking turtle, falling between her thighs as a man falls in a dream.

She smiled a little without opening her eyes. "You're making a pig of yourself," she murmured.

He grunted softly and grinned.

"Would you die if you couldn't?"

"I would," he sighed.

She moved with him, growing involved. In a while she began sporadically shuddering, a Popocatepetl on the brink of eruption. "Mmm," she kept saying. "Mmm, mmm, mmm."

"Mmm, mmm," he echoed. They had grown up like brother and sister. Maybe that's why he enjoyed it with her so much, he thought. Every time was like incest. The idea inflamed him even further, and he drove at the sighing flesh beneath him with fresh vigor.

As the door chimes rang, the clock radio came on. "When I'm holdin' you, feel my heart a-beatin'," a man sang. Sue-Ellen pushed up her head. The door chimes rang mellifluously again.

"Shit," Coulter said, continuing to move in an absentminded fashion. "Let it ring."

Sue-Ellen dropped back and nodded.

"You're my woman," the man sang.

"Let me on top," she said.

The bedroom door opened. The chimes rang again. The couple turned their heads simultaneously. Their four-year-old son, Jason, stood looking at them in silence.

"Hell 'n' shit," Coulter swore softly, attempting an imperceptible stroke. Sue-Ellen clucked and rolled over, spilling her husband as a sow spills a suckling pig. She came up on one elbow and smiled at the boy. Coulter felt it slipping away. "Oh shit!" he exploded.

"Hello, Jason," Sue-Ellen cooed.

The boy turned and padded away. The chimes rang twice, impatiently.

"Sonovabitch!" Coulter said disgustedly.

"Goddammit, Rick!" Sue-Ellen flung back the covers. "Watch

your goddamn mouth." She rolled from the bed and went out, half-closing the door behind her. Coulter lay there stroking himself, hoping against hope for a continuance. He heard Sue-Ellen open the front door. There was a momentary pause. A man spoke and then Sue-Ellen called, "It's the sheriff for you, Rick."

But for this interruption, Coulter's mood that morning would have been smooth and reflective. He certainly wouldn't have burst from the house an hour or so later, like a clockspring, with but one thought in mind: the raven-haired girl at the Ho-Hum Motel.

The Ho-Hum, Cope's only motel, stood off Main Street at the western end, beside the John Deere tractor dealership Ned Seiler ran. In the summer Seiler paraded his tractors on the apron in front of the showroom, a precise row of tall three-wheelers, glinting in the sun, angled like fighters on a carrier deck. But this time of year the forecourt was empty, and the drab tufts of grass pushing through the cracks in the asphalt rustled in a cold wind that gusted through the town.

The Ho-Hum was set back from the road a little, so they hung out the name in pink neon on a sky-blue board that stood in a cairn of cemented rocks hauled from the Big Lost. The motel, built in the mid-fifties, was three sides and two stories of white-painted cinderblock about a center parking lot with a lifeless patch of grass in the middle and an empty swimming pool with cracked sky-blue sides. A black railing stood around the upstairs balcony, and the door to each room was painted a different color.

As he pulled in, Coulter spotted the girl standing behind a service cart on the balcony, dressed in a white nylon uniform, sorting through clean linen. She looked down. He was something, tall and broad and built, with a fine face like one of those cigarette cowboys and smoky eyes full of good times and a head of cute, tight chestnut curls that bustled out from under the black hat with the Mercury dime band he always wore. She held still. He'd been a hero in high school. He had letters for everything and he ran through everyone. They were five years out of school now, but she'd never forget how he was and she'd never believe he'd asked her out. He just wanted to get laid. She knew that really, but still.

Coulter grinned and waved at her through the windshield. She nodded, startled. Coulter felt his mouth growing dry. He parked at the foot of the stairs and bounded up three steps at a time, saliva evaporating like hosewater on a hot sidewalk. She half-smiled as he came out onto the balcony and touched his black Stetson. She was holding a clean sheet. She looked nervously around and he followed her look. The yard below was deserted. So was the office. He made a friendly show of rubbing his hands and shrugging against the cold as he came towards her. She was a slight, stoop-shouldered girl with the shadow of a moustache and dark eyes a little close together. Coulter remembered reading in *True* magazine that girls with moustaches were *really* hot.

She frowned. "You shouldn't come here. My folks don't like me to see people while I'm workin'."

"I had to see you."

"You're seein' me tonight."

"That's it. I can't. I'm goin' huntin'." He came close, leaning slightly over her, right hand on the wall behind her.

"Jesus, you're tall," she said.

He grinned at her. "Let's go where we can talk."

"What's there to say?"

He crowded her good-naturedly. "Well," he shrugged. The air was thick as gravy.

"Well?"

"Well, how about this?" he said, reaching dexterously around her, opening the door behind and nibbling at the lobe of her right ear as it passed his lips.

"You're insane," she said. "You're a cracker-brain."

"I'm dyin' for you. Honest to God!"

"You just may if my dad sees you."

"Let's go inside quick," he said softly and, pivoting gracefully, put an arm about her shoulders and drew her into the room, closing the door with a boot as he did so.

The room was dusky, the curtains still drawn, light filtering in around their edges. Coulter looked quickly about. The bed was unmade, only one side used. White towels lay damp and crumpled on the carpet.

"Please!" The girl seemed bewildered.

He kissed her seriously, with tenderness that surprised her, following her movements insistently. She smelled lightly of Lysol. She squinted at him and saw his eyes were closed. He felt a breast. She filled his groin with her hip. The atmosphere groaned. Charged particles rubbed like day-old chicks.

She broke. "I don't believe you!" she gasped. "Not here. It's crazy!"

But he gathered her, holding her around the waist and at the nape of her skinny neck, an undeniable hold, and kissed and slowly pumped. Now, with growing urgency, standing, hopping, bumping mouths, groping, fumbling, zippering, sliding, they peeled each other to the skin and fell upon the unmade bed. But as they did she tensed, as though she'd felt a rattler in her sleeping bag, and Coulter felt a hand slide through his belly fur, grasp him and then pull back. Wide-eyed, she looked down.

"My God!" she said in awe. "I hope you know how to use that thing."

He looked proudly at it himself. The appearance of it never ceased to intrigue him: this thing implanted in him by genetic grace; this act of God, awesomely sprung from a field of chestnut curls. He regarded it as a father might his herculean son. It sprouted in a monstrous curve, a Beardsley phallus incarnate with a glorious purple, heart-shaped head and staring cyclopean eye.

"Trust me," he told the wide-eyed girl and pushed her gently on her back.

"Not *all!*" she whispered.

He bent over her, arched gracefully. "Shhhh," he said. "You just hush up."

"Oooooh."

"It's okay?"

"Oooh. Mmmm."

"Aaah."

She curled her legs upwards, a rose opening to the sun, and gasped with each invasion.

"Ooooh!" she wailed. "Oooh! Ooooh! Oooooh!"

"Shhh!"

"I—oooh!—can't. Aaaah! God! Oh God! Oh God!"

"Shhh," he hissed into her ear.

"Oh God!" she yelled. "Oh yes please God!"

· "Shhhhh!" he commanded, but her sheer enthusiasm was drawing him inexorably into the realm of reflex. Now he closed his eyes, no longer able to watch the ecstatic face beneath him. It was difficult enough to restrain himself in the abstract, but when he opened his eyes and saw that he was actually fucking this woman and that she was responding to his being within her, then reason departed and he began fornicating like a lion. He closed his eyes again and thought of where he would go hunting and how. It was little help. Perhaps three minutes later reflexive oscillations began, signaling the end. Thus, when he heard a key in the door, there was nothing he could do. Deep within him the discharge was beginning, and all things now would have to run their course. Light flooded the room. Beneath him the girl convulsed triumphantly, clinging with absolute ferocity, arms and legs alike. The cold air played upon his buttocks. He closed his eyes; he clenched his jaw; he thrust magnificently.

A woman screamed, "Rene!"

The girl went limp, gave out an involuntary moan and, almost in that breath, cried out, "Oh Mother. Oh God." She pushed strongly at him. "Rick!" she yelled. "Get off!" He rose half up. She withdrew her hips and he snapped out of her. Her mother stepped forward in time to see the dreadful fluid brimming over, rhythmically spurting from that awful eye upon the soft, pale belly of her beloved daughter. Her baby. Her only child. And still, as Coulter's pelvis flapped, majestic as a white stork's wing, mother and daughter froze an instant to admire this miracle enacting itself before them: this blind functioning of the unconscious beast, before the mother screamed out again.

"Rape!" she howled. "Rape!" And she ran out onto the balcony.

Rene bounced off the bed in pursuit, Coulter sat up, feet on the floor, raw stick still upright at the confluence of his thighs, and savored his climax a precious moment before he dashed for his trousers, noticing on the way the brilliant orange sheen of the mother's housecoat as she leaned over the railing, as far out as she could, screaming like some garish cockatoo from the jungle treetops.

"*Louie!*" she squawked. "*Louie!* Bring your gun, Louie. Rene's being raped!"

At that instant, Rene ran naked onto the balcony and with surprising strength dragged the woman back into the room and slammed the door.

"For Christ's sake, *shut up!*" she yelled. She was crying, a strangely determined kind of crying.

"Oh, baby. Poor baby," her mother sobbed. Then she caught sight of Coulter standing in the corner beside the bed, tall and white, balancing on one leg, threading his shorts. At the sight of him her face contorted. Coulter hopped around, away from her, as she came on, charging him, spitting. "You filthy *pig!*" she screamed. She began hitting him, slapping his back and shoulders. "*Pig, pig, pig!*" she screamed.

"Pardon me, ma'am." Coulter reached down for his trousers.

"*Pig!*" the mother yelled, slapping him hysterically.

"*Stop it!*" Rene shrieked, coming after her mother. In the mirror above the bed, Coulter saw bare breasts jiggling as she came. The girl's mother, seeing that her pummeling was ineffectual, pulled back, shrugged off her daughter, and stepped defiantly on Coulter's hat. Coulter, now trousered, sprang over and pushed her away.

"Dammit, woman," he growled. "Don't hurt my hat."

"He pushed me! He hit me!" the mother called, opening the door and flapping onto the balcony once more.

"*Louie!*" she screamed. "*Louie!* He attacked me. Louie, where *are* you?"

Coulter stuffed socks and shirt into parka pockets, zipped up, and stooped for his hat. Rene was buttoning her nylon smock. "Jesus!" she hissed at him.

He shrugged. "I'll call you," he said and left.

He was aware of people standing on the balcony and faces down below him, looking up. The girl's mother was leaning over the rail, yelling loudly. She didn't see him go. The stairs went down through the building so that once he was on them, he was out of sight. He was halfway down when an older man in gray flannel pants, a gray sweater and bedroom slippers turned the corner and started up. He was carrying a .38 as though he were afraid it would go off. Obviously, this was Louie.

"You Louie?" Coulter called immediately.

The man looked suspiciously at him and nodded. Coulter kept descending easily. He inclined his head up the stairs. "They're calling for you."

Louie grunted.

"Don't let him see you gotta gun."

"No," said Louie. He stopped and stuffed the gun into his waistband. He pulled his sweater down to cover the piece. "Can you see it?" Louie asked.

Coulter leaned back and looked. "Perfect," he said.

"Has he gotta gun?" Louie asked.

Coulter shrugged. "I doubt it, but you never know. I'll go call the cops."

"I did already. That's what took so long."

Coulter nodded and started down again.

"*Louie*, where are ya?" the mother's voice came again. "He's got away." A door banged.

Louie said, "Oh no," and hurried on up the stairs. The gun fell out of his trousers and clattered back down. Coulter stopped and picked it up. Louie turned and Coulter handed it up to him.

"Thanks," the father said, wheezing.

Coulter nodded and left. He jumped the last four steps, one hand on the rail. Walking to the car he heard the father shout, "It's me. Louie." Looking up through the windshield, he saw Louie standing outside the door, pounding on it. Rene must have locked her mother in, he thought. The guests stared in disbelief. Some were watching him.

"Open the door!" Louie was shouting. "Open the door!"

Coulter backed his pickup out of the stall and drove casually across the courtyard to the highway entrance. He waited a moment and then pulled out, heading downtown.

"God," he said aloud. "The trouble a man can get into over just a natural thing."

He turned on the radio. Lynn Anderson was singing "Rose Garden."

"Hell, honey," he said. "Don't you ever sing anything else?"

He cruised downtown. Cope was maybe six blocks long, from the phone company depot beyond the John Deere dealership to the Standard station, and not all the blocks were built on. There were a couple of general stores and a hardware store and Larry Charles the attorney and Dr. Hardcastle's office and the VFW hall with the Sherman tank, hatches welded closed, and a flagpole flying the Stars and Stripes out front on a concrete plinth. A hundred yards farther, where the Snake River road T-boned Main Street, right next to the drugstore, was the Two Ball Inn, the focal point of this scrawny mountain town.

Coulter drove through town to the Standard station at the other end and Buck Meyers, rawboned and hunched in a Levi jacket, came out to serve him. Coulter sat staring blankly, feeling remarkably relaxed, listening on the radio to some really smooth pedal steel guitar. He rubbed his nose thoughtfully. It was all up to the girl, Rene. She'd be all right, he thought. And the guests would all leave town. A '55 Ford panel wagon in gray primer pulled into the station, rumpled as a morning pillow. There was an Indian driving it. In his thirties somewhere. He pulled up at the far pumps, looked across, caught Coulter's eye, and looked away. Buck Meyers came up. Coulter paid him and Buck ambled over to the Indian, blocking Coulter's view of the man. Coulter left, driving slowly back down Main Street to the Two Ball Inn. He pulled up right outside and went in.

Greg Sanders was working the bar. They did a ham and eggs for six bits on Saturday mornings. Sanders came and stood opposite him across the bar.

"What'll y'have?" he asked, peering through his fine gold-rimmed spectacles.

Coulter undid his parka as he considered.

"I'll have a beer with it," he said. "A Lucky."

"Got dressed in a rush this morning, I see?" Sanders said, peering at Coulter's chest with a trace of admiration. Coulter looked down and realized his shirt was still in his pocket.

"As a matter of fact, that's right. I did."

"Love 'em an' leave 'em, eh, Rick?"

"I don't have to take your shit, Sanders."

"You don't have to show me no stinkin' badges," Sanders said and went to get the beer.

Arizo got directions to the Big Lost Valley trailer park while he was gassing up. This was the address he had for Lumpy Weldon. Buck Meyers told him that the park was maybe three miles north of town, and he drove out through the sage that grew among the volcanic rock under a gray sky. A cold wind blew across the road. Behind the wheel, Arizo hunched his shoulders and huddled into his parka.

A laundromat, a small store, and a bar like a big square packing crate set down in the tules with a red neon cocktail glass hung out front, sat by the road next to the trailer park. There was nothing else in sight. Arizo turned the Ford in through a screen of scrawny cottonwoods, under an archway of galvanized pipe and rusting wrought iron that looked ready to collapse, and pulled up alongside the manager's trailer. The manager was a pasty man with a sour-looking face and an asthmatic wheeze. He stood on the trailer steps holding the aluminum door ajar and looked down at Arizo with suspicion. From inside the trailer came a roar of TV laughter.

"You a friend of his or somethin'?" the manager asked.

Arizo nodded. "From California." The old man grunted and looked past Arizo, squinting at the license on the Ford. A woman on the TV screamed hysterically, and then there was an explosion of applause and a man's voice yelling above it. "She's got it! She's got it! *She's won twenty-five thousand dollars!*" The manager pursed his thin lips and nodded, satisfied. Then he said: "Weldon left here a month ago."

Arizo looked at him and gave a half laugh.

"What's so funny?"

Arizo shrugged. There was a dense roar of laughter from the television inside the trailer.

"Ruth! You wanna turn that thing down some!" the old man yelled. The sound vanished abruptly.

"He said he was goin' to Vegas," the manager said.

Ruth appeared in the doorway behind her husband. She wore a sky-blue bathrobe, and her bleached hair clung to her head in tired ringlets. She stood peering at Arizo over her husband's shoulder. "There's no work 'round here this time of year," the manager said.

"There's no work anywhere this time of year," Arizo said, nodding to the woman.

The manager squinted. "You don't want to get sore about it. When I was like you, there wasn't work summer nor winter."

"That's right," Ruth agreed. She had a peculiarly metallic voice. "Gettin' sore about it'll eat you up worse than havin' no work will. There's a bunch of them outta work in the park already. But your friend didn't complain any. He was a good boy. Never complained. He said they were hiring in Las Vegas right now. Maybe you oughta go down there. Your friend said they needed dealers. He said he'd go to dealer's school maybe, and maybe get a job at the Thunderbird. He said they're hiring for the winter season right now, was what he said."

Arizo nodded. Weldon always said that about Vegas. He was always going to deal craps. "How can a man admit he's goin' to Vegas to wash dishes," he'd say.

Arizo drove slowly back across the flatland towards town, listening to some Cajun music. He had driven all night and hadn't eaten since dinner. It was beginning to tell. He'd eat and then sleep and then make up his mind what to do. In the Standard station, Buck Meyers told him to take Main Street to the Snake River road and follow that down a little ways to the Bluebird Diner.

Main Street was busy with ranchers come to do Saturday shopping. Arizo's dimpled gray panel wagon slowly tailed a tall white Ford four-by-four pickup with Wyoming mudflaps and three cowboys brim-to-brim across the front and a 30/30 in the window rack. Arizo squinted. It was a Winchester 94 with a lever action, the same as he had in the back. He nodded to himself and made an appreciative face. He turned down the Snake River road opposite the Two Ball Inn; a split-log cabin, painted fire-station red, standing on an elevated sidewalk ten feet above the road.

It was shortly after noon when he reached the Bluebird, a chrome diner under a stand of tall, bare poplars. The sun was breaking through. He sat by a window and gazed flatly at the row of poplars that stood like bound hearth-brooms against the sky. Beyond the poplars, the desert plain spread to the foothills on the horizon, dull and mottled as a hen pheasant. Arizo yawned and turned the back of one hand idly in a shaft of sunlight, studying the fan spread of tendons and network of veins showing beneath the copper skin. He'd been a damn fool to go chasing Weldon. Maybe he'd go to Bakersfield and forget about Vegas. Vegas was depressing unless you had a big roll.

This new possibility stirred him. He opened the menu and thought of Maxwell Patterson, the ship's cook, his Aunt Jolene's lover, the frail black man with the soft face, the steel gray nap, the pencil moustache, and the dark double-breasted three-piece suits with pleated pants pressed sharp as paper folds. He made a great omelet, Maxwell. He had a steady hand and steady eye. Untroubled. He never raised his voice to Jolene, provocative as she could be. There must have been a time, but Arizo couldn't recall it. Not even when Maxwell was drunk and Jolene was yelling at him with tears of anger and despair.

Arizo became aware of the waitress standing over him. He looked up. She was really pretty and smiling, with a smooth, open face, dark hair, and turquoise eyes. The color of eyes didn't usually strike him, but this girl's did.

Looking too long, he flustered: "I didn't make up my mind," he said.

"I'll come back."

"No. I'll take the fish fingers."

She looked surprised.

"What is it?"

"They're not very good."

He shrugged. "I don't feel like meat," he said.

She smiled again and left. He watched her go, easy and grace-ful, and shook his head at the way he'd been with her. They'd seen into one another, but he couldn't just let it be. He would leave for Vegas after he had eaten. He looked out of the window, thinking of how frustrated Jolene would get at the way Maxwell accepted things. He hadn't been able to understand it himself then, but he did now. He hadn't been able to see how Maxwell could keep drinking when the destruction was so obvious. Now he could. It hadn't always been this way. When he first came to live with Maxwell and Jolene, Maxwell and he had spent some good time together. The best he remembered from all his boyhood. Maxwell mostly sailed between Honolulu and San Francisco, so he wasn't gone for long the way most of them were.

It was fun to have Maxwell at home. He balanced Jolene's seriousness, and intensity. Jolene felt responsibility, carried it like a weight. Not just for the boy, but also for Maxwell. Maxwell never felt it. That was obvious in retrospect. The way he lived, there wasn't room for worry. At least none that Arizo ever saw. Maxwell enjoyed doing things with a flair. That's what he concen-trated on.

The waitress was suddenly putting food before him. He looked up. She smiled mostly with her eyes and turned away without a word.

He watched her walk down the aisle between the crowded booths, the white fabric of her dress moving on her. He watched her go and slowly began to eat, thinking of Maxwell's flair. When Maxwell made an omelet he broke an egg and separated white from yolk all with the fingers of one hand. And as he did he gave an exaggerated flourish and flashed a smile as if he were a conjurer turning a dove into a white silk scarf. Sometimes he'd croon words from Al Jolson's "Mammy," and do a soft shoe around the kitchen, catching Jolene up in his arms. Sometimes he'd sing roughly, imi-tating Jelly Roll's coarsely sung "Dr. Jazz," standing at the wash basin in his under-shirt, suspenders hanging emptily from his waist, while he carefully shaved his sallow cheeks.

One morning he told Arizo: "Boy. You don't worry 'bout

school this mornin'. I'se gonna be your personal professor and chef." And he made them a lunch and they took it in a brown bag and rode the bus over the Big Bridge, through Treasure Island to San Francisco. It was a clear, fall day and from the bus they could see over the railing. The city rose in white steps from the water. The piers were busy. Pointing to one ship after another, Maxwell told the boy where it was bound, and the boy's mind seethed with images of strange ports and towns and people and he felt excitement and held tightly to Maxwell's hand.

In San Francisco they took the Potrero bus out to Seal's stadium, which sometimes lay literally in the shadow of the Hamm's brewery. On the brewery wall that overlooked the ball park was a neon beer glass three stories tall, which filled, blinked out and refilled with golden light.

They sat behind first base. It was a scruffy sort of field, big for a minor league park. It seemed odd to the boy that they had come to watch a contest in this field between grown-up men. The Seals were playing the Hollywood Stars. The boy wondered how the men were going to look. Maxwell took a pint from his jacket pocket, then took his jacket off and carefully folded it and put his Seals' cap on. The afternoon sun was good and warm. Maxwell leaned across to the boy. "You imagine," he said. "You imagine a supergiant like Joe DiMaggio playin' right here on this field, which he did for the Seals 'fore he was a Yankee. You imagine it." The boy was imagining a supergiant in a baseball uniform when the teams came out. The men did seem very large. The pitchers began warming up. They did everything fast and with a great deal of force. "Lefty O'Doul was manager here twenty years," Maxwell said. The name was strange to the boy.

"Lefty's lifetime average was about three hunnert and fifty an' in twenty-nine, when he were with the Phillies he hit three ninety-eight. Three ninety-eight. Phew!" Maxwell exhaled sharply. "That is somethin' boy. He had a hunnert and fifty-six hits and if he'd 'a had but one more. One more. He'd 'a hit four hunnert." Maxwell stopped and took a long drink from his pint. He wiped his mouth on the back of his hand. "Damn," he said. "Imagine that? Imagine havin' to go through the whole rest of your life knowin' that if you'd hit one more lousy time, you'd have batted four hunnert 'long with Babe Ruth an' all them others?"

"It wouldn't have worried you," the boy said.

"No. That's because I never worried 'nough to even get up there in the firs' place." He grinned broadly. "Wouldn't catch me," Maxwell said emphatically. "But I could have though. Let me tell you, last time Lefty played he was sixty. He put hisself in as pinch hitter 'n' he hit a triple. Afterward *all* the newspapermen they come 'round an' ask him, 'Lefty, what's the secret to hittin'?' Same damn fool question newspapermen is always askin' hitters. As if there's some secret. 'Well,' says Lefty, 'I tell you,' an' he looked real serious an' he went into his hittin' crouch an' they all gather 'roun' waitin' for the big secret. 'Well,' says Lefty, real slow, 'the secret you gotta remember is when you get up . . . you gotta make the pitcher laugh so damn hard he can't throw for shit!'" And Maxwell nudged the boy and leaned back and laughed so hard the boy was embarrassed.

The Seals won the game in the bottom of the ninth. Jim Moran hit one out over centerfield. The boy would always remember how powerfully the ball rode and the man with the bat looking after it as it arced. There were no bleachers in centerfield. There was no room. The ball carried the screen and landed in the street. It was that much of a hit. Maxwell stood and yelled and shook his fist. The boy watched.

On the bus going home Maxwell said, "Did you want to do somethin'?"

The boy looked at him.

"I mean with your life. Not like me."

"I don't think you do nothin'," the boy said. "You sail on ships."

Maxwell was a little drunk. He nodded. "But somethin' important. Somethin' of significance. Because if you do, you got to do what that Moran did jus' now. You got to go for *the fence*." He sat back and looked out of the window at the city. "I shoulda had someone tell me that when I was your age. But I'm tellin' you." He leaned across and the boy recoiled from the smell of his breath. "There's no one gonna blame you if you take a good cut," he said, "an' miss. But you take a third strike . . . That's what most of us do," he said. "We just stand there an' take."

"Do you want me to heat that up for you?" the waitress said. Arizo looked up.

"Shall I heat your coffee?"

She was beautiful. He thought of the world of men who could look at her with a right to their fantasies. It was best if he didn't even pretend to be a part of it. Best because then there was not wishfulness or regret, no frustration.

"I'm sorry," she repeated, "but did you want more coffee?"

"I'm half-asleep."

"You're from outta town?"

"Yeah."

"You stayin' over?"

"I don't believe so."

She poured him more coffee. "I wouldn't blame you," she said.

"Maybe I'll go to Vegas."

"Tonight?"

"I was thinking about it."

"You should sleep first."

"Are you from here?"

She shook her head. "I'm from Gallup."

"You Indian?"

"Part, I think." She stood looking down, smiling. Her eyes were clear with understanding.

"I think I'd better have my check, please," Arizo said. She nodded and left.

When he had finished eating, he went on down the road and pulled the Ford over at a place beside the river. He was full and sleepy. He locked the doors, climbed onto the mattress in the back, pulled a quilt and a blanket over himself and slept.

When he woke, it was dark. He lay for some time on his back, warm and comfortable, listening to the river. Then he struck a match and looked at his watch. It was only six-thirty. He would get a drink at the bar he'd seen on Main Street and then head for Vegas.

The Schlitz sign stuttered red-eyed as he breasted the short hill
and came to a halt on Main opposite the Two Ball Inn. He
parked the gray Ford around the back, nose in among knuckly
pickup trucks. The barroom was smoky and crowded and smelled
warm, damp, and stale. He made his way towards the rear,
through hair and hats and wool coats, until a stool emptied as he
got to it. The men on either side had their backs to him. Behind
the bar three large mirrors were framed by an ornate Corinthian
facade of amber-colored wood. He sat on the stool and looked up.
The ceiling was an amber-colored cream, stained by tobacco
smoke. The bartender looked incongruously frail, with blond hair
and fine gold-rimmed glasses. Arizo caught his eye and ordered a
draft, aware as he spoke of the man on his left turning around.

"An' give him some J.D. to chase that," the man said. He was
drunk. Arizo glanced around and nodded his thanks. He didn't
want whiskey, but neither did he want an argument. The man
was young, early twenties. His face was broad and good-looking.
His eyes twinkled. His hair was a froth of tight brown curls, and a
black hat rode on his shoulders. He looked intently at Arizo. Arizo
saw the gleam of smooth flesh and realized that the man wore
nothing underneath his parka. Then he saw the waitress from the
Bluebird Diner peering around the cowboy's shoulder at him. She
wore a russet shirt with pearl snaps and her hair was down, settling
on her shoulders, amber in the light, rich as the rest of her. She
was smiling at him again, and she lightly raised an eyebrow—in
mock surprise, he thought. He allowed himself to grin and immediately felt foolish. It was such an entirely inadequate gesture. The
man saw the grin and nodded. "I'm Rick Coulter," he said, tapping himself on the chest. "Schtick close to me, frien'." He put an
arm about Arizo's shoulders.

"You're an Injun, yes?"

Arizo gave the slightest nod, more of understanding than as-
sent, and Coulter plowed on.

"Saw you come into town," he said. He was weaving slightly on
his stool and now he began wagging a finger in Arizo's face while
holding onto his shoulder with the other hand. "Well, listen.
Injuns sometimes get into trouble in here Saturday night."

"Don't you worry," Arizo said. The girl was still leaning forward, watching him. He felt confusion.

"I'm Rick Coulter, and I wanna say you're lucky to have me along. Because five years ago they'd hang yer ass for sellin' likker to an Injun anywhere in this whole goddamned state. You know that? Huh? You know that?"

"It doesn't surprise me."

"But I can kick ass."

"So?"

"So?" He looked surprised. "So you're lucky to have me along. They haven't all forgot that yet."

"Forgot what?"

"About Injuns and likker. There's some of them here who're a lot more than five years behind the times." Coulter turned to the girl.

"Isn't he?"

"What?"

"What? Lucky to have me along."

She nodded. "We all are."

"Wha'sat?"

"We all are."

"Tha's right. We all are." He patted them both on the back. "Tha's right." He turned to Arizo. "This's Sandy Brown." He looked blank. "I forgot your name."

"Mike Arizo."

"Mike Arizo," Coulter said triumphantly. "This here's Sandy Brown." He peered at Arizo. "You married?"

"No."

"Huh? Tha's great. Because here's a wife for you. You wouldn't have this opportunity, 'ceptin' I already got one." He kept his arms about them both. "Where you from?" he asked Arizo.

"California," Arizo said, aware that he was carrying on the conversation only for the girl.

"A *Californicator!*" Coulter roared, banging his beer bottle on the bar.

The man on the other side of Arizo turned around. He was tall and tight-looking, in his early forties with very pale, watery eyes and, Arizo realized, a harelip, a caving-in that created a small shadow beneath his nose. He stared at Coulter.

"Hush up, Rick," Sandy said. "You're drunk."

"It's only Poulsen. Poor ol' Poulsen," Coulter said.

"What you thay?" Poulsen said.

"What you thay?" Coulter mocked him.

Poulsen spat on the floor and stared hard at them before he turned away.

"You came to hunt?" Coulter asked Arizo.

"I'm just passin' through."

"Hey-y-y, pass me by if you're only passin' through," Coulter half-sang and half-shouted. "Remember that? Tha's Johnny . . . Johnny Ricardo."

"Rodriguez," Sandy said.

"Ricardo," Coulter yelled.

The bartender appeared. "Rick," he leaned across the bar. "Please."

"Hey. Another round."

"You've had enough."

"For my friends. My friend from California. Larry, this here's Ricardo Rodriguez."

Larry nodded to Arizo and pointed to his glass.

Arizo motioned to Sandy. Sandy shook her head. Arizo nodded and pushed his glass towards Larry.

"You a hunter?" Coulter turned back to Arizo. "You hunt?"

Arizo nodded.

"You gotta rifle?"

Arizo nodded.

"Then by God you can come huntin' with me in the morning," Coulter said. "I need someone to go huntin' with. You gotta rifle?"

"I don't have a license."

"Shit." Coulter screwed up his face. "Sheeeit. Who needs a fuckin' license? I can get us in an' outta these mountains if the airborne was tryin' to stop me."

Larry set a beer and a shot down and took the money from the stack of bills on the bar before Coulter.

"Lis'en. You wanna go huntin' with me?"

"I'm headed for Vegas."

"First hunt, then go."

"I'd sooner be . . ."

"Huntin' with me!" Coulter finished the sentence loudly. "Right on, baby. Right on, baby," he repeated. "Tha's nigger talk. You ever hear nigger talk? You ever hear them talk, niggers?"

"I was raised by a nigger," Arizo said evenly.

"We don't get so many niggers up here. Fact is we scarcely get a one. It's too cold for them up here."

"I imagine it is," Arizo said.

"There's not many that'll go huntin' with me. You know that? I mean, I can't find anyone to hunt with me, 'ceptin' my Pa, an' he can't go that good anymore. The rest, they don't care to." He peered closely at Arizo. "An' you know why?"

Arizo leaned back and saw Sandy smiling. He didn't smile back. He simply let himself look at her face, let it seem she was a woman he could have. He enjoyed the sight of her in a way that stirred fragments of memory from a world mostly forgotten. He smiled.

"Tha's right," Coulter yelled. "*Tha's right.* It *is* funny. But not the way you think."

"Rick," Sandy urged. "Rick, cool it."

"It's goddamned funny," Coulter yelled, ignoring her. "You wanna know why they won't hunt with me? This here's why." He suddenly stood upright on the rungs of the bar stool so that he towered unsteadily over everyone. Then he cupped a hand over his sex and shook it. "'Cause I got what the ladies want." He looked down at their upturned faces. Conversation died. "More of it than anyone in this county. So I'm a freak. An' they don't want to get too close to me 'cause they don't want me near their old lady case she gets hot. Tha's why," he yelled and threw his arms outspread in a dramatic gesture that caused him to lose his balance and topple to the floor with a crash, legs hooked in the fallen stool. There was a roar of laughter. Arizo helped him up. Coulter looked suddenly maudlin.

"I think you had enough," Arizo said quietly. "I'll buy you coffee someplace."

"*Coffee!*" He faced Arizo, and Arizo was aware of all the faces turned on them. There was no way out. He had the feeling that always came with the realization that he was at the beginning of something most unpleasant and unavoidable.

"I'm tellin' you something important, and you're talking about coffee." Coulter's voice was strong. He had only Hank Williams on the jukebox to compete with now.

"You don't believe me." Coulter was still talking to Arizo, but looking at the crowd around him. "Well, I'm tellin' you the truth. They all know what I got." He grabbed himself again, his voice rising, "An' the women they all wanna see it an' get it up an' see how much they can take, even." The crowd stirred and some giggled. "I hear them a-titterin' everytime they see me come an' the men peekin' over in the u-rinal. They all love it, but they can't tell me." He shook his head. "No, sir. No, sir. They got to treat me like original sin 'cause I am attached on the end of this thing, see." He was shouting now. "An' they don't want it out that they even think about this stuff." He paused. "An' I'm married to the only woman in town that knows 'bout all you assholes. That knows it's this them women want. Not me." He gave it another shake. He looked about to cry.

"I'm too goddamned big for this prissy-ass, shithole, two-bit town. I should get outta here like that faggot, Tony Danudo. 'Cause you assholes don't know a *man* from a *cock*."

Poulsen came off his stool. "That'th enough of your thit, Coulter." He was very red in the face.

Coulter spat. "S'matter, Poulsen? You talk about it with your fuckin' buddies. You don't wanna talk about it with me? Huh?" He lurched towards Poulsen. "I'm too big for this town, Poulsen. Want me to show ya?" He began fumbling with his fly. "Want me to show ya what your old lady likes most? Huh? You wanna see it, too?"

Poulsen knocked him down with one punch. Despite himself, Arizo was impressed. He hadn't often seen it done, particularly among drunks. Coulter caromed off two bystanders and fell among dusty boots beside the pool table. The bare light shone on his contorted face. Sandy went to him. Poulsen snatched a pool

cue and started in, but Arizo blocked the big man, who stood hesitantly, then went back to the bar. The talk began again.

Arizo and Sandy took Coulter home in the Ford. When he got
out of the car, Coulter kneeled in the cold night and started
retching on a patch of lawn outside his house. The front door
opened, and Arizo saw the silhouette of a large young woman
standing in the light.

"That you Sandy?" Sue-Ellen said.

"Brought your man home."

After a moment's pause, she said, "Thank you, hon. You want
me to fix you coffee?"

"No, thanks. Sue-Ellen, this here's Mike Arizo."

"Glad to know you."

"Likewise."

"Ain't you even gonna ask me what kinda day I had?" Coulter,
still on his knees, suddenly called to Sue-Ellen.

On their way back to the bar, Arizo and Sandy Brown drove
side-by-side in silence, acutely aware of each other, but not finding
anywhere to begin. They pulled into the lot where Sandy's car was
parked. "This is dumb," she said. "Where you staying?"

"I'm not," he said. "I think I'll go on."

"Come and have coffee with me before you go."

"Maybe I'll just go on."

With two fingers on his shoulder, she turned him to face her.
In the glow of the headlights, she saw he was frowning. She
smoothed his forehead. "It's okay," she said. "It's only that there's
so few men in this town to *talk* to."

He smiled awkwardly and nodded. "I'd like to," he said. "Only
I didn't want to say that I did."

He followed her car. She lived in a small cabin close to the
river. There was a short dirt drive. Cottonwoods came up in the
headlights on the right of it. Inside the cabin it was warm. The
floor was carpeted in Navajo rugs, very fine and naturally dyed,
browns and grays on ivory from Two Grey Hills and Crystal.
Against the wall to the right was a sofa, and at the far end a small
wood stove, wooden chairs, and a sink. The walls were natural

pine, and the roof, too, and there were heavy sackcloth drapes and potted plants hanging in rope cradles from the rafters. It was civilized and personal, a place such as he was unused to.

"In the winter I come home after work and light the stove," she said. "Even if I'm going out." She smiled. "But I don't go out much in the winter."

She put a kettle on the stove, pulled up two chairs, and they sat before it. "When I get it real hot," she said, "it'll boil water from cold in seven minutes."

"We're pretty high up."

She shook her head. "Not really. Just two thousand feet. But it feels like more in the winter."

She opened the firebox and they watched the flames while they waited for the kettle to boil.

"Why are you here?" he asked.

She shrugged. "Why are *you* here?"

"An accident."

"Me, too."

"But you stayed."

"Doesn't seem to make much difference."

"No?"

"I go back into the mountains in summer."

"And now?"

"Nobody goes there now."

"Coulter wants to."

"He's crazy. The snow's coming."

"So soon?"

"It's October," she said. "Are you going with him?"

"I haven't hunted for a long time."

"He's a good hunter."

"Maybe I'll go then."

"He'll call here before it's light. He wants you to go."

"He's got a nerve."

She nodded. "He's all right. He needs someone to take him seriously."

"I didn't want to get caught up in it."

"You already are."

Arizo thought about this. "I sorta like him," he admitted.

"He's crazy."

"Is it true what he was sayin'? About no one huntin' with him an' all?"

"Yeah. And the rest."

He was silent.

"You're like him," she said. "Maybe that's why."

"Whatta you mean?"

She reached down and picked out another piece of wood from the pile behind the firebox and pushed it on while he watched her. "You both seem like you're sort of wandering around," she said eventually. He looked at her, surprised. "You in one world and him in another. But in the end . . ." she hesitated. "You know what I mean?"

"I hear what you're saying."

"I didn't mean anything insulting." She reached out and touched his sleeve. "I like you."

"No," he said. "It's okay." He sipped his coffee and they were quiet a moment. Then he said, "What about Poulsen?"

She sat hunched towards the fire. Without moving, she offered: "Vern's a real straight guy. He has a ranch outside town. He's got two kids and his wife, Marlene, that he's real crazy about. I mean jealous. I hardly know him—just what I hear. He doesn't come in the diner much, just sometimes on Sunday."

Arizo, too, had leaned forward, elbows resting on knees, face glowing in the firelight. "He's real sensitive 'bout his ol' lady," he said.

"Yeah. Wouldn't you be if you had his problem?"

Arizo shrugged. "Is it that much of a problem?"

"Well," she said. "A man can have worse, I guess."

Arizo straightened up and wiped his mouth on the back of his hand.

"She's a good-lookin' woman," Sandy went on. "I heard from Coo-Coo she doesn't go out on him, but Vern's real scared. And when he's scared, he can be mean. Everyone knows it. Nobody goes after Marlene."

"Who's Coo-Coo?"

"He's this real young cowboy in town. I did a thing with him once that I wish I never had. I know his father. He comes in the diner a lot. He was a miner from Kellogg, up north. He got some trouble with his health, came down here an' bought a place, an' then it got too big for him an' he sold it to Vern Poulsen when Vern came to town."

"You know all about this place."

"Workin' in the diner you get to hear a lot," she said quietly.

It was late when she pulled out the sofa into a double bed and made it up for him. When she went into her room in the back, she left the door open and he lay listening to the sounds of her getting ready for bed. She turned out her light and in the dark the sound of the river came to him and he lay feeling the weight of his body on the bed.

"Good night," she called.

"Good night," he said.

He lay on his back, staring up into the darkness, letting his muscles go. In a while, she asked softly, "What happened to you?"

He was startled for a moment and didn't know what to answer.

"I split up with a woman."

"That's all?"

"That's all."

"Were you with her long?"

"Long enough."

"Don't take it so hard," she whispered.

He wanted to cry. The sadness washed over him in small waves. Then suddenly she was beside him in the gloom. She got into the bed and lay near him, so close that he could feel her body warmth and hear her breathing. At first he felt confused and remote, but when she demanded nothing, he let himself be held.

"Sleep," she said gently.

"It's best I go to Vegas in the mornin'."

"Is that what you want?"

"I don't know what I want." He turned on his back and rested his hand on his forehead. "I don't think too much about it. If you don't think, then you don't get all excited about somethin' that never happens, and you don't get down about somethin' that does." He wished it were so; he was thinking about Baby Zeus.

"Yeah," she said, almost in a whisper, "but if you never think at all, then the sky falls down on your head when you least expect it."

"It does anyway," he said, and they laughed together in the darkness.

The telephone was ringing. Arizo felt a body stir against him and woke with no idea of where he was. It was still dark.

"It's Rick," Sandy said, slipping out of bed. He heard her pick up the phone and come quickly back across the room in the cold.

"Yes," she said. "He's here."

He felt about in the blackness for the phone, thinking how strange the whole thing was.

"Mike." Coulter's voice was energetic. "This is Rick. You ready to go?"

"To Vegas."

"Look. I screwed up last night. At least come have coffee with me and drop me at my truck on your way outta town. It's still at the bar."

They went hunting. They drove out through the sleeping town in the Ford, and Coulter directed them to the road over the Sun Valley pass into Copper Basin. At the summit they got out to watch the sun swelling behind the far peaks and the valley settle for a moment deeper into the last blue shadow of night. The air was sweet, and Arizo breathed it deeply into him. When the sun exploded over the ridge, light flashed on roofs and windows in Cope, a thousand feet below. They sat on an outcropping, watching the golden light chase down the slope beneath them in a broken line.

"You should stay here awhile," Coulter said.

Arizo looked at the ground beneath his boot. It had a fine, sandy crust, dark with moisture. He worked his boot heel gently until it broke through the crust to the ground beneath. He felt strong and clear in himself, extremely capable. It was being with

the woman. It was being with her and in the mountains that
made the difference.

"At least stay until the deer season ends."

"When's that?"

"December one."

"I need work though."

"I can get you work," Coulter said. "They need a guy where I
work. I can get you on."

Arizo dropped Coulter off outside his house on A Street shortly
after noon. Coulter opened the front door roughly, twisting it
with his hand and prodding it with his boot, arms full of beer
cans and clothes and his rifle laid over the top of the pile. Sue-
Ellen was stretched royally on the sofa watching a large color TV
in a shiny walnut veneer console—a wedding gift from her parents. She wore her hot-pink nylon robe and fluffy matching
slippers and was pulling on a cigarette as he opened the door. In
the other hand was a can of Diet Pepsi. The room was hot as Au-
gust and stuffy. Coulter recoiled. She turned her head.

"Get anything?"

"No," he said. "You need it this hot?"

"I like it hot." She smiled a small cherubic smile that barely ex-
panded the wealth of smooth flesh around her delicate chin,
pushed away the newspaper, a heap of unfolded wash, and Jason's
plastic building blocks on the sofa beside her and patted the seat
invitingly. Coulter took off his parka and threw it over the back of
the chair by the table under the window. The table was crowded
with breakfast dishes, cereal packages, a carton of milk, a frying
pan heavy with cold grease, beer cans, a half-empty six-pack of
Diet Pepsi, a large black ashtray, and a round goldfish bowl with a
floor of colored sand and one small goldfish. Coulter picked his
way through toys, clothes, shoes, and cardboard Pamper boxes on
the floor and sat beside her.

"I gotta call Pops," he said, looking distractedly at the television. A young couple were sitting side by side under a parasol on
the edge of a Beverly Hills swimming pool in an elegantly land-
scaped desert garden shaded by King palms.

"How's that?" Sue-Ellen said, cracking her gum and keeping her eyes on the screen.

"I got to get Mike on at the quarry."

"It's best this way," the woman beside the pool was saying.

"He's staying?" Sue-Ellen asked.

Coulter nodded, eyes on the screen.

Sue-Ellen stretched out a little further and made a weary grimace. Coulter reached across and squeezed the nearest of her swelling breasts appreciatively.

"Goebbels called again for you," she said. "He said the sheriff wants you to stay away from the Ho-Hum Motel. He said you was up there foolin' with that girl, their daughter. What's her name?"

Coulter had missed something. The man who had been beside the pool was now running up a fire escape pursued by two others. All three carried guns.

"Don't know." Coulter shrugged.

"Don't give me that bullshit."

"Ellen, I think. No Rene."

"You think? You oughta know at least who you got it into." A TV chase was now being carried on over the roof of a factory. "You oughta at least know how old they are." They both stared ahead, watching the television impassively.

"I stopped by there 'cause Gowdy's Coke truck was outside and I wanted to get a cheap case for you and she came out and just got *all over* me."

The man by the swimming pool had now fallen through a glass skylight and was hanging by his armpits, his pursuers closing in fast. It looked hopeless.

"She won't admit you raped her. That's all you got to worry about," Sue-Ellen said.

"Me raped her!" Coulter looked for a moment at his wife. "Jesus. I should hope not."

He slid a meaty, callused hand beneath her robe.

"Hold it," she said. He looked at the screen. Police had arrived on the factory roof.

"He *was* a narc!" Sue-Ellen said with mild surprise.

Coulter's small eyes twinkled, and he softly bit Sue-Ellen's perfect ear. She giggled.

"If there was another woman in the country that'd put up with
me . . ." he began.

"You'd be humpin' her," Sue-Ellen said.

"How come you put up with me?"

"It's no big deal," Sue-Ellen said. "I mean, some poor bitch's
gotta prove once a week she can still turn a guy on. Some of them
is curious about what you got. It's not such a big deal." She
paused. "And if you think it is, then you're more damn fool than
they are."

An elderly lady was selling them a preparation for hemorrhoids.

"I can get a man if I want him," Sue-Ellen said. She looked at
him, making a round and sensual O with her lips and drooping
her eyelids. "You don't think so?"

"Sure I know it," Coulter said generously.

"You're damn right, baby." She moved over to press her bosom
against him. "Us women are like hot sauce," she whispered, licking his ear with her sharp little tongue. "Only there's no such
thing as hot sauce." She pushed him back onto the sofa, her hand
fluttering to his groin. She loomed over him, a hot pink sperm
whale breeching, unfastening him. Her robe fell open. Suddenly
the sky was filled with loosened hair and pearl-colored flesh descending upon him like hanging gardens. "There's no such thing
as *hot sauce*, honey," she repeated softly. "Only weak men."

The winter sun warmed pale as a stepmother's love. On the
high sidewalk outside the drugstore, beside the Two Ball Inn, the
old men sat in bundles on the bench watching the traffic pass
below on Main. Behind Main, tall poplars, spotted with the last
small leaves of summer, grew in narrow avenues on Stein and
Parker. These ill-tarred streets ran away from Main up through a
small patchwork of wooden bungalows to give out at the foot of
the mountains half a mile away.

The old men watched a battered gray Ford panel wagon climb
the rise of the Snake River road to the junction with Main,
directly below where they sat, and turn right. The driver was an In-

dian they didn't recognize. But beside him was the Brown girl, and that set off a gust of conversation among them.

At Sandy's direction, Arizo pulled up outside the Speedy Mart. The weather had already blanched and cracked the plaster storefront. Standing beside the smooth, dark wood of Boyer's handsome fifty-year-old feed store, the supermarket was a sorry monument to changing values. In the Speedy Mart they bought pippins, sharp cheddar, hot pastrami, mayonnaise, a cottage loaf, scallions and a cold six-pack of Coors. The young boy behind the meat counter in his Bruce Lee T-shirt and Peterbilt baseball cap chewed his gum violently and eyed Sandy's crotch helplessly. Sandy gazed admiringly up at Arizo, and Arizo, in his threadbare Levi's, down-at-heel, pointy-toes boots, old green parka and white hat, grinned that broad coppery grin at her while the boy looked on and swallowed, his Adam's apple bobbing awkwardly.

As they came out of the store, Arizo grinned at her. "I believe that boy's got some sorta crush on you." He held the lunch in a shopping bag under one arm.

"You could say that."

"Uhuh," he grumped. She looked up at him. He seemed to have drifted away. As they climbed into the Ford, she said lightly, "That's just the Boyers' kid. He's always real hot. But I don't believe he'd even know where anythin' went."

He grinned at her, not much of a grin. "Where are we headed?" he asked and started the engine.

"Up the canyon. There's a place I go sometimes."

They drove up Stein between the bare poplars and beyond the trees and began climbing steeply into the canyon on a loose dirt road, through a series of switchbacks.

"Tell me about her," she said.

He glanced at her, then shifted his eyes back to the road.

"Your woman."

He shook his head. "There's no sense talkin' 'bout that," he said. "That's finished. Anyway, it wasn't a woman, it was a dog."

"What's the trouble?"

He concentrated on his driving. "Nothing," he said.

"Then why?"

"Because the dog died. Or maybe I killed it."

She was looking at him. "No. I meant why did you go away from me all-of-a-sudden?"

"I did, didn't I?"

She was quiet a moment. "Must've been some dog," she said.

"Yeah. He was." He was disappointed that she had given up the other line and that he had let a chance to talk about it with her get away. "Yeah," he said. "He was a very special dog, to me."

"Will you tell me someday?"

He looked at her and nodded and grinned. There'd be another chance. He could only tell her once, and what was the point of messing up a good time before you had to?

"I'll tell you," he said. "But not right now."

The road left the canyon bed and cut over the shoulder to the left, where the canyon broadened out through sparse sage and stunted single pines. It was rough and Arizo drove carefully.

"I like being with you," she said.

"Yeah. I like it, too."

"I wish it would always feel like this."

He shrugged. "You wouldn't want it always the same."

She reached out and touched his arm. "Yeah, that was a dumb thing to say."

He grinned at her. "I wish it was always this way, too. I feel like a kid."

"Then let's not let it change," she said.

"How do we do that?"

"We take care of it real good."

"It's okay by me," he said.

They stopped beside a small flat shaded by piñon trees. From their feet the loose, sandy ground fell gradually away into the canyon with increasing steepness. Through the canyon mouth they saw the town and beyond it the dun plain reaching to the faint blue lip of mountains on the eastern rim. Round clouds like cream puffs sailed above the peaks behind them. The town lay just beyond the debris spilled from the canyon mouth. A blueness

in the air softened the lines of the buildings. Cars crawled like
ants. Around where they sat, small birds fretted in the sage and
the air smelled sharp and clean.

Arizo handed her his knife. It had a large single blade with a
polished handle and a silver heel. She cut the bread and laid it on
a stone while she made sandwiches. He sat looking out, drinking a
beer.

"Do I make you shy?" she asked.

He shrugged. "I was never with anyone like you."

"I *am* strange," she said. She grinned and sucked the mayonnaise off her fingers. "One time I was at a fair in Salt Lake and
these two guys took a Polaroid of me. Here." She handed him a
sandwich. "And the picture came out with white all around my
head. They got real excited and kept saying, 'She's got the spirit.
She's got the spirit!' They wouldn't let me have the picture. I really wanted it, but they wouldn't let me have it."

Arizo didn't know what to make of that. "What do you think
it meant?"

She shrugged.

He grinned. "Maybe you're an angel," he said, "one of them
fallen angels. You know? My father always used to call women
that. Fallen angels." He was thinking of Maxwell talking about
his Aunt Jolene after she'd gone at Maxwell about his drinking.

"When I go someplace new," she said absently, "I always hear
the local radio station in my head for maybe the first two or three
days I'm there. I can turn on the radio and the tune'll be playing
just like it is in my head."

He lay back on his elbows, looking down at the town. It was as
if they hadn't come from there at all, but had crossed the mountains at their backs and found this thinly cultivated patch of civili-
zation where there had been nothing before and where there
would be nothing afterwards.

She stretched out beside him and he turned on one elbow and
looked down at her. They had not seen each other so openly, so
closely before. Her face was finely formed, her skin the lightest
shade of olive, rich and smooth, her eyes a little sad and infinitely

tender, inquiring of him with constant minute movement. What did they see?

She reached up and pulled him to her, pushing off his hat. They stretched out and lay comfortably holding one another, silent, still, unseen, small in the mountain's fold, minute on the skin of the earth, clinging, eyes closed in a moment of timelessness.

So Arizo decided to stay on in Idaho, at least for the while.

Arizo moved easily among the people there. He instinctively knew their values, and he was careful to leave a few distinctive tracks. He was in love with a woman and she with him, and he knew now what that was worth. He kept a room at the Hermans' place but stayed with Sandy in her cabin. He made his money working with Coulter at the quarry for Pops Bivaletz. Coulter was his friend and he Coulter's. They worked together, and once or twice went shooting quail and sage grouse together. But aside from these occasions, Arizo spent all his spare time with Sandy.

In this atmosphere of love, deep and mature, the thing occurred which forever after Arizo would regard as a miracle: that part of him which he had so long regarded as no more than a useful appurtenance to piss through, slowly, weakly at first, but with gathering strength, like a bear in spring, came back to life. Arizo's joy was indescribable. Satisfaction that he had thought certain was denied him forever had been returned. Everyone he came in contact with felt his elation and rightly put it down to the power of love. The lovers exercised and strengthened the convalescent member, and as its strength and stamina returned, Arizo remarked to Sandy, "Seems like you don't ever get a thing till you quit tryin' for it."

"Now we got it," she said demurely to him, "you have to make up for all them years you lost, an' I want you to make them up exclusively on me."

"You want a contract?"

For a moment, she didn't know how to take this. She looked at him seriously and hesitated.

"Aw," he said. "You don't need one."

"Maybe it *would* keep you honest."

He smiled and said no more, and the incident seemed to have been forgotten. Only it wasn't—by either of them.

There was only one aspect of his new life in Cope that troubled Arizo, and that was his friendship with Coulter. Coulter had become like a younger brother to him. Not having a brother, he found it at once a flattering and disturbing experience. For although Coulter clearly admired him, Arizo felt in some way responsible for him and got the feeling, from what little contact he had with the other people in town, that they felt he was responsible, too. Sandy put it quite clearly. "Coulter," she said, "is Cope's hot potato, and they're just happy as hell you got him."

On the morning of the first Saturday in November, Coulter delivered three tons of half-inch gravel to the Poulsen ranch. Vern Poulsen and his man, Chuck Gould, had gone to a cattle auction in Twin Falls and wouldn't be back until dark. The Poulsens' older daughter, Tissa, was away studying oral hygiene in Boise; the younger, Vickissa, thirteen, was on a half-day ride with the Future Farmers of America.

Marlene Poulsen sat alone at the kitchen counter looking out across the drive at the drab fields and the faintly purple mountains beyond, waiting, wondering about Coulter. As always, when she considered another man, she thought of her husband, Vern. He had been a struggling rodeo cowboy, glad to quit the circuit when he got her pregnant. She was on the circuit, too, at that time. Today she would be called a groupie. Then she was just a fan, a polite though not entirely adequate description, since she had, in truth, worked under some of the best bronc busters, calf ropers, and bull riders in the business—if only in the moist twilight of their motel rooms. It was strange, she thought, how she had ended up with Vern, the only harelipped rodeo cowboy anyone had ever seen and the only one she had sworn never to lay.

Vern must have wondered about it too, for he had jokingly called himself the darkest horse since Willie Mays. But once she'd made up her mind, she had easily overwhelmed his doubt with her affection. She always remembered how, just as eagerly, he had accepted the congratulations of his fellow cowboys; congratulations that had been all too rare for his performance in the ring.

They were married by a judge in Carson City, Nevada, when the rodeo came to Sparks. "Do you, Vern Nathanial Poulsen, take Marlene Rose Miller to be your lawful wedded wife?"

"Yeth," he'd said. "I mean, I do."

She had closed her eyes a second, as if in thanks, and thought to herself, "Dear Lord, what have I done?"

But life with Vern had not turned out so badly. His father owned 60 acres of California in the Santa Clara valley near San Jose, and on his father's death in 1966 Vern had sold the land to housing developers for enough to buy 250 acres of Idaho bottom land outright. He had turned out to be a pleasantly assertive man and easy on her, for a cowboy.

In turn, she had weathered well. At forty, she was handsome and cat-slender in boots and jeans, with a tight ass, they all said, a proud arch to her back and small breasts—for which, at last, she was profoundly grateful.

Only now she sometimes wished she weren't this way, for as time went by, she seemed to become more attractive; while he, who had never been much to begin with, grew less so. It was when he saw this that the jealousy emerged. It had always been there, but in the last few years it had become impossible. She could scarcely leave the house. She felt stifled, but reasoned, with mixed feelings, that it must get easier as time passed. When she was stirred sexually by other men, she turned her feelings inward and kept silent. She had been inflexible for years, but now she was beginning to feel that this inflexibility was not right.

She rose and went into her room to dress. The truck would arrive soon. She had seen Coulter eyeing her for some time, but ironically until Vern punched him in the bar that night, she hadn't thought of sleeping with him. When she heard the truck, she went out to meet it, perhaps forgetting her coat. A wintery sun was shining. He leaned from the cab window, black hat riding on broad shoulders, looking down at her appreciatively over his elbow. He grinned and switched off the engine, and the truck gasped and sucked into silence. He looked her in the eye, and, still with that open grin, he said, "Where d'you want it, ma'am, back or front?"

She raised an eyebrow. "Oh," she said. "My husband just said to spread it around."

Coulter laughed. "Well," he said, inclining his head. "You better show me where to begin."

Then it was easy enough. But after he'd spread the gravel, when she invited him in for coffee, she was trembling. He climbed down from the truck and slammed the door and followed her into the house, boots crunching on the new-laid rock. It was a large neo-Spanish split-level, dustless house with french windows in the living room that opened onto a stone terrace overlooking the place where the Big Lost and Snake rivers ran out onto the plain. He left his gloves on the table. They were fancy gloves to cover his work-torn hands.

She faced him. Of course she had heard the talk, heard the girls tittering in Miss Peta's Beauty Salon, and her friend Josie Seiler, whose husband Ned ran the John Deere outlet, had admitted screwing him. "It was just one of those weak moments, sweetie," she said. "But oh God!" She had lowered her eyes at the memory.

Now, as Coulter stood in the palpitating silence of her living room, it was the sight of his hands, broad, tanned, cracked as Bryce Canyon walls, that aroused her. And when she drew them over her neck and shoulders, the sensation revived memories that would alter all their lives; memories shortly reincarnated on her gold-quilted marriage bed with the window cracked open behind drawn curtains and two yards of new gravel to warn of any approach. Memories rekindled by the unspeakable sensation of Coulter's omnipotent phallus as he manfully plumbed the depths of that divine confluence belonging to a former Sweetheart of the Rodeo.

Marlene's cries only fed his hunger, her ecstasy drove him on, while her husband made an honest buck stamping his cold feet on the concrete floor of the Twin Falls cattle barn, keenly regarding the auctioneer.

Afterwards she had abruptly ejected him. "Baby," she said,

sweetly, encouragingly, "we'll meet again—when your truck isn't parked out front."

All brown curls and laughing eyes, he smiled. The inherent goodness in him showed when he smiled. It was reassuring.

"I shall return," he said.

"Oh you shall," she whispered, "you shall."

He bowed gallantly, hat in hand, and left. She heard the truck start up and listened to it pull away.

She closed the window and then returned to sit on the bed, hugging herself, rocking gently back and forth in an aftermath of pure rapture, reviving roundup days in Oklahoma City, Dallas, and Cheyenne, and the quick, hard feel of all those exuberant, wild young men she had so sweetly tamed. She lay on her back and watched them cross her mind, waiting behind the chutes in the afternoon sun, under the lights at night, brown and lean and always laughing. Tears came to her eyes then, and the images of young cowboys now twenty years beyond their prime swam in her regret for time gone forever. Filled with fear, she crawled beneath the golden quilt, curled up, and slept.

When she woke it was growing dark. Nervously, she straightened the bed and then soaked in a bath. At five o'clock Vickissa came home and went straight to her room. A little later as Marlene lay under the sunlamp in the bedroom, she heard Vern. He came into the bedroom holding Rick's black gloves. Unsmiling, he held them up. "Who?" he asked.

She shrugged. "Someone who came to see you, I imagine," she said.

He shook his head. "Only young men wear glovth thith thin in November," he said. He stuffed them in his coat pocket, and she watched him do so with peculiar alarm. The past had compounded simple jealousy for Vern. This was why she had dismissed Coulter so quickly afterwards. It was her gesture to her husband, to the way he felt and the things he did for her.

"How did it go," she asked from under the sunlamp, proffering her lips.

He ignored her.

"Come on, babe," she said. "Come here."

Still with his back to her he said, "I got rid of them. The twenty head." Then he said, "So they brought the gravel. It lookth good."

The day afterwards, Vern Poulsen walked into the bar in mid-afternoon. Two men were playing pool and a third sat watching at a side table. Coo-Coo Catlin was at the brass rail. He saw Poulsen in the mirror behind the bar. Poulsen was the last person he'd have expected in here at this time of day. Coo-Coo was a square-faced boy, light-complected with short blond hair. He was good-looking, with downy cheeks and red pimples by his mouth and he had unusual, chalky-blue eyes. He wore Levi's, a rust-colored parka, and a new hat.

Poulsen nodded and sat down on the next stool.

"You outta work?" he said.

Coo-Coo smiled respectfully. "I was workin' for this house-trailer outfit in Twin Falls, an' they laid me off Friday. It's the Christmas season. Always gets slow this time of year."

Poulsen nodded. Knowing this was the first year the boy had worked, all he said was, "How'th your pa?"

"Good. You wouldn't have work up at your place maybe?"

"I dunno," Poulsen said. "We're gonna bring the cattle in pretty quick."

"Yeah?" Coo-Coo looked eager.

"Maybe," Poulsen said. "But you know, I just noticed that Injun fellow."

"Arizo, you mean. Mike Arizo."

"Yeah. The one in that old Ford panel wagon."

"Yeah. I seen him around."

"Well I jutht heard Pop Bivaleth put him on at the quarry. Maybe he'th hirin'."

"He's been on there a month. It beats me how that sonovabitch got work."

"Maybe Coulter got him on."

Coo-Coo looked sore. "I don't get work in the winter," he said. "An' I *live* here."

"Who you kiddin'," Poulsen suddenly switched on the boy.

"You don't wanna work in the winter. You're pithed off about him and that girl Thandy you wath datin'."

Coo-Coo shook his head emphatically, and his blue eyes appealed for belief. "I don't care about her anymore," he said.

Sanders, the bartender, stood behind the counter, folding a washcloth and listening. He looked at them intelligently through his gold-rimmed glasses. "I imagine it was old Dan Coulter got Mike on," he said. "I think he wanted Mike to be around Rick as a steadying influence. Mike's a pretty solid guy."

Coo-Coo, who suspected Sanders was gay, and was confused by this, said, "Coulter thinks the sun shines out that Injun's ass."

"Really?" Sanders raised his eyebrows.

Coulter's name was poison to Poulsen. Since the fight in the bar, everyone knew that. So when Coo-Coo saw Poulsen with a distant, tight-faced look, he suspected that an image of the lissome Marlene spread under Coulter's lunging body burned on his brain. It was that obvious, and it made Coo-Coo feel depressed, too. It made him think about Sandy Brown. The mood was infectious.

A column of sunlight slanted to the window from the floorboards. Poulsen turned on his stool and absently watched the dust particles swimming in the light. Coo-Coo nudged him as he got up to play the jukebox. Coo-Coo liked to play country music when he was down. It made him feel like he wasn't alone. Sanders watched Poulsen staring grimly into his drink. That morning Vern had challenged Marlene directly and she had laughed at him as if he were ridiculous. "You think I screw *everyone!*" she said, and he had winced. Charlie Pride sang from the jukebox: "Once I Lived a Life of Wine and Roses." At least Poulsen thought it was Charlie Pride. Coo-Coo returned and sat down beside him again. One of the pool players sank the eight ball by mistake and slammed the heel of his cue against the floor.

"Did anyone pick up the glovth?" Poulsen finally asked, lifting his chin towards Sanders.

"What gloves?" Coo-Coo asked.

"I found a pair of glovth in my plathe," Poulsen said casually,

"and left them here in cathe anybody wanted to claim them."
Then, to Sanders: "If nobody did, I'd like them mythelf."

"Oh yes," Sanders was drawing a beer for one of the pool
players. "I forgot to tell you. They were Rick Coulter's." He
handed the beer across the counter and licked the foam off his
fingers.

Coo-Coo suddenly expired into confession. "I gotta admit that
Sandy's goin' with that asshole half-caste really screwed my head
up good."

Poulsen wasn't listening. A powerful scarlet feeling was blos-
soming in his stomach like a giant, carnivorous anemone. He
couldn't speak. He could barely breathe.

"That's what got me so worked up. The thought of it." Coo-
Coo clearly felt better having made the admission. "You know
what I mean?" He turned on his stool and looked at Poulsen for
support. Poulsen gathered himself. His mouth was tight. He nodded slowly.

"Jealousy?" Sanders looked at them and raised an eyebrow.

"That'th my fuckin' *wife!*" Poulsen screamed, and hit the bar.

The others looked at him, momentarily confused. The pool
players stopped and looked, too. Coo-Coo sympathetically attempted a recovery: "I'd like to kill that asshole," he said. "You
know that?" Only it wasn't clear who he meant.

Sanders wiped off the bar and looked at them, and once more
raised his eyebrows. "You two should get together," he suggested.
"Form a club or something."

"Form a posse," Coo-Coo said. "That'd be more like it."

"Well, then you could probably get them both at once,"
Sanders said acidly. "They hang out together all the time. Ex-
ceptin' nights, of course."

"Enough!" Poulsen yelled suddenly and hit the bar again. "I
heard thith athhole enough. If there wath another bar in town,"
he shouted at Sanders over his shoulder as he stormed out with
Coo-Coo trailing, "I'd be in it."

"Me too," Sanders said brightly.

On the sidewalk, Poulsen, making a considerable effort to keep
it together, said to Coo-Coo, "Forget the Injun. It'th not worth

your trouble. You'll ruin your life if you try to get him. Believe me, you could, eathily."

Coo-Coo nodded.

"You'll looth the girl, too," Poulsen added.

"I already did."

"Let me talk to Pop Bivaleth. Maybe we can do thomething without her knowin'. That'd be good. Maybe I can get Popth to lay the Injun off the job."

"The guy's a fuckin' bum," Coo-Coo said suddenly. "You know that. I mean that's what gets me. Her hangin' out with a busted-ass bum like that."

"Yeah," agreed Poulsen. He seemed suddenly agitated, as though he had just thought of something.

"Arizo's got a bed in the back of that busted old wagon he drives," said Coo-Coo. "I seen it. I wouldn't ask my fuckin' dog to sleep in it. He's a drifter, Vern. I swear to God he's no good. He's a low-life, no-account drifter goin' nowhere, without a pot to piss in. I can't believe her."

The pool players walked out of the bar behind them. Poulsen glanced at them and nodded stiffly. "Wait awhile," he cautioned Coo-Coo. "Okay?"

"What about you?" Coo-Coo asked.

"Me?"

"Yeah. What about Coulter? We should fix the two of them."

Poulsen shrugged. "Aw, it probably ain't nothin' with Coulter," he said. "It'th probably all in my head. You know what I mean?"

Part III

THE STORM

THAT YEAR, a melancholy autumn lingered deep into November. Thin mists drifted across the high desert, rain fell softly in the mountains, wet clouds blanketed the sun for days. In the town, eaves dripped unconsolably and the spirit ebbed.

The people seemed to pause, waiting for the accustomed harshness of winter, caught in anticipation. But after the rains came only a clear, sharp cold that grew a brittle crust upon the ground, leaned the grasses stiffly, like frozen soldiers on a winter front, and made the air so clear that it drew the mountains rising behind the town close enough to touch with a finger. For the second time since the snow should have come, the moon rode full and none came. It made them tense in the town, this change in the rhythm of life. It imposed subconscious strain. They had laid in food and money, wood and oil, and now they waited, outwardly exulting in their good fortune at winter's delay, but inwardly worried as they watched the sky.

On the last night of November, Lou and Sherri Pejasky threw a housewarming.

Coulter decided he would go alone. Sue-Ellen wanted to watch "Vanishing Point" on TV; Arizo and Sandy just wanted to stay home. Coulter told Sue-Ellen he wouldn't be late, because he and Arizo were going hunting at five the next morning, which was Saturday, December 1, the last day of the deer season. They were going for one day to Bartlett Creek, which runs into the Big Lost River. They were going the long way in—a way Coulter hadn't been before—because the higher pass he usually used was blocked by a slide. They were going despite what anyone said. Coulter argued that venison would be a necessity once winter deepened, the ground froze too hard to work, and the price of hamburger climbed beyond the reach of an unemployment check. But in truth the economics were merely a justification for one final visit to the mountains before winter clamped them down.

After work, they drove Coulter's pickup directly over to his father's place to get gear and the .303 rifle Coulter had lent his brother. Dan Coulter lived in one of the oldest houses on the north side of Main, almost at the foot of the mountains. The house leaned away from the wind, a dark, wooden single-story place with moss on the lee side and a porch with a swing chair. In the yard, dead grass stood between rolls of rusting wire and the iron spokes of a broken harrow. Blackberry brambles crawled over the chassis of a prewar truck, an abandoned baby carriage, and artifacts of long-forgotten usefulness. The front gate hung on its bottom hinge, forever open.

The old man sat before a beer can at his kitchen table, a wizened, dried-up cowboy with hollow cheeks and a crackling eye. He'd been on his way to California early in the 1920s when he ran out of money in Salt Lake and took a job. His father had been lost in the sinking of an ore carrier on Lake Ontario when he was a baby. His mother put him into a Detroit foster home, saying she would return. She never did. It was the Rockies that stopped Dan Coulter's westward drift. He came to Cope as a ranch hand. He'd been a cowboy, a carpenter, a hunter, a homesteader, a father. He'd become a Mountain Man. He married Rick's mother, Eileen, because she was there and because she reminded him of his own mother. Eileen bore two sons and then went on a visit to San Francisco in the spring of 1949 and she, too, failed to come back.

So Dan raised his boys alone. And now that all the Mountain Men had become pack guides and the explorers were reduced to surveyors and the cowboys to dude wranglers, he was safe with his memories, and he was part of a myth. He had done what there was to be done when it could be done, and in terms of self-respect that was better than money in the bank.

He shook their hands and pointed to chairs. "You boys don't have no business in the mountains this time of year. You know that, don't you?"

Coulter pulled up a chair opposite him and rested his elbows on the table, smiling energetically. "How's you, old man?" he said.

"You're a damn fool," Dan said and Arizo saw fire in his pale eyes. "I gotta tell you that."

"We're goin' to Bartlett Crick."

The old man glimmered. "Remember that? That's where you got your first buck. I can still see him comin' around the path we was on. I didn't know who was more shook, him or you. Remember?"

Coulter went to the refrigerator beside the sink for beer. The father leaned across to Arizo. "He's a good enough boy," he said.

"I wanted to thank you personally for havin' a word with Pops and gettin' me on," Arizo said. Dan nodded.

"Keep an eye on him," Dan urged, watching Rick, who was closing the fridge, a six-pack in his hand. "I can't keep up with him anymore. He's still real young. He needs someone. He's a wild boy. Like to get his head blowed off."

"Like you did," Coulter said, sitting down and sliding the six-pack into the center of the table. "An' I ain't so young. I'll be twenty-three."

"I heard what you's doin'," the old man said, and his lined face was very stern. "With that Marlene, I mean. If you get caught, boy, watch out."

"Who'd you hear from?"

"I ain't mentionin' names, but they know about it in town, an'

it'll be just a short while 'fore he does. An' then you're in for it.
Believe me, I know'd that man all twelve years he's bin here. I
seen it before." The old man coughed a couple of times. There
was silence.

Coulter tore a beer can from its plastic harness and slid it across
to Arizo. Arizo saw the father look at him as if there was something in particular he wanted to know but had decided in that
moment not to ask. Instead, the old cowboy looked out of the
kitchen window and said casually, "I don't know what's happen
to the snow. Used to be we had twenty foot up against the house
by this time. Used to drift clear to the top of the house on that
side." He waved his arm. "Every winter. Regular. That's why she
leans some. I'll tell you," he said confidentially, "when it does
come late like this, it comes good."

Arizo nodded. Coulter looked admonished. Arizo had never
seen him subdued like this.

"Last one was in forty-eight. That was when they begun testin'
them atom bombs down in Nevada. We never had no more big
snows after that. Haven't had a one since."

"You figure it changed the weather?" Arizo asked.

"Well, maybe it was a coincidence. But not by me."

"That was the year my ma left, too," Coulter said.

The old man looked at his son and nodded. "She left in the
spring after that last bad winter we had."

Arizo hesitated. Then: "She didn't like the winters?"

"She didn't like the Mormons. That's what she didn't care for.
Them an' me, I guess." The old man's voice trailed off.

"Is there a lot of Mormons 'round here?"

"You're lookin' at one." The old man brightened. " 'Round
Idaho Falls, Pocatello, all in there, there's a mess of us." He
winked at Arizo. "We ain't so bad."

"I read where the Mormon Church is one of the fifty biggest
corporations in America," Coulter said. "Makes a million bucks a
day."

"Maybe," his father shrugged. "But I tell you, when that Teton
Dam went, it was the Mormons that come in there an' took care
of all them families. They had rescue trucks comin' out of Salt

Lake before Washin'ton ever knew'd it was happenin'. They had a whole disaster center set up at the college there in Rexburg 'fore anyone else did a damn thing. 'Fore it got dark even."

Arizo was impressed.

"If you're gonna be a good Mormon, according to the *Book of Wisdom,* you ain't gonna smoke, drink, cuss, nor do a damn thing but be fruitful and multiply. That's what Brigham Young said to do." The old man looked at his son and wheezed with laughter. "I'm afraid your ma thought I was takin' that bit too serious."

"You got to be 'sealed,'" Coulter explained to Arizo. "Everyone's got to be 'sealed.' The husband an' the wife is 'sealed' to each other, and their children is sealed to them, an' them to their ancestors an' so on to the Last Days, an' then everyone that's sealed gets eternal life."

"An' the rest that ain't sealed?" Arizo inquired.

Coulter looked at his father and shrugged.

"You'd have to ask President Kimball 'bout that," the old man said. "I'm a jack Mormon myself." He held up the beer he was drinking. "I ain't a good one. You can see for yourself."

"So what about the bomb?" Coulter said and tore another beer from the plastic harness.

"Hell. They killed a lotta Japs is all I know," the old man said. "For my money, they'd been better off sendin' in MacArthur. I never held with all that killin'. But I recall when they done it. Me and Bill Sturgis was up near Bogus Basin after antelope. We got ourselves a couple an' was comin' back over Lemhi when we heard it over the radio that Sturgis had in his Studebaker."

"You got antelope?"

"You could take antelope then. There was all you'd want. Elk, too. That was before them hunters began comin' from California. They'd shot everythin' down there, I reckon, and now they come to shoot everythin' here, too."

"Mike's from California," Coulter said.

"Then he'll know what I'm sayin'. Used to be you never saw a California man here from one year to the next. Just local people. The Californians and the people from Detroit an' the east took everythin' outta this place for themselves. They took the lumber, they cut every decent Ponderosa there is. They took the silver an' even the water, an' they took all the young people that we raised here even. There wasn't no one considered in his right mind that wanted to stay here in the country. Everyone wanted to be havin' a high ol' fast time in the cities, an' they thought we was a bunch of no-account ol' boys that didn't have sense enough to know how to start a brush fire." He took a drink and put the can down slowly, turning it on the scrubbed wood tabletop, watching what he was doing. He looked up at Arizo. "Now it's all different. Ain't it? Now we ain't such goddamned fools after all. Now they screwed up California an' them other places. It ain't fit to live back in Buffalo and New York an' them places, so they wanna come back here and screw up this place."

"You get hippies come up here?" Arizo asked, surprised.

"Some," Coulter said, "but it's too cold for them to come in winter."

"Burt Meyers tells me he thanks the Lord for every winter," the old man said.

"Who's he?"

"The sheriff."

"Oh yeah."

"We got dope smokin' up here anyway," Coulter said.

His father snorted. "Not like in California. An' we don't have a big drinkin' problem like they do there either. When I was in Frisco one time lookin' for your ma, there was a bar on every corner of every block. I swear it. See," he gloated, "they're startin' to find us Mormons was right about drinkin', too." He lifted his beer.

"I'll drink to that," Coulter said.

"If you boys is truly gonna go to Bartlett Creek tonight, you best go," the old man warned. "If you'll listen to me, you'll stay home, but I guess you ain't gonna listen to me."

Coulter looked at his watch. "Shit," he said. "We gotta haul ass."

As they rose to go, Arizo saw the old man's bandy legs and the old man caught him looking. "Rickets," he said. "That's what kept me from killin' Japs, an' that's how come I can't keep up

with this boy no more." He shuffled between them across the
kitchen to the door, a dried-up cowboy. They dwarfed him. He patted Arizo's shoulder. "But *you* can," he said. "There's not so
many people in this town appreciate him, but he's okay. He was a
helluva athlete in school an' real popular. But he's got in some
trouble since. Maybe someday he'll amount to somethin', though.
Maybe he'll show 'em."

"You bet I'll show 'em," Coulter said. He rested an arm on his
father's shoulders. "I'll get to Hollywood soon as I save train fare,
an' then I'll be the new Burt Reynolds."

"Burt Reynolds," the old man said. "Who in hell is Burt Reynolds?"

Coulter drove Arizo back to Sandy's place and went on to his
alone.

It was very cold. Too cold for snow, Arizo thought. From behind the cabin he could hear the gentle sound of the river. He
walked in darkness to the cabin, went in and turned on the light.
It would be a little while before Sandy came home from the diner.
He closed the door behind him and saw that she had changed into
her uniform in front of the stove and left her clothes draped on a
chair and her boots beside it. The boots were worn and very small.
He smiled at the sight of them. Then he saw she'd left him a note
on the table. She'd weighted it down with a silver dollar he'd
given her. He took off his boots and crossed the cabin floor to
read it:

> Put on the music,
> Get out the wine,
> When I get home, babe,
> We'll have ourselves a time,
> I love you.——S.

He held the note and read it again, grinning. Then he stood
and gazed about him. This was now home to him, this 15 by 15
cabin. He was better off in this little square of ground than anywhere he'd ever been. "One square's a bad time, another square's
a good," he said aloud, thinking of the square under the lights

where Baby Zeus had fought, thinking of how bad he'd felt. Now
he felt extraordinarily good. He blew Sandy an imaginary kiss
and went out back. In the light from the door he split some wood
and brought it in and made a fire. When it was burning well, he
heated a kettle and washed the dishes, whistling to himself as he
did, now and then looking out the window whenever he thought
he heard the sound of the car bringing her home.

Coulter knew the Pejasky place. He'd delivered material when
they were building. It was a fancy house, built around a furnished
courtyard roofed with glass.

The Pejaskys were as comfortable as you got in Cope. Raised on
adjacent ranches, childhood friends, high-school sweethearts, they
were most generously endowed upon marriage by delighted parents who, on both sides, were more into beets than potatoes.

It was already crowded when Coulter arrived. Sherri Pejasky
greeted him. She was thirty and seven months pregnant. Some
pregnant women were sexy to him, but she wasn't. He'd once had
a girl who said she was six months along. Sherri was nice, but she
looked like a goat, he thought: swept-back, rounded nose and jaw,
swept-back forehead. He took a drink and wandered around the
periphery, looking for an entrance.

He was still standing alone when Marlene and Vern Poulsen arrived. They had had a row in the car on the way over, and Vern
looked tight and intense. Coulter nodded carefully to both as
Sherri Pejasky rolled up to greet them.

He watched Marlene with admiration. She was really a classy
woman, he thought. She wore a clean white hat with her silvery
ponytail hanging down from under it over a chocolate brown
cowboy shirt with arrows at the pockets and brown snaps. She'd a
matching choker and a full brown skirt with big red roses embroi-
dered on it and a slit up the front a little way and scalloped two-
tone Letty boots and American Indian silver turquoise bracelets.
She was knocked out, he thought. He couldn't believe her.

"She fills her clothes real nice, doesn't she?"

Coulter turned. Len Longren, the lean Scandinavian who

owned the feed store, was standing next to him. Coulter nodded emphatically.

"Tell you the truth," Longren said, "I wouldn't half-mind gettin' in there with her."

Coulter raised his eyebrows in mock surprise. "No shit."

" 'Course, Vern would kill anyone that did."

"Yeah. But you wouldn't blame a man for trying."

"Not me," Longren said, shaking his head as he stared with admiration. "Not me."

Marlene and Sherri stood side by side looking around the place. Poulsen had taken his wife's coat to hang it up. The center courtyard was softly lit, hung with large ferns and dotted with *House Beautiful* indoor garden furniture with thick bamboo frames and covers of banana yellow with a bold print.

"Honey," Marlene gushed to Sherri. "It's simply wonderful!"

"Well," the hostess answered, twisting her hands, "we certainly like it. 'Course it's not finished yet. That there"—she pointed to a large window boarded with plywood—"is gonna be the nursery." She laughed nervously. Marlene was watching Coulter from the corner of her eye and thinking to herself how damned stupid it was that here she was near forty and her mouth still went dry whenever she saw the man.

"But of course," Sherri Pejasky was saying, "we still have a couple of months before it arrives."

"Who's that?" Marlene asked, and then saw the girl looking fondly at her belly. "Oh," she said. "Of course."

"Let me show you the rest," Sherri said and led her off.

Vern Poulsen got himself a tumbler of Wild Turkey from the bar and lurked by the group surrounding Lou Pejasky, feeling that he ought to say hello. Being under the same roof with his wife and her suspected lover rendered him utterly ineffectual. He felt desperate and sick and wanted to take Marlene home, except that that would cause another scene and he'd be even more depressed when he got there. So he decided to get drunk.

Someone put on some fiddle music. Lou Pejasky broke out of the circle and took him by the elbow.

"Vern!" He sounded delighted.

"It'th a heck of a plathe you got here," Poulsen lisped.

His host slapped him on the back. "Dammit, Vern, me and Sherri, we like it well enough." Lou Pejasky was dressed in red and white. He wore Footjoy golf shoes with fringes and white uppers. He had a good belly on him, glasses with thick rims, and his round red face perspired with excitement and alcohol. He turned back to the group. Poulsen saw Don Puccinelli, who ran the auto-parts house, Fred Meyers, Len Longren, the Seilers, and Clark Payne, the president of the VFW chapter. The whole town was here, he thought. The Pejaskys could certainly draw.

"I was just tellin' these folks 'bout the disaster we had with our new septic tank," Pejasky explained. The others dutifully turned to listen, except Poulsen, who looked around for his wife and couldn't see her.

"So we got the leach lines dug all right," Pejasky was saying. Poulsen felt his stomach gnawing. "And they were workin' real good until we had all that rain. Even then it woulda been all right, 'cept that Chuck Gould, my good buddy, he come along and parks his goddamned D-37 clean on top of the thing an' leaves it overnight. When we come out the next mornin', that big ol' cat had just squeezed the shit right outta everything." Lou Pejasky looked around and led the laughter.

Poulsen drifted away. He couldn't see Coulter either. He was feeling sick again. But then, to his relief, Marlene appeared with Sherri, and he found himself in the group around Joey Leonard, talking bird dogs.

"An' then there was just a prick of a water test," Leonard was saying. He had a wall-eye and long, flat silver sideburns. "I mean just a bastard of a thing through a real scuzzy log pond with all this loose slime an' everything. An' when I saw it, I said, 'That's it. That's the end of the line for my dog Malarky.' Because he'd never saw a thing like that in his whole life before." Now Coulter appeared, too, talking to Ned Seiler's daughter. "But I'll be damned if Malarky didn't just jump right in there and cleaned it and come up with his bird like he did it everyday." Leonard pounded one fist into the other. "I mean, he just dived into that pond and came up with logs rollin' all around him, and he didn't

bat an eye." Leonard shook his head and stuck out his jaw to
show the dog's determination and his own amazement. The
others grunted their approval. Even Poulsen found himself listening, though he didn't like Leonard.

"You got Chesapeakes, haven't you, Vern?" Leonard asked,
turning to him.

Poulsen nodded. Leonard knew perfectly well he had Chesapeakes.

"Vern's a maverick," Leonard laughed. "Everyone knows Lab-
radors is the *only* way to go."

"I need another drink," Poulsen said, looking for a way out.

Marlene was suddenly there offering to get him one, but instead
of answering her, he said to Leonard, "Chethapeake'th got power.
That'th what I like."

"Bullshit," Leonard said.

Marlene left and Poulsen saw her go and was angry with himself and her.

"You hear 'bout the Electrician bein' put on the roof of his
truck by a pair of Chesapeakes he was training?" Leonard asked
the group.

"Who's the electrician?" Clark Payne asked.

"The Electrician is this ace guy who trains with electric collars,
remote controlled," Leonard explained. "Anyway, these two Chesapeakes figured where the shocks was comin' from an' put the
Electrician on the roof."

Everyone guffawed and Poulsen said, "Right. The Chesapeake
ith no fool. They're bright, I tell you."

The courtyard was hot and smoky. Leonard began to tell another story, but Lou Pejasky came over and interrupted him to
tell his story about Gould parking his D-37 on the septic tank.
Poulsen sought refuge in the bar and got himself another tumbler
of Wild Turkey. He stayed there and drank it. He swirled the
bourbon in his glass and watched the liquid grow light at the
edges. He had another drink and began to feel better. He was getting on top of it. He couldn't see either Marlene or Coulter, and
he didn't give a shit. He was beginning to notice some of the
other women.

He backed Josie Seiler up against the wall. Everyone knew she went off the rails now and then with out-of-town salesmen.

"You know," he said, "I'd really like to get to know you a little better."

She looked at him blankly.

"I mean, we been neighborth thith long and . . ."

"Want to take the Broncos and six points?" Poulsen saw Josie Seiler smile. He turned. George Herman punched his arm. "Well?" he said. Herman had on his plumber's hat. Even when Herman got dressed up, he looked like a bum, Poulsen thought.

Josie Seiler excused herself.

"You know thomething, Herman?" Poulsen looked the good-natured Herman coldly in the eye.

"What's that?"

"I don't give a thit about football, and you jutht ran off the lady with your goddamn talk."

"Jeeze," said Herman, amazed. "Jeeze, I'm sorry."

Poulsen shook his head and went off to get another drink. On the upper level of the house, some of the guests had begun dancing. The men were jerking about, bent at the knees, asses sticking out, grinning stupidly with raw faces. Poulsen thought they looked ridiculous.

They were out of Wild Turkey at the bar, so he drank J.D. instead. Bobbie Fraser was at the bar, a nice young blond kid. Poulsen told her a partially true story about how he was stomped by a bronc at Calgary, departing further from the truth than usual, but pleased with his creativity.

He slapped Gladys Herman playfully on the rump, and he beat Longren's kid arm-wrestling on the kitchen table. He had another drink and wandered into the living room. He still couldn't see his wife or Coulter. Near the front door he saw the Seiler kid, Frances, a pale, serious-looking girl with straight blond hair and a long neck.

"When's Tissa comin' home, Mr. Poulsen?" she asked.

"Call me Vern."

"Vern," she said shyly, confused by his drunkenness.

"Thoon, I hope."

"She's so beautiful."

"I think tho, but I'm prejudithed."

"She takes after Marlene," the girl said.

He leaned towards her. "What'th that?"

"She takes after Marlene." The girl raised her voice above the music.

At that moment there was a sharp crack. A splintering sound that stilled the party. Poulsen saw the girl's serious face swivel on its long neck like a Chinese goose, and he followed it around to see the temporary plywood panel covering the nursery window falling towards him. The whole frame was coming with it. Bricks were tumbling from the sill. Air rushed past him. The girl had her hands up to her mouth. As the leading edge of the board dropped, Poulsen saw a black Stetson sliding forward over a wide pair of shoulders. It was Coulter's hat, followed by Coulter, face upturned looking wild-eyed at them, arms outstretched, grasping for balance, toppling forward. Under him, Poulsen saw with peculiar momentary detachment, was his wife, her ponytail spilling across the plywood, her mouth agape, upturned eyes blinking in the unaccustomed light. The board hit the carpet with a bang. The struggling couple, who had evidently been leaning against it from the other side, were cantilevered across the sill as if lying along a teeter-totter and Poulsen realized he was looking at Coulter wedged between the delicate, well-splayed legs of his wife, whose skirt was somehow about her waist and from whose right boot—now thrust kicking high into the air—flapped the white panties of surrender.

And in the awful instant of silence, as the onlookers gasped at the reality of it like fishes sucking desperately at air, the recorded voice of Patsy Cline sang: "You walk by and I fall to pieces," stretching out the final notes in a heart-wrenching quaver.

"I guess Poulsen's looking for me," Coulter said as he came in. Sandy saw his mouth was tight and his eyes nervous and knew it was serious. Arizo looked at Coulter and rubbed his nose with the back of his hand. She hadn't seen either of them like this. There was a sudden anxious sharpness to them.

"He caught you, huh?"

Coulter nodded. "Half the town did. Everybody at the party. I think maybe we should leave for the mountains right now. That way we can start hunting at first light, an' it'll give Poulsen time to cool off some."

"He's real mad?"

Coulter grimaced. "You kiddin'?"

Arizo looked thoughtful and said, "We should leave your truck off this side of the river an' take the Ford."

Coulter was relieved. "I don't have gas anyway."

Picking up his coat, Arizo went into the bedroom to get his rifle.

The phone rang.

Sandy picked it up before it rang again. She brushed the hair back from her eyes. "Yes," she said. Coulter was watching her. Arizo came out of the bedroom carrying the Winchester 94 by the stock. When Sandy hung up, she turned to him, a little breathless. "Vern and Coo-Coo Catlin were just at Rick's place," she said, and then to Coulter: "Sue-Ellen says Vern's got a rifle an' he's crazy. She said he searched the house for you."

Coulter said softly, "Sonovabitch!"

"Maybe he'll come here," Sandy suggested.

Arizo was watching them. Coulter shook his head. "No," he said. "They'll go to the bar."

"That won't take them a minute," Arizo said.

"I don't think you should go, Mike," Sandy said and her words came quickly, edged with fear.

Coulter looked at Arizo and stepped closer. "We go for the day, Mike, like we planned," he said. "What's the difference? Vern'll be cool by tomorrow. Long as he don't see me tonight, there won't be no trouble." Now he reached out and, taking Arizo's elbow, softly drew him forward. It was the slightest gesture.

Arizo nodded. "Okay," he said. "We'll go huntin'. We'll be back Sunday, hon." He touched Sandy's cheek.

"Well, I'm goin' to the Hermans' place," she said.

"They were at the party," Coulter said.

Headlights suddenly swung across the far wall of the cabin.

"Holy shit!" Coulter yelled and crouched near the window, clutching his rifle.

Arizo went quickly to the window and peered out. "It's the Hermans come back next door," he said.

Sandy laughed with relief. Coulter got up looking angry.

"I'll meet you at the quarry," Arizo said. "We'll leave your truck there. He won't find it."

When Coulter had closed the door, Arizo turned to Sandy and held up a hand as if to stop her.

"I know," he said. "You were right."

She came to him and put her head on his chest. He held her. "You're his friend," she said.

"He makes me real angry. We all told him this would happen."

"He's a boy."

"He's a damn fool."

"He's gotta be looked after."

"He's gotta learn."

"He doesn't have another friend."

"Neither do I. 'Cept you."

"Yeah, you do," she said. "A lotta people in this town like you. Especially the women. I hear them talk in the diner."

He pushed her back a little and studied her upturned face.

"That's right," she said. "An' Pops likes you, an' Dan Coulter."

"Yeah?" He was pleased.

"They're important people in this town. I trust their judgment." She grinned at him.

"I better go."

"Yeah." She laughed a little. "This's ridiculous. We're spoonin', and there's a psychopathic killer huntin' for us."

"I'll be back real soon. But first I'll take you over to the Hermans' place."

She nodded. "I love you," she said.

He hugged her to him. She smelled of coconut oil. "I love *you*," he said.

"You take care, you hear?"

"I will," he said. "You know me. An' when I get back," he added, "let's get outta here."

She pushed back further and looked at him.

"I'm serious," he said. "I told Rick that first day I'd stay till the end of the deer season. That's tomorrow."

"Well, we could," she said slowly and smiled at him as the full possibility dawned on her.

"Damn right we could. I don't wanna struggle through a winter here. We could go to Florida or Texas."

"Someplace where it's warm." The delight in her eyes filled him with pleasure and he kissed her. "Oh God, I love you," she said and hugged him, clasping as much of him as she could embrace.

He laughed. It welled out of him.

"I best go take care of the boy," he said lightly. "I'll be right back."

Arizo held the Ford in the shadow at the foot of the rise, looking up at the signal that swung over Main Street, waiting for the green light so they wouldn't have to idle in the glare outside the Two Ball Inn. They had to come through town. There was no other way across the river that was accessible. As he saw the yellow, Arizo grunted and accelerated up a short rise, and turned right looking out keenly over the blunt nose of the Ford as Main Street straightened out to meet them.

"This's it," Coulter said.

"I'd like to think."

"Thirty seconds an' we're gone. Thirty Seconds Over Tokyo."

They were both looking about. Main Street was deserted, a ghost town tapering to a point in darkness.

"We don't have much money," Coulter said loudly and slapped Arizo's thigh, "but we sure have fun."

Arizo was silent, but Coulter didn't seem to notice. He turned on the radio. Waylon Jennings was singing "Think I'm Gonna Kill Myself." Coulter turned it up.

Arizo snapped it off. "Watch," he said. "'Cause we're bein' watched." They were almost out of town.

"What's the matter with you?" Coulter was indignant. "There's nobody saw us."

"There was some old woman outside the hardware store for openers."

"Eleanor Holmes. Gone around to service ol' Meyers. She done that every Friday night, I remember. You're just paranoid."

"I'm just pissed," Arizo said.

"Shit," said Coulter and turned away. "I do a girl one favor, an' you're pissed." He watched out the window until there wasn't anything but sage beside the road.

"It wasn't just me that warned you."

"Oh shit," Coulter said wearily.

"You're a damned fool. You know that? I was feelin' sorry for you. I figured they picked on you in this town but they're right," Arizo said. "You're a damn fool that only thinks about himself."

Coulter stared ahead and said nothing.

"You know the rules," Arizo persisted.

"You always stick to the rules?"

Arizo's anger rose again. "I don't fuck another man's ol' lady. That's for sure."

"You never did?"

"I never did."

Arizo had let his speed drop.

"Well, that's your loss."

"I already got enough trouble."

"That's for sure."

"Supposin' somebody screwed your ol' lady?"

"They never would."

"Yeah?"

"I'd be pissed as hell."

"You're damn right you would. You'd kick ass."

"Too right."

"So?"

Coulter stretched. "Virgin worship is the trouble," he said. "If we didn't worship the Virgin, it'd be all right to get laid."

"Seems to me that's all anyone does around here anyway."

But Coulter wasn't listening. "When you think about it, when you really think about it," he said, "gettin' it on with someone, when you're really *cookin'* together, that's a *high* thing. I mean it's holy. It's as close to God as you can get. Think about it."

Arizo thought about it.

"An' I can't see a damn thing wrong with it." Coulter muttered, half in memory, half in regret. He thought a moment and came on a different tack: "Some people you go fishin' with because they're good to go fishin' with," he said. "Some people you fuck with because they're good to fuck with." He looked at Arizo, thoroughly pleased with his deduction. "Fishin', fuckin', fuckin', fishin'—what's to get so excited about?"

"The white man has one god," Arizo said. "One god and one woman."

Coulter leaned against his door and looked across at Arizo's silhouette lit in the backglow of the headlights. "Huh," he sniffed. "What's this 'white man' shit. You're no fuckin' Injun."

Arizo took a hand off the wheel and touched his hair. "Well, I sure as hell don't feel like a white man," he said.

"Whattya mean?"

"I mean if I look halfway pissed at the bar, they eighty-six me."

"That's true," Coulter admitted. "They scared you might get drunk and start yellin' and cut their throats. They're scared of you."

"Look out," Arizo said tensely. His tone had changed. Coulter saw him looking in the rearview mirror and twisted around. Well behind were headlights gaining on them.

"They're comin' up real fast."

"Yeah," Coulter said. "An' it ain't the heat either."

The lights came close up behind them and stayed.

"Shit," Coulter said. "This isn't so good." He settled in his seat.

"No," Arizo said. "When it's the heat, at least you know what they're gonna do."

Eleanor Holmes closed the back door to the hardware store and, as she went carefully down the steps, heard Fred Meyers turn the key in the lock behind her. Carrying an empty loose-knit nylon shopping bag, she walked down the concrete drive beside the store with a tired, swaying motion, staring at the pathway a

few feet ahead of her. When she heard the sound of an engine,
she looked up and saw a gray Ford panel wagon accelerating up
Main. It was that Injun fellow, she thought to herself.

As she entered the area covered by the street light, Fred Meyers
turned off the light over the back door. The weekend had begun.
She sniffed and turned left on Main. A truck pulled up outside
the Two Ball Inn and stood with lights on and the motor running. She had gone a few steps farther when she heard a short
blast of music as the bar's door swung open and a man hurried
out. He climbed into the waiting pickup truck and the truck
started to move before the door slammed. She heard the man
swear at the driver, ". . . an' you're fuckin' insane." As suddenly
as it was accelerating, it braked and stopped opposite her. The
driver's window went down and in the half-light she recognized
Vern Poulsen's face.

"Hey, Eleanor," he called across the empty street, "I'm lookin'
for a friend. You thee anyone drivin' by or anythin'?"

She stared at him. He was smiling, but seemed very strained,
and she wondered whether to say anything. She shrugged. "Just
that new Injun fellow is all," she said. There could be no harm in
telling him that.

"In that old Ford panel wagon."

"Well, I dunno what you'd call it."

"Goin' thith way?" He pointed ahead.

She shrugged again. "Looked like it."

"Well, okay," Poulsen said. "I wondered if he knew the way,
that'th all. Good night, Eleanor." He wound up the window and
drove off, moving hard.

Eleanor Holmes, in her shapeless woolen overcoat, her wool
scarf tied about her wrinkled little chin, wiped her nose on her
coat and turned down the Snake River road. Out in the darkness,
well down the road, she saw the lights of the Bluebird Diner. The
lights were reflected by the roof of her old Buick, parked a short
way down the slope. Fred didn't like her to bring it any closer. As
she got into the car, she was remembering, as she did every week,
a time when there was real fire in her for him. Only he had always
been so sure someone better would happen to him. She sniffed and

started the car. But now she shared his life anyway, she thought. It was hardly as she had wished, but she had become indispensable to him. Without her, she thought as she started off, half-looking over her shoulder, his life would come to pieces. That was for sure. And that was enough for her.

Sandy Brown walked slowly up the steps of the Bluebird Diner, head bent, listlessly watching the lift of her thighs. Chloe, silver hair stacked like Little Egypt, blue eyeliner squirting from the corners of her eyes, saw her come and met her.

"It's okay, sweetie," she said.

"Were they here? Vern and Coo-Coo?"

Chloe nodded and lightly rested a hand on Sandy's arm. "Listen, darling," she said, "you don't worry. Your guy Mike will take care of 'em all."

Sandy smiled a little.

"He's a good guy, Chloe. Isn't he?"

"Best that come to town."

"Do you think they'll be all right?"

"Hell yes, honey. It's just bucks rattlin' horns."

"I don't feel good about it," Sandy said. "Something in me says it's all goin' wrong." And she began to cry, quietly, hopelessly.

The embalmed face of the newscaster flashed upon the screen before Sue-Ellen, who reclined like a Rubens madonna upon her sofa. She cracked her gum with displeasure, set down her diet cola, and pumped the button on her remote changer with a plump, petite hand. The face of David Janssen appeared, gazing with melancholic sincerity at a browbeaten beauty across a candle-lit dining table. Sue-Ellen settled back on the sofa and reached down for her drink.

In his bungalow on Parker, Sheriff Burt Meyers pushed back his mahogany Naugahyde recliner and between his slippers watched David Janssen hand the sad-eyed heiress an airline ticket. Martha, the sheriff's wife of thirty years, was fussing in the kitchen. At sixty, the sheriff was tall and gaunt and grim. His eyes were deep

set and chronically suspicious and his jaw stuck out like Florida.
He had been sheriff of Cope County for twenty-three years. He
regarded its denizens as his own. The people from beyond the
Snake River plain, the people of the cities, were his nemesis. He
dispensed justice regally. His need for arbitrary power over others
was considerable. His view of morality was prudential in the extreme, and he snored terribly.

The telephone at his elbow rang. With hoary hand he placed it
to one elephantine ear.

"Dan," he said. "Uh-huh . . . Uh-huh . . . Uh-huh . . . You
oughta had that boy fixed. . . . Mmm . . . Uh-huh . . . I
thought you said that Injun fellow was gonna quiet him down.
. . . Uh-huh . . . Uh-huh . . . So what the hell you want me to do
about it, Dan? Was they drinkin'? . . . So's I can put out an APB
an' have 'em busted for drunk driving is why."

Between his bedroom slippers, he saw David Janssen put a hand
on the grieving heiress's shoulder. "I'll do what I can for you,
Mrs. Wallace," Janssen said. He didn't look optimistic.

"Well, you know me well enough, Dan, that I don't have no
sympathy for these boys. If they been drinkin', they deserve whatever the hell they get. It's the devil's own poison. I spent half my
life fightin' it and gettin' shot at on account of it, so don't ask me
to get worked up for your boy if he's been drinkin' an' gone made
a horse's ass of himself. But I'll do what I can for you, Dan."

David Janssen was driving down Sunset Boulevard in an old
convertible with the heiress beside him. The sheriff watched im-
placably. "You understand? Uh-huh. That's right. Good night,
Dan. Get some rest." He hung up and called into the kitchen:
"Martha?" His voice seemed to come from deep in the weathered
folds of skin under his chin. "Bring me a toothpick when you
come. I got that goddamned steak stuck in my teeth."

David Janssen was being beaten up by two black men. The
sheriff's eyelids drooped.

"We don't know it's them," Arizo said.

"I'll bet you paychecks."

"If it's them, how come they didn't try anythin'?" Arizo was steering with one hand, gazing into the rearview mirror. The lights were perhaps 100 yards behind, where they had been for the past half hour.

Coulter sighed heavily. "I don't know. It spooks me."

"If it's them, they got some other idea," Arizo said. "To let this drag on, he must be real mad. Otherwise he'd've run us off the road or took a shot at us at least."

"Yeah," Coulter replied wearily.

"It's really gettin' to you, isn't it?" Arizo glanced across at him.

"I guess it is." Coulter shook his head and turned on the radio. He heard Lynn Anderson singing "I Never Promised You a Rose Garden."

"Terrific!" Coulter said to her and turned her off and hunched around in the passenger seat to look back and then turned forward again and slumped.

The road was climbing now. To the right, the land dropped off sharply to the river. To the left was the face of a cut that showed up light, almost sand-colored, in the headlights. Above them, they could now feel, though they could not see, the black pressing presence of the mountains. Through the top of the windshield, Arizo saw the stars scattered over a clear sky. The Ford's tired engine clattered a little as it pulled in the thin air. The heater fan whirred.

"Next place I see," Arizo said suddenly, "I'm gonna pull over an' let them by."

"Okay." Coulter reached into the back and picked up his rifle, worked the action, and then stood it between his legs, the muzzle pointed away from them. They rode in silence a few hundred yards more, and then the road opened slightly and there was a turnout. The transmission growled as it slowed and stopped. Coulter was looking over his shoulder and Arizo was watching in the mirror. The lights behind them hesitated, it seemed, but then accelerated on by, swinging over to the far side of the road.

A high, light-colored Chevy four-by-four whipped by and continued up the far side of the road, accelerating fast, quickly disap-

pearing into the darkness until the taillights were put out by a
corner. Coulter said emphatically, "It's him."

"Yeah?"

"Yup."

"How come he didn't stop?"

"How the hell do I know?"

"What plates were they?"

"I didn't get to see. But it sure looked like him."

Arizo got out and stood beside the car. Coulter got out, too.
They closed their doors and stood in the darkness, listening. The
air was very sharp and cold. In the wedge of sky between the rows
of peaks that rose steeply on either side of the river was a great
wealth of stars. From below, the sounds of the Big Lost came like
a far-off wind. Occasionally they heard an engine, faintly. They
listened in silence for some time, then Coulter said, "He's still
goin'."

"Sounds like it," came Arizo's voice.

"It's cold," Coulter said and got back into the car, slamming
the door. Arizo heard the sound fly out into the darkness over the
river and sink. His hands were like ice. He put them in the
pockets of his parka, hearing the rustle of the material. Had she
gone to bed or was she still up, talking to the Hermans? He saw
her in the circle of warm light around the kitchen table, talking to
them. When she was not with him, she was a completely different
woman, self-reliant and independent. He had stood once on the
steps outside the windows of the diner at night and watched her
through the glass, laughing and talking and moving about among
the people at the tables. He saw the way men looked at her when
he was not there. She was strangely exciting. Freshly so, even to
him. It was odd how people chose each other among all there
were and then stuck so firmly to their decisions, he thought. He
never could understand it. When he had seen her that first time,
watched her walk away between the booths, he had felt something
different to the feeling he had had when looking at a thousand
other women. She was pretty, and there was every reason why he
should love her. But why did he? Because he sure as hell did. He
squirmed his shoulders in response to the feeling in his belly that

came when he thought of her. He thought of everything in terms of her. Everything he was and everything he did and everything he wanted and everything he felt. He wasn't his own person anymore. He was hers, and he liked that more than anything.

"Hey! What are you doin'?" Coulter called from the car.

Arizo got in and closed the door. "All right. Whatta we gonna do?"

"You wanna go back to Sandy?" Coulter inquired.

Arizo thought of his plan to leave soon with her. It meant that he and Coulter would have no more time together after this. He thought of his promise to hunt with Coulter and he shrugged and said, "No. I said I'd go. Let's go."

"If we go back, he'll be waitin'—if that wasn't him that went by."

"It doesn't feel like that was him anymore," Arizo said.

"No," Coulter agreed. "It doesn't, does it? Feels like we're sprung now. Feels good."

"How far are we from Mackay?"

"Fifteen miles, maybe."

They started up and pulled back onto the road, Arizo working the old Ford carefully through the gears as it pulled the slope. The lights of Mackay, a few points in an ocean of darkness, appeared below and to their left as they came over a crest a few miles further on. They were rolling down the grade into the town when Arizo said, "Damn. Where'd he come from?" Coulter looked urgently.

"Is it him again? That him you think?"

"I dunno." Arizo was still looking. "But we'll soon find out."

They were on the edge of the town now. It was a small place: a general store, a few shops, and in the center a brightly lit Shell station. Arizo signaled and pulled across the road into it. Coulter turned around as he did, wound down his window and looked back. There was no sign of the lights now. "He's gone," he said, surprised. "He must've turned off."

They both got out and stared back up the road from the blaze of light on the station apron to the darkness on the edge of town. There was nothing. The road was empty to where it was lost in blackness, but they both felt the tension prick them as they looked for movement and both started when a station wagon with a load on the roof came through, going in the other direction. It was an old wagon sagging tiredly and was full of people looking out at them.

"Huh!" Arizo shrugged and turned away. Three boys sat around a radio in the office listening to loud rock. One of them finally got off the desk and came out; a scrawny kid with acne, dark eyebrows, and a weak chin.

"You wanna fill it with regular and get the windshield?" The boy nodded and Arizo went to the john.

Coulter asked the kid, "You live here?"

"Sure I live here," he said, cleaning the windshield while the pump filled the tank.

"You know the way into Copper Basin, then?"

"Sure. It's the third left outta town. It's a dirt road. Through some white gates. There's a cow guard."

They counted the turnings. Beyond the second, about a half mile out of Mackay, Arizo said, "Look." Coulter pivoted fast, holding his breath, and studied the lights through the rear window. "That's not the same," he said.

"No?"

"I don't think so."

"We ain't the only people on this road, y'know."

"Is that the turnin'?"

Coulter swiveled back. "Yeah," he said. "White gates, the kid said."

Arizo spun the Ford in through the break in the fence, between high white steel posts. They crossed a cattle guard, and the wheels made a hollow drumming sound on the metal bars. Beyond was a hard-packed dirt road running away to the left and slightly downhill, across a high meadow. Coulter had turned around again, and Arizo was watching in the mirror. The vehicle on the main road was moving normally. They watched its headlights approach, and it seemed as though it was ignoring the entrance. But at the last moment brake lights glowed red and it slowed to a crawl and

turned in after them. Its headlights swung across the drab
meadow grass picking up the Ford and holding it, faintly lighting
the interior and their watching faces.

"Fuck!" yelled Coulter and smashed his fist against the dash.

Poulsen's pickup rumbled tightly across the grid and, high behind the wheel, Poulsen felt suddenly that he was entering an
arena. He even sat a little straighter and looked out at the dark
folds of the mountains silhouetted against the night sky and saw
them as an amphitheater. Across generations lost, sweat gathering
in the cleft of his lip, eyes shining peculiarly hard, he felt the
thrill. Even Coo-Coo Catlin, slumped beside him in the glow of
the cab, sensed a difference. On the road from Cope, Poulsen had
seemed first rashly furious, bursting dangerously with uncontrolled
anger. This mood had slowly given way to an almost casual one as
they had waited, hidden, beside the road beyond the summit
above the town and then in the driveway at Mackay. It seemed to
have become a game, then, and Coo-Coo had relaxed a little and
even begun to enjoy it. Now it was different again.

He saw Poulsen wipe his mouth on the back of his hand without lifting his eyes from the taillights bobbing on the road ahead.
There was an open box of .30-30 shells on the seat between them.
Coo-Coo picked one up and turned it in his fingers. "So whatta
we do when we get 'em?"

"Kick ath," Poulsen said.

Coo-Coo looked at him, somewhat afraid, somewhat in defer-
ence. "That's it?"

They were starting slowly down the dirt road after the Ford,
moving up perhaps twenty miles an hour, keeping the station a
hundred yards back.

"If a guy took a crap on you," Poulsen said slowly, "what would
you do?"

"I dunno," Coo-Coo hesitated. "Sandy wasn't my wife or anythin', so it wasn't that tough for me."

"Right," Poulsen said fiercely, turning to him. "I'm through in
Cope. You know that? My children are gonna laugh at me. My
wife ith a whore. You know what a cuckold ith?"

Coo-Coo shook his head, wanting but not daring to look away.
"Well, you're lookin' at one. I worked hard all my life, Coo-
Coo," Poulsen whined in his low, hard nasal voice. "An' now I'm
through. It'th not my fault. But I'm through."

"It ain't that bad," Coo-Coo said, despite himself.

Poulsen's voice dropped lower still, and he spoke with contempt. "What the fuck d'you know, boy? You didn't thee it. You
weren't there. And you're about the only thonovabitch in town
that wathn't."

Coo-Coo sat back and stared hopelessly through the windshield.
The Ford's red lights glowed ahead of them. Off to the right in
the edge of the lights, he saw white traces of a snow fence. Coo-
Coo Catlin, seventeen years old, squat, ham-fisted, well-meaning,
good-looking, slouched on the seat beside this man, one boot on
the dash, chain-smoking Camels. He felt morose, tired and depressed as hell. When Poulsen pulled him from the bar an hour
ago, he'd had a heat on. Now that edge was gone, and he'd
never had the degree of fury that Poulsen had. He was used
to not seeing Sandy anymore. It had been once, and beyond
that only in his imagination. She was gone. There were other girls
in town he'd been with. If she wanted to screw a half-caste,
he was sorry, but it was her business. He didn't care that much
anymore. He'd nearly had the courage to say no to Poulsen
when Vern first came looking in the bar, but he'd been afraid of
the older man's towering anger. And anyway, Poulsen was his father's friend and owned a ranch and said maybe he had work.
Right now he wished badly that he had said no. He felt the man's
craziness and didn't know what to do. He felt angry with his own
hesitancy.

Poulsen didn't know any of this and didn't care. The sweat kept
gathering in the hollow of his upper lip, and he kept wiping it
away. He never took his eyes from the jiggling red lights ahead.
He followed them into the dark mountains that stood waiting to
receive them with a peculiar sense of triumph. He followed as an
executioner follows his prisoner into the yard at the appointed
time.

Coulter was pissing into a jar. "Go easy," he told Arizo.

Arizo slowed the Ford to a crawl and looked in his mirror at the lights behind. He shook his head. "Jesus, these guys are serious."

"I guess." Coulter was head-down, preoccupied.

"So whatta we gonna do?"

"I dunno."

"Well think."

"Well, shit, all we can do is go on, go back, or stop."

Arizo abruptly stopped the Ford. Immediately the lights behind them stopped.

"What you doin'?" Coulter looked at him alarmed.

"I stopped," Arizo said. "They didn't try anythin' on the main road. Maybe goin' off like this is just doin' what they want." He was watching in the mirror for signs of movement. Coulter twisted around in his seat and then turned back. The road in front of them was still tending downhill slightly, and the snow fence off to the right was getting closer. He looked up at the stars for a while and then announced, "We're headed wrong."

"Yeah? Who says?" Arizo sounded completely fed up.

"We're headed southeast and we should be headed southwest."

"You know this road?"

"No."

Arizo groaned and started off again. The truck behind followed.

"Now whatta you doin'?" Coulter asked, emptying the bottle out of the window.

"Well, we can't stay here, an' we can't go back."

Coulter thought about this. "At least we got plenty of gas," he said.

Neither man spoke. In a while, the road crossed a narrow wooden bridge and began to climb through sage and higher foothills. A light appeared on the left.

"Let's stop here," Arizo said. "Maybe that'll scare 'em off."

"We could call the sheriff."

"And tell him what? There's somebody followin' us?"

A narrow track led off from the road towards the light. They climbed a short grade in low gear and then the headlights picked out a bungalow with a scraggly-looking corral beside it. When they got out, Coulter saw the lights of the truck waiting below at the foot of the rise, still on the road. A man in a loose-fitting thermal vest half-opened the bungalow door. He had a yellow dog with him, and he kept the chain on. They saw he only had one eye. The other was an open empty socket. He said nothing, just stood there looking at them.

"Hi," Coulter said, rubbing his hands together and hunching his shoulders against the cold. "We're looking to get to Copper Basin."

The single eye stared at one of them and then the other and blinked. They waited for him to invite them in, or to speak, but the man and the yellow dog just looked.

"Is this the best road?" Arizo asked.

"This here's the Burma road," the man said hoarsely. He cleared his throat. "You best git back."

"We can't do that," Coulter said.

"How's 'at?"

The yellow dog growled.

"We got someone on our ass," Coulter said and looked back down the hill to point out the lights to the man. Only the lights were gone.

The three of them stared into the blackness.

"He must be set down there waitin' for us," Coulter said.

The man was squinting at them both. "You best git back," he repeated. "This road goes into the Basin, but it's likely blocked by now. You're too late." He closed the door and threw the bolt loudly.

"Hey," Coulter called, leaning on the door. "Can we use your phone, mister? We'll pay you for it good."

"You git away or I call the sheriff m'self."

"That's all we want," Coulter yelled excitedly.

"You better git," the man shouted through the door.

"Ain't you a Christian, buddy?"

"I'm leavin' myself tomorrow," they heard him say.

As they walked back to the car, Coulter said, "I'm sorry I got you into this. You should be home right now."

"We came to do a little huntin'," Arizo said. As they got into the Ford, Coulter called over the roof, "Right now I believe we're *bein'* hunted." He laughed.

They sat in the car.

"You think they're down there?" Coulter asked.

"Somewhere."

"Maybe we scared 'em off. Maybe he figured we rang the sheriff."

"Maybe."

The man with one eye appeared in the window of his cabin. He held a rifle and motioned them away. Arizo started the Ford and swung it around. The lights cut out deep across the dark. They looked hard for the glint of metal, but there was none. They started down the slope. Still there was no sign of the truck. When they reached the dirt road Arizo turned right, back towards the highway. They ran down the grade. It was quite a steep slope, so their headlights didn't cover much ground ahead.

"Hey," Coulter called to Arizo lightly. "I think it worked. I think they got scared."

"You think?" Arizo was driving faster now.

The Ford reached the bottom of the slope and was leveling out to cross the bridge when both men were blinded by lights that suddenly came on, high and straight at them. The truck was parked in the center of the wooden bridge.

Arizo skidded to a stop fifty feet away.

"Don't move," he said to Coulter.

"What are they gonna do?" Coulter whispered above the idle of the engine.

The high beams of the truck had been supplemented by spotlights on either side of the cab. The lights from the old Ford were like candles against all this. But they were enough so that from inside the Ford they could see the outline of two men leaning from the windows of the truck cab with rifles trained upon them.

Arizo threw the Ford into reverse without thinking and spun it around. It was flat where they were beside the river, so they made it. They started back up the hill, scurrying without dignity, Coulter looking back all the while.

"They're comin'," he gritted. A moment later, he added, "I

could easy shoot their radiator out. That'd stop them soon
enough."

Arizo shook his head. "Screw shootin'. That's all we need."

They reached the turning that led up to the one-eyed man's
bungalow. He thought for a moment of taking it, but kept on
uphill. "No," he said, thinking of what the man had said. "We
don't have to do anythin'. The man up there said this road goes
into the Basin, right?"

"Yeah."

"An' we shoulda' come in from the other end. Right?"

Coulter brightened. "That's right. It makes a loop. We keep on
this road, an' it'll take us clear 'round the long way, back to the
main road. That's it. Far out!" He shook his fist in the air.

"How far is it?"

"Thirty, forty miles, outside, I guess."

"We got enough gas."

"For sure. An' we got all night." Coulter laughed and looked
around at the lights coming slowly up the hill behind them and
made a defiant, disparaging gesture, using both arms and a fist.

Beyond the ranch the road grew worse. They made a long, slow
climb, higher and deeper into the sleeping mountains. In the
headlights they saw scattered pine out among the pale sage.
When they reached the first shoulder, there were patches of snow
about and two small drifts lay across the track. They had no problem with them, but they began to discuss the possibility of their
having to use chains. "If we gotta fit them," Arizo said, "I'll turn
the car around and then get out so he can see it's me an' then I'll
keep the door open an' fit the back wheels with the door coverin'
me."

They descended and climbed a second ridge and the road came
around to the southwest and Coulter said they were headed right.
There were outcroppings of black rock among the sage now. They
were cheerful now. They joked and laughed, and Arizo felt
buoyant at the thought that he would be home in three or four
hours. He would surprise Sandy, crawl into bed while she was still
half-sleeping and curl up with her, maybe make love to her. "God,

it'll be good to get home," he said. Coulter laughed and wound
the window down to put his face out.

"It's not that cold," he said. "It's freezin', but we must be up to
seven, maybe eight thousand feet."

Arizo only nodded.

Close to an hour from the ranch, they came slowly through a
switchback, running downhill, and saw the glare of more snow in
the headlights. Arizo stopped. This drift was larger than the
others, maybe thirty yards long.

"Whatta you think?" Coulter said.

Arizo shrugged. Coulter looked back to see that the truck had
stopped above them on the ridge. Its headlights shone out into
the dark, lighting a patch of fir a couple of hundred yards beyond.

Coulter studied the snow ahead. "We can make it."

"We sure as hell can't go back," Arizo said and he jammed the
gas pedal. The Ford surged forward, fishtailing as it climbed onto
the snow. Arizo worked the wheel quickly to keep it straight, but
almost immediately the rear began slipping sideways down the
slope and the engine note rose while the car lost speed.

"Shit!" Arizo grunted.

He accelerated again, but the Ford dragged to a halt, the
off-side rear wheel spinning with a fierce whine. They were no
more than eight feet short of the far side. Arizo let up on the gas
and slumped on the wheel.

Coulter looked at him in the dim light. "It's high centered," he
said.

"No shit!"

"Whatta we gonna do?"

"You want to get shot at in the dark while you're diggin'?"

"Jesus!" Coulter moaned. "You know what? I left the goddamn
shovel in the truck."

Arizo was silent for a while. Then he turned off the engine and
put out the lights. He was close to tears, and Coulter sensed his
disappointment and said quietly, "Jesus, buddy." Arizo rubbed his
eyes. "What time is it?" he asked, his voice very tired.

"About three, maybe."

"Screw their games. I had enough. Let's get some sleep. Tomorrow is soon enough to take care of them assholes."

"You sleep—I'll watch."

"There's no sense us all stayin' up. They ain't gonna come in the dark. So let them watch, and we'll be ready to go in the mornin'."

"You got some nerve," Coulter said, and his voice was full of admiration. "I swear to God you take the cake."

It jolted them in the truck when the lights below went out. Poulsen quickly turned out his own and killed the motor.

"Wind down your window," he ordered Coo-Coo.

They listened in silence for a moment and heard nothing but a soft wind in the firs beside them.

"Let's get outta here," Coo-Coo said. "If they're comin', they're comin' for the truck."

They moved away from the truck into the firs on the uphill side of the road, carrying their rifles, keeping the branches from their faces with free hands, bent double, moving as quickly as they could. Fifty feet from the truck, they lay down beside each other on pine needles under the branches at the edge of the stand, so that they were looking out over the hillside where the Ford had stopped. They lay on their stomachs, cradling their rifles.

It was warmer than either had thought it would be. Only their hands grew cold. Coo-Coo pushed his into the elastic-bound sleeves of his parka. They could see nothing, and there was no sound but the wind brushing the fir tops above where they lay.

They waited.

After half an hour, Poulsen told Coo-Coo to sleep if he wanted.

"It's two thirty-five. I'll wake you at five-thirty," he said.

Coo-Coo turned gratefully over on his back.

Twice Poulsen caught himself on the verge of dozing, and jerked up his head. The third time, his head didn't rise. He lay across his rifle and began to snore.

In the air above, ice crystals were accumulating around the sea salt, particles of dust and microorganisms held by the clouds. Clustering uniquely, they finally fell softly onto the mountains

and into the broad canyon where the four men lay asleep. The big
snow had come at last.

Coulter woke with a feeling of panic and no idea where he was.
He sat up, looking about. A weak light filtered through the frosted
glass.

"Jesus!" he said looking about in horror. He shook Arizo. "Hey,
man, wake up," he said. "It's late already." He climbed clumsily
into the passenger seat.

Arizo sat up. "Look out what you're doing," he hissed. "They
could be waitin' to shoot your ass."

Coulter shifted into the driver's seat, slowly opened the window
half an inch and peered out.

He whistled.

"What?" Arizo was crawling in.

"Look. We ain't goin' anywhere today."

Coulter moved into the other seat and Arizo hurriedly took his
place. He looked silently for some time, then he said, "Maybe it'll
melt."

"Not till the spring, it won't. You see anyone?"

"No."

"Let me get out there."

"They could be waitin' on the roof."

Coulter started and looked at Arizo, then grinned and shook his
head. "You asshole," he said. "They're neither of them that
smart."

Coulter opened the door slowly. The light flooded in, and for a
moment they sat blinking stupidly. The car was stuck midway
down a gently dipping snowfield. Two hundred yards below, a
spidery line of larch and willow trees marked the creek bed. Beyond, the ground rose in an equal slope to a steep, dark belt of
snow-dusted firs. The firs gave way abruptly to an unruly bed of
huge snowcapped boulders from which a sheer, black granite wall
rose two thousand feet to a dome, on whose shoulder sat the
morning sun in a fresh blue sky.

The two men crouched, looking through the doorway in silence.

"It's got us," Arizo said at last. "It sure got us."

Coulter climbed out, still crouching, and looked down the slope. "We must've got twenty-four inches in the night," he said. "There's no more road."

Arizo joined him, careful to keep his head below the roofline, assuming their pursuers were still up the slope. The powder came to their knees. Everything sparkled in the morning sun. Holding their breath, squinting against the glare, they saw that across the slope, behind and slightly above the Ford, was a canyon mouth, a missing tooth in the mountain wall. Below, beyond the nose of the car, the creek ran down about a mile and slipped to the right behind the shoulder of the hill. Above them, where that same shoulder finally ran into the trees, was the superstructure of the black pickup. This was their introduction to Muldoon Canyon.

As they looked, they saw three deer just starting up the rise from the creek, emerging from the blue shadow, a stag leading two does towards them. Coulter slowly slid the rifles out of the back. They waited for an easy shot. The animals came cautiously across the open ground, coats like wet slate against the snow, hopping elegantly, making their way down out of the mountains to forage on the plain now that the big snow had come. Every few yards they paused, standing motionless, heads raised, ears pricked, poised, regarding the half-buried Ford.

At fifty yards, the men beside the car, squinting down the barrels of their guns, fired.

Above them, the two men in the truck had been watching the Ford for some time. They had seen the door open. They had watched the deer moving up from the creek. Now they saw two black shapes kicking grotesquely in the snow as the life ran out of them, and a third animal, bounding with incredible leaps into the purple shadow by the creek. The two onlookers sat cradling their weapons behind a low bank of snow that had formed on the edge of the road beside the truck, and they heard the rifle shots echoing from the mountain face.

Coo-Coo was mostly hungry. He had gotten over his distaste and was now warming to the adventure. "Whatta you think?" he said to Poulsen.

"I think I coulda got all three. An' I think they're gonna go out there in a bit an' clean them." Poulsen sniffed and pinched his nose with thumb and forefinger. "Then we'll thee."

"We'll just scare the hell outta them. Right?" Coo-Coo asked. He looked at Poulsen intently with his chalky blue eyes. "Right?"

Poulsen nodded. "Right," he muttered.

"Now what?" Coulter asked.

"Let me take a look." Arizo crawled around to the rear of the Ford. When he came back, he said, "They're sitting by the truck, waitin'."

"They're still crazy mad."

"You think?"

"Yeah, I think."

Arizo put Coulter's black hat on the end of his rifle and held it barely above the rim of the roof. In three seconds there was a shot, and the hat trembled slightly. Then the echo cracked back at them again and again off the mountain wall. Arizo pulled the hat in and looked at it.

"You're one dead sonovabitch," he said.

Coulter turned to Arizo, eyes wide, badly shaken. "They really wanna kill me," he said. "Those sonsofbitches."

"It sure as hell looks that way."

"I don't believe this." Coulter looked dumbly at Arizo, appealing for reason.

"What'd you think?"

Coulter shrugged, still speechless, then he too moved to the back of the Ford and peered up the slope at the two riflemen. When he came back, he was panting a little. He licked his lips. "Soon as it gets dark, let's go up there an' get 'em." He seemed all efficiency now, but Arizo didn't trust the speed of the change. He looked closely at him and inquired, "How we gonna get 'em?"

"Disarm them."

"How far from the main road you think we are?"

"Thirty miles?"

"Which way?"

Coulter pointed to the mountain. "Over there. East."

"An' how far from where we said we'd be?"

"I dunno. Maybe five, ten miles. We're for sure south of Bartlett, but I dunno if these mountains is the White Knobs or the
Pioneers."

Arizo squinted. "If we just take it one thing at a time, it'll be
okay. First we get them off of our backs; then we get outta here."

"How many cigarettes you got?"

"Half a carton."

"Let me have one."

Arizo shook two out, gave one to Coulter and lit his own. He
exhaled, leaned back against the Ford, and studied for the first
time the niches and faults on the sheer mountain wall.

They made a simple plan over the smokes. At dark they would
circle around the back of the truck, staying together to avoid
shooting each other.

"And if we draw a blank, we'll at least know where they are,"
Arizo said.

"Where?"

Arizo tapped the Ford. "Right here," he said. "Waitin' for us."

Coulter stroked the stubble on his chin and grinned.

"Is this all we got?" Coo-Coo asked, holding up the bottle.

"Take a hit," Poulsen said. "It'll hold you."

Coo-Coo took a good shot from the half-empty fifth of bourbon. He had been shocked by Poulsen's shooting at the hat. Vern
had said it was just a hat, but Coo-Coo couldn't believe his part-
ner was sure there wasn't a head in it until afterwards. Even now
it was possible he'd hit someone, for the hat had disappeared with
the shot.

Coo-Coo handed back the bottle. "Whatta we gonna do, Vern?
Let's call it off now, man. We scared them enough already.
Okay?"

Poulsen shook his head. "We can hold 'em down eathy till
dark."

"Then what?"

"We'll think of thomething. I wanna thake 'em up thome
more."

There was a shout: "*Vern.*" Coulter's voice.

Vern-Vern-Vern came off the mountain. Poulsen said nothing.

"Ain't you gonna answer?"

Poulsen shook his head.

"*Vern,* I'm sorry," Coulter called.

Sorry-sorry-sorry-sorry.

Poulsen squinted down his rifle, looking for movement.

"*Vern, I'm sorry, I truly am.*"

"Come on Vern," Coo-Coo said. "Answer him. You gotta, man. This isn't no fuckin' game anymore."

"You keep quiet, boy." Poulsen's face was grim. "You hold your tongue, you hear?"

A pair of crows, ragged, in labored flight, came out of the trees beside the creek; black shapes flapping over the brilliant snow.

"*Vern. We're all in this together now!*"

Poulsen was considering a shot through the top of the roof, figuring Coulter to be sitting in the doorway.

"He's right," Coo-Coo said, his voice rising. "Answer him, Vern. It's enough, I tell you."

Poulsen glared at Coo-Coo, and his lips were tight. Coulter's voice came again: "*Coo-Coo, you hear me? Talk to Vern, Coo-Coo.*"

"Vern, please pack it in," Coo-Coo pleaded. "I know how you feel, but—"

"My ath you do."

"*Stay down, Rick,*" Coo-Coo called to the pair below. Rick-Rick-Rick . . . He looked at the man beside him.

"Screw you, Vern, you're crazy. I'm gettin' out."

Poulsen fired three times in rapid succession. In the confusion of echoes clattering across the canyon, the crows flew up again, squawking a warning.

Coulter's voice came angrily now: "*All right Vern, goddammit!*"

As he watched, Poulsen saw a little movement at either end of the snow-covered Ford. Then the shots came fast, smashing into the truck behind them. The windshield fell out immediately, and the passenger window. Poulsen began returning the fire. He scrambled a few feet along the bank to change his location, lying on his stomach and firing hastily, scarcely looking where, kicking up the snow.

Coo-Coo shouted in horror—"*Vern!*"—staring at him across the ten-foot space between them, eyes wide with disbelief. Poulsen fired again, grunting, not lifting his head from his rifle as it jerked against his cheek.

More shots came from below, banging into the truck. Poulsen looked back at it, twisting his head. "That truck'th brand-new," he screamed in rage, and went back to firing. Two shots more, and his rifle clicked empty. He swore and went to the box of shells that lay beside him, swearing, growling, stuffing the clip with fumbling, shaky hands that were red with cold.

Coo-Coo watched him, afraid to speak. But finally it burst out of him: "You said we was just gonna scare 'em, Vern," he shouted with an anger and strength that surprised them both. "You're fuckin' crazy. You're gonna go to jail for this, man. You'll do time."

Poulsen had finished reloading. He worked the bolt as he looked across. "You're behavin' like a goddamn woman!" he yelled. Taking his hat off, and pushing up until he could see over the ridge, he fired again.

He was almost bald, Coo-Coo realized. He had never seen Vern without his hat before.

"I'm goin', Vern," Coo-Coo said, calmer now. "I'm leavin'."

Poulsen didn't look around or even lift his head.

Coo-Coo crouched. There were more shots.

"Get down!" Poulsen yelled madly.

"*Don't shoot!*" Coo-Coo shouted down the hill as loudly as he could, and he started for the trees behind them. Instantly there was a shot, and Poulsen heard a hollow *sock*—a strange wet sound. In the corner of his eye, he saw the boy go down, saw it at the edge of his vision, as a camera catching the edge of movement, an essence without detail, the flesh blurred, the shadow halted suddenly upon the snow. The boy fell forward and sideways, against the hill. He lay as if still in the act of running, head forward, face pressed into the snow. Sprinkled around the head Poulsen saw what seemed to be a handful of geraniums.

Poulsen stared with hostility and then swore and turned back to look down the hill. No further shots came. He looked for some sign of Coulter and Arizo but could see no movement. He fired a couple of rounds, tempting them to reply, but they did not.

Sandy awakened knowing there had been a change and afraid without reason. She lay on her back, covers pulled up, staring at the familiar knots on the pine-board ceiling, then raised herself cautiously on her elbows, as though she had heard someone, and stared past the open bedroom door into the darkened cabin. The place was empty, and the air was cold and still. She saw it for what it was without him being there: small and poor and lifeless. She turned her head sideways, listening. There was no sound but the faint muffled running of the river. No sound at all.

She fell back impatiently, frustrated at the thought of a day before he would return. She tried to relax herself by rubbing the back of her neck and organizing her day, but soon found herself staring at the light leaking onto the ceiling from around the curtains, unusually pale and diffuse. In that moment she knew what had happened.

"God!" she called softly, and flinging back the bedclothes, she stood and drew back the curtain in what seemed a single motion. The glare outside was dazzling.

"Oh God!" she said, louder this time, and with an edge of panic. She dropped the curtain and began pulling on her clothes and boots. "I must call," she said aloud. "I must call. Oh God."

She ran awkwardly, splay-legged in the snow, some fifty yards across the slippery ground to the Hermans' bungalow, and beat on the door. Her breath came in clouds. Gladys opened to her and stood looking, glasses dangling on her bosom from a rhinestone string.

"Gladys! We've got to call. We've got to do something. The snow's got them! They'll be stuck." Sandy broke down as she heard herself. "Oh God, Gladys," her face crumpling, "why did this have to happen?"

Gladys had not known what to do until Sandy cried. Now she stepped forward instantly and took the small body to her, clucking and stroking the girl. "You hush," she said, "you hush. There's nothin's happened 'cept a little snow. Those boys are no fools. They're no babies. They'll be home soon enough."

"You think so, Gladys?" Sandy sniffed into the older woman's gray sweater, smelling the musty smell of her, feeling the softness of the wool and the warmth.

"Yes, child," Gladys said, "I certainly do."

Her husband was standing beside them now, wearing a soft plumber's hat and absentmindedly holding a newspaper by the corner of a page. Gladys nodded to him. George Herman stepped deferentially around them. "You better go inside, Gladys, an' let me close the door. You're letting all the heat out."

Sue-Ellen answered on the second ring. "Ya-lo," she said. Sandy could hear the TV in the background.

"It's me, Sue-Ellen." She was trying to be calm. "Have you heard from them?"

"Honey, three foot of snow fell in the Basin last night. I wasn't expectin' them home just yet."

"Shouldn't we call the sheriff?"

"They're not scheduled back till tonight."

"I'm afraid something's wrong."

"What?"

"I dunno. Somethin'."

"You wanna call Sheriff Meyers and tell him that at eight o'clock Saturday mornin', you go right ahead, sweetie."

Sheriff Burt Meyers, filled with orange juice, sausage, buckwheat pancakes, toast, strawberry jam, and black coffee, sat at his desk in a pool of Saturday morning sunlight, a grizzled, contented peace-keeper.

He liked the office on Saturday mornings. The slackened tempo had the feel of being aboard ship in port after a strenuous passage. He was reading the Twin Falls *Times-News*. The Denver Broncos were twelve-point favorites over the New York Giants. He grunted with satisfaction, rolled his left cheek off the chair, and farted. He was no great lover of the gridiron, but he fiercely loathed New

York. He'd never been there and he would never go. New York City was, in his mind, a stopped-up crapper spilling drugs, smut, pornography, homosexuality, and prostitution all across the country. America was ankle-deep in New York's old shit and toilet paper. That was what he liked to tell parents in his antidrug lectures. Now, this excrement had even seeped onto his preserve, right into Cope County, which was geographically larger than all of New York City. It polluted the county's four thousand resident souls. It hadn't only made his job more difficult: it had changed it and altered his very way of life. Used to be poaching, rustling and a bar fight Saturday. That was it. Now? Bad enough the divisions of frustrated, cooped-up city game hunters who swarmed over his territory in the fall, not knowing the difference between a bull moose and a coffeewagon; bad enough the pale-skinned army of fire-setting, ankle-busting, boot-sore suburban backpackers that preceded them. But, infinitely worse were the drugs they brought with them. A bunch of them killed themselves on drugs up in the mountains every year. He'd find them frozen in fancy dress, half-eaten by coyotes, or wandering around lost with that crazed dope-look. Drugs riddled the high schools despite his ceaseless round of lectures. Drugs were undermining the society he had gone to war to preserve and for which many who had been boys with him had died. Now the whole goddamned U. S. Army was addicted to marijuana, he'd heard. Drugs had lost the war in Vietnam. Who left in the ranks would obey without question? Who would sustain the fight? Who would not flinch to make that final sacrifice? He put the paper down and stared through the window at the sky. The generals no longer had any alternative, he thought. They had to finish it quick. Drugs had brought them to an ending of the free world. He had known it would happen so.

There was a knock, and Sergeant Jarl Goebbels entered the sheriff's large, spartan office.

"Burt," Goebbels began, "we got four hunters went into the basin Saturday."

The sheriff looked at Goebbels, at his tidy stomach comfortably swelling his crisp khaki shirt, his blond hair brushed neatly back, his blue eyes bulging like his belly, his pink cheeks puffed like some painted cherub on a church ceiling.

"Goebbels," the sheriff said, "I just realized somethin'. Somethin' pretty goddamned awful. What are the generals gonna fight with come the next war, Goebbels? If every fightin' man is busy smokin' pot, what are the generals gonna fight with?"

"I hope there won't be another war," Goebbels said angelically.

"Hell!" exclaimed the sheriff and shook his head at such idiocy. "The only question is when. And the only thing the generals have left to fight with is the bomb. They're gonna drop the big one, Goebbels. What else can they do? No goddamned junkie is gonna risk his neck. The junkies have pushed us to the wall worse than the Japs did in forty-one. You realize that?"

"Yeah, I see what you mean," Goebbels said and scratched his bottom. "What shall we do about this business in Copper Basin? I think maybe I'd better get the Mountain Rescue Posse set up for Monday." He scrutinized the sheriff's face, which was as flat and cracked as old mud, and saw nothing in those dusty eyes.

The sheriff squinted and scratched his jaw.

"They had twenty-three inches in the Basin last night," Goebbels persisted.

"It's Coulter's kid and that Injun fellow, isn't it?"

"How'd you hear?"

"I didn't," the sheriff lied. "I just know'd they were headed for trouble." He leaned back in his chair and gazed sternly at Goebbels, whose eyes popped like corn.

"Vern Poulsen and the Catlin kid is missin', too."

"They're probably in there together," the sheriff acknowledged. "That Coulter's boy's been foolin' around with Poulsen's wife, you know."

Goebbels raised his eyebrows.

"Call a meetin' for tomorrow night if they haven't showed by then. I don't want our boys goin' off bustin' ass searchin' in the mountains while them four is gettin' drunk at the Cottontail ranch."

Goebbels nodded and went out. The sheriff never ceased to amaze him. He knew what was going on in town before it ever

happened. Goebbels shook his head. In moments like this he surrendered his ambition. He'd never make a halfway decent sheriff
by comparison. He didn't have that touch of brilliance Burt had.
He would have had the whole posse out there, maybe even today.
He shook his head and sighed with relief.

When the door closed, the sheriff picked up the phone and
called his deputy in Mackay.

"Lieutenant Kule," he said. "It's Burt."

"Yes, sir."

"Lieutenant, get some of your Mountain boys alerted, will you.
I believe we'll need 'em Monday morning. I believe there's some
boys got caught up there in the Basin."

In Copper Basin they waited for darkness, weighing stratagems,
considering eventualities, watching the shadows change on the
mountain wall as the sun moved across the sky.

The silence and isolation nurtured their enmity, for there was
no one to bring reason, interrupt, or bear witness. Only the overwhelming mountain looked down, impassively. Being men, they
took from its grandeur and applied nobility to their wretched
cause. And that then made them all the more serious.

Poulsen did nothing to retrieve Coo-Coo's body. It lay where it
had fallen, half-submerged in fresh snow, arms outstretched, face
down. From time to time Poulsen glanced at it as if for confirma-
tion of some private reality, for some support. He sat behind the
low snowbank leaning against the wheel of his truck, watching the
car below, nursing his rifle and occasionally drinking from the bottle. He was red-eyed and stubbly and looked ten years older. His
stomach was afire with hunger. He thought about Marlene, but
without any great emotion, for he was obsessed with what he was
doing, with maintaining that aggressive edge which was the thing
he always enjoyed about hunting.

There being no time for some parts of the mind, Poulsen had
decided as he lay there what he should do.

They would come up the hill and circle around him as soon as
it got good and dark. While they were doing that, he would take
the unguarded center and walk down to the Ford. He would get

into the back, and when they tired of searching for him and returned exhausted and unguarded, he would be waiting for them.

Sheltered from his sight by the Ford, Coulter and Arizo sat
largely in silence. Occasionally they checked the hill behind, uncomfortable with hunger. But all that moved, beside the clouds,
was the pair of crows that roamed the creek below them. Coulter
fidgeted, drew in the snow ceaselessly with a stick, and kept meas-
uring the progress of the sun. Arizo seemed largely absent and did
not move for long periods at a time.

Each man had his own vision of what the night would bring.

Towards mid-afternoon the wind picked up and clouds came
from the direction of the canyon mouth, closing rapidly. The men
put on their parkas as the temperature fell sharply. The sun went
quickly, and within an hour or so, the last blue sky had vanished
to the east and snow had begun falling. The gathering wind
kicked up the loose powder on the ground; the line of trees that
marked the creek bed vanished and the temperature fell steadily.

When he could no longer see the Ford below, Poulsen climbed
into the bed of his truck, which nosed, with shattered windshield,
into the weather. He sat with his back against the cab, clasping
his knees, and saw the snow eddying about the sides and top of
the cab and beginning to settle lightly upon him.

Below, Coulter and Arizo lay side by side on the mattress in the
Ford, blankets pulled over them, listening to the growing sound of
the wind rushing down from the canyon mouth, feeling the power
mounting against them.

It was clear now who would be the hunter on this night.

By six that evening, the storm had settled fully upon Cope. The
wind blew hard up Main Street from the west. The snow strung
through the yellow light above the junction of Snake and Main in
stinging horizontal lines. The wind hurried Eleanor Holmes along
the deserted street as she carefully made her way past the hardware store and turned down the driveway immediately beyond the
building.

She let herself in the back door with her own key, stamped her feet on the mat, took off her woolen scarf, and went up the stairs, listening for some sound of him. He was sleeping on the cot, curled on his side facing the wall. The empty baby bottles lay about him on the bed. The bed was wet.

She woke him slowly, shaking his shoulder, undressed him, and led him to the shower. She ran the water until it was warm and when he had washed she held out a towel and then fetched him clean pajamas. She led him back to his own room and helped him into bed. He stared at her, saying nothing. She kissed his forehead and tucked him in. Then she set his alarm for six-thirty, and left, softly, turning out the light. As she began closing the door, he called out: "Leave it open."

Half-turning she said, "Good night." It was the end of the weekend ritual. The following morning he would open the store at 8:00 A.M. as he did every Monday morning. On the dot.

The storm blew with a hushed roar along the canyon walls, gliding from its mouth across the slick surface of the snow, twisting strongly in gusts that would take a man off his feet. Lying in the blackness, Coulter and Arizo felt the wind buffet and tremble the thin steel shell surrounding them and heard its chilling howl.

Poulsen felt his body heat draining, hour by hour. His limbs grew stiff as the cold soaked into him. At first he crouched motionless and afraid, but then he looked up into the darkness and screamed in rage at the storm, pounding the wall of the truck with outstretched arms. Once he dared this, he found an ecstasy in the storm's magnitude. Its force was an exalted expression of the madness in him, and he yelled scornfully at it, challenging it to blow harder. Then suddenly he stood and climbed stiffly over the side of the truck. He fought his way into the wind until he stepped on the stiffened body lying half-buried on the ground. He unzipped Coo-Coo's parka and pulled it roughly off the unbending arms. In the truck bed he wrapped the parka about his legs and knees, curling into it, and, with this newfound security, raged and laughed hysterically until the laughter turned to sobbing and his head fell forward in release onto his knees and fitfully he dozed.

So Poulsen survived the night, seeing the light grow and, as it did, finding the bed of the pickup half-filled with new snow.

He sat for some time watching the darkness fade. The gale had fallen off to a strong, fresh wind. When it was quite light he decided he must eat somehow and climbed clumsily over the side of the truck. He would go downhill and find the deer. This was all he thought about. He left his rifle buried in the bed of the pickup.

There was still a good ground blizzard blowing. He couldn't see more than thirty feet ahead. With each step he sank deeply into the new powder, breaking immediately through the light crust made by the wind. Going down the hill, he slid and fell and struggled up—only to fall again. Each time he came floundering to his feet, spitting snow from his mouth, wiping it from his eyes, he would say aloud, "One, two. One, two. One, two." And then he would slip and fall again. Soon he was panting hard, gasping in the thin air. His breath froze on the cheap dog-fur trim around his hood, snow stuck to his eyebrows and to the stubble on his face. He held his arms out for balance. His focus dwindled with his strength, and he became concerned not with where he was going, but only with the task of moving.

Sometimes, fretfully, like an old man who continually sees he has forgotten, he would mutter to himself and, standing in the drifting snow, pause and look about him and change direction. A few steps later, he would do the same. And so he wandered about, going nowhere, feeling his strength slip from him.

He sank suddenly to his armpits, crying out and floundering for support. The wind-driven snow that flurried low along the ground blew blindingly into his face and he threw up an arm to shield his eyes and turned his head away. He struggled out of the hole, gasping and moving slowly and heavily. He was feeling warmer now. He turned his back to the wind and looked at his watch. Then he sat a moment to rest, leaning his head upon his knees. He raised up his arms as if in supplication and saw the swirling whiteness going past, the pieces losing themselves in one another as they danced away from him. Slowly his head began to sink once more. But at that moment he saw the shape of the Ford.

He saw it dimly in a world of faint shadows; a uniform, unnatural shape, a dark mound sticking up only a foot or so above the surface, staring at him, sightlessly. For some time he stared back and then he struggled to his feet. The fine reasoning of the higher brain was gone now. Only the ancient roots beneath still functioned, that part assigned to the reflex instinct for survival. He looked at this shape as an ancient man contemplating a sleeping mammoth: carefully, suspiciously, but hungrily. He began to move towards it, unaware of his stumbling, his mouth agape but his eyes filled with purpose.

They heard a thud against the driver's door and sat up, listening in terrified disbelief. It came again; a slow, repetitive thumping, and then a muffled yelling and the sound of someone repeatedly trying the door.

"It's him," Coulter whispered. "My God, it's him!"

"Must be." Arizo fought to be alert.

"Whatta we gonna do?"

"Let 'im in."

"Wait. He could be blastin' us. He's crazy."

Arizo had a vision of being shot in the face through the opaqued window. The muffled thumping and pulling were still going on. He figured whoever was outside would have fired already if they were going to.

"Who's there?" he yelled. "Who's there?" He felt ridiculous.

It stopped. They listened, but there was only the wind.

"He's goin' around to the other door," Coulter said.

Guns ready, they listened for a full minute, but there was no further sound.

"Shit," Arizo exclaimed. "I'm goin' out. If they were gonna shoot us, they'd just shoot through the side."

Nevertheless he opened the door very slowly. All that he saw was snow driving past. But then, as he opened the door further, the body of a man lay face down beside the car. It was quickly being buried. Together, Arizo and Coulter pulled him inside and laid him in the back. Ice had formed in his hair and on his eyebrows. It was Poulsen.

"He was sweatin'," Coulter said.

"What now?" Arizo looked at Coulter. Poulsen was unconscious.

"About him?"

"Yeah."

"Well," Coulter hesitated. "What the mountain posse does is, you take his clothes off, and you take your clothes off, and then you both get in a sleepin' bag together till he's thawed out. He looked at Arizo in the dim light. Neither man moved.

Arizo began to undress Poulsen. Then he stopped. "You do this," he said and began undressing himself, taking off his parka, and hastily crawling under the blankets where he continued. "C'mon, for Chrissake, get him under here." They tugged and pushed the dead weight of Poulsen until he and Arizo were naked beneath the covers. Arizo, embracing the icy figure, said to Coulter, "You go out an' see if you can find Coo-Coo. But don't go outta sight of the car."

Coulter nodded. "You know what I think," he said.

"Yeah, I know what you think. But go look anyway," Arizo told him.

Later that morning, as the storm was still clearing, Coulter shot the last two deer to come out of the mountains by way of Muldoon Canyon. Poulsen was still sleeping, and Arizo had dressed but continued to lie beside him. Coulter had moved into the front seat at full light, despite the intense cold. He couldn't bear to lie next to Poulsen, listening to him breathe as he slept. He found it completely unbelievable that this man, whom he and Marlene had ridiculed and deceived, was jammed up here against him. So he had gone to sit in the front, saying quietly as he went, "I can't handle this, Mike. We got to get outta here soon as it lightens up outside."

Arizo was lying on his back. He grunted agreement.

"I'm gonna go crazy otherwise with him in here."

When Arizo heard shots, he sat up and looked. Coulter was bent over his rifle in the driver's seat, the muzzle of the .303 resting on the half-open window. A deer was jerking spastically in the snow some eighty yards away.

"You get it?" Arizo blurted.

"Hell yes, I got it," Coulter yelled excitedly. "I got the both of them. See, there's the other. What'd you think, man?" He pushed at the snow against the door and clambered numbly out. Arizo glanced down at Poulsen and was a little shocked to see the man's eyes open, watching him. "He's got some deer," Arizo said as if he was speaking to a child. Poulsen's expression did not alter. Arizo, too, got out of the car, being careful to take his gun with him.

They cleaned the animals in the lee of the car where the snow was packed more firmly. They lashed the hind legs to the door frame and stretched out the carcasses belly up. The belly fur was chalky white, thin and flat and coarse to touch. They slit both bellies open and intestines spilled out, steaming, onto the snow, richly colored and oily. The stomachs in turn burst out a tan puree which Coulter examined with his knife.

"They were gettin' real hungry," he said.

"Yeah?"

"When they get to eatin' bark like this, you know they are."

"So how come they stayed up here so long?"

Coulter shrugged and grinned and wiping his knife blade on the belly fur, he said, chuckling, "I guess they're dumb, too."

Arizo suddenly stopped. "Jesus!" he said. "We completely forgot about Coo-Coo. Did you look before you shot these deer?"

"Well, I was wonderin' about him, but we need food first, and . . ." Coulter trailed off and Arizo snapped his knife shut and climbed back into the car, kneeling in the front seat.

"Vern," he called. "What about Coo-Coo?"

There was no answer. Thinking he was asleep, Arizo called him again, louder. He was oddly reluctant to crawl into the darkened back where the man lay. He hesitated a moment and then he backed out and walked around to the rear, cleared away the snow and pulled the back door open. It was like turning a rock and finding some insect beneath. Poulsen lay under the blankets, haunted black eyes staring at him, helpless, blinking in the light.

"We gotta find Coo-Coo," Arizo said. "Let's go." He heard

Coulter coming around to stand next to him. The three men stared at each other. Poulsen's eyes were at once determined and afraid.

"Maybe he's sick," Coulter suggested.

"How do you feel?" Arizo asked.

Poulsen only looked at them.

"Screw it!" Arizo said. "We'll go look ourselves."

Arizo fetched his rifle and he and Coulter walked together cautiously up the hill towards Poulsen's truck.

The truck was a shell, with the windshield shattered and the cab and bed half-filled with powder. The two stood beside the passenger door, staring.

"I'll be damned," Coulter said. "Where'd he spend the night?"

"In the back, maybe." Arizo stepped to his left and looked into the bed. He pulled out Coo-Coo's parka.

"Look at this." He held it up. Then he leaned his rifle upright against the side of the truck and put his hand in one of the pockets. He came out with a letter in an envelope folded in half. Coulter stepped closer. Arizo flattened out the envelope. It was from the Sun Valley Mobile Home Co., in Twin Falls, and it was addressed to Mr. Coo-Coo Catlin. There was a moment's pause, and then Arizo stuffed the letter back into the pocket. He picked up his rifle and, carrying the parka, started off past the front of the truck. Coulter stood still for a moment more before he followed.

Arizo had gone perhaps fifteen feet when he stepped on the body. It was buried under a few inches and frozen hard. Coulter stood back a little as Arizo brushed off the snow. The body was hatless. Ice and snow had crusted in the fair hair. Arizo reached down and took the outstretched left arm that was frozen stiff as a branch and rolled the corpse part way over as if it were a log. The right side of the face was like a pomegranate exploded and then frozen. He heard the sound of retching and looked around. Coulter was throwing up.

Arizo turned the body back over, using the arm as a lever. "We should go finish cleaning the deer," he said, and they started hurriedly downhill.

As they went, thinking of Coo-Coo, the sky was clear and the sun well over the mountain. Everywhere the snow glittered freshly, dazzling in its brightness. Squinting, they followed the track they had made coming up, and both were puffing by the time they reached the car. They looked in on Poulsen. He hadn't moved. He lay looking at them with animal intensity.

"You knew he was dead," Arizo said. "How come you didn't tell us? You could've saved us a lot of grief."

Poulsen said nothing.

"Fuck him," Coulter said, and they went back to cleaning the deer. They put the organ meat in a plastic bag to store separately, and when they were finished, they started for the creek to gather firewood. They left their rifles but took the bolts with them. They had gone a few yards from the truck when Arizo stopped. "God we're being dumb," he said. "Where's their rifles?"

"Must be up by the truck."

Arizo went to the rear door, Coulter walking behind him, and pulled it open.

"Where's the rifles, Vern?" he asked.

Poulsen didn't respond.

"I need them," Arizo said evenly.

He had thought at first the man must be too weak and ill, remembering the ordeal Poulsen had been through. But his sullen look was insulting. Arizo found himself growing impatient and angry. When Poulsen still said nothing, he reached down suddenly and pulled the covers off him in a single movement and then, putting a foot on the doorsill to brace himself, he grabbed Poulsen by the feet and dragged man and mattress violently out onto the snow. In his nakedness, Poulsen rolled with surprising quickness and struggled upright. As he did, Arizo slapped him across the face so hard that the man went down again. He lay curled in the snow, naked, shivering, and Arizo stepped over him. "You sonovabitch, you tell me where the fuckin' guns are or I'm gonna hog-tie you till you do."

"Tie *him* up," Poulsen said hoarsely, motioning to Coulter with his head. "He'th the fuckin' animal." And suddenly he scrambled up and, almost in the way a woman would, lurched forward and

attacked Coulter with flailing fists, making a shrill chilling whin-
nying sound that didn't seem human. Coulter was surprised, but
recovered and caught Poulsen by the arms, twisting his tall, thin,
white body and throwing him back down into the snow. He stood
over him, breathing hard. "Don't ever touch me again, man. Else
I'll kill you. I swear to God."

Poulsen began to weep, a strange gasping sound. He covered his
face with his hands and drew his knees up to cover his stomach.
The two stepped back, hands at their sides. Poulsen could not
control his grief. His sobbing nearly stopped, and then broke out
again. Finally he rolled onto his stomach and came up on his
knees in the snow, looking away from them, across to the foot of
the mountain.

Then he stood and went quickly to the Ford without looking at
either and quickly dressed and in the surprising warmth of the afternoon sun, led them up the hill to retrieve the missing rifles. By
the time they had returned to the car, it was clearly too late to go
down to the creek, so they gathered the tops of the sage that still
stuck up through the snow in places, stamped down the snow beside the car and made a fire in a hubcap. They cooked the venison
very rare and ate quickly, in silence. Afterwards Coulter and Arizo
lit cigarettes, but Poulsen went back into the car without speaking. They looked at one another, questioning, when he did. They
crouched outside, around the blackened hubcap, a while longer,
and then Coulter said what he had been thinking: "It was self-
defense."

Arizo looked blankly at him.

"Coo-Coo, I mean."

Arizo was surprised. He had been wondering whether Poulsen
might not have shot the boy in his anger.

"You're my witness."

Arizo nodded.

"Ain't you gonna say something?"

Arizo shrugged. "We all know what happened."

"I didn't mean it. I was defending myself."

"It's okay. Keep it together. I just started livin'."

"Understand how I feel, Mike." He was whining a little.

Arizo nodded.

"This ever happen to you?"

"Did I ever kill somebody?" It hit both of them powerfully when he said it.

Coulter's attention wandered a moment. He nodded.

Arizo saw Baby Zeus grinning up at him. "Sort of," he said. "Once." Coulter looked almost relieved, but Arizo changed the subject. Pointing towards the Ford, he said in a low voice, "We should still keep the guns away from that one."

"Think so?"

"Yeah."

"I think he's already had the piss took outta him," Coulter said. "I don't think he'll hurt us none."

"I'm not scared of myself, but if he blows himself away, it'd really screw us."

"You think he might?"

Arizo shrugged. "He could do anything. He's half-psycho."

Coulter seemed alarmed. He hadn't thought about that possibility.

"So keep your rifle empty," Arizo whispered.

Coulter nodded and got up, brushing off his Levi's. "My pants is wet," he said. He crouched down again, forgetting his pants. "So whatta we do?"

"Now?"

"Do we stay or walk?"

"Like I said—where are we?"

"I told you. Five, maybe ten miles from Bartlett Crick."

"How far is it to walk out?"

"If we didn't screw up, maybe twenty, twenty-five miles."

"It's probably best if we stay here right now. The car's easy to see, an' we can at least get outta the wind. We got food here, an' walkin' around out there has got to be a whole lot more dangerous than sittin' here."

"Maybe *he* knows exactly where we are," Coulter said. "Hey, Poulsen. Where are we?"

There was no answer.

"Hey, asshole," Coulter said louder. "You asleep? Where are we?"

Arizo was looking at Coulter, shaking his head, looking pained.

There was no sound from the Ford. Arizo peered in. Poulsen was lying down in the gloom, his head to the front. He didn't look around at Arizo when he spoke: "I think we are in the White Knob Mountainth."

"You don't know for sure?"

"Could be Pioneer. I dunno how far we came."

"So you're not sure?"

"Where were you goin' huntin'?"

Arizo relayed the question to Coulter, who walked over and said, "Where I always go. Well, mostly this time of year. To Bartlett Crick in Copper Basin."

Poulsen overheard the reply and said flatly, "Well, Bartlett Crick ain't in Copper Bathin. It'th maybe forty mile north."

"You sure?"

"Uh-huh. Bartlett'th on the Big Lotht."

"That's what Rick told me," Arizo said. "But in Mackay at the gas station he asked for Copper Basin." He looked harder at Poulsen. "You gotta be wrong about this, Vern."

"I ain't the one that'th wrong." Poulsen said, almost triumphantly.

Before dark, they made an inventory of all they had: ten books of matches, six packs of cigarettes, a half-pint of maple syrup, four peanut butter sandwiches, a small cooking pot, a skillet, a half-pint jar of pancake flour, a half-pint jar of milk and eggs, a small can of shortening, two sticks of margarine, some coffee, sugar, a loaf of bread, and a half-pint of plum jam. On the mattress were two blankets and two quilts.

At Arizo's suggestion, Coulter started a log. "No one's gonna believe how this whole thing went down," Arizo said. "Maybe writin' it will help." He was also thinking that it would give the restless Coulter something to do. Coulter found a work log and a pencil in the glove compartment and, on Sunday, December 2, wrote laboriously in the cold: *Three feet of snow last nite. This a.m. Vern found us. Coo-Coo is dead. We have decided to stay*

with the car until we are rescued. Cold & blowing again now. We
are praying they come tomorrow."

"Jesus Christ," Coulter said. "It's Monday." He sat up, leaning
on his elbows and looked down at Arizo. Coulter had slept the
night in the middle. They had agreed to rotate the center spot,
since it was warmest. "What's Pops gonna do with us both off
work? I got eight stops today."

Arizo lay with his hands laced behind his head. "It does feel
kinda strange," he said. "But there's plenty of guys laid off right
now that can drive a truck."

"That's right." Coulter was disturbed. "If we don't get our asses
outta here right away, we're gonna be outta work. You know
that?"

Arizo nodded and picked his teeth with a thumbnail. Poulsen
lay with his back to them, unmoving. Arizo was thinking of the
morning Coulter first drove him out to the quarry to see Pops
about work. It was early, about seven o'clock, a cold morning early
in October. There was a gray light on the mountains, and the sage
was covered in frost. The quarry was about seven or eight miles out
on the Snake road. He hadn't figured why it was called the Snake
road when it ran along the Big Lost, and he hadn't remembered
to ask. He remembered the conversation. . . .

"His real name is Shlomo Bivaletz," Coulter, who was driving,
said. "Can you imagine that? We call him Pops. I think he escaped from Hitler or something, but they got his folks an' his
brother. I think maybe my pa must've helped him when he first
came, but they don't ever talk about it. I don't know why. Maybe
because Pops is the only Jew in town. Probably the only Jew in
Idaho. I think he's had three heart attacks."

"How old is he?"

"Seventy."

"I never worked for a Jew before."

"No?"

"No. I guess Jews don't farm so much."

"He's the most honest sonovabitch I ever knew."

The office was a small wooden shack at the head of the quarry. Pops was at his desk. Arizo watched him squint at them as they came in. He was small and skinny, in a gray wool sweater and gray pants, with gray hair that was hardly allowed out of his scalp. He looked very fragile, like a newborn bird, Arizo remembered, but for the eyes. The eyes were strong and humorous. Right away you could tell he wasn't someone you put things over on. He got up from behind the small desk as they came in. There was a brass reading light with a green glass shade on the desk. The office was dusty. An old electric stove was glowing on the floor. On the wall was a color poster of a rocky seashore at Caesarea, faded to a lifeless blue. Arizo remembered wondering where Caesarea was. There was also a pinup calendar from a builder's supply yard in Salt Lake City—a platinum blonde in a black cowboy shirt that was falling open around her tits. She was sucking a red popsicle and winking at you.

At the sight of Coulter, hustling in, curls bustling from under his black Stetson, eyes dancing, the old man smiled.

"I brought your new man, Pops," Coulter said.

They shook hands and Pops asked, "You would like some tea, perhaps?"

"Thank you," Arizo said, surprised.

The old man walked slowly over to a sideboard where stood tea things and an electric kettle, saying, "Oi, oi, oi. It is terrible to be an old man. You cannot know how terrible it is. Never be an old man."

Coulter reached up and turned the pinup calendar to the wall. "If you're feelin' bad, Pops, you shouldn't be lookin' at things like this," he said. "That'll kill you quicker than anything."

From the sideboard Pops turned and looked over his shoulder. He was grinning slightly. "Regard," he said. "One thing I can tell you. I shall never die young from this. You? That is not certain. But for me?" He shook his head. "I am dead already."

"But how can a dead man talk?" Coulter asked with exaggerated puzzlement.

Pops shrugged and said, with that same slight, sly grin, "That's what I ask myself. 'Ow can a dead man talk? I sink it is a miracle. No?"

Arizo grinned as he remembered the exchange.

Pops turned to him. "Regard," he said. "If you 'ave ever been in prison, you will like it 'ere. 'Ere we do ze same sing zey do zere, but," he paused, "'ere in the evenings you may go 'ome." He squeezed his eyes closed and nodded emphatically. "Mr. Coulter will show you what eez to be done. Yes? An zen, regard. You will receive a 'undred an' fifty dollar each week an twenty-five if you work a 'arf day on Zaturday. Oi, oi, oi." He rubbed his eyes again and turned back to his tea things. "It is terrible to be an old man. You cannot know."

"I can imagine," Arizo said.

"No," said Pops flatly. "You cannot. I will tell you a story to show you zis. Regard. When Napoleon was one time in Russia"— he screwed up his face as if he were concentrating on some unimaginably difficult question—"'e was caught by some Russian soldiers and zey, sinking 'e was just an officer, prepare to 'ang 'im. But zen, regard, zere is a junior soldier wiz 'im and 'e shows zem zis man eez, in truth, ze General Napoleon. So zey do not 'ang 'im and afterwards Napoleon escape and comes back to Paris. When 'e does, 'e call for zis soldier an' 'e make him a good job an' say, 'Regard. You are my friend for life.' Zo, zis man, 'e say, 'Sank you, mon general. But one zing I would like to know: Of what do you zink in zese minutes when zey prepare to 'ang you? When you knew you would die?'"

Pops' face clouded over. "Zen Napoleon become furious and 'e shout at ze man, ''Ow dare you ask me such a zing? 'Ow dare you ask ze general such a personal question? Who you zink you are?' An' he say to ze guard, 'Take zis man away an' 'ang 'im immediately. Now! In no more zan fifteen minutes. Do not delay.' So ze guards take 'im away and 'e is crying for mercy. But Napoleon, 'e is mad. 'E is furious, yes? So zey take ze man an' zey prepare to 'ang 'im an' zey put ze rope 'round 'ees neck. An' ze man 'e is crying for help. An' at zis moment Napoleon appear and say, 'Is enough.' An' to ze soldier 'e say, 'Now you know.' You ask me a question I cannot answer. Zere eez only one answer to zis question. You must know for yourself. No man can tell you." Pops looked sideways at Arizo. "So you see," he said, "you cannot know 'ow it is to be an old man." He rubbed his forehead again and grimaced.

Arizo laughed and said, "I never knew Napoleon was in Russia."

Pops shrugged. "There are many things you cannot know," he said, "but what can you *do?*"

"About everything," Arizo said.

"Some of everything and not a whole bunch of anything," Coulter said and laughed.

"Regard," said Pops. "You must take off your 'at when you speak zo, for on zuch men I zink zey 'ave made America."

Coulter slid into a body builder's pose and flexed his biceps. "We don't have much money, but we sure have fun." He grinned broadly.

"On his muscle and your brains," Arizo said.

Pops nodded. "On such zings, Mr. Rockefeller 'as become a rich man."

"And you," Coulter added.

Pops closed his eyes and lifted his head slightly. "I?" he said. "I am making less zan you an' working more."

"So what satisfaction do we all get?" Coulter asked.

"You 'ave made Mr. Rockefeller a rich man," Pops said. "And you 'ave a place where zey do not come in ze night and kill you."

"If anyone comes for me, they better not come in the night," Coulter said and winked at the old man.

Pops shrugged. "I am surprised someone 'as not already come for you," he said. "An' now. Regard. You will please to show Mr. Aritzo . . ."

"Ar-*I*-zo," Coulter corrected.

"Excuse me. Mr. Arizo. You will show 'im ze place, an' I will return to my work."

Now Arizo looked at Coulter, propped on his elbows beside him, staring absently into the morning twilight that filtered through the snow-covered rear window of the Ford. "Pops will let us hang onto our jobs," he said.

Coulter wasn't so sure. "How long d'you think?"

"Long enough so it won't make any difference to you if he doesn't," Arizo said.

He rolled out from under the blankets. "Jesus, my ass is stiff," he said. "My back, too."

"You gonna see what it's like outside?" Coulter inquired.

"No," Poulsen said, unexpectedly. "He'th going to thee if we got any mail."

Coulter looked over at this sarcasm. Poulsen was still facing the wall. "So what the fuck's eatin' you?" he said. "Didn't you have a nice night or somethin'?"

"You kept me awake all night with your beatin' off," Poulsen said.

Coulter was so surprised that he could only shake his head weakly and say, "Shit."

At eight o'clock that same morning, Sheriff Meyers stood outside the door to his main office listening. Beside him in the foyer, plaid wool hunting jackets and parkas were piled on the receptionist's table, and black rubber overboots stood in pairs in snow puddles on the vinyl floor. Beyond the frosted glass, the sheriff's temporary deputies were complaining vigorously. They were grousing about the money they were losing by being off their jobs, about the sheriff's parsimony, about their wives' frigidity, about the stupidity of the people they were about to go looking for.

There was always stupidity involved when someone got lost in the mountains. In the winter it was usually fliers the Mountain Rescue Men went after. Pilots in aircraft overdue for service, drunk pilots, pilots who ignored the weather. In the summer it was mostly the city people, so hated by the sheriff. In the fall it was hunters from the suburbs of Salt Lake, San Jose, San Francisco, Seattle, or Pasadena. Whoever it was, the sheriff thought, they got into trouble because they hopelessly overestimated themselves and hopelessly underestimated the suddenness and power of natural forces.

The sheriff had been exposed to this during the depression, the war in the Pacific and twenty-five years in the Sawtooths. This ineptitude, and the sight of mankind becoming daily more sepa-

rated from God, Nature, and Reality by its appetite for technol-
ogy, drugs, and alcohol, had brought him to trust no one's
judgment but his own and to perceive his fellow men, and particularly the people of Cope County (whom Goebbels insisted on re-
ferring to as "his subjects"), as malleable children. To his credit,
he had not surrendered to cynicism. He had, for instance, organized a high school antidrug program that had been written up in
the Idaho State magazine. He had risked his career more than
once to make Cope a dry county. And he had taken this crew of
roughneck beet farmers and ditchdiggers lounging beyond the
door and turned them into a paramilitary mountain rescue squad
that was in demand all up and down the eastern Rockies.

It was with a concealed sense of pride, then, that he opened the
door and slowly entered. They took boots off desks, conversation
died and a couple of them called out, "Hey, Burt." He walked between the desks to the blackboard and turned to face them. There
were eight of them, plus Dan Coulter, their equipment manager,
and Sergeant Goebbels, who stood beside the sheriff at the blackboard, hands on hips, stomach thrusting significantly forward.

"One thing we got goin' for us in this," the sheriff said. "The
boys we're looking for is some of our own. So that'll remind you
all not to go takin' liberties. We're lookin' for boys that ain't no
jackass hunters. They know'd the mountains good as anyone, and
they were still caught."

" 'Cept they had women on the mind," Red Lewis said. "I
mean, you know what they were doin' up there, Burt? You know
about Coulter humpin' Marlene Poulsen at the Pejasky place an'
all that?"

The sheriff nodded. "You boys don't need to worry none," he
said. The sheriff barely moved his lips when he spoke. "They'll be
cooled out by the time we get 'em. I guarantee it." There was
laughter.

"An' the one we bring out gets the chair," Joey Leonard said.
"Be the first time we saved one for the chair." There was more
laughter. It was easy for Leonard to get a laugh. With his silver
sideburns and walleye it was somehow enough to make you laugh
if he just looked at you and grinned.

Buddy Lane said, "I'd as soon freeze."

Dan Coulter cleared his throat and said, "I believe they broke down."

"If that was my kid, I'd believe it, too," Leonard said, and they guffawed again.

"Was your boy drivin' in that Injun's ol' Ford?" Buddy Lane asked.

Dan Coulter nodded with a long face. "I believe."

"Then I'm with you; it was a breakdown," Lane said and got the best laugh yet.

"They ain't nothin' wrong with Fords," someone protested.

The sheriff held up his hand. "It ain't no joke. There's thirty-six inches fell in the mountains already, an' a bunch more comin'."

"You got the Forest Service?" Len Longren asked.

The sheriff nodded. "They'll meet us in Mackay," he said. And then, turning to Goebbels: "You got the map, Sergeant?"

Goebbels unrolled a topographical map of the Bartlett Creek area and hung it over the blackboard. "This here's the area of highest probability." The sheriff pointed to a red-shaded area. "We work two-man teams. If we start going off the roads much, we'll go to three. Each team gets a mile of road. Go back in three hundred yards each side. And—"

"When you've done it once, go back and do it again," Leonard sang out.

The sheriff turned narrowed eyes on him. "I don't give a damn how many times you heard this, Leonard, you gonna hear it again, 'cause you ain't none too fuckin' smart. Fact is, Leonard, if I was lost out there an' I knew it was you lookin' for me, I'd smoke my ass 'fore I froze it to death."

The others chortled and Leonard looked indignant.

The sheriff wasn't finished. He paused and surveyed the room. "This ain't no time for you boys to go thinkin' you can bite them mountains, 'cause if you do, I guarantee you're gonna get bit right back." He glared at them in silence. Then he said, "You'll work back three hundred yards on either side, 'less you see somethin'. Their vehicles will likely be buried now, I reckon. We'll work on Channel B of your talkies, and you bring your own food. Right

now I got enough to buy gas, an' that's all. If we don't find them
right away . . ."

They grumbled, as always.

"Sergeant Goebbels, hand out the topos."

When that was done, Sergeant Goebbels gave the sheriff a list.
The sheriff studied it a moment, then said, "Okay. Section One-A
is a lot of sidehilling. Who wants it?"

"Me and Seiler'll take it," Red Lewis said.

"Spangler and Rose, Two-A," the sheriff intoned. "Leonard
and Longren, Three-A. That's a steep one. Me an' Sergeant Goebbels will take Four-A, the Forest Service and Lieutenant Kule will
handle five and six, and Dan"—he looked at the missing man's
father—"you'll run the base. Okay?"

"Supposin' they're shot up?" Lewis said.

The sheriff regarded Lewis and rubbed his long chin and
shrugged. "Then plug the holes and call me. Let's go, gentlemen."

The meeting broke up. They were in good spirits, secretly
pleased to be off work and extremely optimistic. The sheriff
watched them for a moment and, as he turned to go, he said to
Goebbels, "Just don't let 'em know what kinda weather we got
comin', okay, Sergeant?"

"They'll see it on the TV," Goebbels reminded him.

"The TV is one thing," the sheriff said, patting him on the
shoulder. "You an' me is another."

Sheriff Meyers' Mountain Rescue Posse searched the Big Lost
up as far as Bartlett Creek that first day. They found nothing. By
the time they gathered under the lights in the parking lot outside
a diner in Mackay, it was suppertime. There were sixteen men in
all now, counting Lieutenant Kule's team and the men from the
Forest Service. They pulled up in a dozen high pickups, hauling
snowmobiles lashed under tarps and plastic covers. It was a subdued gathering, like a losing locker room. They were tired and
hungry and disappointed. They had expected to find at least a vehicle.

"I guess they're further up the road than we could get today,"
the sheriff said, and his breath steamed around the rim of his hat

in the neon glare. "Or maybe they went up North Fork. So to-morrow we'll go up North Fork and some of you will take Summit Creek." The men were huddled about him, stamping their feet, shoulders hunched.

"Are there any questions?" There were none. "Does any of you have anything to say?" Nobody did. They wanted to go home. "Then unless you get a call, we'll meet here tomorrow at seven A.M."

At 5:00 A.M. Lieutenant Kule called the sheriff at home. "We got Force Eight up here, heavy snow and zero visibility," he said.

"What's the long range?" asked the sheriff.

"Maybe it'll go twenty-four hours."

"How cold did it get last night?"

"With the wind an' all," Kule said in a casual way, "probably forty below in the Basin."

The sheriff sighed. "Those boys ain't gonna last long in that."

"We ain't gonna do much good in there today 'less some sonovabitch runs over 'em," Kule added.

But the old sheriff led them in. They roped their machines together to beat the ground blizzards. They wore full masks, and some of them helmets to keep out the cold. With considerable courage, Longren, Leonard, and Seiler got as far as the summer ranch midway between the main road and the mouth of North Fork, maybe twelve miles in. But it just kept blowing harder and there they were forced back. The next day it was the same. Their going out at all was tokenism, and they knew it.

Back on the road, that afternoon, Leonard told Sheriff Meyers, "Those boys aren't gonna make it. You know that, don't you? There's no one gonna stay alive out there too long 'less they were set for it, an' these boys weren't. Shit, they was drunk an' comin' from a party. I think the sonsofbitches are gone, Burt, an' that's the truth."

"You wanna quit, then?"

"I'm just tellin' you what I think."

"You're a good boy, Leonard," the sheriff said. "But I don't care that much what you think, an' I'd just as soon you keep it to yourself. You'd be surprised how bad a man can wanna live, Leonard."

"Maybe so," Leonard said. "But I'll be goddamned surprised if anything comes out of there that ain't in a bag."

That night when Sandy Brown called him, as she did every night, the sheriff was a good deal more optimistic than he had any reason to be. It was still blowing, and there was no sign of a break in the weather front.

"The main thing," he said to her, "is that they're stayin' with their vehicles. That's the main thing."

"But how do you know?" she said.

"Well," said the sheriff, "that's what I figure."

"But you don't know."

"That Coulter boy was brought up in the mountains, ma'am. He's no fool."

"I'm not so sure of that," she sighed.

She hung up and sat looking at the phone. She had thought Rick Coulter fun when she first came to town. She was attracted to him. They sat up one night, alone in a friend's house, and debated whether to sleep together. She had decided not to. She did so because she had misgivings about what was true or substantial behind the fun of Coulter. She was wondering again about that now. She had a feeling there wasn't much. If she was right, and she trusted her feelings, he could be a real danger to Mike or anybody else in the mountains, she thought. He could be a greater liability there than he was in town. Wherever he was, she realized, his mercurial temperament made him a liability. The most she could hope for was that this experience would push him into making a change. It might even make him a man.

She wasn't worried about Coo-Coo. He would do what he was told, and he was basically strong and a good kid. She wasn't worried about Vern Poulsen either. She was, she realized, assuming they hadn't killed each other. When Vern came around looking for Rick the night they disappeared, he'd been angry all right. He'd told her he was going to give Rick a whipping. She got up, filled with sudden anxiety. She was always avoiding this issue in her mind. She stood over the stove and poured herself some coffee.

Vern's got too much to lose to go crazy, she thought. He's too methodical. He had built up a family and a farm, carefully, consistently. He wouldn't blow it now. Not for Marlene, not for anyone.

Coulter was the danger. It was a waste for Mike to spend his time with him. Mike was right: they should get out of Cope. She wished she'd thought of it before. Mike had the qualities of a man. She'd begun to think no men existed in the world she lived in. She just met boys. All afraid to be gentle or quiet or tender until they were old. For some time she had had two older lovers because of this need. Men in their fifties. Mike had been saved from becoming like all the county boys because of what he saw as his problems. In fact, she thought, those problems had set him apart and made him special. Her own father, a heavy-equipment operator in Reno now, called it "case hardening." When he called a man "case hardened," it meant he was fixed some way or other for good. In that regard, Mike was still a virgin.

She sat and drew off her boots. She normally took them off by the door, but she had come in and run to the phone without thinking. Mike was the first thing she ever had in mind now.

"I'm definitely in love with you," she said aloud. She got up and went over to the mirror above the drainboard and studied herself. The darkness and softness of her face pleased her. How vain she really was. She looked into her own turquoise eyes and winked.

"You're in love," she told herself solemnly. "You know that, you fool?"

She thought she saw a blemish on the olive skin of her cheek. She pushed out with her tongue to tighten the skin and examine it closely. It wasn't. She then sat down by the fire she'd built in the stove. But it failed to warm or console her. Where was his voice? When would she hear him coming? She listened, trying to make it happen. Then she looked around the cabin for something of his, finally going to the bedroom door and switching on the light. His few clothes hung from a rod in the open closet, his Sunday boots below. She stared at them, all so empty. She turned off the light and came back to her chair by the stove, opening the firebox to see the orange flame. It wasn't economical or sensible—the wood would burn faster, the water for her shower not be as hot. But why in God's name should she shut off the color and life of the fire to make it last a little longer.

Coulter was the key. She came back to it again. He had brought all of them together, and yet he was set apart. Like Mike. But unlike Mike, Coulter fought all the time to get back in. Or at least to get revenge. Mike didn't seem to fight, she realized. He seemed to accept things that came down on him. He was a passive sort of guy—maybe too much so.

But then what had he had to fight about? He wasn't part of anything, as Coulter was. He had no town or family. He didn't seem to have any faith, even. But he had his life. She rose, felt the water tank, came back to sit before the fire again and pulled off her socks. She had to get some Desenex. Standing all day at the diner made her feet sweat and get sore. But when you were alone, she thought, it was easiest to be passive. That would change now that they were together. That was the most important thing about being with someone: you had someone to see yourself by.

Sergeant Goebbels announced that Rail Catlin, Coo-Coo's father, was on the phone. The sheriff spoke to him. "They weren't where they said they'd be, Rail. We checked to the turnaround at Bartlett, and they wasn't there."

"Whattya think?" Rail Catlin asked. There was always resignation in his voice. After he got sick and sold out to Poulsen, the price of land skyrocketed. Now he worked as a driver for Coors beer in Arco and rented a place. The guy was beat, the sheriff thought.

"I think that leaves us with about twelve hundred square miles," the sheriff said.

"It's not so good for my boy, then?"

"He'll be okay."

"I reckon."

"Stay in touch."

"If I gotta call *you*," Catlin explained, "I know it's for nothin'. But I can't stand around just waitin'. How long d'you give 'em?"

"Who knows?"

"Well, I wouldn't give 'em more than ten days, outside," Catlin said unemotionally. "An' they already had five."

"What am I gonna tell you, Rail?" the sheriff said, which was his way of agreeing. "Soon as it clears, I'm gonna put a plane up."

He booked the plane, but Thursday, the sixth day, the weather was worse than Wednesday. The men went out on the ground. They wanted to get as far as the east fork but it was useless. As Epke put it, staying on the trail with a snowmobile was like riding an icy log in a wind tunnel full of freezing chicken feathers.

There was a break in the front Thursday, but it came in the afternoon, and eight hours later another storm came through. The second was more severe than the first. It pinned the rescuers down Friday and Saturday and now they were all of them losing heart. They were Mountain Men. They had seen the paths of avalanches that snapped the largest firs at mid-girth. From five miles off they had watched the wind blow huge snow clouds from the ridges. They had found men frozen, curled like stillborn fetuses. The mountains were never still. They moved too slowly for a man to see and too fast for him to run from and always with more power than he thought possible.

In the car they hung on. They plugged every crack and door-jamb with newspaper rolled into thin strips. They cooked stew over a fire built in a hubcap inside the car, breaking wood into pencil-sized pieces, coughing and choking in the smoke, cooking the meat until it was only half-raw. The smoke from the fire stung their eyes and settled in their clothes, and the smell of it permeated their blankets. Hour after hour they lay side by side without talking, listening to the wind. They were always cold, always hungry. The days were gray, the nights pitch-black. They pissed into a jar and poured it clumsily out of the window and mercifully stayed constipated.

"Don't you ever have anythin' to say?" Coulter asked Poulsen after a prolonged silence.

They were eating half-raw venison. Poulsen regarded Coulter and chewed on, contemptuously.

Coulter looked pale and stark, and there were blue rings under his eyes. He turned to Arizo. "He's a weird sonovabitch, isn't he?"

"I don't know what there is to say myself," Arizo said.

Coulter gave a short laugh. "We could talk football," he said. "Or different places. I dunno. Anythin's all right with me." He shrugged and laughed nervously again. "Whatever you like."

"I thought maybe we should make a sign on the snow," Arizo said.

Chewing too hard to speak, Coulter nodded agreement.

"But I figured it'd get covered over with the ground blizzards every few hours."

They lapsed back into silence. After a while, Coulter said again, "Keep talkin', okay? Sometimes it makes me real nervous when we're all quiet like this."

Poulsen turned toward him, and his look was black and bitter. "I prefer to save my energy."

Without speaking, Coulter took his piece of venison and climbed into the front seat and sat eating there, his back to them. The hours passed slowly. Occasionally Coulter tried the radio, but the storm created incessant static. Once he began to pound the radio frantically until Arizo shouted at him to stop and then Coulter screamed angrily and accused them both of being useless and chickenshit. Once he pounded the sheet-metal wall of the Ford, bringing down a shower of thin ice that had formed from the condensation that dripped on them incessantly and shouted at unseen people outside to come and get them. Soon after, Arizo thought he heard him sobbing.

When Poulsen realized what was happening to Coulter, he began to speak, but only when it was absolutely necessary. He was, Arizo realized, moving in to help him out. Coulter was getting hard to talk to. If Poulsen had gone on the way he was, being bitter and crazy, it would have been all over. It was difficult enough to keep his own head straight, Arizo thought. He did his best not to think of Sandy because that only made it more difficult. He slept as much as possible, and when he was awake, he

listened. When he did start thinking of Sandy, he would deliberately switch to someone else, and he found himself thinking a lot
about Poulsen. Poulsen lay almost all the time with his back to
them, staring at a side panel of the Ford. Arizo found himself
feeling sorry for the man. Of them all, Poulsen had the most to
lose and had already lost the most. It was true what he said: that
he was washed up in Cope. Maybe he had set himself up for this,
but they were all of them set up. If you really cared for anything
or anyone, you were set up, Arizo thought. It was like him and the
dog. If he hadn't cared that much for Baby Zeus, what the hell, it
would just have been experience. Instead, here he was in this car
in the mountains with men he hardly knew and all broken up
over a woman and probably going to die. The thought jolted him.
But you got to face it, he said to himself.

Anyway, that was how it was with Poulsen, he thought. The
man had a family he was scared of losing, and a woman he was
scared of losing, and that set him up. Marlene definitely wouldn't
have been something Rick was so crazy about if Vern hadn't set
her off limits by being so afraid. He looked over at Poulsen's head.
Vern was just asking for it with Rick. Getting scared of something
is another way of asking for it.

Arizo felt dislike for Rick, and it worried him. This wasn't the
time or place to turn off to someone. And then he heard the wind
outside and remembered he was supposed to be listening to it. He
caught its varying pitch, trying to pick out a pattern for himself
within the sound. Doing this for hours was crazy, too, he thought.
But it was something to do.

In the long nights and twilight days of moaning wind and brittle cold, Poulsen, too, looked into his life as he had never done before, and at the bottom of it saw how he had trapped himself by
his own fear.

This was one reason for his silence. The slow anger of years, cul-
minating in this flare-up which had taken him so out of himself
that he would have killed them both, had left him drained so that
he saw for the first time over his own defenses and within himself.
The anger, the chase, the killing, and the storm had hardened

him, and now when he saw how he had trapped himself, it shattered him.

It was his lip, Poulsen realized. He had always been afraid that people would not accept him because of it. It seemed so huge a thing to him. It dominated him when he was a boy, filled him with years of fear that he would be unable to attract a woman, have a family, achieve what his father had achieved. It seemed insurmountable, his lip. It became outside him, an overwhelming and remorseless enemy. Sometimes he was afraid of it, as, he imagined, was everybody else. Certainly he tried too hard to make up for it, to balance it out, as if this would hide it. He had forced himself to ride the rodeo circuit. And this, he realized now, had only made his lip more obvious. He winced at the thought of it. Still, this effort had won him Marlene. But then he saw that even when he had won what he never thought could be his, it had made no difference. He had never fully enjoyed his wife and children because he had been so afraid of losing them. He knew that if she went, she would take them with her. Thinking of these things in the car, he desperately wanted to be back with them, to have a chance to show them he knew now what he had, to show them how different he could be, how open, how loving, how gentle a father, husband, man.

This was when he began to speak and to help Arizo with Coulter. For this was the time—more than any in his life—that he wanted to go on living.

In the town below, they waited, too. Some waited with their lives at a standstill. Some waited to go against the mountains, like paratroopers waiting to scramble, occupied not with the men they were going to rescue, but with the logistics and stratagems of battle. These would-be rescuers constantly watched the weather maps, called the airport in Twin Falls, called each other, checked the sky, prepared their equipment and stood by for the storm to let up. Weather changes very quickly in the mountains. A good man anticipates it, and a lucky man anticipates it correctly.

There was little communication between the women at this stage. Sue-Ellen Coulter was unconcerned, and that was it. She said she never could see the sense of worrying. She was interviewed in the Twin Falls *Times-News* saying just this. Her nonchalance was talked about as much as Marlene's disgrace.

There was a great deal of talk. In fact, there was little else. Some found themselves suddenly caught up in the play through no reason but happenstance. Eleanor Holmes, for instance, who had directed Poulsen after the two hunters and was able to tie them together unequivocally and to say that Coo-Coo was also in Poulsen's truck as he left town, had had only a walk-on part in town until this. Now she was a major figure, and she was loving it.

On Friday night, when she walked to the hardware store with her packages in the string shopping bag, she looked about her in the empty street, re-enacting the scene in her mind's eye. There was snow on the pavement now, though, and that made it difficult to imagine. Also, the snow made her feet cold.

She turned down the driveway beside Meyers' hardware store and when she reached the back door stood, shivering and annoyed because she had been foolish and because her lover had the place locked and would not let her use her key except on Sunday night. Fred Meyers came to the door, opened it, and took the packages from her.

"Can I come in?"

He shook his head briefly. It was too dark to see his face. "Not tonight. I'm afraid they're watching you. There's been a lot of talk about your being here this time of night, you know."

"This time of night!" she repeated, disgusted.

"Next week, when it's calmed down," he said. "Good night."

She walked slowly back up the driveway to Main once more, carrying her empty string bag, feeling dejected. This time she crossed the street without hesitation and went into the bar.

In the hardware store across the snow-filled street, Fred Meyers, the sheriff's younger brother, locked the door behind Eleanor and went slowly up the narrow flight of stairs that led to the apartment above his shop, clasping a brown paper bag beneath each arm. As he came up the stairs the bulb hanging on a bare wire above the well threw a small bright circle of light on his bald pate.

At the top of the stairs the bedroom door was immediately to his right, the living room door, open, on his left and the kitchen, which was small and had no door, lay three steps ahead. He went into the kitchen softly whistling "The Streets of Laredo," and set the bags down carefully on the counter beneath a wall cupboard. He opened the cupboard doors and, reaching up to a high shelf on tip-toe, began taking down baby bottles, two and three at a time. He checked the shelves to be sure there were no more and then lined the bottles up. There were fourteen of them, in different colors, each with a teat. Now he unscrewed the teats, methodically, and, with the nimbleness and exactitude for which he was known as a storekeeper, put each opposite its bottle. Then he took from the two paper bags three fifths of Jim Beam and breaking the seals carefully, decanted each fifth in turn into the waiting baby bottles, filling them to the brim and then screwing the teats back in place.

He placed the bottles on a large green, tin tray decorated with a picture of a wall-eyed pike, put the three empty fifths in the garbage under the sink and carefully closed the counter doors.

Then he went next door into the bedroom and reappeared minutes later dressed in blue flannel pajamas decorated with red airplanes and fire engines. He lifted the tray and, careful to turn out the kitchen light and shut the bedroom door with one foot, went back into the bedroom.

There was a small bedroom, from which came the only light, off what would be called the master bedroom. He carried the tray in again, carefully closed the door. It had the feeling of a sanctuary, the small bedroom. The roof cut off one wall and there was a single window at the end. It was carpeted in blue and the walls were blue and the only furniture was a high-sided child's cot against the high wall, above which was a shelf. It was an old cot, wooden, with a warm varnish under which, on the headboards, were decals of nursery rhyme figures and two or three bluebirds. Above the cot hung a ceiling light with an orange bulb and shade, controlled by a pullstring, and on the floor glowed an electric heater.

Fred Meyers rested the tray on the cot side while he arranged the baby bottles in an orderly row on the shelf above. Then he slid the tray beneath it, let down the side by releasing the spring handles at either end, climbed in, and pulled up the side again. He had to curl up in a fetal position to lie. He arranged the blanket over him, tucking it beneath his upturned ear, then reached up for a bottle. When he had arranged it on the pillow so that it was at the proper angle, he pulled the string that turned out the light and the room was filled by the glow from the electric heater and now and then the gentle sound of sucking.

On Saturday morning, Tissa Poulsen called her mother from Boise, where she was studying oral hygiene, to say she was coming home to stay until her father was rescued. Marlene said she would meet her bus if she could get out of the driveway, and that if she couldn't, Tissa should take a taxi.

"I had the drive cleared yesterday afternoon when the snowfall stopped," Marlene said. "But it's been snowing again since last night, and if I can't get a-hold of Chuck Gould, I don't think I'll be able to get out by this afternoon."

She did get hold of Gould, and at 2:30 P.M., with chains on the wagon and the driveway cleared, she went to pick up Tissa at the Greyhound stop. She was urgently in need of her older daughter's company. She felt guilty and desperate in her confusion. Even Gould couldn't look at her straight. Men were always thicker with men when you got right down to it, she thought.

She backed carefully down the driveway. It was the first time she had left the house since Vern had gone. That was what she struggled with. He had gone and he hadn't come back. It had started routinely enough at the party. They'd had a row. All perfectly normal. He had got drunk and rejected her in public. A little thing. Probably nobody much noticed, she thought. But Coulter had been there, so she had taken revenge.

She peered through the driving snow, and when she reached the main road, turned right.

"Well, it was a pretty unreasonable thing to do." That's what Gould had said. Unreasonable? What was unreasonable when there was no reason anyway? Vern had been unreasonable all along. For goddamn *years* he was so jealous it made her want to scream. She stretched her face a moment to relax it. She often did this; otherwise she feared she would get worry lines. It said so in *Woman's Day* or *Redbook* or somewhere. His being so unreasonably jealous was what had made her do it. When you were left alone with the birthday cake, you had to stick your finger in the icing and have a taste, right? In the end she had *had* to do the thing he feared most. *That* was reasonable.

Still, she regretted it. Going into the nursery with Rick Coulter and locking the door. In the dark, hearing the party through the wall so clearly. All those people saying anything while they wondered how the other would be. And the two of them actually doing it on the other side of the wall . . . what everyone else was thinking about. They giggled so much at first they almost gave up. They could hear bits of conversation: "Oh, I sure think so . . ." "I'm so pleased . . ." "That's right!" "No, no . . ." "Uhuh . . ." "It's the *best* . . ." "She is, isn't she?" Exclamations.

Then the fire caught, and they became too intent and lost themselves. She shifted herself behind the wheel as she thought of it. Frowning now, she followed in the tire tracks through the snow in her lane. The windshield wipers were clacking frantically. When the temporary plywood wall began to fall, she had not understood what was happening in that first moment when she perhaps could have done something. And of course Rick was out of it. God knows, nothing was going to stop Rick. You could have run a train over him right then, and he wouldn't have noticed a thing. As the partition fell, she was trying to get him off her. It was eerie, like falling in your sleep. The party hubbub vanished as they slowly toppled. It was like a dream sequence in a movie. On the way down, she had seen them all clearly just for one instant; half the people she knew in the world. She heard Vern's bellow of rage. Rick, jarred loose from her, had picked himself up and run out, tugging at his pants, leaving her to face the laughter, the gasps, and Vern.

She hadn't seen Vern after that. He had vanished. The things you couldn't prepare for that changed your life always frightened her. It wasn't necessarily what *happened;* it was that your life could be changed like that. In a moment. As if it wasn't yours at all.

With a roar and splash of snow, the bus from Boise overtook her going at twice her speed. When she had recovered, she hurried after it, but gradually it disappeared into the falling snow, and she sank back into herself again.

She was angry and she regretted it. She wished to hell she'd never seen Coulter. But some part of her wanted him again, even now, and she had to battle with that, too. The other strange thing was that Vern was up there somewhere in those mountains, actually doing something this instant.

Thank God, Tissa was coming. Marlene got along with her better than she did with Vickissa, their younger daughter. And Tissa got along with her better than she did with Vern. She'd been home all week with Vickissa and found it difficult to talk to her. There were a lot of things she desperately needed to talk about, but Vickissa was too young. Not only that, but Vickissa adored her father and blamed her, Marlene knew, for what had happened. Mostly it wasn't any good trying to tell your children the reasons for the things you'd done. They had their own ideas and when you spoke to them, they were just listening for echoes of themselves, like everybody else.

She saw the big red taillights of the bus through the snow. It was pulled over a few yards before the Two Ball Inn, four or five people standing beside it watching the driver bending into the luggage bay to pull out their bags. She saw Tissa, a tall girl in an orange coat and calf-length black boots, her collar turned up.

Marlene pulled the station wagon over to the side and stopped. She kept the engine running and the wipers on. Tissa saw her and waved. She picked up her case as the driver put it down and came running picking her boots high through the snow. Her mother waved at her to walk. She was so pretty, Tissa, with an almond-oval face and dark eyes full of unusual concern. Marlene leaned across and opened the door and the girl pushed her suitcase into the back and plunged into the front seat beside her mother. They held each other in a long silent embrace. Then, still hugging,

Marlene began to cry, sobbing into her daughter's dark hair, "God, Tissa, I did a dreadful thing."

On Sunday, December 8, the weather let up again, and the search parties got in a good day. They checked the North Fork of the Big Lost almost into Blaine County, and they went up Summit Creek as far as a vehicle could go and down the East Fork of the Big Lost as far as the Johnson Ranch.

When they met in the sheriff's office that night to debrief, they were a subdued lot.

Red Lewis, twirling the hairs of his beard between thumb and forefinger, said what the others were thinking: "They didn't go where they said. Unless we're plain lucky, we're never gonna find them 'fore they freeze."

Ed Epke looked up and spat out a fingernail. "If they're waitin' for us to come get 'em, they could hold out some more."

"They're still alive," Dan Coulter said quickly. "They all of them know enough to keep alive this long, easy."

"It's been a week," Lewis said.

"I wouldn't wanna have been up there this week," Longren said and hunched his shoulders, shivering.

"Not this week, not any week in winter," Bill Rose agreed.

"Whatta we waitin' for?" Dan Coulter asked.

"Burt," Joey Leonard said. "What else?"

"You think they got into it up there, Lewis?" Spangler asked.

Lewis shrugged. "How do I know? Someone did that to my old lady, I sure as hell would."

"What a fuckin' mess," Epke said.

"What about the Injun?" Leonard asked.

"Whatta you mean?" Lewis looked at him.

Epke took his pipe out of his mouth. "He's no fuckin' Injun," he said. "He's a half-caste. He was just hangin' onto Coulter for the ride."

"He's more than that." Dan Coulter stood up. He looked tired and gray. He turned on Epke. "You don't know what you're talkin' about, Ed. You're always shootin' your goddamned mouth

off without knowin' what you're sayin'. You been doing that ever
since you was a kid."

"Hey, hey, hey."

"Take it easy, you two."

"He's right though, Epke," Rose said, getting off the desk and
stretching his short, powerful body. "You do shoot your mouth
off."

"I know what I see," Epke said.

"Where would you have gone if you was them, Red?" Leonard
asked, turning his head to look at Lewis with his good eye.

"I wouldn't have gone anyplace," Lewis said. "If I'd been Rick,
I'd've stayed an' took a beatin' right here. Those sonsabitches
Vern and Coo-Coo were crazy mad, I tell you."

"That's right," Rose said with authority. "They were fightin'
over a woman, so they mighta done any goddamned thing."

"That boy of yours stuck everythin' in town," Lewis said to
Dan Coulter. "He had it comin'."

"Jealous?" Leonard looked at Lewis and punched his arm and
laughed.

Lewis ignored him. Lewis didn't like to be kidded. He could get
very angry.

"Who knows where Rick's been." Spangler sighed.

"Well, ol' Vern didn't, that's for sure." Epke sat forward and
shifted his pipe as he spoke. "Like they say, Vern was the last to
know."

"I couldn't believe he didn't know," Lewis said.

"He knew," said Leonard. "He just couldn't admit it to himself
is all."

"What a fuckin' mess," Epke groaned again.

"Yeah," said Lewis. "Ain't it, though? And here we are bustin'
ass on account of it."

"I'm so goddamned sore I can't hardly walk," Epke grumbled.

"I tell you, Bill," Leonard called to Spangler. "If you was a
halfway decent carpenter that nursery wall wouldn't have busted,
and we'd all be home gettin' some right now."

The rest looked at Spangler and laughed. Spangler was a tall, thin man with an elongated face and nose. He was slumped in a chair. He waved his hand. "You're full of it, Leonard," he said. "An' you couldn't find your ass in the dark with both hands. There's nothin' wrong with my carpentry."

"Not if you like party tricks," Leonard said, and they all laughed again. Even Dan Coulter.

"What they doin' in there?" Dan Coulter nodded towards the sheriff's private office where the sheriff and Sergeant Goebbels were conferring.

"Talkin'," Leonard said.

"Well, don't it concern us?" Jeff Seiler inquired. He was eighteen, Josie and Ned's kid, the youngest man on the Mountain Rescue squad.

"If the sheriff wants it to concern you," Epke answered, sucking on his pipe, "it'll concern you."

As if on cue, the door opened, and Sergeant Goebbels, serious as a cardinal preceding a pontiff, preceded Sheriff Meyers into the room.

"I'll tell you what we decided," the sheriff said quietly so that they strained to listen. "But first I want to thank you all for the fine job you done so far." He looked around and smiled faintly. His men were clearly pleased to be congratulated. "Now, if there's some of you got to get things took care of tomorrow, let me know an' I'll get some B-Team men in. But I need to know tonight. Otherwise," he said, "tomorrow morning we start goin' in the other end of the Basin. Up the Burma road as far as Muldoon Canyon. That clear?" He looked around.

"Good," he said. "We'll meet up in Mackay at eight o'clock."

"That's thirty miles from where they said," Epke had been figuring. "They won't be that far off."

"I said, 'Is that clear?' " Sheriff Meyers repeated.

Lewis said, "But I tell you one thing, Burt, we gotta find these boys real quick, because I used up my sick leave, an' tomorrow I'm startin' in on my vacation."

The sheriff looked at him thinly. "What's a vacation, Lewis?" he asked.

On December 12, a Wednesday, Arizo woke from one of the few dreams he could remember: He was guiding a group of crippled children across a desert of sand, scoured by hostile nomads. The sands were red and purple, fine and warm, and a soft wind drifted over them. The children moved in a column, and he ran up and down beside them with effortless, bounding strides. He felt free and insuperable, as though he could fly. The children were deformed and grotesque, but they turned their faces to him and kissed him, and for his part he loved them all. But then he was somehow parted from them. Still running in this easy, floating way, he came to immensely steep dunes and stood at the top, afraid. When he started down, he found the dunes had a loose velvet skin that slipped into folds and made it easy to descend. At the foot was a band of nomads sitting around a fire with rifles. He approached them secretly, thinking he would have to fight, but they laughed and welcomed him and made a space for him to join them and he sat with them and shared their food.

He opened his eyes feeling relaxed and found himself staring at a skin of ice on the steel wall of the car, inches from his face. He felt the blanket scratch at the lengthening stubble on his face, the wind gusting against the car and—once more—the cold. He shifted his legs slightly. They were stiff and his feet ached with cold. He lay still and closed his eyes, looking for sleep again. Coulter was at his back. Coulter always slept in the middle now; when he was on the outside, he became fretful and restless and prevented the other two from sleeping. It wasn't so bad. Poulsen had never cared for sleeping in the center anyway.

Arizo listened for Coulter's breathing to see if he was asleep. There was only the wind. But then Coulter called his name softly. "Mike," he whispered. "Are you awake?"

Arizo didn't answer. Coulter had become utterly pessimistic. It was very difficult to deal with him.

"Mike, are you awake?"

"We all are now," Poulsen said testily.

"Uhuh," Mike said.

"They're never gonna find us in this."

"In what?" Arizo sat up. Coulter was lying on his back staring up at him. Arizo scratched vigorously. The dry cold made his skin peel and itch madly.

"In this."

"Did you go outside already?"

"No."

"Then how'd you know?"

"Listen to the wind."

"I *have* been."

"I thought you were asleep."

"No."

"I didn't know Vern was awake either."

"All night, I think," Poulsen said. He lay with his face to the other wall. "The wind ith gettin' better now. It wath real bad in the night."

Arizo crawled into the front. Coulter sat up and watched him, but Poulsen lay still. When Arizo wound down the window, wisps of snow drifted in. He peered out, squinting against the glare. The few hairs on his brown face sprouted unevenly. His black eyes narrowed.

"Can't see much," he said. "There's too much driftin' snow on the ground." He pushed the door open and climbed onto the roof of the car. Ice cracked and fell in a thin shard from the ceiling. Coulter followed him out. Like a dog, Poulsen thought. On the roof they were just above the ever-rising snow, and visibility was good. There were clouds, but these were high and thin.

"They'll put a plane up today," Arizo said.

"I don't think so. Too much wind."

Arizo was annoyed. "Get the rifles. An' bring the blankets."

"Here." It was Poulsen's voice. They turned and looked down. Poulsen was holding a rifle on them. It gave both men a shock. Poulsen stared at them a moment, enjoying his advantage, then smiled crookedly and handed the rifle up, butt first.

They waited on the roof of the car until it was past noon.

The wind died, and, stripped to the waist, they lounged in the sun, waiting. They were in good spirits, all three of them for the first time together. The shadow of the mountain retreated until the sun was shining on its face. The light was brilliant and clear. The air smelled of pine.

They were reluctant to leave the rooftop in case someone or something should appear. But shortly after noon hunger prevailed, and Arizo told Poulsen to come with him to the creek to fetch wood. Coulter would stay and watch. This seemed to Arizo the best division, even if it meant leaving Coulter alone. They left the rifles with him.

As he stepped into the snow in the lee of the Ford, beyond the point where they had packed it down with their walking and cleaning of the deer, Arizo sank to his thighs and yelled a warning. Poulsen followed him closely, arms outstretched for balance. Powder crystals floated up around them and stuck to the hair on their faces and they called to one another as they went down the slope towards the creek. They carried Arizo's laundry bag with them. In the thin air and deep snow, it took them half an hour to reach the creek and by then they were exhausted and had to rest for some time. They gathered branches from two dead willows and a jack pine. It was difficult and dangerous to do, for they had no real idea of the course of the stream and as Coulter warned, ice bridges will form among trees, sometimes over them entirely, like a canopy, become covered and hidden with snow, and then collapse under the weight of a man.

There was also the danger that in the places along the bank where the snow was thinner, it might conceal a spring that had not frozen. Neither man had snow boots on. Poulsen wore the fancy Lama boots he had worn for the party and Arizo wore lumping boots, ankle-length, with crepe soles. A wet foot now would be disaster.

They started back on the track they had already made. As they left the trees, Arizo stopped. "Look," he said, pointing towards the Ford. In the distance they saw how small was the figure of Coulter sitting on the roof of the car. They looked up the slope into the canyon mouth two miles or so to their right and down the creek bed two or three miles to where it turned behind the shoulder of the hill. There was no movement, no sound.

"It's hard to believe there's anyone else in the world right now,"

Arizo said. "Feels like we're all that's left, doesn't it?" Arms filled
with wood, he turned to look up at the mountain, twisting his
head. The afternoon sun glazed the wall above the rockpile.

Arizo felt his insignificance and nodded slightly to the mountain. It was almost a bow. It had seemed they were so large and
obvious to any rescuer, but in this instant he saw how truly small
they were. The mountain rose like the thick neck of a giant, and
they were like flies' eggs in the hollow of its shoulder.

"Let'th go," he heard Poulsen say.

Arizo went on up the slope through the deep powder, clasping
his pitifully few sticks of wood, slipping and panting hard. When
he had felt large, he had been separate from the mountain, as he,
a man, felt separate from everything. Being apart, he could even
feel superior to the mountains, to anything or anyone. But struggling beneath it now he saw that he was not separate; the mountain was his father. They were of the same whole. He felt better
when he understood this. He felt kinship where there had been
enmity. He turned to speak to Poulsen, saw the strain on the
man's face as he stumbled in the snow in his fancy boots, and felt
compassion.

They cooked a meal on the roof. The sun slanted lower towards
the canyon mouth, the breeze grew cold. Poulsen and Coulter
spread a blanket across their backs and sat side by side to block
the wind. They stood the hubcap on four small chocks of wood
that Arizo used to prop up the passenger seat. Poulsen held the
steaks over the fire on the end of Arizo's knife while Arizo fed it
slivers of wood. They talked of whether someone might still come.
They were charged with expectation. After the meal the breeze
shifted. Arizo and Poulsen climbed back into the Ford, but
Coulter stayed where he was, sitting, clasping his knees, staring
out, straining his ears, waiting until it was quite dark.

In the morning he woke the other two, throwing off the blankets and crawling rapidly to the front towards the light that came
through the frosted windshield. "Look," he called. "It's clear. It's
beautiful. They'll come today. See?" He was in the driver's seat
now, pushing open the door against the snow that had drifted
against it in the night. "See?" he said. "Like I said."

Arizo watched him. He was like a kid.

They all climbed stiffly onto the roof once more, red-eyed and rumpled. A fresh fall in the night had covered the tracks to the creek and all lay wind-smoothed and even in the shadow of the mountain. There was no life, not even crows. The sun stood off behind the peak, firing its silhouette in gold. They brought up blankets from the car and waited.

Later the wind came up, increasingly fresh and cold, and the night's soft powder blew up around the car. They decided that only one need stay out. Arizo remained, and it was he then, who first heard the drone of two-strokes, growing, fading, a faint tinny sound. Snowmobiles! He pounded on the roof with his fist. "They're comin'!" he yelled. "They're comin'!"

The others spilled out of the car, clutching their rifles and Coulter a box of shells. They stood together on the roof looking down the canyon. The wind had come around and blew steadily into their faces, kicking up the lacy flakes around their legs. They stared down the creek bed towards the elbow and listened.

The small sound of the two-strokes came and went.

"They're around the turn," Arizo said. "But they're coming this way."

Coulter shrieked and waved his rifle above his head, clutching it in two hands, and fired twice into the air.

"Hey!" he yelled. "We're here. *We're here!*"

Arizo put an arm on Coulter's shoulder and they listened again. The engine sound was more even. Coulter fired again and again. He turned to the other two. "shoot!" he shouted. "Whatta you waitin' for? *Shoot!*"

Two machines crawled around the point, far below. They were very small and black and they inched over the snow, cautiously. They came out perhaps a hundred fifty yards from behind the shoulder and then stopped and the riders dismounted and stood side by side staring up the valley towards them.

All three men began firing. It was a celebration more than a signal. "Oh-o-o. I fuckin' don't believe it," Coulter yelled. "They came at last. The sonsabitches are here. I can't fuckin' believe it." He turned and hugged Arizo, lifted him off his feet and jiggled up

and down on the roof of the car until the metal buckled loudly
and the two began to fall. Poulsen made a grab for them as they
went, but it was too late. Arizo shouted out, half-laughing, "Hey,
you fuckin' turkey!" as they went over the side into the snow that
was thick and soft on the uphill side. They crawled back onto the
roof, spitting out the snow and still laughing, while Poulsen kept
firing. As they came up onto the roof, Poulsen said, "They didn't
thee uth yet."

"It's this fuckin' ground blizzard," Arizo said.

"An' we're downwind," Poulsen added, firing again.

"Bullshit!" Coulter shouted. "They gotta hear us." He was
standing up again, waving both arms and screaming, "We're up
here! We're here!"

"Let's fire all the rifles at once," Arizo said. They did, but the
two figures below showed no response.

"Tie something on the end of a rifle and wave it," Poulsen
suggested. "That way we'll get above the thnow." They did that,
too, using Arizo's shirt. But there was no sign of recognition from
the small black figures, who still were stationary, scanning.

"Here. Get on my shoulders and wave the shirt and shoot the
rifle," Arizo told Poulsen. Poulsen scrambled onto his shoulders.
They all three felt the time getting short. Coulter kept firing and
yelling. "Hey, you blind fuckers. We're right here. Hey! Hey-y-y!"

Then the figures began moving again. One of them walked
down into the creek bed for a minute as if examining something.

"They're lookin' to see if they can cross," Arizo said excitedly.
"If they can get across, they'll come up our side." The snow was
not drifting as badly where the two searchers were, so it was easy
to watch them as one man came up out of the depression formed
by the creek bed. The wind blew hard into the faces of the men
on the car, and Arizo felt its bitter cold on his bare chest. Now
the searchers turned again and looked up towards the canyon
mouth. Coulter emptied a whole clip in rapid succession, but the
wind shipped the sound away. The searchers began walking towards their machines. They climbed on, and suddenly the snowmobiles were moving again, creeping over the white expanse

slowly, inexorably towards the shoulder of the hill. They disappeared, and the sound of their engines began to die.

The men on the roof were all yelling now, and Coulter was growing hysterical. As the machines disappeared behind the shoulder, he stood arched like a rooster, face to the sky, uttering one final, despairing howl that broke midway. He slumped to his knees and hammered the metal of the roof with his fists. The two others stood staring after the snowmobiles. Arizo fired a few more desultory rounds.

When the sound of the engines had gone completely, they all sat on the roof, Arizo pulling on his shirt and parka over his freezing skin, the wind gusting the snow about them. Coulter stared at his boots without seeing or moving.

"They'll be back," Poulsen said finally.

"Maybe they went back down the creek to where they could cross," Arizo said without conviction.

"We better wait here," Poulsen decided.

"What else?" Coulter mumbled.

"On the roof, I mean."

"They ain't comin' back. I don't give a shit how long we wait. They ain't comin' back," Coulter said.

Arizo put a hand into the pocket of his coat and came out with a pack of Camels. "I got the last cigarette here," he said. "Maybe we should do it now." They sat in silence and smoked, suffering the wind. Occasionally, as the cigarette went around, Arizo lifted his head and listened.

Eventually he said, "We're downwind, on a white car, hidden in a ground blizzard."

"And no fire," Poulsen said. "We maybe could have uthed a fire."

No one answered him. A few minutes more and Arizo, shivering, said, "We're gettin' cold for nothin'. Let's go in."

It was as they were getting into the car that they heard the sound of another engine, this time crisp and flat and growing fast, filling the air.

"A plane!" Poulsen shouted. "They're comin' back! They saw uth!"

The plane broke over the ridge above them no more than 100 feet off the ground. It was a small high-wing Cessna, red and white, and as it appeared it banked sharply to its left, so that in the snowfield the men getting into the Ford were presented with its belly. It flew up over the treeline towards the canyon mouth.

"They're lookin' by the treeth!" Poulsen shrieked.

"They're gonna miss us," Arizo yelled frantically.

Coulter was firing into the air again, and so was Arizo, and they were all of them waving. The plane banked on its wingtip as it neared the head of the canyon and came down the creek towards them. For a moment it was level, and they saw the pilot and copilot's faces behind the windshield. Then it abruptly dropped its left wing so that the pilot could scan the creek bed, and the men on the car were again watching its belly.

"Motherfucker!" Coulter screamed with rage. "We're *here*. We're *here!*" In that moment, as the plane was opposite them and not more than 150 yards away, Coulter came up with his rifle, led the plane by 20 yards and fired three rounds. It made no difference. Coulter raged at it again as it zoomed away from them. He took his rifle by the muzzle and flung it, and they watched it cartwheel slowly in the air and kick up snow 30 feet away. The plane followed the creek to the bend, banked again, and vanished behind the mountain's shoulder. The sound of its engine faded rapidly.

The other two became aware of Coulter standing with his arms dangling at his sides, tears running down over his face, staring into the empty sky, pleading in a hoarse, broken voice. "Come back. Come back. Please don't leave us here. For God's sake, don't leave us."

Arizo moved beside him and put an arm about him and drew him close. "It's okay, Rick. They'll come back. And if they don't, we'll get outta here without them."

The wind blew harder against them, as if reasserting its claim. Poulsen suddenly laughed a short bitter laugh. "Now we can get down to it," he said. "Now it'th the real thing. Huh?" He grinned mirthlessly at them. "That enough for you two?"

"There's three of us. We can't just leave each other. We gotta stay together. Let's take a vote. Okay?"

"I don't wanna fuckin' vote," Arizo yelled. "I'm freezin'. I wanna go."

"We all do, Mike," Poulsen said strongly.

The wind screamed beyond the gully's mouth a few feet away. It seemed insane to Arizo to go anywhere at that moment. He felt them waiting, reproachful.

"So okay," he said when the wind noise died. "We'll vote."

"Our food an' everythin's at the car," Coulter reminded them. "I'm for the car."

"I'm for the car, too," Poulsen said, but as he said it, the wind rose again and Arizo yelled, "What?"

Poulsen waited for quiet and reconsidered.

"We could try an' dig in here," Arizo's voice came to him, pleading. "We could give it a shot anyway. We did come three hours' distance. We don't want to waste that."

The wind shrieked again.

"We'd be outta the wind in the car," Coulter hollered. "An' supposin' it blows like this for a week like it did before? We'll be fucked out here."

"Yeah, but maybe we'll find a cabin or somethin' farther down in the Basin," Arizo said.

"There's nothin' down there. I know this place," Coulter called out, his voice cracking.

Arizo was stamping his feet again. It set Coulter off. "We know where the car is. If it clears, we can go out again tomorrow." He tried to sound calm and reasonable.

There was silence from Poulsen. They waited for Arizo.

"Let's go back," Poulsen said.

"You lead," Arizo said shortly.

Once they cleared the head of the gully, the full force of the wind coming down the canyon struck them. It was like crossing the bar. Poulsen and Coulter had wrapped the blankets around face and head. Arizo, at the rear, just kept his face down. Coulter had inserted himself in the middle spot as they headed along the field that sloped upward to the car.

"Keep movin' your fathe," Poulsen shouted back to them. As they headed into the wind, visibility was cut to zero. Thick driven snow flew well above their heads. Poulsen reeled in the first full blast. Turning away, Coulter tried to catch him, and was turned, too. They staggered like blind men, almost losing one another, fighting for balance.

Arizo took the lead then. He no longer thought logically about it. He went as though there were no alternative to what they were doing. He shouted to the others and grabbed them and pushed them into line behind him. Again Coulter insisted on being in the middle. They walked in Arizo's footsteps, clutching. Sometimes they stopped briefly and huddled, like exhausted football players, arms about each other's shoulders, faces inward to rest from the stinging wind. They did not speak. They moved as if in a trance, automatically, not thinking or speaking. Arizo led them directly to the car. It was an extraordinary thing, uncanny. They almost collided with it before they saw its dark top against the slightly less dark snowfield.

They climbed in with no excitement, no sense of victory, grunting and pushing in their hurry to get out of the wind. They had just come to a place without wind. A place that stank of smoke and piss, a metal box lined with ice and a sweaty mattress. In the gully, Coulter and Poulsen had seen it as a warm, comfortable place. Now they said nothing. They lay on their backs, effigy on a tomb, feeling lucky to have the breath still in them and the wind without.

Then Arizo was sitting up, they realized, fumbling with his boots. In a moment he asked Coulter to strike a match. Poulsen sat up, too. "What'th the matter?"

"Hold it here." Arizo guided Coulter's hand, their two faces intently staring in the weak light, beards and eyebrows glistening wet. "I can't get these boots off."

The boots were frozen to the socks. Coulter struck another match.

"Jesus, that's weird!" he said, peering. "How's it feel?"

"It doesn't."

"We should get them off quick."

"Maybe if you wrapped them in the blanket, they'd thaw," Poulsen offered.

"Shit!" Coulter said and threw down the match as it burned his fingers.

Arizo wrapped one boot in a blanket and with his knife he cut the other boot off, removing the lace, then slipping the tip of the blade between leather and wool. It was a laborious business. Poulsen burned tapers of tightly rolled newspapers for light. Their eyes watered in the smoke. By the time Arizo was done, the sock itself had thawed out enough to come off. He peeled it off slowly. The flesh was gray. He touched it with a forefinger and whistled softly.

"What is it?" Coulter asked anxiously.

Arizo tapped the flesh at the instep. It rang dully, like china. Poulsen held the taper closer.

"Holy shit!" Coulter said in awe.

"It's froze," Arizo said.

"What can we do?" Poulsen asked quietly.

Arizo had been leaning forward over the foot. Now he sat up and blew out his breath at length. "Jesus," he said. "I dunno. You guys live in the mountains, whatta you do? I never had this before."

"I was only frostbit on the end of my nose once," Coulter said. "It hurt like hell when it thawed out."

Arizo looked at him. "Yeah?"

Coulter backed up. "I could handle it," he said. "My Dad said they used to use paraffin wax an' get a piece of wood."

Arizo didn't understand. Poulsen turned the taper vertically. "What's the wood for?" Arizo asked as he began unwrapping his other boot.

"I dunno. I guess maybe it's to bite on," Coulter said.

There was an awkward pause.

"I heard you thould pack it in thnow," Poulsen said. "I remember now."

Coulter shook his head. "That's what they used to say, but it's no good. You gotta get it to thaw out. That's the thing."

Poulsen lit another taper.

When Arizo got the second boot and sock off, the other foot was just as bad. The others looked at him not knowing what to say. Arizo knew it was very bad, and he was close to tears. He bit his lip and lay back down. "Omigod!" he said hopelessly.

Tears welled in his eyes. He stared at the ceiling, blinking, not seeing the other two looking down at him. Coulter pulled the blanket up over his chest. Arizo nodded his thanks. The wind had quieted.

"It'll be okay, Mike," Poulsen said softly. "They'll be better in the mornin', an' we'll get outta here even if we got to carry you."

Arizo was still chewing his lower lip. "I know, Vern," he said. "I'm sorry to get so bummed out."

Coulter started to get under the blankets.

"I shouldn't have held them over the fire, I guess," Arizo said. " 'Cept they were so fuckin' cold."

The taper was burning very low, and Poulsen's eyes began to water from the smoke.

"Okay?" he asked, to console himself, as much as Arizo.

Arizo nodded.

Poulsen pinched out the taper and the darkness fell on them.

It was like waiting for a bomb to go off, lying in the dark listening to the wind, waiting for Arizo's feet to thaw: for the distending ice crystals that had formed within each tissue cell to melt and permit sensation to find and excruciatingly report the damage. Poulsen sat with his back to the doors and insisted that Arizo warm his frozen feet against his bare belly. But once the feet began to thaw, Arizo smashed his fist against the steel walls of the car and bit his other hand and jerked them away. In the darkness Poulsen wriggled over to lie beside him and Coulter found Arizo's mouth and stuffed a piece of firewood between his teeth. "Bite on it," he said, "else you'll bite your tongue off."

It lasted for some hours. Arizo pounded the wall and cried out around the short stick between his teeth. The other two urged him fiercely and continuously to hang on and Arizo grunted and cursed the pain. Poulsen climbed on the far side of him, Coulter held one hand and forearm, and when the pain was worst, they wrestled with him, afraid he would otherwise lash out and damage himself or them in the darkness.

Towards dawn Arizo abruptly told them he had to go outside to piss. They argued with him, but he insisted and refused their help. "I can make it," he said. "I ain't no fuckin' cripple."

He crawled to the front seats. They felt the freezing draft as he opened the window. Outside the wind had died, and all was strangely hushed.

"What the fuck you doin', man?" Coulter asked.

When there was no answer, Coulter lit a match. As it flared they saw Arizo lying across the front seats, his feet thrust out the window, his face oily with sweat and the wood still between his teeth.

"You crazy?" Coulter said, incredulous.

Arizo took the wood out of his mouth. "I'm freezin' them again," he said slowly. "What else is there to do?"

In the morning Coulter crumpled up the note taped to the steering wheel and left with Poulsen to fetch wood from the creek. When they had gone, Arizo crawled out of the car and tried to stand. The instant he let go of the car door, he began to fall. It was like trying to stand on two bowling balls. He could feel nothing below his ankles. He sat on the edge of the driver's seat, bare feet buried in the snow. The mountain seemed uncaring, unchanged and remote in the gray overcast. He stared at it and squinted. "You motherfucker!" he said under his breath. Sandy came to mind and he wept. She didn't know this had happened, and he couldn't tell her. He crawled into the back and lay down and felt tremendous bitterness as he listened to his companions shouting to each other by the creek.

Having no way to talk to her was the worst thing. It was like being dead.

He thought of Maxwell. There were a lot of things he wanted to talk to Maxwell about. Above all, he wanted to show him that the boy had heard and remembered what he had been told, that the time he gave had been worth it.

He heard them again. The sound carried in the stillness like a voice across water. He shouldn't be in here, he thought, looking at the black shell around him. This was a retreat, and Maxwell wouldn't have approved of his lying here with his head down. "Come on, boy," he said aloud to himself, "get it together, get it together."

He pulled himself outside, using his arms for the most part, not wanting to get his feet bumped because of the way they felt. When he got onto the car's hood, he saw that Poulsen and Coulter were starting back, their heads and shoulders moving slowly, black against the snow, emerging above the creek bed. Coulter was ahead. He stopped, looked up and waved. Arizo, sitting on the hood, waved back. It would take them a good thirty minutes to reach him. He had that much time to himself. He leaned back against the windshield and thought of her. He considered various occasions and chose the evening of the first day they were together. They had come back from Piñon Flat in the canyon late in the afternoon. They came to her cabin beside the river and stood for a moment watching the reflection of the evening sky on the black water. Behind the cabin a cord of piñon and a cord of juniper were stacked beneath a shelter. In the twilight he took an ax and easily split some logs and broke kindling across his knee, his breath rising. He came into the cabin, arms full of wood, and closed the door behind him with a boot. She was at the counter fixing something. He saw her in jeans, the angle of her hip, the curve of her thigh. He laid a fire, mixing the wood. It started quickly and burned with a bright orange flame. She turned and came towards him. He saw each movement, each expression. They sat on a rug on the floor in front of the open stove. The curtains were drawn. There was no other light in the cabin but the fire.

"These are my favorite woods for burning," she said. "They smell so sweet."

"They smell of you," he said. "They do."

"That's where I get my smell from. The smoke."

She leaned against him, and they were silent. Such moments had been so rare in his life. He had always thought that everyone else must have them often. When he heard the late-night deejays talking softly on the radio as he drove somewhere, he thought of all the lovers they were talking to, sprawled warm in firelight. You could have the impression of the world being that way, but in truth most people he knew were lonely most of the time. And being close was when you could be most lonely. Otherwise you got used to being alone. Nothing was the way you thought. That's what he had told her that night in front of the fire.

"One thing I always find, however you think it'll be, that's not how it works out," he said.

She half-turned. "How do you want it to be?"

"Like it is now."

"So here you are."

"I thought I was going to be with Lumpy Weldon, and then I thought I was going to be in Vegas."

She shook her head, her hair brushing his face.

"What do you know?" she said.

"Nothing."

"I know something."

"What's that?"

She sat up and turned around and put her arms round his neck and kissed him, slowly and softly, a kiss of reflection, of consideration.

"I know that you're a good man."

He smiled. "Yeah?"

She nodded. "I *know* these things. Let me tell you what happened when I was a kid."

She turned around again and settled against his shoulder and looked into the fire. "My mother and I never got along. We were strangers from the start. So when I was fourteen, she sent me to San Diego to live with my grandparents. You know San Diego?"

"Sure."

"They had a house in the hills by the ocean. It was way up on the hill and down below, next to the water, was an airfield. My room looked out over the town and the airfield and across the sea. It had big windows, and in the summertime I kept them open, even at night. I was lying in bed one night, waiting to go to sleep. I had the radio on. They were broadcasting a concert of classical

music. It was really sad music. I remember it. I was half-asleep
when I heard a small plane taking off. I listened to it coming, and
it flew across my window, climbing. I saw its lights and I was
afraid. I was shaking. I couldn't believe it. I started to cry because
I knew that the man in the plane was going to die. It just came to
me. I knew it. I ran to the window and I watched the lights of the
plane till they disappeared into the dark, and I went back to bed
when I couldn't see it anymore, still scared and shaking. But nothing had happened, so I told myself I was being stupid, and I lay
down and I curled up and tried to go to sleep. Still the same
music was playing. After a while, I was drifting off to sleep and
then I heard the plane coming back, and right away I got this
same awful feeling and I was shaking and shivering. And this time
I suddenly knew that when the plane was right opposite my window, the music on the radio was going to end and right when it
did, the man in the plane was going to die. I lay there, listening to
the plane coming, the engine getting louder, and I put my hands
over my ears to shut myself out of the thing because I thought I
was making it happen, and if I could stop doin' it, the man
wouldn't die. But the plane kept coming, getting louder, and the
music went on and I couldn't stop and I got so terrified and sick I
couldn't even call out."

She paused and slid forward onto her knees and put wood on
the fire. Then she came back and lay beside him again.

"As the plane came close, I stayed in bed. All stiff. Listening. It
didn't sound like the music was going to end, but right when the
plane was opposite, there was this brilliant flash that lit up the sky
and the ceiling and the radio went dead and I screamed. I jumped
out of bed screaming and my grandparents came running in and
my grandmother held me. They thought I'd electrocuted myself
with the radio. All the lights in the house were out. It was dark. I
kept crying to my grandmother that the man was dead and that it
was my fault. 'Course they didn't understand. They said I had a
bad dream. They took me to the window, but we couldn't hear
the plane anymore. My grandmother closed the windows and put
a coat on me and took me in the living room. In the morning we
saw the plane dangling from the high-voltage wires that went

along the hill down below the house. One time I saw a brown pel-
ican flown into some wires, just hangin' dead like that. Just
swingin' there in the wind, all burned up. The next day in the papers they said the pilot had committed suicide. He had left a note
at the airport. Still I felt like it was my fault. Like I had guided
him to his death. For years afterwards I figured that what I was
thinkin' had gone out to him as he flew past my window. It was a
long time before I saw it was his thoughts that came to me."

"That's something to have happened," Arizo said.

"I often see what's going to happen."

"What's going to happen to us?"

"You want to know?"

"No," he said.

The phone rang. It was Coulter to tell him he had got him a
job at the quarry and that they had to be up there the next morning at seven-thirty to see Pops.

"Hey!" Coulter was shouting at him. "Hey!" Arizo turned and
looked across the snow. They were only fifty yards off, panting,
lifting their legs high over the snow, each step a labor, sinking to
their knees.

"I thought you were asleep," Coulter yelled. He was in good
spirits.

Arizo shook his head. Coulter was carrying the laundry bag over
his back. Poulsen had several small branches under his arms. Arizo
leaned back, determined to savor his last moment of privacy. She
must know how it was with him. Something, anyway. He knew
she did, and that was one reason why he had to keep it together.

"How're your feet?" he heard Poulsen ask. Arizo swung his legs
off the hood and dangled them over the fender, facing them. As
he did, they reached the car and Poulsen tossed down the wood
he carried while Coulter dropped the sack. They were both blowing hard.

"Okay," Arizo said.

"We gotta get you help real quick now." Poulsen, his thin face
sweating, came and sat beside him on the fender, looking down at
Arizo's bare feet resting in the snow. Arizo examined them, too.
They were swollen hard, and the skin was cracked.

"This is the only way they feel good," Arizo said.

"I figure they'll come back to check thith bank of the crick today," Poulsen offered.

"That's what I was thinking," Arizo said, forcing a smile.

But this day, Monday the seventeenth, was the day after the search officially ended. On the thirteenth, the day Leonard and Epke had searched the Burma road on snowmobiles as far as Muldoon Canyon, Marlene Poulsen had called Sue-Ellen Coulter. It was their first contact. "I'd like to come see you," Marlene said. She had been thinking of doing this for several days but putting it off every day in hope the phone would ring and it would be Vern and the waiting would be over.

Only the phone never rang for her. It was always for one of her girls.

"It's funny," she said to Tissa one night, "how when some disaster happens to you, people don't call or anythin' because they don't want to disturb you, an' really, that's what you want more than anything."

"Clem Meyers came 'round."

"I know. Isn't he the nicest man? He told me I shouldn't think a thing about what happened that night. He said it just made everyone in town happy it wasn't them that was caught. He said I should just be a good spirit for Vern an' think about nothin' else. I thought it was the nicest thing anyone said."

Tissa nodded. "Joey Leonard calls," she said.

"You know what *he* wants."

"You're not serious!"

"Sure."

"Really?"

"Uhuh."

"That pig." Vickissa shook her head while Marlene pulled her bottom lip.

Marlene had thought of calling Sandy Brown, particularly after Tissa told her what they were saying in town about Sue-Ellen.

"Sue-Ellen's actin' like Rick's just stayin' in Twin Falls workin' nights," Tissa said. "That's what they say. She just says he's comin' home sooner or later an' there ain't nothin' to worry about."

"Probably she just won't admit to herself what's really happened," Marlene said. "That's what it sounds like."

They were sitting at the kitchen counter, Marlene staring out the window. It was snowing lightly. Vern was out there in it, somewhere. Or maybe he wasn't anymore. She shuddered. "There isn't a helluva lot to be cheerful about," she said glumly. "Not right now, as far as I can see."

Tissa shifted slightly on her stool. "Were you guys gettin' along?" she asked.

"Sure." It was reflexive and just as obviously it was inadequate. "Like we always did."

Tissa just nodded.

"Vern's done good by all of us," Marlene said.

"But?"

"Well," Marlene forced the word out and sighed and looked at her painted fingernails. "It was all pretty even." She realized with a shock that she'd used the past tense, and she quickly added, "Until now, that is." She thought of a flat line on an electrocardiogram with just a regular beep like they had on all the medical shows. That was her life with Vern. As if to atone, she said, "This whole thing's my fault." And then tacked again: "But when you get to be my age an' you see the wrinkles comin'—" she made a helpless gesture with her hands and put her head down and began to cry. Tissa got off her stool and went to hold her.

"I just want to *live* a little more," Marlene said in agonized apology. "Before we were married we . . . It was like I was free. You never knew what was gonna happen. . . . That's all I wanted."

Tissa began to cry, too.

Later on, feeling purged, Marlene called Sue-Ellen and went over. As she stood waiting on the step outside the front door, she heard the sound of television. Marlene was touching the back of her head, nervously pushing her hair up a little, when Sue-Ellen opened the door, wearing a chartreuse nylon housecoat and matching slippers with puffy balls on the toes. When she smiled, Marlene saw fine teeth, small and set in perfectly even rows.

Sue-Ellen looked Marlene up and down. "Well, sweetie," she said. "You look great. It's no wonder he went for you."

Marlene blushed.

"Come on in. It's gettin' cold in here."

They closed the door and went into the cluttered living room. Marlene couldn't remember seeing such a mess and found herself wondering why she had come. "I came to talk serious about some things," she fumbled.

Sue-Ellen sat on the couch without offering Marlene a seat. She looked up and cracked her gum. "Honey," she said, "you shoulda said that to yourself before you come on to my ol' man."

Marlene nodded. "I know. I'm here to tell you I'm sorry."

Sue-Ellen cracked her gum again. "You ain't the first," she declared. "Have a seat an' I'll fix some coffee."

Marlene sat on the edge of her chair. "You know, they're talkin' about callin' off the search," she said to Sue-Ellen, now in the kitchen.

Sue-Ellen stuck her head back through the door and grinned. "I heard they was bitchin' about how bad it is up there."

"You know Sandy Brown?"

Sue-Ellen nodded.

"How is she?"

Sue-Ellen disappeared again. "I don't see her. She's a pain in the ass."

"You think they're all right?"

"I just *know* Rick's comin' home."

Marlene realized that she didn't feel that way about Vern. "It doesn't do a damn bit of good feelin' any other way," she ventured.

Sue-Ellen appeared again, chewing on her gum with her front teeth. "They'll be okay," she said. "This weather'll cool 'em off."

"You think they'll stop lookin'?"

"If they don't come up with somethin' soon. The guys are losin' work time now, an' they mostly won't have work all winter, anyway."

"Why doesn't the sheriff pay them?"

"Shit," Sue-Ellen said, "he can't even pay their gas right now."

"He said they're gonna have a meeting this week maybe."

"Well, Burt wants the search to go on three weeks. He says the weather's been so bad, half the time they was up there was a waste."

"That's what he told me."

"But there's a bunch of them wanna call it off."

"Right now?"

Sue-Ellen fussed with her housecoat. "It's the women," she said. "They don't want their old men up there. It's dangerous."

Marlene sighed and nodded tensely.

"But Meyers will hold the line," Sue-Ellen resumed. "They'll do what he says. This is his town. His county, in fact. Been that way since I was a girl. Want some coffee?"

Marlene nodded.

The phone rang.

Marlene sat on the edge of her chair and watched Sue-Ellen gather up the instrument. She wasn't just a big woman around, she was tall, too.

"I'll tell her 'cause she's right here with me," Sue-Ellen said into the phone. "Yup. Thanks. Good-bye." She hung up and turned to Marlene. "That was the sheriff. They're gonna have a town meeting Friday an' vote on it."

"Vote on what?"

"Whether to go on with the search."

"But that's tomorrow."

"Yup."

"What if they call it off?"

Sue-Ellen shrugged. "The boys'll be on their own." She smiled reassuringly. "But they won't. They won't go against what Burt tells 'em to do."

Two days before the meeting, Pops Bivaletz went to the Bluebird Diner on his way home from the quarry. He ordered coffee and cookies. Chloe Tippet was surprised to see him. Pops very rarely appeared in public. His visit was not a random event. If

there were seemingly chance aspects to his life, it was usually because there was more distance between cause and effect than the
observer was capable of detecting. That's to say that Pops Bivaletz
had noted how things, once set upon their right course, work
themselves out best without further interference. If this made his
life appear as colorless as his cheeks, it was, again, because the observer did not truly understand economy of effort.

So, when Chloe Tippet poured him coffee and in reply to his
inquiry told him that Sandy Brown was taking a vacation, he
smiled understandingly, carefully bit into a cookie, and wiped the
corner of his mouth with a paper napkin.

When Sandy Brown called him the following evening and
asked if she could come and see him, he was pleased but not surprised.

"Come," he said. "We shall 'ave some tea."

Pops' bungalow was on Parker. An old cast-iron lamp threw a
weak light upon it. The porch was half-hidden behind a laurel
bush that crowded the front steps. The tiny patch of front yard
was covered with snow. He met her at the door, a slight, smiling
figure in a gray woolen sweater, gray trousers, and carpet slippers.
He went ahead of her down a dark hallway to the kitchen, towards the light. There was no other light on in the house but the
bulb over the table in the kitchen, harshly reflected under a plain
white porcelain shade.

The chairs were plain wood, the table covered by a plastic cloth
of faded design. A large ivory-colored ashtray in the shape of four
skulls stood in the center. He fussed about Sandy slightly as she
sat, pulling her chair out for her. Then he crossed to a samovar
and poured tea into glasses that stood in old silver holders. They
had belonged to his mother's grandmother in Russia, he explained. He talked about his mother as he put white bread and
butter, cream cheese, jam, honey, plates, and knives on the table.
Then he sat opposite her, beside his radio, and grinned and spread
his hands towards the food: "This is my dinner," he explained.
"Please."

She accepted because she wanted to join with him. He turned
the radio beside him up a little. It was ten o'clock. They listened

to the headlines while he made toast. She spread the butter as if
she were taking communion. "Do you always eat this late, or did I
hang you up?" she asked.

"Always," he said, chewing. "For an old man zere are no more
days and nights."

He looked at her appreciatively.

"Don't look at me," she said, smiling apologetically. "I'm all
washed out. I look terrible, I know."

"You are a fine woman," he said.

She blushed.

"An old man can say such sings, vizout ze proper introduction.
Yes?"

She didn't know what to say. She didn't know exactly why she
had come, but she felt comfortable with him. He made it seem as
if there were nothing beyond this kitchen and the two of them in
it.

"I 'ave a sister," he was saying. "In Haifa. I came to America,
she to Israel. Zen it was Palestine, yes? Ze British were zere. So,
regard, two years ago I go to Israel to see 'er, an' we 'ave a meeting
of all ze people in Israel zat come from our village in Russia. Zere
are many. I go wiz my sister, yes? But when I look at zem I want
to go 'ome, to leave. My sister says 'Why?' an' I tell 'er, 'Look at
all zese broken old men.' " He grinned and purposely looked senile
and grotesque. "I 'ave always known zem as boys. In my mind,
yes? So strong, so fast. I tell 'er I sink it is best I remember zem
zis way." He stopped.

She smiled.

"But zen," he said dramatically, leaning towards her across the
table as if he didn't wish to be overheard. "I see Freda. Freda,
from our village. Zis girl I loved when I was sixteen an' she was
twelve. She was so beautiful you cannot imagine." His face was
filled with consternation. "An' now, I am seventy an' she is sixty-
six, yes? An' I see so many wrinkles I cannot believe. But I go to
'er an' I say to 'er, 'Freda, when we were so young, I loved you.' "
He leaned forward, holding out a hand for emphasis, "An' she say
to me, 'But Shlomo (Shlomo, zat is my real name), why didn't

you tell me?' An' I look at 'er an' I say, 'Per'aps I was afraid. Per'aps. I am not sure.'"

Grimacing, he sat back and rubbed his forehead vigorously with the heels of both hands. "Oi, yoi, yoi, yoi," he sighed, in his way of mocking himself. "I am learning wisdom at seventy years an' dying a fool."

When he looked up, she was crying. He made a sad face and tipped his head. She sniffed and wiped her cheeks. "I'm sorry," she said. And then, gathering herself, "Did you ever marry?"

He lit a cigarette, shook out the match, and drew back to avoid the smoke. "No," he said. "But what I tell you is zis. Regard. If you 'ave somesing, you 'ave 'ad it. You know always 'ow zis is. If you never 'ave something . . ." He leaned back, the cigarette dangling from his lips, his eyes mere slits. "You 'ear what I am saying? Yes?"

She nodded.

"You 'ave to give sanks you 'ave not been so foolish as me. Also you must 'ave courage"—he pronounced the word as though he were speaking French, in the same way that he said "regard." "You must 'ave courage, ozervise you are not so worthy to be viz a man of such courage as 'e 'as."

She dabbed at her tears and said brightly, "It's true."

"I shall make more tea I sink. Yes?"

"Please," she said.

Shortly after she left, Pops called the Hermans. If there were any problems, he said, he would like it if they let him know. If things were becoming difficult for Miss Brown, any way in which he might help. Gladys Herman thanked him and said she understood.

After he had hung up, he put the bread back into the bin in the cupboard beside the table. He wrapped the cheese and butter and put them away beside it. He wiped off the faded tablecloth and washed the two glasses at the sink. When this was done, he came slowly back to the table, sat down in his chair, and turned on the radio beside him. He found a news program, lit a cigarette, and stared across the room.

They held the meeting that night after Leonard and Epke had got back from their search of the Burma road as far as Muldoon Canyon.

It was a town meeting, held in the VFW hall. Marlene was the only one of the three women who went. Sue-Ellen said she knew what was going to happen anyway. Sandy, who was now staying with the Hermans, seemed not to care about the logistics of the rescue effort.

Outside the VFW, spotlights lit up the Sherman tank with the concrete bung in the barrel and the welded hatch covers that memorialized Cope's World War II dead. The snow that was piled up beside the pathway had frozen hard. Marlene found herself in step with the sheriff. He wore his usual grim face.

"I appreciate what you're doin' for us," Marlene said.

"Wait till I do it," the sheriff replied.

"I feel real bad about what happened."

"I would, too." The sheriff spoke gruffly out of the side of his mouth.

Marlene dropped back, and when she saw she was alone she returned to her car and drove home again.

The VFW hall smelled warm and damp. Gray metal chairs with rubber-tipped legs were arranged in rows before the stage. By the time the sheriff arrived, the hall was full. There were snowmobilers from the Challis and Mackay clubs who had been involved in the search and beet farmers from the plain who hadn't lifted a finger. And there were women from all over, too. The issue was an interesting one for these people. The tradition of independence in Cope County goes back to the days of the territory. But there's also a strong tradition of law-and-order. On the Fourth of July, the John Birch Society runs at least two floats in the parade.

The issue of the missing hunters, as they had become known, pitted the one attitude against the other. The search had lasted two weeks. The sheriff said go on. The wives said stop. The men were caught in the middle. Both sides were serious.

There was a taste of frontier to it, of propriety tinged by lynch-mob vestiges. Would they cut these boys off or not? Pull the plug? Whether life remained in the mountains was fast becoming the mootest point of the winter. If there was, abandoning the search now seemed absolutely certain to extinguish it. This became a sore point, touching upon western values these folks fancied they still lived by.

It was the wives who had brought about the meeting, the wives of the men who were searching—which made the men variously proud, bashful, fearful, and angry. They made jokes about women's lib, but for the most part they wriggled ineffectually in their seats, locked in the grip of the vaginal vise.

Lucy Leonard, Joey's wife, opened the meeting. She was short and well built. "Us wives has had enough worry. It's a bad business for those with loved ones that's been lost, but it's gettin' real dangerous for our men in there, an' I don't want to see us go losin' some more for nothin'."

There was a ripple of applause.

Rosalind Rose was encouraged to say: "They ain't where they said they'd be, an' now they could be anywhere. Maybe they ain't even in the mountains at all. Nobody knows for sure. Another thing is they know'd better than to go gettin' into the mountains this time of year in the first place." There was longer applause this time. "I got to speak my mind," she went on, and held up her hands the way she had seen Johnny Carson do so often on TV. "It's gettin' to be Christmas. There's four kids in my house. We already lost a sled up there while my husband was lookin'. That's six hundred dollars. Burt here can't even afford to buy us gas anymore, an' he still wants us to go on. Heck, I can't buy presents to give the kids; can't afford a turkey even. We got to get these men back to work while there still is some."

Now there were whistles with the clapping.

It was an hour or more before Sheriff Burt Meyers stood up. He didn't want to waste his piece in the early going. Some of the men had spoken in favor of going on. They were getting ready to vote.

"There's about three things I wanna say." The sheriff looked about the hall, eyes half-closed, as if he'd been napping. "Imagine it was *you* up there before you vote this thing. Imagine it was you or your husband. You gonna cut him off so quick? We been lookin' two weeks, okay. But how many real clear days we had?

About four or five, maybe. An' there's just one more thing." He paused and glared right at them. "I give the order for this search to be continued for another week. If there's any member of the posse don't show up like I told him, he's gonna be charged under Article 2501 of the Code for disobeying a peace officer." With that, he sat down slowly. There was a mixture of boos and applause. Epke, who was next to him, took the pipe out of his mouth and leaned across. "I'm afraid you're pissin' in the wind, Burt," he said.

"Wouldn't be the first time," the sheriff replied without looking around.

When the door chimes rang, Sue-Ellen was lying on the couch in her aquamarine housecoat, painting her toenails and watching "The Little House on the Prairie."

It was 10:20 P.M. She had no idea who would come this late, but she opened the door with no preliminaries to the tall, gaunt figure of the sheriff.

He came in and took off his hat. He had a hangdog look, his whole frame was stooped a little, and his stride seemed short. She'd never seen him this way before in the eighteen years she'd known him, and she found herself concerned. She also was impressed and elated by his presence in her living room.

"Let me take your coat," she said. "I just made some coffee."

He handed it to her. The green serge of his shirt was shiny with starch. His gun hung in its black holster from a heavy, black, webbed belt that creaked when he moved.

They sat at the table in the living room with the goldfish bowl between them.

He glanced around. The living room looked like a bomb had hit it. "Everythin' all right?" he asked.

She nodded. "Things didn't go so well at the meeting, did they?"

He shook his head and sipped his coffee. "They're not goin' on with the search. Not past Saturday."

"Did you expect them to?"

He rubbed his chin and she saw that he was more upset than

she would have imagined. He leaned back in his seat and looked straight at her, his left eyebrow raised critically.

"I'll tell you," he said. "I never expected no posse of mine to walk out. Twenty-three years, and you'd think they'd figure I know what I'm doin'."

"It's the women, you know."

"Yep."

"Can't you do anything?"

He shook his head. "Nothin' that's gonna help them boys in the mountains."

"Maybe they'd go back if you—"

He made a sour face. "They're gonna have to live with themselves, an' if they can do that, there's sure as hell nothin' I can do to them." He rubbed one bloodshot eye. "Fact is, I'm thinkin' they can find themselves someone else to run this county. I've had about enough, I tell you."

She nodded calmly, amazed and thrilled that he would come to her and say such things. She wondered, wanting to help him. Jason stirred in his sleep on the floor in front of the TV.

"Would you give me a hand with puttin' him to bed?" She motioned towards the boy.

"Sure. You want me to carry him?"

"He's gettin' too big for me without wakin' him up," she said.

The old sheriff knelt, pushed his gun back out of the way, and lifted the sleeping child in his arms.

"This way," she said softly and led him through her bedroom to the room in back where Jason slept. The sheriff put the boy onto his cot and they stood beside him, looking down.

"That takes me back some," he whispered.

She looked up at him and smiled. "Come," she said.

She led him to the door, let him through, and switched off the light, drawing the door closed behind her. When she turned, he was still standing there and they were face to face in the half-light of her bedroom. She looked up at him, her face soft in his shadow. "You shouldn't feel bad," she said and reached up to place her hands flat upon his chest. "You did everythin' you could." His face was hard to see in the light, and he said nothing.

She reached up her small, soft hands, drew his face down to hers, and kissed him long on the mouth.

The sheriff responded slowly; his hands came hesitantly to her sides and felt the nylon slide over the swell of her hips. She pushed him gently back, shook her shoulders, and her housecoat slipped off. "Come," she said to him softly and drew him down, knowing in her way that the surest antidote to serious depression and defeat is unexpected conquest and not being unwilling in the least to give him that.

The morning after the meeting, Gladys Herman was wondering whether to tell Sandy Brown the news. It was front page in the Twin Falls *Times-News*. She tried to discuss it with George at breakfast. George drowned his buckwheats in boysenberry syrup and shook the last drops from the bottle. "Hell, if you don't, she'll find out an' figure she doesn't have *any* friends in this town," he said.

"If she asks, I'll tell her."

"I don't see it'll make a difference."

"How d'you mean?"

"I mean she's that upset already."

"George . . ."

"Gladys." He waved his fork at her. "I heard enough."

She couldn't discuss anything with him. She didn't know why she kept trying after so long. It was either the way he wanted it, or nothing. It was like being married to a traffic cop, she thought. Or a stop sign.

She stood in the doorway and watched him walk to his pickup. His soft-brimmed hat was pulled down well over his ears against the cold. The snow crunched under his boots. He slammed the truck door and shook his head at her through the glass. She waved a little and shivered and, closing the door, turned into the silent house. She had tried to explain to him what she felt about Sandy. She had spoken to him of a vigil that should be undisturbed, but she hadn't properly expressed what she knew. George had looked at her like she was soft. She lingered now in the peace that settled over the house. She had been stupid to expect his understanding.

This was a matter for the female, a matter of love and deprivation. She could see how it had come to Sandy. It was the shadow
side—the lost side of her moon. The side that sometimes woke her
crying in her childlessness. She looked about her at the place
where she lived, at George's coats hanging by the door. This was
the side of her that gave meaning to the nonsense of her life, the
caring side. It was the thread connecting her to all her sex, to all
experience. And in this woman now in her house it was pure and
predominant. It had come entirely to the surface and she must protect it. For there is much to harm the spirit come so far into the
light.

When she looked in, Sandy was sleeping. She lay on her stomach, arms outstretched, one leg extended. The bedclothes lay on
the floor; the sheets were crumpled. She could have slept little.

Later in the morning, when Sandy came in and Gladys told her,
as gently as possible, that the search would be called off after Saturday, Sandy nodded as if she'd been expecting it.

Newly diagnosed terminal cases generally respond with disavowal and later with anger. Marlene Poulsen was now angry. The
morning after the meeting, as Sandy Brown lay sleeping and Sue-
Ellen sat at the breakfast table with Jason, humming the theme of
"Mr. Ed," Marlene Poulsen was on the telephone, bitterly attacking the citizenry of Cope, while her two daughters sat watching
her across the kitchen table in awe.

"An' you can tell that worthless sonovabitch from me that if
he's shit-scared to get his ass into the mountains and keep lookin'
for his 'old buddy'"—she put a great deal of derision into the
term—"then I'm gonna find me someone that will. An' when Vern
gets home, I'm gonna direct him to lay one up alongside his head,
real fuckin' good, so he'll wish a mule had kicked him instead."
She banged down the receiver.

"But I don't think it was Red's fault, Mamma," Tissa said carefully. "You said yourself—"

"The hell with what I ever said, girl. Your papa's stuck up there
in the goddamn mountains freezin' to death if he ain't already,
an' they're sittin' 'round on their fat asses, pussy-whipped."

Vickissa began to cry and Tissa tried to comfort her.

"Hell-an'-shit," Marlene swore and picked up the phone. "I want the number for the governor's office."

But the governor was on Christmas vacation, and so was everyone else at the capital who might otherwise have told her there was nothing they could do to help her.

Marlene hung up the phone and lit a Marlboro. She was looking terrible. She stared at her youngest daughter, Vickissa, and Vickissa looked sullenly back. Marlene shook her head. "It's no use cryin' about it, hon," she said. She called the sheriff. "Sheriff," she said, "this is Marlene Poulsen."

"Yes, ma'am."

"Sheriff, since the official search has been called off, I'd like to organize my own search which I will personally finance. Can you advise me how I should go about this?"

"Yes, ma'am." The sheriff sounded comfortable. "But before you go to the trouble, let me tell you that since the meetin' occurred, I have decided that I'm gonna carry on the search during my off-duty hours an' on weekends together with a group of boys that feels the same way I do. I have spoke with them this mornin', an' it's all set."

The morning after the meeting, they decided in the car that Poulsen should attempt to walk out alone. Arizo shaped the decision. He didn't reckon Coulter could handle the walk, and Poulsen didn't seem to be afraid of going.

They fed him up and made him rest. They fed him liver and heart from the deer, meat high in nutrient value. Coulter cooked it carefully over a tiny fire in the hubcap in the back of the Ford.

Arizo pulled himself out onto the fender to avoid the smoke. Clouds covered the mountain almost to its base and formed a swirling lid over the hollow of the canyon. He sat with his bare feet buried in the snow. It was cold—about freezing, he thought. He pulled his feet out and examined them. They had turned black. In some parts around the ankles it looked like bad bruising, but the rest was pretty much solid black. He couldn't wriggle his

toes at all anymore, and the skin around them was beginning to
flake off as though they'd been badly sunburned. But what concerned him most were the cracks opening in the skin. They were
large and deep, and they didn't bleed.

When Poulsen came out of the car, Arizo said, "Look at this,"
as if he'd found a curio. "They don't bleed, even. They must be
froze clear through."

Poulsen bent a little and squinted in dismay. "Do they hurt?"

"No." Arizo pointed to the cracking. "I guess they're dead. I
guess that's why they're black."

Poulsen straightened up. "We gotta get you outta here real
fatht," he said.

After the meal in the car there was a moment of awkward silence.

Arizo said, "So you'll stay near the treeline?"

Poulsen nodded.

"We should've done that before," Arizo said.

"Thnowth too deep by the crick," Poulsen said.

Coulter was playing with his knife, balancing it by the point on
the toe of his boot. His eyes shifted to Poulsen.

"Whattya gonna tell 'em?"

Poulsen looked blankly trying to avoid it.

"You know. About Coo-Coo."

Poulsen shrugged and regarded the two of them openly. "I
dunno," he said. "Whatta you'all think?"

"It was a accident," Arizo said. "Much as there's accidents."

"Yeah," Poulsen agreed.

"I didn't mean it," Coulter said slowly, trying to read Poulsen.
"You know that, don't you?"

"He only come here on my account," Poulsen said. "An' now
the poor thonovabitth ith dead, anyway you look. How d'you
think I feel, uh?"

"The sheriff's gonna ask you exactly what happened," Coulter
said. "We gotta agree exact, or I'm fuckin' hung." He looked
nervously to Arizo for agreement, but Arizo was studying Poulsen.

"We were uphill," Poulsen explained, "him an' me, we were

huntin', an' he come outta the treeth an' you thought he wath a
deer."

"He was comin' down from the canyon. Like he'd been searchin'
the canyon." Coulter's face was alive with anxiety.

Poulsen nodded. "I never thaw it," he decided.

Arizo changed the subject. "What you gonna do 'bout the
glare?"

"I got real dark glatheth in the truck. I forgot about them."

"You'll stick to what you said, Vern?" Coulter begged.

Poulsen nodded. "Yeah, of courthe."

Arizo shifted his legs and winced. Poulsen reached across and
patted Arizo's thigh. It was an unexpected gesture. For all the
proximity, or rather because of it, they had none of them touched
each other unless it had been unavoidable. And they had spoken
very little to each other even after the animosity had begun to dissolve. What there was to say was so obvious they didn't need or
want to say it. That was clear to them. They had both of them
seen him staring unseeing, eyes vacant even face to face, disengaged, lost in some impenetrable private world at the back of his
head, carrying on some conversation with himself even he was unaware of. And they had both held their breath that he would not
break here. Neither mentioned it though. They had seen each
other watching, so there was no need.

Now Poulsen, arm still resting on Arizo's thigh, said offhandedly, "When we get together after, you know, I gotta ranch.
Maybe you'd come give me a hand?"

Arizo smiled. "After we get outta here, we won't any of us
wanna see the other again." He took Poulsen's hand in a brotherly
shake. "But thanks anyway, Vern."

"Jesus, are they gonna get a shock when they see you!" Coulter
said suddenly to Poulsen.

There was an awkward pause. Poulsen kept the initiative: "In
case they come when I'm gone, I'm gonna thtay on the high
ground till I can thee my way clear to the river. An' when I get to
the river, I'm gonna go downththtream, whether it'th the Big Lotht
or the Thalmon. Okay?"

"An' if we don't hear anythin' after four days," Arizo said, "Rick's comin' after you."

"That's right," Coulter said.

"At night," Arizo cautioned, "dig yourself a snow-hole but be sure you got somethin' in there with you so's you can dig out if there's more snow in the night or a drift or somethin'."

Poulsen nodded, flexing his fingers, getting psyched up.

"You go to the shoulder with him, Rick," Arizo said.

Outside the car, Poulsen wrapped a dirty woolen blanket around his shoulders. The sky was a heavy gray now, and the light very pale and flat.

"You mind you don't get up a sweat with this." Coulter touched Poulsen's blanket.

Poulsen nodded and turned. "I'll thee you in a bit, Mike," he said. Arizo had pulled himself to the doorway. He grinned. "Good luck," he said.

Arizo climbed out with difficulty to sit on the fender and watched the two of them trudge up the slope to the shoulder. They walked slowly, with much floundering, although it looked easier for them as they got closer to the treeline. He watched the way they moved through the snow, breathing in gray puffs. It was a strange thing, walking, he thought. He hadn't ever really seen it happening before. He hadn't really thought a thing about it.

It went so well at first that Poulsen forgot why they had stayed so long in the car. The temptation to push was strong, and he was careful to pace himself, afraid to sweat. He had read about sweat-soaked clothes freezing as the body cools.

He worked along the side of the hill, at the treeline, for the first couple of hours. It was slow going, but still nowhere near as bad as it had been lower down by the creek. Where he was, beside the firs, the snow was no deeper than two or three feet, except where it had drifted. Beyond the first shoulder, where he had parted with Coulter there had been a second. When he reached this, he saw the ground spill away into the full spread of the Basin. It was hard to tell distance, for the light was flat and the sky and snow merged in a dreamlike uniformity of color more beautiful than anything he remembered. Near where he stood was a fallen tree.

He brushed off the snow and sat. The clouds of his breath were all
that moved. The Basin tilted slightly away from him, away from
the ridge on which he sat which curved away slowly at right angles to the slope. He worked it out. The Basin drained to the
northwest and the ridge ran northeast to east, to where he could
see the ground rising softly into a cloud. He guessed correctly that
these were the White Knob Mountains, which ran to maybe
13,000 feet. He would have to cross the Basin, sticking to the rim
to avoid the deep snow, to where it drained into what he again
correctly guessed was the east fork of the Big Lost. The Big Lost
cut through the White Knobs to the Mackay road. This was his
way out. And now was the time to cross the creek below; the same
creek beside which the cars were stranded maybe four miles farther up. While there was still a slight elevation on the far side,
where the snow would be shallower. He studied it all for a moment more, checking his calculations. Then he rose and started
downhill, away from the trees, a very small and solitary figure.

Quickly, the snow became deep once more, and he began to
flounder. He grew panicky and wanted to turn back. His chest was
tight. This crossing, he told himself, was more than he could do.
So he stopped and stood still, staring at the disturbed crystals of
snow around his thighs, looking across the snow's smooth surface
to where definition was lost in the mist of warm gray cloud, waiting until his breathing grew easier and he became calmer. And
then he went on, sometimes sinking to his hips. There was, he
thought, some definite number of steps he must take that would
bring him to that solid one, when he would stand upon the road
that lay there, waiting for his foot.

A car came towards him through the hard granules of powder
drifting across its glassy surface. He heard Marlene's voice on the
telephone; he saw his daughters' faces. He was coming home.
Now he stood facing the rise on the far side, at its foot. The snow
would get less deep now. He had made it. He went on.

There was a sharp and loud crack. As he twisted about looking
for its source, the ground went under him like an elevator starting
down. The surface started going up. Snow was sliding towards
him. He was, he saw, at the center of a slowly collapsing cone.

Something sharp whipped his face. Something hit his thigh and pivoted him. Snow was falling on him. There was nothing to grasp, and it was all happening very slowly. It occurred to him that he was falling through a tree.

He hit the ground awkwardly, landing with all his weight on his left foot, feeling his ankle turn and break. He went down on his back and lay looking up at the sky through a hole fifteen feet above him, glad to be still, his heart pounding. He lay on broken willow branches and fallen snow. He saw he had fallen through a screen of ice that had formed a roof over a stand of willows. Beyond his feet, a bank rose steeply into the darkness. On either side were two or three more willows and then, dimly, a wall of snow.

"God-in-hell!" he shouted. "God-in-hell!" And he beat the ground beside him, red-faced, veins thrusting in his neck. He stopped abruptly. His foot hurt a good deal. He looked down at it and saw it was turned at a stupid angle. He reached out and touched it gingerly, pushing it a little back in place. Then it hurt a great deal. He swore again and dropped back onto his elbows and stared at the patch of gray sky through the hole. He said aloud, "Vern boy, you're goddamned through. You know that? You're all done, boy."

He dropped his head on his chest. Gradually his shoulders rose as despair filled him until it spilled over and he wept in long, convulsive sobs. He would have cried his life out in those tears if he could. He wished for it. His hands closed mechanically upon snow and twigs.

And in that moment he heard the sound of an engine. He looked up and saw in an instant the shape of a plane crossing the patch of gray above him no more than a hundred feet above the surface—a dark, oblique shadow that was gone as he saw it. But the noise was real, and he screamed up at the sound dying so quickly as though he were calling to someone out of a window, shouting, "You tell 'em I tried, okay? You tell 'em, sonovabitch."

And then he lapsed into silence.

He looked at his hands, lifted them, and brushed the gloves together to rub off the snow. Then he studied the sky as though he had some purpose in mind. It was losing its brightness. It must be close to four o'clock, he thought. He listened to the wind, which was beginning to pick up. Soon it would be dark. It would begin to freeze.

Poulsen had been gone three days and the sun hadn't shone. The clouds had been high and ragged, with mists below that swirled about the base of the mountain and thickened the gloom.

They had been lying side by side, silent, always hungry, weak and half-asleep, when the plane came the first afternoon after Poulsen left. Arizo had started up, forgetting his frozen feet, and blocking Coulter's line to the door for a precious moment. The sound of the engine filled the interior of the car, but when Coulter broke from the door, waving and screaming angrily, the aircraft was already halfway down the creek and about to bank for the dogleg that would take it out of sight. Coulter leaped into the snow after it, shouting, screaming.

For a full day afterwards, he would not speak to Arizo. Then he began going in and out of the car at every imagined sound, moving restlessly, fidgeting, like a man with hours to wait who looks at his watch every minute, and complaining about the stench every time he came back in from the outside. Arizo looked blankly at him and said very little. He lay on his butt until the cheeks grew numb and sore. Then he turned on one hip until that got sore and then onto the other. Everything was made worse by the cold. He was always cold. The cold and the fact he couldn't exercise made the muscles in his legs so stiff that it was painful to move them in the least. For long periods of time he would lie perfectly still, listening to the wind outside, feeling himself growing increasingly uncomfortable, trying to estimate the point at which the discomfort of lying still would exceed the discomfort of moving.

Sunday morning, a little after it got light, Arizo crawled awkwardly into the front, sat on the driver's seat, and buried his bare feet in the snow outside the door. More snow had fallen in the night, and it was still drifting down lightly now. Sitting in the doorway of the Ford, he could barely make out the patterns of bare branches along the creek. The flakes fell thick in breathless air. He sat watching, finding it soothing. It was impossible to tell the hour of day from the light. He wondered whether Sandy was awake yet. He thought of her in the bed, warm and slight and supple, drowsy with sleep, curled on her side with a future stretching away in front of her. He looked down at his legs. His feet were buried to the ankles. He had rolled up the legs of his trousers to stop them getting wet. Now he heard Coulter moving, pulling himself up to rest his elbows on the back of the seat, looking surly.

"Do they hurt?"

"No. Just around the ankles they itch some."

Coulter was silent a moment. "This is fucked. Vern never made it," he said.

When Arizo didn't reply, Coulter pushed open the door a little wider and stared at the snow around his feet. Arizo slowly and carefully lifted them out of the snow. From the ankles down, they were black and purple as an eggplant.

"Jesus Christ!" Coulter said.

The skin was cracked open, and around the toes it was sloughing badly.

"You could get gangrene," Coulter said.

"I already have."

Coulter shook his head. "You'd be dead if it was gangrene."

"Only if it was infected."

They continued to stare, as if hypnotized, at Arizo's feet.

"They're dead," Arizo said. "All the skin an' everythin'. That's why I don't feel nothin'."

"So how come you keep freezin' them?"

"So they don't get infected."

Coulter nodded slowly.

"I guess I've lost them," Arizo said. "Isn't that a motherfucker? I can't imagine it, even."

Coulter could think of no answer.

Arizo shifted his weight and slowly pulled himself over onto the passenger's side. Now he could see that Coulter was crying, looking out of the open doorway, the tears falling, and he reached over and put an arm about his friend's shoulders and roughly, clumsily

kissed his cheek. It was an impulsive gesture that took both of
them by surprise.

"It's okay," he said. "No big thing."

Coulter struck his palm against his head. "Jesus, we're a poor
bunch of slobs!"

"Make a fire," Arizo said, "an' we'll cook a meal."

They broke sticks and laid them over paper in the hubcap, and
Coulter lit the paper and then turned around to put the frozen
venison bits on the snow into the pot. All the meat that was left
now had hair on it. While he was doing this, the fire went out,
and when he saw this, he broke into tears again. Arizo held him
again. "I'm sorry," he said. "I should've been tendin' it myself."

Coulter straightened and sniffed. "I shouldn't have let it die.
We only got six matches left. Ain't that goddamn pathetic?"

Later that afternoon, when it was obvious no one would come
that day, Arizo said, "If they don't spot us tomorrow, you gotta
go."

Coulter rubbed his face with a grease-caked open hand. Arizo
had been growing more depressed as the day wore on, and it made
him nervous. He wanted to do something for him, but didn't
know what. It was a bad thing being unable to relieve a friend's
suffering.

"We're outta everythin', just about," Arizo said.

"I know, I know we are. I got to go."

Arizo was silent, lying on his back, hands behind his head, staring at the ceiling.

"The day after tomorrow is Christmas," Coulter observed.

Arizo nodded.

"I guess it's takin' Vern longer than he reckoned."

"I hope to God he's gettin' there."

"You think I should go the same way he did?"

There was no answer.

"Well there's only one way out. Down the canyon, like we already said."

Still Arizo said nothing.

Coulter was hesitant. "After that I guess I go east."

"Yeah, I suppose."

"What about you?"

"I'll be okay."

"Is there something we should do?"

"What for?"

"Your feet."

"I been thinkin' I should cut them off."

Something went off inside Coulter's head which told him Arizo was serious. At the same time he heard himself saying, "Yeah. I can imagine you'd feel that way."

"They're killin' me." Arizo said it softly, a little distantly. "I mean, I'm lyin' here watchin' myself die."

"How d'you mean?"

"It's spreadin'," Arizo said. He was looking away from Coulter, at the wall. "It's spreadin' up my legs."

Coulter shifted. "I better go right away," he said.

"I already told you, the soonest you should go is Christmas morning. They could come tomorrow, an' you should rest up."

Coulter sighed heavily.

After a long silence, Arizo said, "Maybe you'd help me?"

"Sure," Coulter said without thinking.

"With my feet."

"You ain't serious?" Coulter felt a touch of terror. "Why'd you wanna do a thing like that?"

"Why?" Arizo's voice suddenly rose. "Because they're no use anymore. You know that? I'm never gonna walk on them again." All at once he sat up and pounded the metal sidewall nearest him with the heel of his fist. Then he turned and Coulter saw that he was crying. "They're just"—Arizo searched for the words and then yelled it out—"they're just rotten meat eatin' me alive."

Arizo was fumbling at his belt. In a moment, the knife with the silver heel was in his hand, and he was pulling at the blankets.

"I'll show you!" he yelled. "You don't fuckin' well believe me!"

"I do. I believe you. Honest to God, Mike." As if the admission would stop it. But Arizo had the blankets off his feet now and was slashing at the dark flesh with his knife, cutting and stabbing.

"Holy Mother!" Coulter screamed and grabbed his arm. Arizo

twisted free and cut again. "See, Rick," he said in morbid triumph. "There's nothin' to be scared about. They're gone."

Coulter was at him again now and they wrestled briefly on the
mattress in the gloom of the car for possession of the knife. Then
Arizo went limp with Coulter across him and again was sobbing.
Coulter sat up slowly, shaken, and Arizo rolled towards the wall,
putting his hands to his face. Coulter lay on one elbow, a hand
resting on Arizo's shoulder, not knowing what to do.

After a long while, Arizo wiped his eyes with a corner of one of
the blankets. "I don't see there's much point to all this," he said
quietly. "Sometimes, like right now, I don't see why I'm makin'
such a big deal about hangin' in there. For what?"

"For Sandy, for openers."

"She's not gonna want someone that's lame."

"How d'you know?"

"Shit, she ain't gonna be spendin' the rest of her life with a
goddamn cripple!"

"Hell, you won't be a cripple. You'll be walkin' around an'
everythin'."

"If we get outta here, maybe."

Coulter was quiet for a while and then he plunged in: "Look, if
you think it'll make the difference, I'll help you with your feet,"
he said quickly.

Arizo thought about it in a less passionate light.

"Whatta you think, really?"

"I dunno. If you think that leavin' it the way it is is gonna be
more dangerous than the other, then I guess we should."

"It wouldn't hurt me none."

"Yeah?"

"Probably it'd feel better, and when they get me out, that's
what they're gonna do anyway."

"I dunno."

"Maybe it'll stop it from spreadin'. Let's light a fire," Arizo
said. "We should keep the knife hot all along."

Coulter clambered out to where two small branches lay by the
Ford. He brushed the snow from them and broke them across his
knee, one by one. They were dry in the cold. The snow was falling

again, vertically, in still air. Behind this veil the mountain was like an awful bride. Coulter looked straight up, the flakes falling in his face, then looked down at the sticks held by his hands and wondered what all of this had to do with him.

"Rick?" Arizo called.

He stooped to enter the doorway.

"We best do it quick," Arizo said. "It'll be too dark otherwise."

He flinched at the smell. The way he always did, and it was a moment or two before Coulter's eyes adjusted to the light. When they did, he saw Arizo propped against the far side in the corner by the back door, watching him.

"Supposing it starts to bleed?" Coulter asked.

"How can they? They're dead." Arizo's voice was weak and flat.

Coulter threw the wood ahead of him and climbed into the back, over the seats. He began breaking the branches up.

"Here," Arizo said, "let me help you with that."

When the pieces were small enough, they lit another fire.

Arizo rolled up his pant legs to the knees. "Keep the fire goin'," he said. "We have to keep the knife sterile all along."

Coulter held the blade into the flames and Arizo watched and thought of Sandy spreading sandwiches with it by the piñon trees in the canyon that first day.

"You think this'll be enough?" Coulter asked, turning. When he saw Arizo's face he said, "Jesus, you're cool!"

"It's not so tough."

"I can do it," Coulter said. "It'll be better if I do."

Arizo nodded again. "Take your time," he said. "It's no big deal."

"Where should I start?"

They looked at Arizo's black and swollen feet. Arizo put a finger across the top of the instep, right under the ankle. "You got to get as much of the dead stuff as you can," he said.

Coulter held the knife, ready to cut. His face was sweating.

"Well?"

"This is fuckin' crazy," Coulter said, shaking his head. "I can't do this. You're crazy to think about it."

Arizo compressed his lips and leaned forward. "Here." He held out a hand. "Lemme see that knife."

Dec. 23, 23 days. Both feeling pretty bad. Doesn't seem like Vern got thru. Not much wind today, but cold and cloudy. Thought about Sue-Ellen and Jason. Guess they aren't having much of a Xmas. Pray for Vern, pray someone comes tomorrow.

Coulter didn't mention Arizo's feet. He felt self-conscious about writing anything down because the log was a common one even if he kept it. He didn't really know how Arizo felt about his feet, and he was afraid to ask.

Arizo had quickly given up his idea when the cut began aching and oozing a very dark and viscous blood.

"Jesus!" he said, pulling back the knife.

"What?" Coulter wasn't looking, couldn't look.

"It's bleeding."

"The knife was clean," Coulter said.

Arizo moved for the door.

"Here," said Coulter. "Let me give you a hand."

Arizo shook his head. "I can make it."

Coulter returned to his log: "*Whatever happens, tomorrow will be our last day together in the car,*" he wrote.

Next day it dawned clear. The mountain re-emerged in fresh glitter, and the crows were back along the creek.

"Who knows what those birds find here this time of year," Arizo said. They were sitting on the hood of the car, watching. "I'm goin' down to get us some wood," Coulter announced.

Arizo shook his head. "Stay here an' rest up," he said. "I'm even gonna cook today. It's in my own interest."

Arizo made a stew and after they had eaten, they went back out into the sun and sat together on the roof, facing down the canyon, feet on the hood. The silence was not easy. A time for going had been set; the next thing was the going. All that came between was fill.

Eventually, Coulter said, "You think they're still lookin' for us?"

Arizo sat on his coat with his hands between his legs, round-shouldered, his swollen feet bare. He screwed up his face.

"No," he said. "Maybe weekends, some."

"They must've gave us up for dead."

"I never could work out how come the guy with one eye we saw that night at the ranch never said anything."

"He couldn't have."

"Except he said he was leavin'."

"Whatta you think they're sayin' about us?"

Arizo shifted his weight and looked away, up at the mountain. "That we were goddamn fools, I guess."

"We were, weren't we?"

"People that work for wages are all goddamn fools."

"Yeah?" said Coulter, surprised. "I park the truck at five an' go home an' forget it. Whatta I want with all the shit Pops goes through, an' longer hours?"

"Did you ever try to figure it out another way?"

"I reckoned I could be a stunt man," Coulter said. "I read about it once in *True*, an' I could do it easy."

Arizo nodded. He was thinking of Baby Zeus, but he didn't say anything. Thinking of himself back then it was already as though he were thinking of another person.

"We could sell our story to the movies after we get out." Coulter burst out with the thought as it came to him.

Arizo half-grinned.

"We could get a million bucks. That's what some of them get."

"Yeah?"

"Like those guys on the football team that crashed in the Andes. Remember?"

"Where they ate each other?"

"Yeah."

Arizo saw for an instant a spark in Coulter which reminded him of how much they had changed in the weeks they had been there.

"Whatta you thinkin'?" Coulter asked.

"How we changed from when we first come up here."

Coulter nodded. "It's not ever gonna be the same when we get out either. I keep forgettin' that."

"You forget about Coo-Coo?"

Coulter shook his head.

"I can't believe how it's gonna be for me," Arizo said. "With the hospitals an' everythin'. I was never in one before, except when my pa died."

Coulter nodded, and looked away.

Arizo was thinking about Maxwell. Maxwell never made a fuss. Maybe that was because he drank, or why. At night, when the aching in his feet kept Arizo awake and thoughts crowded him, he wished he had liquor. He noticed it was what he was *not* going to be able to do that preoccupied him.

And he remembered Maxwell. . . .

Maxwell's drinking got so bad that in the end Jolene couldn't watch it anymore and left. Maxwell was sitting in front of the TV watching a Monday-night ball game when Arizo came home from his first job, which was with Union Pacific, and learned Jolene was gone.

Maxwell's soft face under the gray nap of hair looked sad and his eyes were teary, although he didn't cry. He just said that she was right to go and that he missed her already.

Arizo was sixteen then.

The following morning, Maxwell sounded hoarse and announced, as he drank a Rainer's Ale for breakfast, that he was going to the doctor about his sore throat. In the evening when Arizo came home from work, Maxwell said he had some codeine syrup that was fine.

Soon after that, Arizo left the apartment on Campbell Street in Oakland. Union Pacific had track to lay in Bakersfield, so he went down there to live.

"When you git to L.A., fetch me a Dodgers cap," Maxwell said. "I got all these caps, but for some reason I can't figure, I never did get me a Dodgers cap. Can you imagine? That constitutes a serious gap in my collection."

Arizo had been down in San Diego about fourteen months when he got a call from the Veterans Hospital that Maxwell Patterson was seriously ill there. Arizo drove up overnight, worried and angry that Maxwell had said nothing.

Maxwell was in a ward with two other men who were also dying. His bed was in the middle. When Arizo came into the room, the smell hit him. He reeled around and went out into the hallway and threw up. When he came back in, Maxwell didn't seem to have noticed. He looked fragile and gray. There was a white plastic tag around his wrist, and he wore one of those short-sleeved cotton hospital gowns that tie at the back.

"How come you never told me?" Arizo said.

"There wasn't anythin' to say." Maxwell's voice was softer than ever, and he didn't lift his head off the pillow.

"What can I do?"

"You can listen close. I bought a bunch of linens an' towels at the Emporium. They was havin' a sale. I got them real cheap, an' they're in the closet where the heater is."

Arizo nodded impatiently.

"Another thing that's important," Maxwell said. "I jes' had the vacuum cleaner fixed."

"Look, Maxwell—"

"Cost me forty dollar. I busted it 'cause I overheated the motor. I ran it with a bag in there that was too full, an' it overheated an' busted."

Arizo was bursting to interrupt but he didn't. The discourse was oddly sacrosanct. Maxwell had had nothing but time to think of what he wanted most to say, and how he wanted to say it.

A crow squawked by the creek, rousing Coulter, and both men turned their heads and watched its lumbering flight. Arizo spread out his coat and lay back, Maxwell's sallow face before him once more.

"So when you use the thing, be sure an' keep the bag fresh. Check it after you're done. Don't forget now. It's a good cleaner."

"I want to thank you," Arizo said.

Maxwell looked to the men in bed on either side of him and grinned. "You hear that?" he said. "When we get outta here, we gonna get this boy to give us a good party. Right?"

The man on the left winked feebly, the other one appeared to be asleep.

Arizo made himself smile.

"Did you get me that Dodgers cap?" Maxwell asked.

"I did," Arizo lied, "but I left it at the house. I'll bring it to-morrow when I come."

Maxwell nodded. "I gotta get some sleep," he said. "Thanks for comin'." Arizo leaned over and kissed his cheek.

When he came back the following afternoon, Arizo went straight to Maxwell's room, his work boots squeaking on the gray linoleum floor. He had gone out and bought a Dodgers cap. A nurse was bent over the thin black man. Arizo saw where the tops of her white stockings began on her heavy thighs. She stood and turned as he came in, and he saw a hypodermic in her hand. She had blond hair and a puffy face.

"I'm his son," Arizo said and then, when she looked at him strangely and he remembered Maxwell was black, he added, "Sort of."

"You'd better see Dr. Albright," she said.

They went out into the hallway, which was cool and dim and loaded with silence.

Dr. Albright's face was sunken and ashen and overworked, and he bit the corners of his fingernails. They stood by the elevator. "So he didn't tell you?" the doctor said.

"He didn't say nothin' to me."

"I told him ten years ago he'd have to cut down on his drinkin'. We had him in here twice working on his liver, you know. Finally I told him I wasn't going to go on taking hospital space from people who really needed it for someone who was creating his own problems. But he said, and I'll always remember it, 'Doc, you carry on looking after my liver. You're doing a good job, and that ain't what's gonna get me. Something else is.'" A nurse came up and the doctor told her he'd be with her in a moment. "So then he got diabetes."

"I never knew about that either," Arizo said.

Dr. Albright bit at the inside of another nail. "About a year ago, he came to see me with a sore throat, and we found he was shot through with cancer."

Arizo grimaced.

"We wanted to bring him in, but he insisted he was going to stay on in his apartment and go on as long as he could."

"That was his place," Arizo said. "He had the TV an' the ball games an' his beer an' sometimes a neighbor woman would stop by."

The doctor continued, "I told him it was going to get difficult for him and he said it was simple; that when the time came, he'd just give himself an overdose of insulin."

"So what happened?"

"He let himself get too weak to give himself the shot."

"And now?"

"When he came in, he said he wanted to see you, and afterwards he asked me to make him comfortable. That's all."

Arizo shook his head slowly.

It was clear that Dr. Albright liked Maxwell. "When I came in a while ago and saw him sleeping like that," he went on, "I said to him, 'Maxwell, is this really the way you want it? Are you sure?' I want him to wake up and tell me once more that it is. Even though I know there's no alternative, I wish he'd answer me."

"I didn't know anything about it," Arizo said.

The doctor shrugged slightly.

"I should have got that cap earlier."

"He mentioned you were bringing it."

The doctor had ordered Schlesinger's solution for Maxwell: morphine and Thorazine, four grams every two hours. He never woke up. Four days later, Dr. Albright called Arizo to say that it was over.

On the car's hood, Arizo rubbed his eyes and looked about. The sun was slipping and the air beginning to chill.

"I'm goin' inside," Coulter said. Arizo watched him go.

Maxwell never made a whole lot of fuss about dying. Maybe he was sloppy in some ways, but not about losing his life. He went cleanly and didn't make a big thing of it. Dr. Albright had said that kids died that way, not expecting more of life.

Arizo pulled on his coat and prepared to follow Coulter into the Ford. Going back in was something he liked to postpone as long as possible. The sun was falling at his back, and the cold blue shadow was reaching out towards him from the mountain. He had often put Maxwell in to bat for him when it got tough. He'd imagine how Maxwell would handle a situation. After that he could handle it himself without any trouble.

Coulter was huddled in the passenger seat, hands in his coat pockets, shoulders as tense as his face.

"I'm scared about leavin', I tell you," he said as Arizo began to pull himself in through the driver's door.

Arizo stopped and looked at him.

Coulter avoided his eyes. "If it was you an' me, okay. The two of us can handle anythin'. But it's a lotta country out there for a man by himself."

"Depends on the man."

"Vern was one brave sonovabitch the way he went. He said, 'Well, I'll see you in four days,' an' went off."

Arizo came all the way in, raising himself on the seat back and the door frame and swinging his useless feet into position before he lowered himself onto the seat.

"That's the way to do it," he said. "If you start thinkin', you're through."

"It's like buck fever."

"That's right."

Coulter seemed a little cheered at being right.

"The only thing to think is where you're puttin' your foot."

"Yeah."

"You can do it easy."

"I guess so."

"It's both our asses if you don't."

There was a full moon that night. It rode high over the mountain, and the snow and the air glittered blue diamonds. With no cloud cover, the still air was cold beyond belief. When Coulter stepped outside the car, the hair in his nose crackled and froze with his first breath and he knew his spit would freeze before it hit the ground.

He stood in the snow and looked down the canyon, wondering about Vern. Whether he was frozen somewhere like a side of beef or sitting by a fire with a cup in his hand and a glow on his face,

telling the story. He thought of them in Cope, sitting around
their fires in houses half-buried in snow. Shelter was all he, Mike
and Vern needed, and shelter was what they hadn't been able to
get together properly in the car. They hadn't tried living in the
mountains like the Mountain Men used to. They had only waited.
It was like in football, he thought: You get hurt when you were
scared, and that's how they'd been all along. They'd waited to be
hit, and they'd been hit. They'd relied on someone else to get
them out, on machines, as they'd relied on machines to get them
in. They couldn't keep warm. They didn't know how to build a
shelter anymore, how to feed themselves off the land. They didn't
know how to live, only how to work for the man. To get up early
and go to bed early and get drunk Friday.

So Arizo was huddled in the stinking pisshole with his useless,
blackened feet, while he stood here shivering in the snow. They
were crouched down here in the vastness of God Almighty's Rocky
Mountains with their problems so huge inside them there wasn't
room for a damn thing else. Coulter gave a short laugh, rubbed the
tip of his nose, blew on his hands, as he took them from his pockets, and climbed back into the car.

After a while, the thin sound of two men singing poorly came
from shadow thrown by the moon on a canted field of snow, a
thin sound rising up into the mountains that jostled imperceptibly
around them. They sang to obscure this awful scale of time; they
sang to obscure their fear; they sang in defiance; they sang to be
worthy of love; they sang until they could sing no more.

They sang:

> *You'll never know, dear,*
> *How much I love you.*
> *So please don't take my sunshine away.*

They sang:

> *I came from Alabama*
> *With a banjo on my knee,*
> *I'm going to Louisiana*
> *My true love for to see.*

They sang:

> *Irene goodnight, goodnight,*
> *Irene, goodnight*
> *Goodnight Irene, goodnight Irene,*
> *I'll see you in my dreams*
> *Sometimes I live in the country*
> *An' sometimes I live in the town.*
> *An' sometimes I have a great notion*
> *To jump in the river and drown*

They sang all the songs Maxwell had sung as he softshoed about an Oakland kitchen while his lover, a butt end stuck to her lower lip, and the coppery half-caste boy they lived with, clapped in time and grinned.

They sang every scrap of every Christmas carol either could recall, running out early with "Silent Night."

"That's all I remember," Coulter said.

Arizo laughed. "I'm hoarse anyway."

"Not a bad Christmas, considering."

"Whitest I ever had."

"First time I ever cooked Christmas dinner."

Arizo laughed again. "You did good," he said.

They sat in silence. The light from the moon that came weakly through the windows turned the air silvery blue.

"We better turn in," Arizo said. "You got a ways to go in the mornin'."

They lay down beside each other, back to back, touching for warmth. Arizo reached around and put a hand on Coulter's shoulder. "Sleep good," he said.

By mid-morning Coulter was ready to leave. The sun came through a high rack of broken cloud, the soft snow spread smoothly across the broad canyon, and all the shapes it made were symmetrical and round. It was terrain as hostile and yet pleasing to the eye as any on earth. Coulter stood in the snow a few feet from the car, beguiled by this beauty. Now that the time had come to leave, he felt for a moment, oddly calm, with none of the frustration and urgency that had filled him all the other while he had been here. Suddenly, on this bright morning, he had no desire to start out, to begin anything, until he had marked the ending of something else.

Arizo's call broke his reverie. "Trade coats with me," he said. "Mine's warmer." Coulter shook his head, but Arizo insisted. He also insisted that Coulter take his .30-30 since Coulter wanted a weapon, and it was considerably lighter than Coulter's own .303.

Arizo came out painfully and sat on the hood of the car. He pointed up the hill. "Stay by the timberline, like Vern did," he said. "Stay out of the deep snow all you can. When you get to the Big Lost that'll take you out."

Coulter nodded. "I left you the log," he said. "I got another pad. There's a pencil in the glove compartment."

"Good," Arizo said.

Coulter seemed to hesitate a little. He turned away. Then he said, "What's it like when you're freezin'? I mean, what do you feel?"

"Good," Arizo said. "You get real sleepy an' warm."

"That's all?"

"Far as I know."

Coulter shifted his weight in the snow a few feet from the car. "Well, I guess that's all," he said.

"Don't go tryin' to figure things out all the while," Arizo advised. "Sometimes you can't ever see the answer if you're tryin' to figure it. Gets your brain all full of stuff and keeps you too busy to get an answer."

Coulter remained silent.

"Too much figurin' an' you'll forget where you are," Arizo added gently.

"I know what you mean."

"Bear it in mind," he said. "There ain't nothin' else to say."

Arizo held out a hand. Coulter shook it.

"See ya," Arizo said. "An' if I don't see you in four days—good luck."

"In four days."

Coulter turned and started up the hill, the rifle over his shoulder. By the time he reached the shoulder he was out of breath. The thin air hurt his lungs. He felt dizzy, and the thought of going on was ridiculous. He turned around and stopped. Against the trees, a few yards below him, was the half-buried truck, its windows shattered. Somewhere just beyond lay Coo-Coo.

The sun had wetted the mountain face and the gray Ford was a blemish on the dazzling white apron beneath. Where its blunt tail divided the wind, sickle-shaped troughs were spread out in the snow like whiskers on a white cat's face. Arizo was a small dark figure perched on the hood. Coulter saw an arm raise and slowly wave. He hesitated a moment, then waved back once, turned abruptly, and went on, keeping the trees close by his right.

Part IV

WILD HORSE

For some time after the figure vanished, Arizo sat on the hood of the car staring across the great bowl of the canyon up at the mountain that thrust like an old tooth from a jaw of boulders. This was his place now, his piece of earth. He and the mountain were at last alone, and he felt greatly satisfied. He could be with the mountain as he would. He could concentrate upon it spared of the considerations that must go with company. In another way, too, he was glad to be alone. He could deal more easily with the fact of his feet, for nothing was wrong now that he was alone. Nobody walked. Nobody ran. No one shrank at the sight, for there was none. Nothing was compounded; there was no progress forward or back. There was nothing to judge himself by and no one to comfort him if he should cry.

When it started to blow, he shivered and, working along the fender hand over hand to the door, pulled himself back inside the car.

He was breathing sharply by the time he was done. Back

propped against the seats, he lay with the whole mattress and all
the covers to himself. He could hear the wind picking up and,
lying there, he saw Coulter moving slowly through lightly falling
snow, a small, dark shadow against the trees, uncertain. And he
remembered him saying, "You an' me, we can handle anythin'."

Arizo blinked and snuffled and wiped his wet nose on the back
of a sleeve, staring up at the ice that sheathed the gray ceiling
above him and the cracked plastic cover of the broken courtesy
light. "You an' me, we can handle anythin'," he repeated. Coulter
had said that before. He had said that one Friday night in the bar
where they had cashed their checks. King McGarth, who owned
the place, worked the bar on Fridays. McGarth was a big red-
haired German Scot who smacked men around like boys when
they made trouble. Coulter liked to help him, wading into a fight,
black hat riding on the back of his shoulders, forearms like four-
by-fours, eyes glistening. Arizo would leave after a couple of
drinks. The mere sight of his copper skin was enough to trigger a
fight. Coulter generally ignored this and teased him about wanting to get back to Sandy.

"A man needs to save his strength for the real thing," he'd say.
And to McGarth: "Give this man one for the road, King, he's got
a helluva night ahead of him."

Arizo had wanted to protest, and sometimes he even felt close
enough to Coulter to tell him how it was for him. He almost had
in the beginning. But after it had begun to get better, he was
grateful he hadn't.

One night he had said to Coulter, "Women'll kill you."

Coulter had looked at him and grinned. "That's right," he said.
"An' you know anythin' around here that's better to do, an' I'll do
it with you."

Arizo finished his drink and set his glass down on the bar. "I'm
gone," he said.

That was when Coulter had said it. "Someday you should stay,"
he said. "We could handle it, you an' me. Us two together, we
could handle anythin'."

Arizo had left then. Gone through the door and let it swing
behind him, abruptly shutting off the sound from the bar and

pushing him into the dark. He stood a moment on the high sidewalk looking down into an empty Main Street. The traffic light,
strung on a cable level with his eye above the intersection, clicked
green. It swung gently in the night wind that came down from
the mountains to chase among the dark houses and run away out
onto the plain. An illuminated display in the window of the hardware store across the empty street jiggled repetitively.

He drew breath and watched Maxwell coming towards him, a
little unsteady on the uneven sidewalk, reaching out a hand to
sometimes touch a building. Maxwell, dead for years now. Where
was he if not here? Home?

Home? Where was home if not here, if not with him in this
half-empty town? In any half-empty town, where the shadows
made him uneasy and things unseen compounded trouble for
him. Decay was in things compounded. They should go on, this
woman and he. That was what he had felt. But where to? He
shivered and turned up his collar and put his hands back into his
pockets. What had he learned, if not that one place was as good
as any other? He walked slowly around the side of the building to
the parking lot. If not that you couldn't take anyone along with
you. He climbed stiffly into the Ford.

Through this very ice-crusted door he now stared at how he had
come. He had closed it by that handle and started the engine and
driven home to Sandy, abandoning all to forgetfulness. He had
come to her and she had run to him, across the cabin, calling his
name, kissing him a welcome home.

Home. He began to cry.

                                                              •

Coulter would have told you it was the physical dangers he
feared, and it was these he was alluding to when he told Arizo in
the Ford that he was afraid because "there's a lot of country out
there for one man." But far more dangerous to a man in Coulter's
condition were things he might suspect and fear, yet in reality
know nothing of. Buried in Coulter's remark was clearly the seed
of understanding, but it remained intuitive—that is, subconscious
—and when things began to take hold of him, it was too late for

him to do anything. For the first thing to go was judgment, and the next, reason itself.

He was hungry and weak and scared from the moment he came over the second shoulder and saw the same thing Poulsen had seen: the extent of the Basin stretched out at his feet. It was more or less a circle formed by a ring of mountains. He could just make out the mountains on the farthest edge. The way out lay through them, through the mouth of a valley that was just a shadow from here. He must cross the Basin to reach it. He could not keep to the rim; he would have to go down into the deep snow at some point because the valley crossed the Basin, too, and was apparent only as a faint depression where it crossed the center of the ring. Down there in the Basin, he knew, beneath the evenness, the snow had drifted into gullies fifty and sixty feet deep.

Like a horse that shies, he breathed out sharply and lifted his head. His feet ached with cold. Curiously, he lifted one boot up out of the snow and looked at it, cocking his head sideways. And then, as if by some signal, he turned and began walking again. But with three slow steps, he felt the snow give way and sank to his thigh on one side. He panicked a little, afraid that all might go. His other leg broke through, and suddenly he was in up to his hips. He shouted in alarm and anger.

Bent forward from the waist, he literally crawled out on his hands and knees. He tried to stand, and in a moment broke through the crust again and was floundering. He swore shrilly and, half-walking, half-wading, he managed to get closer to the trees where the snow was harder packed. As he reached them, he came out of the snow like a wader reaching a shelf. He stood there gasping, looking down at the disarrayed tracks he had left. He was hot now, sweating and trembling. He put his hands under his armpits and hugged himself and blew a freezing drop from the end of his nose. When the adrenaline wore off, he felt exhausted and sat down in the snow and looked out numbly from the ridge, neck buried in his shoulders, hands still beneath his armpits. Then he lay back against the snow, still panting, and looked up at the clouds. The sun seemed likely to break through the overcast. The

glare was strong. He closed his eyes against it and at once realized
how badly he wanted to sleep.

But he mustn't sleep. Mike had warned him about that. And
Mike was depending on him. An image came to him of Arizo
waiting, hovering over useless feet in the semidarkness of the
stinking Ford, listening. He sat up quickly. The image frightened
him, and the fear turned to anger against Arizo.

"Fuck it!" he cried in an exhausted voice and lay back against
the snow once more and closed his eyes. He just wanted sleep.
If he were by himself, he could have slept anyway. But he opened
his eyes finally, before it was too late, and forced himself to his
feet. The immense Basin was still there. He hadn't gotten closer
to anything while he rested. His teeth began to chatter. It seemed
so hopeless when he looked at the size of it and thought how long
it had taken him to come just the last few yards. If he had a thousand years, it wouldn't be enough, he thought. And as he thought
this, he looked down at himself and realized that he was not simply cold, but that his clothes were stiffening on him. Fresh panic
set in, and he hastily took another step, watching the leg sink to
the knee, pulling up the other, lifting it high and around slightly
as a man may do when walking quickly in surf. He must keep
moving. He cautiously shifted his weight from one leg to the
other, watching each action intently, lips pressed together, arms
held out for balance, talking aloud, cajoling, warning, encouraging
himself, moving like a mechanical man.

He stuck as close to the trees as he could, sometimes grasping
the branches that swept down. He took to going from one tree to
another, selecting a particular tree not too far off and then pausing when he got to it, triumphant, providing himself with a constant incentive. Each time he stopped, he would stand and lick
his lips and look around for some sign of Poulsen's passing. But
any tracks were long since buried by snow and brushed over by
wind.

He thought about Poulsen. He would look out across the Basin
for a tiny black figure. He knew it wouldn't be there but he
looked anyway. For he would have given anything to have been
with someone then. If Mike hadn't screwed up so bad with his

feet, if he'd listened to what Vern had told him, they'd all be together now. They'd have a better chance together, he thought.
But at the thought of Arizo he went on again, feeling guilty and
confused.

He passed the spot where Poulsen had begun his disastrous descent three days before. His legs felt heavy now, and he was walking even more slowly. He chose trees that were closer together as
his mark and he rested longer, but it didn't really help. His stomach felt sick and empty. It was not with hunger. He was so used
to hunger that he paid it no attention. In any event, he was not
starved in his belly anymore. The hunger had gone beyond that.
Now the hunger was around his mouth, the mark of true hunger.
The feeling in his belly came from a sense of utter hopelessness.

Still he went on. He became like a man walking in his sleep. He
moved slowly, deliberately, obsessively. His mouth slipped open;
his look was fixed on the snow a few feet ahead of him. As he
went, he no longer looked around. He was too tired to be curious
any longer. Only one thing concerned him and that intermittently: a place to descend from the ridge. He would have to
leave it. It was beginning now to curl away in the opposite direction from the drainage in the Basin, away from the shadow of the
valley mouth on the far side. Still he delayed going down. Whenever it came to him that he should, he would look down the slope
and then go on, promising aloud to Arizo—not to himself, but to
Arizo—that soon the ridge would come around and he would be
on his way.

But it didn't. And now he was headed almost south instead of
north. When he realized he was going in the opposite direction, he
slumped down in the snow again and sat with his arms wrapped
about his knees and his face pressed against them. He stayed this
way, crablike, for some time, struggling against the driving force
of Arizo.

At last he looked up with reprieve on his face. He had to eat.
That was it. He felt in the pocket of his coat and took out some
half-cooked meat wrapped in plastic. His fingers were trembling
badly and were difficult to control. He took off one glove and

unwrapped the meat, staring intently at it, and when he ate it he chewed it fast and long and looked about self-consciously.

He left the business of making himself a snow-hole until it was late, refusing to believe there was no alternative. When it was almost dark, he found a place. He was cutting through a firebreak in the firs when, on the downhill side, he saw a drift about shoulder height built up against a stand of young trees. He moved hesitantly towards it, eyes wide open, and very tentatively began to dig.

When he was finished, it was dark. The moon rose and climbed above the firs to shine down into the break and make faint shadows in Coulter's fresh tracks. It lit a small breath that drifted from a blowhole in the bank, turning to steam as it hit the cold air.

Coulter fought to keep awake, afraid that if he fell asleep in clothes still damp in spots, he would freeze to death. For a little while, he was successful, but then his breathing slowly became deeper and more rhythmical, until it was like the sound of surf.

He dreamed of walking along a sweep of beach under a gray sky. There was heavy surf. The waves rose vertically before they broke. To his left, the salt grass bound the dunes and now, from these, appeared a man, walking directly towards the sea, too far off for Coulter clearly to see his face. At the shore, the man paused and then walked on. Coulter saw the small waves slap his thighs and then a larger breaker rear over him and knock him down. He got up again, the water running off his clothes, and went on, arms held out, ducking one wave but caught by its backwash and dragged out to be buried violently by the next. He surfaced and swam a few halfhearted strokes and then Coulter saw, strangely close, the face upturned towards the gray light, the open mouth and water pouring in.

Lifeguards brought the man in, carrying his limp body up the beach, laying it near Coulter and leaving. He looked down at the face. It was Arizo. Coulter was not surprised.

"What did you do that for?" he asked.

Arizo looked up at him. "Don't let's talk about that," he said. "There isn't enough time."

Coulter understood. This was a privileged glimpse at that inter-
lude between death and the final departure of the spirit, and he
was excited and eager to know of the secrets of death.

"What's it like?" he asked.

Arizo looked openly at him. "I'm sorry to get you into this," he
said.

"You mean what you just did?"

"Yeah."

Coulter frowned and sat beside him. "I'm not involved, I was
just walkin'," he said.

"Yeah, but you are now."

"No I'm not."

"They're gonna blame you for this."

Coulter shook his head, but Arizo only said, "I'm sorry about it,
buddy. Believe me."

"No," Coulter yelled. "It's not my goddamned fault. You did
it. I saw you. No!" And he came bursting up from his sitting position, exploding out of the hole, snow falling over his head and
shoulders. Out into the light he came with a look of terror, shouting, "No, no, no!"

He stumbled and fell forward on his face in the snow and lay
still a moment. When he raised his head, he saw it was daylight
and snowing. There was a gentle but chilling wind. Slowly he got
to his feet. He was cold and stiff and it didn't feel as though he'd
slept. Brushing off the snow, he looked about, biting his cracked
lips and squinting against the glare. All traces of his tracks were
gone. He looked down at himself. Something was missing.

"The rifle!" he cried in astonishment, looking about. He struggled clumsily to the trees beside the ruins of his hole, then turned
back as if remembering something else.

"Shit!" he shouted, stooping, groping about beneath the fresh
layer of snow. "Shit!"

He searched in growing panic until he was exhausted and then
remembered: he must not sweat. He felt fresh horror, grim and
overwhelming, and collapsed panting in the snow.

"Jesus!" he kept saying. The fear fed ratchetlike upon itself,
slanted teeth catching on a pawl. Then he saw the rifle as he was

sitting, hung from a branch where he had put it the night before. Angry but relieved, he went over and picked it off and went on, frustrated at how slowly he must walk, wanting desperately to be out of this place. A small avalanche fell into the snow from a tree behind him, landing with a soft thump. He brought the rifle to his hip and swung about as rapidly as he could, in a clumsy movement, searching for the source of the sound. Dry-mouthed and tense, he waited. He had definitely heard something; something was there. He swore and fired a round into the closest snow cover. Nothing moved, but he felt comforted by the sound of the shot and walked on, occasionally turning quickly without warning to look behind him. Once he crouched behind a tree for twenty minutes, watching his own trail.

It continued to snow. In windless air the giant flakes floated thickly down. The only sounds were the squeak of new snow compressed beneath Coulter's boots at each step, and his coarse breathing and muttering. Occasionally he stopped to listen, holding his breath. He could neither see nor hear anything, but he was certain something or someone was coming after him, tracking him, perhaps. Sometimes he would make small detours, climbing up the ridge a short way, panting and struggling fiercely in the slippery powder, then stop and crouch down to watch and listen in absolute silence. Once as he hid he screamed out, "All right!" and then looked about. But the sound was swallowed, and he was only made to feel more hounded and alone.

The ridge was shrinking now. There were no more trees, and it was small enough so that he could walk along the spine and see below him on both sides the deep snow on the Basin floor. He was like a man walking out into the ocean on a breakwater that was gradually lowering him into the surf.

When this became obvious to him, he stopped and for some time was undecided. Then he turned and began intently going back as one confidently rectifying a mistake. But then, just as suddenly, he stopped and looked up the ridge, studying it through a moving curtain of snow, straining against the silence.

Now he took several more steps and stopped again, holding his breath, mouth agape, eyes straining, a gloved hand cupping his ear forward, the other clutching his rifle by the stock. He licked his lips and stuck his head forward an inch, as if he heard something. Then he pulled his head back and yelled, "Mike!" And again "Mike!"—longer the second time, and then listened. When there was no answer, he shuffled forward a little way and shouted again. Then, peering still, struggling to keep his balance on the steep slope he floundered back the way he had come, a few steps before he paused again and looked up.

"Go back, Mike!" he shouted. "Go back. We can't get through this way. We can't make it." He took a few more hurried steps, swearing and muttering incoherently. Then, without pausing, he called over his shoulder as he went, "Mike, I'm doin' the goddamn best I can. You understand?"

He paused, as if to give time for a reply, and then called out again, "You got to listen—you won't make it in the snow down there. It gets real deep. You won't make it, Mike—I'm tellin' you." Panting, he paused, looking up the ridge, waiting for some reply.

It was snowing harder now. Visibility was no more than ten or twelve feet, and there was still no wind whatsoever.

Again he stopped. "Don't bug me, man," he called. "Go back an' leave me be—okay? I'll get us outta here, Mike, but don't bug me."

No answer. He stood, crouched slightly, unsure of what to do. He turned this way and then that. Deprived of sleep, of food, of human contact, of any usual sound or feel or sight or touch by which it ordinarily monitored and constructed reality, Coulter's exhausted and bewildered mind had begun constructing a reality of its own. Had he been more fortunate, this reality might have been an amicable one, but it was not. Arizo was at his back, driving him. Or so he imagined. And before him and all around lay a sea of soft, drifting snow that could close over him any time and leave no trace.

Looking about him, as if to be sure he was unseen, he now started directly down the side of the hill. He took a few staggering, sliding steps and then fell. When he tried to stand, he actually came up at right angles to the hill and fell again. The third time, still absurdly insisting on trying to stand at right angles to the steep slope, he fell back. The rifle struck him and the forward sight cut into his scalp behind his ear. He rolled over onto his knees, leaning forward, holding his head, wincing in pain, the blood running between his fingers and dripping onto the snow. He stayed thus, not knowing what to do, not knowing what had happened, not understanding why he couldn't get onto his feet. He was bitterly afraid and angry—sure now that nature herself was involved in an active conspiracy against him. He had no idea that he could not stand because, with all visual references to the horizontal removed, the weight of his limbs was no longer enough to tell him which way was up.

He kept trying to stand until, as if to reinforce his notion of a conspiracy, the snow thinned and the cloud began clearing as fast as it had come.

Coulter straightened up in his kneeling position to watch the cloud's retreat. It revealed a brilliant sunset, golden at the core, spreading outward in vague bands of ruby, opal, jade, and turquoise. He stared, childlike.

The sun was half-behind the peak, within moments of going, when he caught the flash below in the Basin to his right. His head swiveled. The flash came again, blazing for an instant, and then was gone. He was left with bits floating before his dazzled eyes and he rubbed them and shook his head and looked again.

It was a roof—perhaps half a mile away and two hundred feet below.

He saw it joyously at first and then with suspicion. He got onto his belly, unslung his rifle and peered at the roof like a scout. Finally he rose and, still in a crouch, clambered, hurrying as best he could, along the ridge to get a better view of it.

For a long while he sat on his haunches in the snow on the side of the ridge and watched and waited. Only after the short twilight had given way to darkness and the moon had come up and hung large and low above the mountains, did Coulter start down the ridge again, towards the building he had seen.

At a hundred yards, he worked the bolt on his rifle and slipped the safety, although there was no light visible in the building. At half that distance, he could see that it was an aluminum trailer house with a small wooden awning over a door in the side. Snow had drifted to its waistline. The moon behind threw the house's face into shadow. The snow sparkled dully; the only sound was the dry, soft crunch of freezing powder.

He roughly cleared the four steps with the butt of his rifle, mounted them, and tried the door. When it didn't open, he stepped down and shot out the lock, feeling oddly guilty as he did so. The shot rang in his ears. He pushed the door open with the muzzle of his rifle. There was no sound inside, no movement. He stepped in. In the blue moonlight he saw a very ordinary trailer house: a table with bench seats to the left of the door, opposite a sink, sideboard, and stove. He turned on the light switch. Nothing happened. He stepped over to the stove, still clutching his rifle and turned on a tap. No sound. He swore, then began rummaging through the closets and drawers above and below the sideboard, pulling things out, slamming drawers and cupboard doors, muttering, until he found a flashlight. He held it up, looking at it closely, and turned it on. It worked. Still muttering, he put down his rifle and went out through the open door and searched about in the snow beside the walls until he found the butane tank. He turned on the tap and came quickly back, slamming the door closed behind him. Now he found matches and lit all four burners on the stove, opened the oven door, lit it, too, and left it open.

He stood over the rings of blue flame, orange at the tip, looking as though he'd never seen fire before. He smiled and held his hands out over them. The light lit his face from below, leaving only the socket of each eye in shadow.

The door banged open behind him. He felt the grope of cold air, saw the circles of flame waver on the stove, and spun around, fear turning to anger. He lost his balance and crashed into the flimsy table. Recovering, he kicked the door shut, but it blew open immediately. This time he took a chair, wedged its top beneath the knob, and stood there panting.

He could get no light and find no candles, but in the blue glow from the stove he turned to the cupboards above the counter and took down two cans of Campbell's rice and tomato soup, a large can of cling peaches in heavy syrup, and two tall cans of Coors beer. He opened a beer and then the other cans and, without pausing to sit, consumed it all, draining the syrup from the can with his head tipped back, the thick liquid spilling through his beard as it overflowed his mouth. Nothing had ever tasted this good to him before. Nothing. He wiped his mouth on the back of his sleeve. It was starting to warm up in the trailer now. There was heat in his belly, heat blowing all around him, and, like any animal, Coulter was less dangerous now that he had eaten. He looked about him and belched. He didn't feel so great, he decided.

Maybe it would be better lying down. He walked across the living room, consciously treading on the carpet in the little hallway, feeling the pile under his boots, touching the walls on either side of him. It was unreal.

In the back bedroom, by the dim moonlight, he saw blankets folded in a stack on the bed. He threw himself down without even removing his boots and pulled all of them over him.

Suddenly he was awake, lying on his back, rigid, straining for a sound. He came up on one elbow and held his breath. There was just the slightest wind. Doubtfully, slowly, he lay back again, feeling his heart racing and the dryness in his mouth. Something, he somehow knew, had made a noise out there. It came again—a thump. Then another. Muffled, scraping, thumping sounds. To his horror, he heard the door rattle and the banging of the chair as it fell to the floor. He tried to swallow. In the first instance, he knew it was a man. Quickly his logic told him it was a bear, but still he knew it was a man.

He scooped his rifle up and worked the bolt. There was a great roaring in his ears. He did not breathe. The hair on his neck was stiff. He moved down the short hallway to the living room, the rifle before him, prodding at the air.

Someone stood in the living room, close by the open door. In the blue light from the rings still burning on the cooker, a figure, shadowy and huge, leaned on a staff. The shaggy head was wrapped about the temple with a thick band of cloth that hung before the eyes and fell at the sides into hair and beard. Its bulky awful presence filled the room and as he came in the figure turned towards him, pivoting awkwardly. Coulter heard a peculiar thump and saw that one leg was wrapped in strips of torn cloth that bound sticks to make a crude splint. The blue light was reflected in burning eyes ringed with black shadow, wide as they beheld him. The arms came slowly up, letting go the staff, which fell with a clatter, and the figure lunged towards him. "Hoi!" it called out. "It'th me."

Coulter stopped dead and screamed: "Get back. *Get back!*"

But the figure took another step.

Coulter fired from the hip.

The figure called out again. It may have been something intelligible—even Coulter's name. It may have been protest, surprise, or pain. But Coulter was beyond listening and, to maintain order, he maniacally worked the bolt, the spent case bouncing with a hollow sound on the plastic tabletop, and fired again. The figure had started to double over with the first shot, but now jerked up, making a supreme effort, and grasped for the doorway.

Its hand missed.

Coulter saw it wave emptily in the air for an instant. Then the figure swiveled to its left into the open doorway, and Coulter shot into its side, driving it out of the trailer. Falling, the figure disappeared below the level of the doorstep. As it fell, Coulter got off a final round.

Then it was gone.

Coulter walked to the doorway and looked down. The black figure lay half on its face at the foot of the steps. The snow was bluish in moonlight. Feeling an enormous tension gone from him, Coulter sat on the step, rifle clutched against his body, and looked out across the plain of snow. It was flat and shining, pale and soft as porcelain, rising gently to a rim of shadowy mountains like barricades on the horizon. Gratefully, he breathed in the cold, clear air and closed his eyes. A slurping, gurgling sound came unexpectedly from the figure at his feet. It was loud and rude in the silence, and it shocked and disgusted him. Angrily he went down the steps, took the figure by the leg that was not splinted, and, straining, leaning away from the heavy form, dragged it over the snow, sinking in with each step, hauling it around the back of the trailer. There he threw down the leg and walked back to the doorway, panting slightly, noticing a dark trail of blood in the snow. When he came back to the stoop he sat again, looking to recapture the feeling he had had. But it was gone. And he got up annoyed and went inside, closing the door, and back to bed. He could rest without fear now. "That's took care of it," he said.

He lay down and covered himself again, still not bothering to remove his coat or boots. But he soon began to feel violently nauseous, and his temperature rose. He sweated and was afraid. He lay still, hoping it would pass, but it didn't. And soon he got up and went quickly to the bathroom and vomited into the toilet, retching until his stomach hurt and he felt so bad he wanted to die. He was sick, vomiting intermittently for several hours afterwards. It was almost dawn before he drifted into an exhausted clammy sleep.

Late in the morning Coulter woke, his stomach sore from retching, his toes aching. He sat up on the bed and took off his coat and then his boots and socks. His toes were frostbitten, pulpy, the skin cracked and bleeding. He looked at them in disbelief. "Sonovabitch," he said. And said it again. He looked about, then got up and went next door into the bathroom. There was a sink and a shower stall and a mechanical toilet. He found Band-Aids and Bactine, and standing with one foot at a time on the sink, he patched the damaged toes. Then he went back into the bedroom and put his socks on. He felt wretched and worn beyond exhaustion, but it was at least warm in the trailer. He made tea. He didn't feel like eating anything. He took the tea and sat at the table by the window and looked out. It was overcast now and snowing gently. He wondered about going out into it. He wondered about his feet. Maybe he should rest up some. It would be better to rest up some than to go out there and blow it. Better for Mike, he thought.

Arizo had suddenly become a far less urgent issue for Coulter. Less real, too. The trailer, the warmth, and the food were what was real for him now. The reality of everything that had occurred before he woke that morning seemed as shadowy as if he had emerged from a high fever that had left his mind a jumble. He was out of it now—why should he want to go back?

Instead he thought about his son. He sat at the table sipping his tea, nursing the warm mug in his hands, staring off into space. He must raise his son in the Mormon faith. He must begin to instruct him immediately and go with him regularly to the temple now that he had been delivered like this from the mountains. It was a miracle, he thought. "I never figured to be involved in a miracle," he said aloud. Then he went back into the bedroom and lay down. When he woke it was dark, and he was shocked and utterly disoriented for some moments. He got up and heated himself some soup and then went back to bed and slept again.

The next morning he found topo maps of the whole Basin in a drawer. He was at Wild Horse, a summer ranger station. The car was in Muldoon Canyon, eight miles away. It was close enough to take food back, he thought, but then he remembered the journey. He had to follow the east fork of the Big Lost to get out. There were two cabins along the fork marked on the map. The third place, a dude ranch at Devil's Bedstead, was marked as having a phone and being open all winter. It was seventeen miles.

"That's a piece of cake," he said when he had worked it out. "I can be there tomorrow. Or anyway the day after." He went to the window and looked out. It was snowing harder than before. He sat on the bed and tried to pull on his boots, but his toes had swollen and it was too painful. He limped to the window. The weather was getting worse. He wouldn't go anywhere today, he thought. He lay back down on the bed and drifted off.

The more he stayed, the less real it all became. His feet were still too swollen the following day and the day after. He slept a great deal and ate sparingly after the first glutting experience. He seldom thought of Arizo. He was doing what he could, he thought. It was no use going out there and getting wasted. That wouldn't do any good for either of them. He had to be cool. Unless Poulsen had made it, he was the last chance.

For the most part he drifted in silence, eating and sleeping and being warm and released from pressure. He would have to live alone when he got out; at least he'd have to have his own cabin.

On the fourth day he went outside. His feet were sore as hell, but he'd managed to get the boots on. He saw there was a flagpole before the cabin. He went back in and found a flag and hung it upside-down as a distress signal.

Shortly before lunch, he left. He took a couple of cans of lunch meat and an opener, although it was only seven miles to the Johnson Ranch. The snow was soft and deep. He had forgotten just how difficult and strenuous it was. After a few hundred yards, he became very discouraged and stopped. He looked back, then up, hung between going on and returning. Finally, when he thought that what he must have was snowshoes, he was grateful to return to the trailer.

He spent the afternoon making snowshoes from plywood shelving, ate more than usual that night, and went to bed early. The following day the weather was bad again, with visibility down to a few yards, and he stayed inside. It wasn't until the morning of the sixth day that he sallied forth again. That morning he wrote in his log: "*Jan. 2. Going on down today. Have dumped out all food in the trailer. Don't want Mike to get sick like I did if he gets here.*"

He closed the trailer door behind him and strapped on his makeshift snowshoes. There was a little light cloud, very high, and a mild wind at his back. He slipped fairly easily over the snow, his legs feeling strong again. To his immense satisfaction, the snowshoes worked well.

Late that afternoon, the driver's window of the Ford wound down. Through the falling snow, Arizo's round face appeared in the black space, peering out cautiously, anxiously, with a look only half-expectant. It was barely possible to make out the shadow of the creek. The mountain was gone, whited out. Arizo stared bleakly for some time and then wound the window up and dragged himself into the back once more. Leaning against the wall on the driver's side, he wrote slowly on a small notepad in pencil, pausing after each word to blow on his fingers.

When he had finished, he held it to the light and read it again very slowly, his lips moving to form the words: "*Dec. 27—Very cold last night. Doubt Rick made it. Pray for him. He has great courage. No wood left for fire, no matches. They will not come today.*" Then he put the pencil back in his pocket and laid the pad carefully under one of the seat blocks they had used to support the hubcap when they made a fire. He lay down on his back, pulled the blankets under his chin, and stared open-eyed at the ceiling. He decided to think of the evening of the first day they had spent together. He didn't allow himself to do this very often because he was afraid the memory would wear thin and become commonplace. To reminisce was now his luxury.

They were in the cabin, and he heard it begin to rain. The first large drops splattered hesitantly against the tarpaper roof. He sat cross-legged on the rug before the fire beside her, looking up at the sound. She sat on her feet at right angles to him, watching his face. When he looked at her and reached out an arm, she came eagerly. They kissed, and her gentleness quickly flared to passion. He followed her, caught at first halfway between acting and desire, aware he was moving precipitously towards the point where that revelation that governed so much of his life was inevitable, aware that he was at last refusing to deny himself whatever it was that was there for him.

But before it was reached, they stopped and she hid her face in his neck. When he lifted her chin, her eyes were wet. He kissed them and pushed back the fine dark hair stuck to her cheek with a forefinger that trembled. They lay down on the rug, and, though they held each other, he felt at a great distance from her, for he saw, for the first time, the power in him—the power grown unfelt in one come to equilibrium from full experience, and thus no longer much moved by that alone. It was the power of father and child. Yet, paradoxically, this same power drew him closer to her than to anyone who had been before because it brought him the perspective to see and honor the unique coincidence they formed in time.

In that moment, he knew they were as close as was possible for two separate beings. It was an achievement without which a life would pass empty, no matter how rich or long. Then he had been humbled. Now he was thankful and made content. Here at least he had gone to the limit of experience. There was nothing to regret.

Silent, she had held him. He felt her tone and quickness, and they were powerfully driven to seek each other as complementary parts of a whole, divided in time lost. They sought to absorb each other, chasing, nuzzling. They rolled back languidly, and her passion was so full and contagious that it carried him at last beyond the remonstrations of his mind.

When she sat up beside him to pull off her shirt, he saw the smooth, young muscle of her broad back, and he reached out like a child to touch it. He would never forget that moment. She turned slowly and with a tumbling of breasts, lay across him. He felt the unbridled milk-warm softness of her, and he allowed the pleasure, experiencing it once more with the incredulity of a virgin.

Yet, when she touched him, his body stiffened reflexively.

She hesitated and looked at him.

"I'm too tense," he whispered.

She kissed him. She did everything a woman may, but to his dismay, he felt himself regarding her caresses as a challenge and not a pure pleasure. He was in conflict with himself and became desperate and angry.

"It's no use," he whispered.

"It's okay. I don't mind," she lied. "I can wait."

She turned him over on his belly and rhythmically massaged his back, feeling broad straps of muscle slowly release, tracing invisible pathways with her fingertips as she straddled him. For more than an hour she stroked him until he was more asleep than awake. Then she put more wood on the fire and lay beside him in the warm light, an arm across him.

"Good?" she whispered.

"Mmmm." He turned his face towards her and barely opened his eyes.

She kissed him very softly and he reached for her, forgetting himself at last, rolled on his back. They moved easily, lightly against one another, arched, hollowed, barely touching and then powerfully together. They were like dancers together, strong but infinitely gentle. When she cried out softly, they were still and he was amazed at the release that came to him through hers, at what existed beyond what he had always thought was the end. He wondered what other worlds there were in him he did not know of. He saw the wetness gleam on her and the fireglow between the rafters.

"You're unbelievable," she whispered. "You know that?"

He smiled with satisfaction. "How's that?"

"You gotta be the only man in America that doesn't think that if he can't get a hard-on, he can't be a man."

"I just now found it out myself," he said.

They laughed, delighted.

The wind squalled and rain swept over the cabin, a murmur rising to a brief fury against the windows. He had seen it out in the night, the rain, splashing the upturned faces of the mountains above them, trickling down gaunt cheeks to quicken the slack river that flowed blackly beside the place where they lay.

When she went to work he watched her dress, then dressed himself, pulled on his jacket, and went walking by the river in the dark. The sky was clearing, the rain had passed, and the drenched ground gave off a fresh scent. He walked the path beside the river, brushing back the willow branches in the darkness, seeing the lights of town up on the bluff to his left. He walked slowly, feeling the wind gentle on his face, the earth give under his step, the flexing of his legs, his confidence. We run about the earth so importantly, he thought, all puffed up, too busy even to see where we are, to see that it's enough just to be here. He saw her face. He still felt her. Even now he could feel her. She spoke to him beyond words. There was a harmony created between them. And when he was not with her, the thought of her made his whole being vibrate like a flywheel out of balance. And only she could reach out a finger and still him with a touch.

The wind was getting up again in Muldoon Canyon. He lay listening to it for a while, his hands behind his head. Maybe they should have buried the whole car in snow right at the start, he thought. That way they would have been insulated. But then no one would have seen them. Well, they hadn't anyway.

Sandy Brown had green eyes. Sandy Brown. He thought about
her name. The sound of it. What the sound represented. Her eyes
were that warm, oily green of old turquoise worn a long time next
to the skin. He'd told her once, sitting over the table at home. She
blushed.

"I try not to think about it," she said. "You know, how I look."

"Yeah? I think your eyes is the best part of you. The prettiest.
They're a little sad though."

"Maybe." She looked at him directly and they smiled together
and nothing else existed.

"When I lived in New Mexico," she said, "I went a whole year
without a mirror in the house."

That's how she was.

By January 2 it had been six days since Arizo had eaten. On
that date he wrote in his journal: "*Worse night than last. Can't
stop worrying about Rick. Wind all night and snow heavy all day.
Made plans for the future with God's help. Found God today and
the way for the rest of my life.*"

At first God had been simply that young Jesus his Aunt Jolene
worshiped: golden-haired, blue-eyed, radiant. His aunt was a
Catholic. She had a shrine to Jesus in the bedroom where she and
Maxwell slept. A small wooden thing with folding doors. It was
his aunt who taught him to pray, taught him "Hail Mary," to
pray for the souls of his departed parents and all the people that
he loved. At various times he would include different friends, feeling guilty when he dropped one, disinclined to mention his aunt
if she had been hard on him that day, yet afraid not to.

Later he would rebel against the tyranny of this God he had as-
sumed. Yet he had the need of one. So, in his teens and twenties,
right up to this moment in fact, he felt confused and overwhelmed
when he thought of God. It was actually physically disagreeable
to do so. Forcing his mind to contemplate the infinite was like
feeling the repulsion of opposing magnets.

Sandy had once called him a true agnostic. He presumed this
meant he didn't believe in God, and that wasn't so. At least he
didn't think it was so. He had always thought that sometime,

some understanding of God would emerge. He didn't think this revelation was something you could just dream up so he had always been content to wait until it came. And he never worried about when.

"I can't *believe* in anything," he told Sandy. "You know what I mean? I believed when I was a kid, and then I changed my mind. So I'm not gonna believe anymore. You know what I mean? I just gotta *know*. And right now I don't."

He remembered the conversation. It was evening, and they were at the table beside the stove in the cabin. The stove was open and there was a fire lit. He thought of the way she had looked at him across the table, nodding her head, the bright eyes looking at him as if he were all there was. Rick was their last connection now, he thought abruptly. "If Rick doesn't make it, I won't see you again," he said aloud, staring at the ceiling of the Ford in the darkening light.

Believing it would come to you was as easy as believing Jolene's Jesus. He switched thoughts. Believing in her Jesus had been easy. You said your prayers to Him and then went out to play or went to sleep.

But what of the real God?

It was easiest, of course, to think he would see Sandy again. That's what he'd been doing. Lying there in the Ford, he'd been planning the future with her, making trips as they said. To California, Mono Lake, Yosemite, Death Valley. To Vegas, where Lumpy Weldon was washing dishes at the Stardust or the MGM or downtown somewhere, probably sending him postcards still and wondering where the hell he was. He'd bet Lumpy was standing right now at a stainless-steel sink in some noisy, steamy kitchen with a damp dishrag tied about his head.

He'd take her into the Valley of Fire, where flamingo-pink sandstone stood a thousand feet high, molded by the wind into feathery shapes, oddly like the colonnades on the Strip outside the Sands and the Dunes.

They'd have a helluva time. Lumpy probably had a girl down there by now, and they could double-date.

He'd get the thing with his feet worked out okay. Hold down a

Sometimes she lay all day on the bed in the room he had taken at the Hermans; sometimes she walked for hours beside the river, always keeping her mind quiet and open to him. Late one night, long after the Hermans were asleep, she sat at the night table beside the bed and wrote to him:

"My dearest Baby,
The Hermans think I have gone crazy. I quit work and stay in your room all the time and so George keeps telling me I should go see the doctor and get some sleeping pills and go back to work and lead a normal life. I tell him this is part of a normal life, but he doesn't see that. And then sometimes I think maybe he's right and I'm crazy, sitting here all these days and nights and not letting anything else happen in my life. But I feel like I should stay open in case you're having a real difficult time. I'd want someone to do that for me.

I know you're thinking about me. I can feel it when you are. It's like you're right here in the room with me or you're suddenly walking by me when I'm at the river. And I know you haven't left your body. I hope the others are okay, too. Everyone says there's no way any of you four can still be alive and they gave up looking for you, except the sheriff and some of his friends who go out weekends. The only person that agrees with me is Sue-Ellen. She tells everyone in town that Rick's coming home no matter what. She even acts like it. She acts like nothing's happened. It's hard to believe her. I don't see her. I don't see anyone excepting George and Gladys, but they tell me what's going on in town. She says nobody in town can believe Sue-Ellen.

I'd like to be that positive, Mike, but sometimes I'm afraid you're not going to come home, and sometimes I imagine them coming to tell me and I get into a real mess. So help me, Mike. Okay? I guess I'm just selfish, but I want more of you. I never knew anyone like you, and I never loved anyone that way either. I wish I was with you, even up there. I'd make it better for you, Mike. I wish you would have listened to me and never gone.

But you're a strong man, Mike. You're the strongest person I ever met. Hold out. Come back and we'll leave here and go where it's warm. We'll go to the sea somewhere and we'll stay on the beach in the sun and not see anyone for days. Come home soon, Mike. And know that I am with you and that I love you.

She signed the letter, folded it, and sealed it in an envelope. Then she wrote his name on the front and let it lie on the wood before her. She sat very still in the silent house and looked at the envelope and let her mind transmit the thoughts in the letter. Maintaining her vigil, now in its thirty-third day.

When he left Wild Horse, Coulter headed down the east fork of the Big Lost at the foot of the White Knob Mountains, which form the northern boundary of the Basin. After several miles the stream left the Basin and funneled into a narrow valley where both the stream bed and the track running beside it were buried under several feet of snow.

The sky was clear, and by comparison with how it had been before, it was easy going on the snowshoes. The leading edges were not turned up, so he had to lift his feet and couldn't just slide over the snow. But at least he didn't sink in. His problem now was the glare, which made his eyes water and ache and the wind that came head-on, buffeting him incessantly. To counter this discomfort, he set up a rhythm keyed to the movement of his body and maintained by voice. Over and over he repeated aloud, "Calamity Jane, Calamity Jane, Calamity Jane." He had no idea where the name came from. He put his right foot forward to the sound of "Calamity," and after a beat's pause to shift his weight, he drew up his left to the sound of "Jane." The rhythm claimed him, beating in him like a slow pulse as he walked. For long periods he did not raise his head and was conscious only of the movement of his legs, forgetting wind and glare.

He reached the Johnson Ranch early in the afternoon, as the clouds were beginning to close again. It was a one-room cabin with a woodshed built on the back. He came over a slight rise and

saw it: a lump in the snow with a belt of shadow between the
snow-covered roof and the snow on the ground. He wiped his eyes
and peered again to be certain. Then he grunted with satisfaction
and quickened his pace, abandoning the rhythm.

A snowdrift leaned against the lower half of the front door. The
door was padlocked. He fumbled with his rifle, blowing on his
fingers, sniffing, shot the lock off, pushed the door open and
scrambled in, spilling snow over the floor. Inside he stood and
looked: there was a single bed against the wall to the right of the
door, an aluminum table in front of him with three chairs around
it and on a side table against the far wall was a cheap TV with a
coat-hanger antenna next to a small, two-burner electric range.
The walls were tongue-and-groove, painted a drab green. A topo
map was pinned above the bed and over the range was a fancy-
shaped barometer from which the veneer was peeling.

Coulter closed the door behind him and flicked on the light
switch. A bare bulb hanging from a joist in the center of the room
came on.

"All right," he said aloud. *"Home sweet home!"*

He closed the door, stooping to sweep out with bare hands the
snow that had tumbled in when he entered. He untied his snowshoes and, leaving them on the floor, walked around inspecting
the place with an oddly self-important air. The barometer read
"Change." He tapped it with a finger. It shivered and stayed the
same. He found an electric heater, plugged it in, and put it on the
table. He inspected the ash inside the Sears wood stove, found two
gallon jugs of Gallo Pink Chablis, opened one, and poured himself a mug. He found a wall cupboard filled with dry food, le-
gumes, spaghetti, cans of vegetables, meat sauce, fruit, and two
whole chickens. He lit the stove, opened a can of chicken, put it
on to cook and turned on the TV.

The TV was an old black-and-white, the kind he knew from
small motels. It took almost a minute to warm up, but when it
did the sound was good and the picture surprisingly clear.

Merv Griffin, legs crossed, pants carefully pulled up, sat talking
to some character actor Coulter had seen in many westerns. Slim
Pickens, he thought, then shook his head in doubt.

He put the set on the table next to the heater, without taking his eyes off the screen. Even when the pot of chicken on the stove boiled over, he looked away only an instant.

After Merv Griffin, he watched a "Charlie's Angels" rerun, the local news, the CBS and finally the NBC evening news. The news evoked no reaction from him. It seemed merely to roll over him, feeding information, unfiltered by intelligence, directly back to his memory banks.

He watched without expression, eyes flat. Even a view at last of the world beyond the mountains did nothing. He was taken up instead by 300,000 phosphorescent dots flickering on and off faster than his conscious mind could perceive. He was electronically invaded and pacified. He was in alpha.

Only subconscious function was capable of interruption. He ate the chicken watching Mary Tyler Moore and during the "Hollywood Squares" abruptly opened a can of beef stew and put it on to heat.

After the "Hollywood Squares," he turned to a Second World War movie: Brigadier Wingate's "Chindits" were fighting the Japanese in the jungles of Burma. The British soldiers wore shorts and bush hats and seemed unnaturally happy about the mud and leeches. Coulter sank back into it, utterly passive, uncomprehending. He did not shift his focus or move his eyes. He made no gesture of intelligent awareness. The conscious side of Coulter was on hold; the subconscious, the dreamer, saturated by TV signals received direct. He became a willing victim of the medium, trading one unreality for another.

After the "Chindits," he watched "Kojak," the late news, Johnny Carson, and then a late movie during which he fell asleep, face down on the table, arms sprawled about his head, oblivious to the white noise issued by the set after the station went off the air, the hum of the electric heater, or the occasional gusting of the wind outside.

He woke at six to the morning news and weather. His back was stiff with cold. He swallowed and rubbed his face, staring at the newscaster, then turned to another channel where a gray-faced farmer in a peaked cap with earmuffs was talking about winter feed.

Coulter switched back to the news. A man had escaped from a California courtroom moments after the judge had sentenced him to fifteen years for bank robbery and had robbed another bank within the hour.

Coulter blinked and rubbed his eyes. He looked at the stove. It had gone out. He turned on the electric range and made some coffee. The "Today Show" would start shortly, he thought. He looked forward to seeing the cheerful face of Tom Brockaw.

Arizo always had hope; but hope, he found, was only the other side of despair. They were the same coin. And, as his body continued to disintegrate before him, he saw he must turn away from too much of either if he were to survive.

The key to maintaining his balance, he realized, was light. The day was comforting. Sunlight was best of all, dusk and darkness the most difficult. So he made his own light: closed his eyes and journeyed to the sun—not in a ship of any sort, but in his own body. Like an adventurer in a Jules Verne story, he drifted among the solar flares, the slow explosions, right into the very core of the sun.

There was no heat. Only light. He would fill his body with this light, feeling it rise up from feet to head as if it were liquid. And when the light spilled over and there was no more darkness in him anywhere, he would allow the outline of his shape, now only a husk separating light from light, to dissolve and he was dissipated and he felt elation greater than any before. He practiced this and began to experience the light as having a granular form and then to experience everything as light in granular form; his body merely a part of it. The differing density of substances showed only as the shadings of the same light. The world became like the screen of a printer's block, but in color and three dimensions. Arizo was free of discomfort or pain; in fact, he felt energized as long as he was in this state.

He considered it daydreaming. Daydreams had not seemed

functional before, but as he thought about them, he realized several things:

The first daydreams he clearly remembered concerned a ten-year-old girl who lived in the house opposite, in Jackson Street in Oakland. At her birthday party he had sat across the table from her. Her hair and eyes were richly dark, her face was beautiful, and in the glow of candlelight he fell in love with that image. And he had been in love with it ever since. He had never fallen in love with a light-haired woman. It had all come from one face.

In his daydreams, thereafter, he saved her from under the wheels of a hundred buses, won for her, died for her. Such dreams, he realized, crossed over into reality. He remembered once telling Maxwell how he had pitched softball so hard that he had splintered a bat. For years afterwards, he was mortified every time he thought of telling such a ridiculous lie so seriously. Maxwell never mentioned it, never challenged it, and so much the worse. But he wondered if Maxwell knew from experience that it was the dreamer in a boy spilling over into the real world.

Later it had been sex. Jolene had a girlfriend who came around, a young woman with huge, high-pointed tits, to sunbathe on the roof of the apartment building. One afternoon he'd gone up there and she was laid out in the sun on her tummy with her halter untied, and he'd seen the incredible fullness of her as she came up on her elbows to greet him. After that his sexual daydreams generally took off from this point and continued with her seducing him, looming over him with an earthy lusciousness, breasts bursting out like soft pink tropical fruit, an unbearable tension in the air, and the sweat would pop out on his upper lip at the thought that she was his aunt's friend and what if they were caught?

This, then, became sex for him: always a forbidden performance, always he had first to be seduced. Not through all the years did it occur simply, without a great deal of tension, until he met Sandy.

Later he dreamed of achievement and recognition on a still larger scale, taking the injustices that were forced upon a man of his education and color and working them into heroic fantasies. He organized fellow workers in the valleys, stirred them with his

speeches, ran with a mob at his back, shouting, beating back the
goons, driving them off the land and claiming it for the people.
He dreamed of being one with Cesar Chavez and Martin Luther
King, even of breaking ground they had failed to break, com-
manding their respect and being greater still.

Such were the dreams that drove him finally to Baby Zeus. He
had somewhere known of it, but never seen it as clearly as this.
He had never understood how strong was the role of the subconscious in his life. Daydreams had always seemed such slight and
pleasant things before.

He still saw this vision he had come to know as a daydream and
not, as it was, a vision of the true nature of things. He saw it as a
dream that brought him from isolation and loneliness to whole-
ness. That much he did see. He saw that the wind he heard blowing constantly outside the Ford, the snow piling up, the mountain
standing over him were not his enemies but part of him. He saw
then that he was made from the stuff of the universe.

When he came to this understanding he wrote in his diary:
"*January 9, Wednesday, 40 DAYS—I have made my peace with
God. I have nothing more to say. From now on I shall just write
the date.*"

On that date, Coulter moved down the valley six miles or so to
the Felton Ranch. He went because he had eaten all there was to
eat at the Johnson place and because he was feeling vaguely restless and dimly but increasingly aware of a world waiting for him
to appear. As he wrote in his journal that day, he felt almost certain that by now Arizo must be dead. So if he had felt curiously
little pressure after that first dazed night at the Wild Horse Station, he now felt almost none at all. He was not terribly anxious
to go back, like a child faced with a party to which it doesn't want
to go. He saw, in gigantic and uncontrollable proportion, the
sounds and shapes and colors of bright and voracious people, plas-
tered with smiles, crowding about him menacingly. He saw a
world filled with them and he shrank. He clung to the world he
was in, populated by friendly faces. He started with Bob Schieffer
on the CBS "Morning News," switched to ABC to watch Rona

Barrett, and back to CBS in time to see Schieffer wrap it up. There were the mellifluous tones of Merv Griffin and Mike Douglas, there was the relaxed, living-room atmosphere of the Dinah Shore show. There was "As the World Turns," and "Days of Our Lives," and then at six-thirty the thing he looked forward to all day: half an hour with Walter Cronkite. Nothing was more comforting than this man's smile, his steady eye and soothing voice. There was a face he trusted completely. He felt massaged after he had listened to Cronkite. Later, there was "Laverne and Shirley," "Alice," "Barney Miller," "The Jeffersons," "All in the Family," "Welcome Back Kotter," "Eight Is Enough," "One Day at a Time," "Starsky and Hutch," Johnny Carson. In one important way, he preferred the crime shows: the sitcoms tended to be part of a series, which left him in frustration, awaiting a resolution.

Coulter was no longer lost utterly to reality. Time passed, and there were longer and longer lucid periods as he became rested and stabilized. By the time he reached the Felton Ranch, January 9, sixteen days after he had left the car, he was essentially out, though by no means free of, the disoriented state he had been in at Wild Horse. But since his observing ego had not been operating while he was lost in this other state, he was as unaware of any transition as he was of the existence of any other state. Now all he knew was that somehow something had gone wrong and he had been sick. There was an entry in his log on January 2 which disturbed him: *"Have dumped out all food. Don't want Mike to get sick like I did if he gets here."*

How could he have thought Mike would get to Wild Horse? Mike couldn't stand up. So, although now he knew he must get help for Arizo, he was peculiarly afraid of re-emerging without knowing what it was that troubled him.

He reached the Felton Ranch late in the afternoon of a very cold day. The valley was deeper and narrower here and the sides quite steep. The cabin was deep in shadow when he came to it. It was as simple as the other place—simpler, in fact. He had to turn the electricity on and there was a television, but no heater. He found a cord of wood stacked under a tarp behind the cabin and made himself a fire in the wood stove.

When it was going well, he opened a can of Spam and a can of sweet corn, mixed them together in the only saucepan he could find, and set them on the fire. He pulled up a chair and sat staring through the open firebox at the flames, wondering what had gone wrong. It was like trying to remember a dream. Every time he closed on it, it slipped away. Angry with thinking of it, he again turned on the TV.

Later that night he wrote in his log: "*Jan. 9, Weds. Made about six miles today. Feet still hurt pretty bad. Very cold outside. Feel real bad about Mike. Sure he must be dead by now. I guess if my feet hadn't got hurt it might have made the difference. Maybe I can go on again tomorrow.*"

He put his notepad away and looked at the video screen. The picture was very bad. He fiddled with the set angrily, switched channels, and jiggled the antenna. Finally he switched it off and watched the light recede to a pinprick and then die, heard the wind blowing down the valley, tugging at the corners of the cabin, felt how cut off he had become. He no longer knew what was happening inside his own mind. If he could know, he thought, his fear would evaporate. He was sure of it. He tried the TV again.

"Maybe Vern got out," he said aloud to himself the next morning as he ate breakfast. It was a bright and sudden thought. "Maybe that s.o.b. got out and they rescued Mike. Maybe they're all waitin' for me, an' they think I got it. That'd be a trip. That'd really be somethin'." He shook his head and got up from the table.

"I can make it to the dude ranch today," he said, talking to himself. He went to the window and stood looking out. It was snowing lightly but he could see the far hill easily and the sky over the valley. He would go. It was only four or five miles to the Devil's Bedstead Guest Ranch. His coat and rifle lay across a chair beside the stove. He shut the firebox down completely, turned off the electricity, pulled on his coat and sat to tie on his snowshoes. The dude ranch was open the year around, and at least there was someone there. They should have a phone.

He walked awkwardly across the floor in his snowshoes and stepped outside. The cold air felt good. He started down the slope, quickly falling into the swinging rhythm of, walking with snowshoes. He crossed the creek by what he reckoned would be the bridge, turned up the valley, and made a couple of hundred yards when the binding on the right shoe broke. He had made the binding by hammering a pair of two-inch nails through the plywood and then turning the heads over the strings and beating them down. When the first nail came loose, the sudden strain pulled out the second. The plywood was only three eighths. He bent down on one knee and fiddled with it until his fingers ached with cold and he could no longer control them.

He stood and tried walking with only one shoe, but that was worse than useless. He took the other off and was floundering deep in the snow once more, with the strange feeling of déjà vu.

He felt tremendously dejected going back. In the cabin, he spent some time looking for nails, then opened up the firebox and got the fire going again to warm his fingers. Now he couldn't find a hammer or anything to use as one until he went outside and saw an ax among the wood.

It was a clumsy business. Twice he hit his fingers with the ax. The second time he broke the skin and the nail bent. All his frustration erupted, and he threw the ax across the room. It smashed the plywood wall and dislodged a mirror, which shattered on the floor. Coulter stared at the broken glass and went slowly to the bed and lay upon it, face down.

He didn't go out again that day or the following one. It blew so hard that he couldn't leave the house. He spent most of his time watching TV. He couldn't make out much of what was happening, but kept it on anyway. He lay on the bed, staring up at the ceiling, listening to the monotonous sound of the set and, intermittently, the howl of the wind.

By this time, Arizo had thought seriously about how long to wait. As with everything, he thought in terms of Sandy. He thought practically: if he lost his legs above the knees, he wouldn't be much use to anyone—an evaluation he felt bound to make.

Thinking this way kicked him into a vast depression. He dragged himself out by reviewing his life in infinite detail, going over the whole thing, pushing himself to remember every moment he possibly could. Once he got into this, he began feeling better, but the depression returned on New Year's Eve, and persisted for days. He came very close to finishing it several times, but some small part of him wouldn't let go the idea that help would come. They could be on the way. Right that minute.

That was the thing about suicide. Supposing there was good news in the mail?

And what would she think about him? What would it do to her not only if he did it, but if he even sat thinking about it? Was she picking all this stuff up? He felt she was. And here he was jamming her with this suicide shit. What would she think about him if he wasted himself? What would she think about life? She'd be freaked, he thought. That was one hell of a signal to put out to someone you loved about how it got at the end. He'd scare her half to death. He'd bum her out so far that she'd never come all the way back.

For these reasons and others he had no notion of, he waited. And in waiting he had found the world of light and slipped beyond the veil that had always seemed to him to be the backwall of reality.

Once beyond, nothing ever hit him so hard as the realization that he had come so close to preventing himself from going through, that he'd so nearly interrupted his natural process because some part of him had said that it was *bad*. What if he had? That's what scared him. What if he'd stopped it, like pulling the plug on the record player in the middle of the song? He'd have been caught somewhere and frozen.

No one ever explained stuff like this to you. When he'd been with Mary-Beth, they'd gone shopping in Chinatown, and he'd sat in the car by the curb and seen the old Chinese men tottering down the street, openmouthed, chicken-necks stuck from collarless shirts, eyes locked straight ahead as they walked with tiny comic steps, and the tourists milling and stepping impatiently around them. They were so lonely and so determined. He'd thought of them as babies on the breast, kissed and cuddled. Where the fuck were they going now, he'd wondered. For what?

It was like Pops Bivaletz rubbing his forehead and shaking his gray head and saying, "Oi, yoi, yoi. I don't know which man 'ave invented zis old age, but if I find 'im, I shall surely kill 'im." If it was so ghastly, why?

Now he felt that he knew. And now another thing made sense. As he became more familiar with the state of dissolution and increasingly caught up in it, as he exercised and increased the capacity of his mind, the importance of personal life dissolved. In the light world there was no past or future. That was what drew him. That was what made him strong.

It demanded constant focus to maintain this place, and periodically he slipped and was brought back. One night, for instance, well after he had found this solution, he dreamed of swimming in the ocean with Sandy and Rick and friends he couldn't recognize in retrospect, when he started to sink. Drifting down into a darkening world of cold and silence he could see and hear them splashing and laughing in the sunlight but there was nothing he could do to return to them and nothing that they in the sunlight could do either.

He woke terrified and depressed and immediately he went traveling again, well out beyond earth.

On Friday, January 10, it was clear in the early morning. Slowly, with enormous effort and frequent rests, he pulled himself into the front, so that his back was resting against the steering wheel and his knees were over the seat. With a small sense of triumph and breathing hard, he wound down the window and revealed the mountain, towering, sailing against the sky, more almighty than he could ever keep in mind, black rock bulging like biceps splashed with snow.

He lay with his head against the wheel, half-turned to look straight at her, thinking of others who had looked at her: redmen long past, Mountain Men then and now, the tourists who would come again in summer when the snow was gone and the willows by the creek were thick with leaves.

He looked at her until his back ached and his body was all numb. He looked till clouds covered the sky. It began to snow, and with gentle modesty, the mountain withdrew behind the drifting veil. Slowly the willows by the creek were hidden from him, too, and when they were gone, a crow flew from them to the shelter of the firs on the hillside above the car and went over him and out of sight. He heard in the silence the cut of its wings through the air. The snow came on, and only long after it had closed off the world completely did he begin the slow business of returning to his bed.

When he was comfortable and his hands had stopped shaking from their effort, he took his pad and pencil and wrote: *January 10, 41 DAYS.*

He was awake through much of the night, bent upon going further, even beyond the light. He made no effort, because it interferes. He was merely a traveler among the suns, the red giants and white dwarves, the young ones livid, the old ones dying, an angelfish among fire coral. In his intelligence was all the universe and there was, he knew, nothing without it. Without his intelligence there were no suns, no stars, there was no God.

Sometime in mid-morning, his body reasserted itself, and he became aware of the wind howling outside, the awful cold and the intense pain in his legs. He had already bared his legs to the knee. Still he pulled up his trousers to uncover more, tucking the blankets tight about his thighs to keep out the cold from the rest of him. When he had finished, he saw Coulter's rifle beside him, took hold of it, lay down upon his back again, and drew it up towards him. There was a round in the chamber. He put the muzzle into his mouth, feeling the coldness of the blue gunmetal, tasting its odd sourness. The taste was like unripe chestnuts. It reminded him of Maxwell.

In the morning Coulter rose, cold and stiff, in clothes worn now for a month and a half. He went to the window, ducking his hands into his sleeves, rubbed a clear patch in the frost pattern, and looked out. The sky above the ridge opposite was clear, a pale, cool turquoise. The sun was still well short of rising. Encouraged, he built up the fire, sat before it, and dressed his toes more elaborately than usual, using Vaseline and the bandage from a snakebite kit. He then made pancakes with Aunt Jemima mix and canned milk, topped with the last syrup.

The sun was still not warming the canyon when he finished eating, so he sat awhile longer by the fire, holding his hands out to the warmth, feeling the pleasure of a full stomach. Half an hour more, and he abruptly tied on his repaired snowshoes, stood and slung his rifle, and left, pulling the door roughly to behind him. It was a four-mile walk to the Devil's Bedstead Guest Ranch.

Coulter crossed the stream bed and started up the short slope to the track. The track was obvious here, for there was a slight leveling in the snow. It was a good fresh day, cold and sharp but with scarcely any wind.

When he came up onto the roadbed, he saw fresh snowmobile tracks and stopped dead. Two of them had passed, headed up the valley towards the Basin. He wondered how he had not heard them, regarding them as if they had some life of their own. He stepped between them and stood staring side to side like a commuter looking for a train. Then he went on quickly down the valley, taken with fresh urgency, sometimes glancing backwards, sometimes talking to himself, rehearsing aloud what he would say when he reached the guest ranch, frightened at the thought of confrontation, half-wanting to turn back. He held in mind the image of his son's face, because it was his boy and not, he would have said, because in this face alone there was no fear of judgment. He hurried towards it.

The valley narrowed, and the tracks wound into a steep-sided cut with black walls. He went easily, smoothly on his shoes, looking up at the walls, listening for the sound of engines returning. And then he rounded a corner and the walls fell back and there, close to the valley's mouth, was the ranch house. Immediately he slowed and began approaching it cautiously. It was a large, robust cabin with dark wooden walls, a dormer window in a steeply pitched, snow-covered roof and wood smoke rising from the chimney. The road ran directly by the building, beneath a window, and the snow was hard-packed and gray from traffic. As he came closer, he saw a figure in red through the window; the silhouette

of a breast; a young woman with short red hair. He was close outside the window before she saw him, standing fifteen feet away.
He was on the brink of calling out, but unsure what to say, anxious not to frighten her.

When she saw him, she slid the sash open and called severely,
"Whatta you want."

At her expression, he stared down at his smoke-blackened
clothes and put his hand to his face to feel his scraggly beard. She
was still staring at him, a plate in one hand. Her face was pained.

"I was lost in the Basin," he began. "One of the hunters . . ."

"Jesus!" the woman said and put her free hand to her mouth.
"You are, aren't you? Wait."

He saw her put down the plate and disappear and in a moment
he heard her voice. "Come around here," she called. He went
around the side of the house feeling foolish in his clumsy plywood
snowshoes.

She stood in the doorway and bent to help him take them off.
She was in her middle twenties. He looked at the wool strands of
her red sweater as she bent and saw the indentation her bra strap
made across her back beneath her sweater. She was still a little
flustered when she straightened up.

"Thank you," he said.

"Is there more of you? There was four, wasn't there?"

He nodded. "My buddy needs someone at the car right away,"
he heard himself say. "You gotta phone?"

"A radiophone."

"Can you call the sheriff?"

She nodded.

"The car's in Muldoon Canyon. Halfway up on the south side.
In the open. Mike Arizo is there."

She ran to the phone.

He went into the kitchen and stood looking out the window
at the snowbank beyond the roadway. The sun came in through
the window, and the kitchen was warm. She had been doing the
dishes, and the water in the sink was steaming. He must call Sue-
Ellen as soon as she was through. He realized he hadn't thought
of this first and gave a little grunt. It was odd—he wasn't frantic

to call her or talk to Jason. He wanted to be by himself. He stared
at the wisps of steam rising from the sink. When he thought of
all the people he was going to have to see, his gut got tight. He'd
just like to stay like this: alone in the cabin with this girl looking
after him. Just the two of them.

"Sergeant," he heard her say excitedly, "one of them missin'
hunters just walked in here. . . . Yeah, this's Jenny up at Devil's
Bedstead. . . . Yeah . . . honest to God."

When she came back into the kitchen, he was sitting on a
stool, leaning his elbows on the table.

"You don't feel so good?" she said.

He shook his head.

"I can't imagine you would. But you are alive. That's unbelievable. We didn't any of us think . . ." She stopped.

"Can I call my wife an' kid?" he asked without looking around.

"Oh yeah. Of course. I'm sorry. What's the number?"

While she dialed he asked, "Also, could I have a bath? D'you
have a bath?"

She nodded vigorously, and handed him the phone. The number was ringing.

"Yalo." It was her voice. But it was strong and light and
confident, and he was taken by surprise.

"Sue-Ellen," he said.

There was a pause. She said nothing.

"It's me."

"*It is*," she said in a low voice, drawing the words out. "Isn't it,
though? It's you, Rick. *It's you!*"

He hadn't heard her that excited, didn't know what to say. He
felt at a distance from her. He wasn't excited, though he tried to
be. They chatted first like acquaintances until she suddenly asked:
"Rick, what's the matter, hon?"

Then he began to cry. Standing in snow-caked clothes, he struggled to pull himself together, but every time he began to speak he
broke down again. He couldn't say a word. He looked around,
helpless, and through his tears saw the girl with the red hair waiting hesitantly a little way off. She came forward and took the
phone from him. "Ma'am," she said into it, "he's pretty shook up

just now. He's okay but he's shook up. The sheriff's comin' to take him to the hospital."

Coulter sat on a stool beside the bath for some time without undressing. Finally there was a tap on the door and he heard her voice. "Are you okay?" she asked.

He reached out and opened the door and looked up at her.

"Hey," she said, "you didn't even get your stuff off yet. Here." She came in and sat on the edge of the bath in front of him. Her nose wrinkled involuntarily. She picked up one leg at a time, set them across her knees, and began to unlace his boots.

Part V

THE SURVIVOR

THE HELICOPTER LANDED in the parking lot beside the Standard station at the far end of Cope. Word was out already, and a small group had gathered at the lot to watch the chopper land. Rumor was that Coulter was aboard. The helicopter was small with stretcher pods fixed to the skids on either side. It was mostly used for lifting injured skiers and climbers out of Sun Valley.

Sheriff Meyers looked dramatically grim as he made his way through the group towards it.

"Whatta they found, Burt?" Don Puccinelli, the auto-parts store owner who looked like Groucho Marx, shouted above the clatter of the helicopter's engine.

Sheriff Meyers glanced at Puccinelli but said nothing. At the edge of the circle he held his hat and ducked under the main rotor blade. Once he was aboard, sitting next to the pilot, a soft, bulky-looking man with glasses and headphones on, the sheriff looked out and saw his brother Fred standing in blue denim bib

overalls under a white linen apron, his hand resting flat upon his
head, and beside him his son Buck in mechanic's overalls, hands
on his hips. Both staring anxiously.

The sheriff waved briefly at them as the helicopter's engine clattered to a crescendo and lifted him abruptly into the air. Puccinelli saw the sheriff squint a little harder as he came off the
ground.

They picked up Lieutenant Kule in Arco because Kule knew
the White Knobs better than anyone else in the department.
They put down in the parking lot beside the Arco diner. As they
came in, the sheriff saw patrol cars blocking the entrance to the
parking lot and the gangling figure of Lieutenant Kule standing
below looking up at them, shielding his eyes with his hat.

They flew west over Mackay and headed for Table Mountain.
The sheriff turned to Kule in the back and yelled, "Who'n hell
checked Muldoon?"

"Rose an' Epke, I think," the lieutenant shouted back.

The sheriff shook his head and narrowed his eyes. "Makes us
look like a buncha assholes," he yelled.

Kule nodded. "Maybe Arizo's hung on."

"What's 'at?"

"I said maybe Arizo's hung on."

The sheriff didn't reply.

They followed the Burma road, twisting below them through
the White Knobs, Lieutenant Kule directing the pilot. There
were faint traces of it beneath the snow; the shape of a cut here
and there, and once the unnatural elevation of a bridge. They flew
directly across the Basin in about three minutes, their shadow
chasing them. The pilot looked down and shook his head. "It's
amazing anyone lived walking across that," he yelled. The other
two men stared out grimly.

Soon they picked up the ridge that marked the western boundary of Muldoon Canyon. It rose out of the white flesh of the
Basin like a collarbone, and in a moment sprouted dark firs, straggly at first but quickly thickening. It was easy to follow the path
of the road here because it occasionally cut small clumps of trees

from the main stand. Now they were flying fast towards a considerable peak that stood over them as they came up the edge of the canyon rising abruptly from a bed of boulders. Kule pointed to it. "That's Big Black Dome!" he yelled. "They should be right below it."

The canyon was turning across them in a dogleg now. They broke out over the trees midway along the upper half of the leg and immediately saw below them on the open hillside the blemish made by the nearly buried Ford.

"How'n the hell did they miss that?" Lieutenant Kule swore.

"It's easy to see if you know where to look," the pilot called over his shoulder.

They landed a little above the Ford, directly between it and Poulsen's pickup, now virtually buried. The sheriff led Lieutenant Kule down to the car, the two sinking into the snow and holding their arms out for balance. Only a slight, sighing wind blew down from the canyon. The sheriff hesitated an instant, then tapped on the side of the car. "Anyone there?" he called.

In the silence, the sheriff looked at Kule. The lieutenant grimaced and shook his head.

"Go 'round the other side while I clear the back door," the sheriff told him. It was very quiet and tense.

The sheriff was still clearing snow from the back door when he heard the lieutenant's voice coming from inside the car.

"Shit, oh shit!"

"What's up?"

Lieutenant Kule's head reappeared above the car on the far side. He had a white, pained look and was shaking his head.

"It's unbelievable in there," he said weakly. "That poor sonovabitch." He shook his head again, his face pulled down and very sour.

The sheriff twisted the handle and pried open the back door.

It was the blackness that hit him. And sticking out of it a pair of bare feet. He didn't recognize them as such immediately because they were black and scaly, grotesquely cracked and swollen. They stuck out from beneath a blanket. For all his years and for all his experience, the sheriff recoiled and Lieutenant Kule, who was

leaning in the driver's door, noticed it. It was a moment before
the sheriff made out details within. Everything was blackened—
smoke, he realized—walls, blankets, everything. It was a small,
dark space, hideous and foul in contrast to the pristine snowfield
glittering all around it. There was in it a smell of stale wood-
smoke, piss, and the damp, bitter smell of death. The lieutenant,
bent in the driver's door, saw the sheriff's mournful face and both
men, having burst unexpectedly into a tomb, into a place where
the quick had no business, were caught silent.

The figure lay on its back, draped in a blackened quilt, clutching a rifle, one hand about the barrel, the other about the neck of
the stock as if presenting arms, still and composed, a recumbent
knight upon a medieval tomb in the transept shadow.

The face was drawn; the dry skin stretched grotesquely; the
open eyes stared upward. From the breadth of the cheekbones the
sheriff knew immediately it was Arizo. The stranger.

The sheriff gazed a moment and then reached in and gently
disengaged the rifle. "You'd've done a whole lot better for yourself
if you'd've used it, boy," he said quietly.

"He didn't, did he?" the lieutenant murmured.

The sheriff, still bent low in the door, shook his head slowly.

"Sonovabitch!" the lieutenant said. "I don't believe it. That
must've been some badass way to go."

The sheriff backed out of the car carefully. "Let's get this man
a bag," he said, waving his hand in front of his nose to disperse
the air.

The lieutenant started up the hill, glad to get away.

When he returned from the helicopter with a green bag, the
sheriff was on his knees alongside the body. He backed slowly out,
careful to avoid touching the blackened walls. The lieutenant,
who was breathing hard, saw that he had left his hat outside on
the snow beside the door. Kule also noted that the sheriff had
closed the dead man's eyes.

"You know this man?" he asked the sheriff. They were standing
up straight, elbows leaning on the roof beside the back door while
the lieutenant caught his breath.

The sheriff shook his head. "Only seen him a coupla times."

"So how come he was with these others?"

"He was a farmhand come up from California, met a girl here and got work with Coulter."

"He shoulda know'd better than to hang out with Rick," the lieutenant reckoned. "Looks like he's a Injun."

The sheriff nodded. "Yeah," he said. "Let's get 'im in the bag. Okay?"

Anticipating a man's weight, they started to draw the body out and staggered back as it jerked free unexpectedly, seeming to leap at them, it was so light. They looked at one another and the sheriff said, "Migod, he can't weigh ninety pounds."

As they pulled again a notebook fell out onto the snow. Lieutenant Kule reached down and picked it up.

"It's his diary."

"It'll keep," the sheriff said impatiently.

The lieutenant ignored him. "Get this, he only died Saturday. He must've, see?" He held the notebook in front of the sheriff, black-gloved finger pointing out a place. "There's Friday's date. He almost made it. Sonovabitch!"

"Let's get him in the bag, for Chrissakes."

The lieutenant pushed the notebook in the pocket of his parka before he bent to the body once more. As he did, he saw the pilot watching from his seat uphill across the snow. The pilot looked nervous, fingers to his mouth. He lowered them as he saw the lieutenant looking.

When they were done and had strapped the body to the near-side stretcher pod, the sheriff told Kule, "You best go check the truck."

The roof of the pickup stuck up about a foot out of the snow beneath the trees a hundred yards above where the helicopter sat. The pilot looked nervous when he heard this. They still stood knee-deep in snow around the body bag. "Let's go," he said. "There's no sense goin' up there now. There's nothin'. This bird runs a buck a minute."

The sheriff turned to him. "You payin' for this, then?" he said sourly.

The pilot didn't lie down. The lieutenant watched in admiration. "We could get caught up here real easy," the pilot said. "Weather can change real fast. We did enough. Let's go." He climbed back into his seat, tapping the snow off his boots against the frame before he drew them inside.

The sheriff turned away and spat. It seemed a habitual rather than an insulting gesture, but the lieutenant knew the sheriff didn't spit.

"You go on up," he told the lieutenant. "Call me if you need me."

Kule slowly climbed the hill. They should've brought snow-shoes, he thought. Only the very top of the truck was above the snow. He stood looking down at it and saw that the windshield was out. Probably froze, he guessed. He stepped to the back. The truck's bed was completely buried. There was nothing he could see, nothing to do. He turned and looked down to where the heli-copter rested on the snow. Burt and the pilot were watching him. He raised his arms and let them fall. Then for a moment he stood and imagined the helicopter gone and looked through *their* eyes. The silence was absolute, nothing moved. Soon it would be dark and the wind would come up. Kule wondered if he would have made it and decided he didn't really know. That was the only honest answer. Of course, he liked to think so, but he was very glad he didn't have to find out.

The sheriff called.

As they took off, the pilot called out, "Sorry to rush you guys, but it's my mother's birthday, see, an' I gotta get her a gift before the stores close." He looked at the sheriff and grinned. The sheriff ignored him.

"I never was expecting this," the pilot said defensively.

"Who was?"

Kule was looking at the log, struggling against severe vibration to read the shaky writing.

"Look at this." He held the diary over the sheriff's shoulder.

The sheriff, who couldn't read without his glasses, said, "It's shakin' too much," and pushed it back.

"Well," the lieutenant said, leaning forward and speaking into the sheriff's ear. "They *both* of them wrote this."

"Who?"

"Arizo kept the last bit."

"What?"

The lieutenant gripped the back of the sheriff's seat and raised his voice. "I said Arizo kept the last bit."

"How much?"

"From the twenty-fifth."

"Christmas Day?"

"Yeah."

"You mean he was alone that long?" The sheriff turned in his seat. Lieutenant Kule saw the pilot watching them.

"Looks like it."

The sheriff twisted around further. "How far's the car off the road?" he yelled.

"I figure Coulter went about eighteen miles."

"Eighteen?"

"Yeah."

"That's all?"

"Well he had to come clear across the Basin, Burt." Lieutenant Kule was growing hoarse.

The sheriff shook his head and turned back in his seat. The pilot glanced at the lieutenant, who was staring at the body bag strapped outside on the stretcher. The canvas rippled in the slipstream. On the snow beneath them, the bag made the fleet shadow of the helicopter look oddly lopsided as it crossed the Big Lost Basin at eighty miles an hour.

Sergeant Goebbels was standing by his patrol car at the center of a fast-growing crowd as the helicopter settled on the Standard station parking lot a little more than an hour after it had left.

The sergeant's eyes bulged. The crowd pressed eagerly about, but the sheriff strode silently to the car, shouldering his way through, while the helicopter climbed noisily into the air behind him. The sheriff got behind the wheel and slid the seat back.

"What's the word on Coulter?" he asked Goebbels as they left the lot.

"The doctors can't find a whole lot wrong with him," Goebbels

said. "They told me he was in amazingly good shape. He got
frostbit some on his toes, but it's not too bad. He won't lose
none."

"What took him so long, then?"

"Whattya mean?"

"I mean he was eighteen days comin' out."

"From where?"

"Muldoon Canyon."

Sergeant Goebbels looked blank.

"Soon as we get back, Goebbels, get me the weather for Challis
every day since Christmas."

The sergeant looked questioningly at his boss but said nothing.

Sandy Brown and Marlene were in the outer office when the
sheriff and Sergeant Goebbels came in. They sat side by side on
the bench along the wall, and their drawn faces were the first
thing the sheriff saw. Martha Meyers was with them, too, standing beyond them near a table. The sheriff was glad to see his wife.
She had taken the phones while he and Goebbels were out; a big,
dark-haired woman in her late fifties with a wide face and mouth
and small, shrewd eyes.

"If you don't mind," the sheriff said to Goebbels.

Goebbels glanced at the women as he went on into the main
office. The sheriff unzipped his old green parka and sat on a chair
opposite the women. Martha walked over, holding a coffee cup for
him, looking into it with unusual concentration.

Sandy blurted out: "They didn't make it, did they?"

Burt Meyers shook his head slowly. "I'm afraid Mike didn't."
His voice was very deep. He paused, seeing a small tightening of
her face.

She held her hands together in her lap and stared at them a moment before looking up at the sheriff. "I knew that," she said.

The sheriff was silent, his lips working.

"He died Saturday," she said distinctly, and her face seemed
calm as she looked at Martha, tears in her eyes.

Involuntarily the sheriff glanced at his wife, too, turning
slightly, the question on his face. Martha was looking at the girl.

"I was very cold Friday night and Saturday," Sandy said, head down again, speaking to her hands. "No matter what I did, I was cold. I knew."

"What about Vern?" Marlene asked coolly.

The sheriff's tone was apologetic. "He must still be on his way. We couldn't see any sign of him up there."

Marlene began to cry. The sheriff leaned forward and picked at a callus on his right hand. "All Rick knows," he said, "is that Vern started out three days before he did, to get help."

Marlene sniffed and Martha stepped forward with a tissue. Marlene blew her nose and asked, "When was that?"

"Just before Christmas."

As though something had caught in her throat, Marlene made a choking noise. "Just before Christmas? God, Burt, that's three weeks ago! Three weeks!" She stood up, arms rigid at her sides and screamed, "God, he's dead then, ya bastards! He's dead!"

The sheriff stood, too, gazing sadly at Marlene, whose body was clenched, all sinew and tendon.

"We've sent men out to meet him," he half-lied, thinking that he had ordered Kule out with a party at first light in the morning.

But Marlene turned on him. "Don't bullshit me, Burt," she yelled. *"Don't bullshit me!"*

Sheriff Meyers put his hands on her shoulders. "You know your man better than I do, Marlene. An' right now you know as much as me. Isn't he gonna make it?"

"Don't give me that crap, Burt," she yelled. "I'm not one of your goddamn high school runaways."

Martha Meyers drove Sandy home. Sandy didn't want it, but it was better to allow the sheriff's wife to express concern than to resist.

At the Two Ball Inn, Martha turned left down the hill. Sandy looked at Cope now with a singular detachment. There was no longer any life in the place for her. She saw it quite suddenly, as they made the turn. It was as if she were driving through some utterly strange town. She almost asked Martha beside her, "What's the name of this place?" Winter had worn the town down: the

grass beside the road was dead and crusted in dirty snow; the land-
scape was gray and brown and black. She found herself longing
for color.

Gladys Herman appeared in the doorway as they pulled up. She
was clearly bursting with news. As they came on, with Sandy leading the way, she said, "He's been on the TV already. They got a
picture of Rick being took into the hospital. He's got a beard, but
he doesn't look bad." Then, as she realized her mistake, her hand
flew to her mouth and she held open the door.

They stood in the hallway. Sandy saw them both, but she
didn't register what they were saying. She was taken with images
of Mike. One after another they came. She looked away. Oddly, it
was a pleasant feeling she had. She excused herself and went out
to walk.

Almost every doctor, nurse, and orderly in the hospital found
some excuse to put their heads into Coulter's room and get a look
at him. There was a steady flow of them. Coulter sat on his bed in
someone else's clothes. He had a straggly dark beard and was very
pale, with black circles under his eyes. A nurse came in pushing a
chrome trolley covered with a white cloth. She was dark, very
young, and had a beauty mark on her cheek that made her seem
faintly exotic.

"I have to dress your toes," she said. "But first get into bed."

"I don't need to go to bed."

She drew a screen across the door and looked severely at him.
"We're not to treat you any different."

"Whatta you mean?"

"Because you're a celebrity."

Coulter stood up, took off his coat and started to unbutton his
shirt. "You think I'm a celebrity?"

"Oh, sure." She folded her arms. "You're a hero and a medical
curiosity."

"Yeah?"

"Put these on." She handed him a coarse pair of white cotton
pajamas.

Coulter was thinking of himself as a hero. He felt lonely and anxious.

"You risked your life for your friends," the nurse said. "Now sit down and let me help you take off your jeans so you don't damage your toes any more."

He hopped up onto the bed.

"Pull your trousers down some first."

He got off the bed and lowered his trousers. He wasn't wearing any shorts. For some reason, the girl in the cabin hadn't given him any. He forgot this until he saw the nurse's face. He pulled the jeans back up again.

"Jeeze! I hope you don't keep that hid all the time!" she said. She handed him the pajamas. "Cover it with these 'fore you start a riot in here. And hop back up on the bed."

Coulter felt nothing. Not even a stir. He carried on the conversation, ignoring the incident. "I was no hero," he said. "If I'd've stayed, I'd've died, too."

"We can't figure out how come you didn't die anyway. Up there in the winter we give people three days outside. That's it."

"We were in a car."

"It doesn't matter," she said. Two doctors and the head nurse came in before she could go on.

"How long are you going to be, nurse?" the head nurse asked.

"I'm just covering them till the doctor sees them." The three left.

"You think I'm a hero?" Coulter asked the nurse.

The nurse stood directly in front of him, holding the dirty bandage he had put on in the cabin. She nodded, her face close. "I think you're incredible." And then she leaned forward and kissed him very briefly. "I'll get you a razor," she said.

Dr. Hardcastle came in with three other doctors and the head nurse and the nurse with the beauty mark left. Dr. Hardcastle looked more frail than ever, his white hair puffed in the light. Coulter was surprised to see him and looked blank. Dr. Hardcastle did a funny little shuffle and put his hand out and said emphatically, "Rick, I told them you'd want your own doctor to give you a check."

Coulter shrugged. "Sure," he said. Dr. Hardcastle may have delivered him, but Coulter had no other reason to thank the man. The one time he'd really been in trouble since, when he froze the back of his throat sucking a bottle of nitrous oxide in the garage with the Meyers kid and had required a tracheotomy, he had rushed to Dr. Hardcastle's office only to see the old man frantically call in his nurse to do the operation. He had often wondered how it would have been had the nurse been out.

"Where's my wife?" he asked the doctor. "Did you come with her?"

Dr. Hardcastle shook his head.

"What about Mike?" Coulter asked the question. "They get him out?"

There was silence. Dr. Hardcastle cleared his throat and looked about at the others. But they were equally still. "They got him out," he said solemnly, and Coulter knew from the way he said it that Arizo was dead. "But I'm afraid he didn't make it."

Coulter looked at them wide-eyed and they looked at him. No one spoke. Coulter bit his lip, tears filled his eyes, and he looked away, sitting there on his bed in his white hospital pajamas, his brown hair straggling, his beard a mess.

One of the other doctors present came forward. He was short and dark and had a pronounced limp. "I'm sorry we brought you this news," he said. "It's obvious from what you did for them how much your friends meant to you. You're a very brave man, Rick. You mustn't blame yourself. You did the impossible, and it still wasn't enough. This was in God's hands, not yours." He put a hand on Coulter's shoulder and stood there looking solemnly down at him.

Coulter wished they would leave. He felt strangled and couldn't speak. He sat on the bed, hands to his forehead, crying like a child. He couldn't stop. Why didn't the fuckers go? They just stood watching him shake and gasp for breath. Finally he sat upright in the bed and shouted angrily, "What the fuck are you starin' at? Get outta here! Please get out!"

They left.

Later, the nurse with the beauty mark came in carrying a small tray, eyeing him with concern.

"What'd they do to you?" she asked, putting the tray down and pulling him forward slightly by the shoulder, rearranging the pillows. He couldn't answer.

She handed him a pill on a saucer.

"What's this?" He picked it up and examined it.

"Quaalude."

"A downer?"

She nodded.

"I'm down enough."

"I know," she said softly. "I heard them tell you about your friend. I'm sorry. But take it. It's a sort of high. Believe me."

He smiled thinly and swallowed the pill.

Sue-Ellen sailed in, her little chin jutting out like the prow of a galleon emerging from a fog, arms outstretched, regarding him coyly. She didn't seem to see the nurse, who started tactfully for the door.

"Baby!" Sue-Ellen cried shrilly. "Oh, baby! Baby! Baby!"

She beached herself on the bed and gathered him into her arms, crushing him to her bosom, pressing his face against the cold buttons of her coat.

"Ouch!" he said.

She stepped back, undid the coat and then embraced him once more. He grasped at her, smelling her Fabergé Tigress perfume, feeling her warmth and softness, properly grateful for it.

When she went to push away so that she could look at him, he only held her more tightly. She struggled a little.

"Baby!" she cried. "I want to *see* you!"

He relaxed his grasp. She leaned back slightly and stared at him.

"I knew you'd be back, baby," she said. "I told them." She gazed on him triumphantly. "I told them it'd take a whole lot more than some dumb ol' mountain to stop you."

He regarded her evenly. "Mike didn't make it," he said. "It's no time for . . ."

She lowered her head. "He almost did. I'm sorry."

"Almost?"

"He died Saturday, maybe Friday night."

"How do you know?" Coulter was beginning to float objectively. The Quaalude was coming on.

"Burt Meyers told me. He said Mike kept a diary."

Coulter nodded, looking down at the gray wool blanket on his bed, rolling up a piece of lint.

"I coulda saved him," he said. "I coulda made it sooner."

Sue-Ellen, sitting on the bed, raised his chin with her hand and looked at him soothingly. "But you couldn't walk, hon," she said.

"I couldn't get my boots on," he agreed, looking away.

"You mustn't feel bad. Please."

"I should never have took them off."

"What?"

"My boots. I shoulda kept them on an' just kept goin'. He'd be here right now if I'd done that."

"Or maybe neither of you would."

"Ah, fuck," he said dejectedly. "I chickened out." He pulled the piece of lint off the blanket and threw it away. "Let's face it."

Sue-Ellen took him by the shoulders and peered harder into his face and shook him. "You quit that kinda talk, Rick. You hear me? That's enough. You're here an' alive, an' you better start gettin' on with it. You gotta son that's dyin' to see you. You set him a good example. Y'hear?"

Coulter gently pushed her away. "I got to talk to you," he began. "I'm gonna go crazy otherwise."

The three doctors and the head nurse returned like a chorus. Coulter sighed.

"We've got to examine your feet now," Dr. Hardcastle said. "I hope we're not interrupting. But you can continue your visit as soon as we're done."

"Three of you for two feet?" Coulter said. He was feeling comfortably high by now.

Dr. Hardcastle smiled wanly. Coulter saw the head nurse peering at him from behind the other two. "Well," Dr. Hardcastle began, "Dr. Hardy here would like to have a talk with you this afternoon about some other aspects of your ordeal."

Dr. Hardy was a beefy man with a network of fine blue veins around his nose and dark eyebrows that ended in a flourish. Coulter noticed he was wearing Letty boots under his gown. Dr. Hardy crossed his right arm over his stomach and, gripping his chin with his left hand, turned slightly sideways and said, tipping his head from side to side, "I, er, just wanted to know how you got on out there." He smiled reassuringly.

"Dr. Hardy here is head of the psychiatric department at the hospital," Dr. Hardcastle explained.

"*Psychology* department," Dr. Hardy corrected.

Coulter looked at them clustered about the end of his bed and grunted. "Well, it was fuckin' cold," he said gravely.

"Oh, I can imagine," Dr. Hardy said.

"No, you can't," Coulter snapped.

"No, I probably can't either," Dr. Hardy agreed.

"Hadn't you better check my feet?" Coulter looked at Dr. Hardcastle.

The doctor nodded. "Oh yes," he said and came forward. They were so deferential. Coulter was beginning to realize for the first time, that at this moment he was truly larger than life. This, he was thinking, was what it was like to be a hero. They were tripping out on him. *Doctors* even. He was somebody. They were scared even, he thought. And as long as that was the case, there was no sense in him being scared of them. Sue-Ellen sat down on the chair beside the bed and watched, intrigued.

The nurse with the beauty mark came in with the dressing.

"You'll be all right," Dr. Hardcastle said to Coulter from where he was working over his feet at the other end of the bed. "You've got the equivalent here of first-degree burns. Second, in a few spots. You're a lucky young man. And a very brave one," he added.

The nurse looked down at Coulter, catching his eye. He looked at her as though she were a filing cabinet.

"How long before I can go home?" he asked.

Dr. Hardcastle didn't look up. "Oh, just a day or two, I imagine. We'll have to check you out a bit more, but you seem in amazingly good condition to me."

Coulter leaned back and eyed Sue-Ellen beside him.

"You know what I need," he said, reaching out and feeling the material of her dress between two fingers.

She turned and grinned at him slyly. "I can imagine."

He shook his head.

"No?" She was surprised. "Well, for sure you need a manager," she said perkily.

"A manager?"

"I keep tellin' you, hon, you're a big hero. A *big hero*." He grinned.

"Don't laugh," she said. "I tell you, here's our chance. They're all outside there now, the newspapers and TV people. They wanna buy your story."

Dr. Hardcastle straightened up. He told the nurse to finish the dressing and said to Coulter, "That's right. I gotta go tell them how you are. And you look out for those people, Rick. They're worse than horse thieves. Believe me."

"Never mind him," Sue-Ellen said as the doctor left.

"Yeah?"

"Yeah." She was a little breathless. "Absolutely, hon. My baby's the biggest hero in the country right now. Honest to God. You wouldn't believe it. An' there's a man downstairs that's an attorney and was one time the governor of the state and he wants to be your manager. Just like Sonny and Cher an' Farah Fawcett an' Louise Lasser an' all them other stars. You got to have a manager, baby."

Coulter closed his eyes.

"Shall I fetch him up?"

He shrugged. "I guess so."

Stewart Kilpatrick had a silvery Vandyke beard, a lean build, and a shrewd look. He reminded Coulter of yacht captains he had seen in South Sea adventure movies.

"I got a log," Coulter said. "I kept it all along."

Kilpatrick pursed his lips. He didn't seem to want to hurry things.

"I got the last part with me. I left the first part with Mike when I left the car."

"I'll get it from the sheriff right away," Kilpatrick said. "The media will be wanting that. They'll pay good money for a log."

"Who will?"

"*Life*, for instance."

"*Life* magazine?"

"Sure," Kilpatrick said. "I've already checked with them. I've got a friend there. They're interested."

"You already checked?"

Kilpatrick shrugged. "Just casually. No commitments yet."

"What happened to Mike?" Coulter asked suddenly.

Kilpatrick was taken by surprise. He looked at Sue-Ellen.

"They didn't tell you?" she asked.

"Yeah, they told me." Coulter spoke quietly, looking away. "But I mean how? Was he in the car? Did he start out or anythin'?"

Sue-Ellen put a hand on his shoulder. "He was in the car."

"Still in the car?"

She nodded.

"Jesus. The poor sonovabitch. It was awful in there."

"Gangrene," Kilpatrick said. "Right up in his thighs. An' so starved, his belly was restin' on his backbone."

"Oh God! Stop it!" Sue-Ellen shrieked. She sat on the bed and took Coulter's hand. But Coulter pulled away, threw off the covers, and got out of bed. He went to the window and stood looking out, standing in his pajamas, the toes of his bare feet bound in white gauze bandages. Outside it was a gray, cold-looking day. Flecks of snow drifted down on the buildings below. It would be a good day for walking, he thought. And then he thought it didn't matter what sort of a day it was anymore. He looked across the town. Over the brown plain and on the horizon he saw the beginnings of the mountains, blue and indistinct. People were in there right now, on sleds poking around where they had been. He felt dislike for them. Derision. They hadn't come when it mattered. Now they were like janitors cleaning an empty house after the last show, guessing what might have happened on a blank screen.

And then he thought of Vern. Vern was still up there, trying for the edge, maybe. Or maybe he'd found a Shangri-la, some-where in the mountains, a place that was better than this. He pondered his own dilemma. What was he going to say to these people who wanted him to tell all? Why should he tell them any-thing? It had nothing to do with them. Eight floors below a red sports car backed out of a space in the lot and a new green station wagon waited for the slot. In the room there was silence.

"Is Vern out?" he asked without looking at them, knowing the answer.

"You know I'd've told you." Sue-Ellen surprised him.

"Did they fetch Coo-Coo?"

"I dunno."

Still he didn't turn.

"They're fetching his body," Kilpatrick said. "The sheriff's com-ing to talk to you about him."

Now he turned. "Sheriff Meyers?"

Kilpatrick nodded, watching him.

"Right away?"

"He's on his way," Kilpatrick said. "There's no one allowed to talk to you before he does."

"So how come you're here, then?"

"I'm an attorney. Sue-Ellen said you didn't have a regular attor-ney, so I thought . . ." He held up his hands.

"He can do both, hon."

Coulter bit at his thumb. "I guess," he said.

"You should have an attorney present," Kilpatrick said.

"You think it wasn't an accident with Coo-Coo?"

"Just for your own protection."

Sue-Ellen vigorously nodded agreement.

"How much d'you charge?"

"Just the regular agenting fee, fifteen percent," Kilpatrick lied. "An' then sixty bucks an hour for legal work."

"Sixty bucks an hour?"

"That's a pretty average figure."

"Jesus!" Coulter said. "You know what Pops pays me?"

Kilpatrick shook his head.

"It doesn't matter."

"No," said Kilpatrick. "I'm sure there won't need to be much legal work."

"They didn't find Vern yet, then?"

Sue-Ellen answered, "No, sweetie. They didn't."

"He left before I did," Coulter said. He gazed out of the window again. He could see the other wing of the hospital. A nurse was unfolding a screen around somebody's bed. A shadow seemed to pass over him.

"I wonder what the hell happened to Vern, then," he said, still looking out of the window. "He must still be out there."

"Probably he'll show up in a day or two," Sue-Ellen said.

"God, I hope so," Coulter said. "It makes me feel weird thinkin' of him bein' out there still."

The sheriff arrived with Goebbels following him in, carrying a tape recorder in a black leather case. The two lawmen seemed large and inappropriate in the hospital room. Their black nylon parkas rustled loudly and their boots squeaked. Their faces seemed raw and violent in this antiseptic place where everything was white except the gray bed blanket and a full-sized reproduction of Van Gogh's *Sunflowers* over the bed.

Before he spoke, the sheriff took Coulter's hand gravely and said, "You sure as hell led us some dance there, Rick."

Bug-eyed, Goebbels stared at the survivor from the end of the bed.

"You look like you're seein' a ghost," Coulter said.

Goebbels swallowed and grinned. The sheriff's weary eyes acknowledged Sue-Ellen and then looked quizzically at Stewart Kilpatrick.

"Mr. Kilpatrick here is my agent," Coulter volunteered.

"Well, you won't be needin' an agent right now," the sheriff said, and took off his hat.

"He's also my attorney," Coulter said.

The sheriff raised his eyebrows. "You'd best set that thing up, Sergeant." He nodded toward the recorder. "An' ask for more chairs."

"*I'll* do that," Kilpatrick said a little too eagerly.

"If you're his attorney, you'd best not leave the room."

When Sergeant Goebbels announced he was ready, the sheriff in his solemn voice identified everyone in the room and the date, time, and the place, taking his time. Then he said to Coulter, "I want you to be sure to answer everythin'. This thing don't record nods, okay?"

Coulter nodded.

"Okay?" The sheriff repeated pointedly.

"Oh," Coulter said. "Yeah."

Sandy Brown walked by the cabin on the path to the river. Wood was stacked outside the back door; an ax, head buried in the snow, leaned against the pile. There was less than half a cord left. She glanced at it, and thought of him standing by the open door in the evening light, split logs held against his chest, looking up at the sky. She knew how it would be inside the cabin, the bed unmade, his navy kit bag half unpacked at the foot, beside his Sunday boots. He had always been half unpacked. She had often wanted to put his things in drawers and hang all his clothes and put his boots away. She had started to do so once, but something stayed her. In a strange way, it would have violated the spirit of his life, denied the quality that gave it distinction. It would have decided something for him that he had not decided yet himself. Not only if he would stay with her, but if he would stay anywhere.

She fought off the temptation to look in through the cabin window, to look backwards. She watched carefully where she trod the path as it went steeply down to the river's edge and when she arrived she congratulated herself for having resisted.

It was a late wintry afternoon. She walked upstream, under the bluff where the town stood. Across the river, half-sunk beyond the crest of the bluff, she saw the rooftops of the houses on Main, turned inward towards one another far away from her. She walked between the bare willow branches, hands deep in her pockets, the hood of her parka pulled up about her ears. Her cheeks and nose were red and, when the wind blew, the cold made her eyes water. At least she told herself it was because of the wind, for she didn't yet feel a crying sadness. The vigil was over and the business done; it seemed only logical to her that he would now come home.

Her memories of him made her laugh out loud sometimes. She saw him standing in the sun outside the Speedy Mart, raising an eyebrow at her over the way the Boyer kid had looked at her breasts. She saw him across the little table in the cabin at dinner.

"If I could rearrange the world—" she'd begun.

He said, "Move that fork."

She did.

"There," he said. "You've rearranged the world." And she saw him grin that vast coppery grin that made the atmosphere glow on every side of him.

She saw him lying naked in the firelight, half-asleep, his skin silky after they had made love.

She saw him at the back door, carrying logs, balancing on one leg, pushing the door closed behind him.

She saw him standing over the stove, his broad back and familiar baggy Levi's, stirring his chili, lifting a little on the tip of a wooden ladle to taste it.

She saw his face over her in the aftermath of lovemaking, the new face of wonder and contentment, the face not seen before.

She saw him running around a bend in the path towards her after work, the strong curve of his body in motion, the arms held up and waving, the exuberance in his face. It made her run a step or two herself.

But then she stopped abruptly and turned to face the river, standing on a small promontory, staring down into it. The water was low and slow moving and very dark. As she looked, the wind gusted, ruffling its face a moment, chasing across the slack water and gone. Like him, she thought. Had he ever been? Truly? She tried to see his face in the water. She crouched down, hugging her knees. She couldn't. She could summon it in her mind, but even then it was a flat two-dimensional image, the edges of it vague, the expression sullen, almost lifeless, as though he were looking at her only half-awake. For a moment, she thought, it might even be contempt, and her heart caught. He had never looked at her that way.

She panicked a little and stood up suddenly. It was growing
dark. She looked about and saw the lights above the bluff. The
town felt strange to her. The river was black and silent. She was
afraid. She hadn't known this man that well. Not really. Perhaps
she had been wrong about it all. Perhaps it had just been an affair,
puffed up in her mind.

She started back, hurrying. She wanted to leave this place now,
to pack up and go tonight. It was a dark, cold, awful place. Her
business with this town was done. She ran a few steps where the
path was even. God, she thought. Had it been her business to de-
stroy him? Was she put here to trap and keep him in this place?
Was this why she felt finished with it, why he looked at her so? Oh
God, this was an evil place. He would never have stayed here but
for me, she thought. He'd be safe now, alive somewhere. She began
to cry, sniffing and wiping at her eyes to see where she was going,
walking the path by habit.

And then she saw him. Standing in the path in front of her. Old
jeans, old boots, old parka, a crumpled hat, smooth face smiling
at her with laughter in the corner of the eyes, broad hands held
out. She stopped and wiped her eyes again. And then she smiled
too and ran towards him, and as she came he turned and, holding
back a hand for her to grasp, led the way home again and she was
no longer afraid. She followed him to the cabin. She had the key
on a ring. Unthinking now, she opened the door and took one
step inside before she realized he was gone again. She stopped,
half-caught, thinking he might have slipped by her and gone
ahead. She took another step, hearing her boot heel on the floorboards, then looked around, her breathing so shallow it was almost imperceptible. Nothing moved. No sound. The place was
just as she had left it.

She took a breath, determined not to be driven off by her own
fear, and walked quickly to the bedroom door and looked in.
There was no color left in the feeble light that came in through
the window over the unmade bed. His bag lay open on the floor,
his boots beside it. Tentatively, she took another step and stooped
to touch his things. As she did, she tensed as though sensing someone behind her. Struggling to control herself, still stooped, she lis-

tened for a sound, holding her breath, the tension spreading in
her chest, the silence growing.

She slowly straightened up and turned around. A hand went to
her mouth. She was straining, her heart beating wildly. It was the
absence of anything that broke her, the possibility of everything.
She gasped a little, took one step, and then scrambled without
dignity for the door, slamming it behind her, running awkward,
gangly, splay-legged in the snow, fifty yards across the slippery
ground to the lights she saw burning in the Hermans' bungalow.
She beat on the door, her breath coming in clouds.

Martha Meyers said, "I must go. I got Burt's lunch in the oven.
If there's anything I can do . . ."

"I'll let you know." Gladys Herman smiled sweetly. Her face
crinkled. "I think maybe the worst's over now though. You know,
it was so strange, but she wasn't sleeping good for—oh, almost
since he didn't come home. An' she's kept pretty much to herself
an' I didn't like to disturb her. I mean, I let her know I was
around and I kep' an eye on her, but I didn't interfere none. You
know what I mean?"

Martha nodded a little impatiently.

"Then Friday night I woke about four an' heard her movin'
about. So I went out an' she was in the linen closet gettin' more
bedclothes. She said she couldn't get warm no matter what."
Gladys paused for dramatic effect. "That was the last night he
was alive."

They stood in silence.

"Burt's over the hospital now, talkin' with Coulter," Martha
said. "He said he didn't see how it could have taken him seventeen days to go eighteen miles."

"Is that what it was?"

"Uhuh."

"Maybe he was hurt or somethin'."

"Burt said he was in real good shape considerin'."

"Oh," said Gladys. "Well, I guess it won't make no difference
to Sandy anyway. And however long it took, I think Rick's a real

hero makin' it at all. He would've gone quicker if he could. Those two were like brothers."

"It's a pity," Martha lamented. "Seems they was really in love, him an' Sandy."

"Oh, they were," Gladys agreed. "You never saw anythin' like it. It was the best thing I saw since . . ." She couldn't think of anything. "Even made George remember a little, so you know it was somethin'."

"I guess it was," Martha said. "I wish I'd seen it myself."

"It was a beautiful thing," Gladys mourned. "It truly was."

There came a frantic pounding at the door.

As Marlene pulled the truck up outside the house, her two girls appeared on the front step, standing on a mound of snow, watching their mother's face. Marlene struggled for composure at the sight of them. She smiled and gave a little wave as she gathered the shopping in the paper sack beside her on the seat.

"Is he all right?" Vickissa called out, straining from the doorway.

Marlene avoided her daughter's eyes as she opened the door and stepped down from the pickup.

"Is he comin' home now?" Vickissa was making little jumps of excitement.

Marlene took two steps towards them and looked at Vickissa and tried to smile again and, as she did, slipped on the ice and fell, dropping the bag. It split open. Green apples and vegetables spilled onto the snow. White paper packets of meat and cheese fell out, and a quart jar of orange juice exploded as it hit the ground. Marlene fell among the debris. The fall jarred loose the tears, and she sat there weeping. Her two daughters ran from the doorway in their stockinged feet to help her.

Coulter told the sheriff what they had agreed on in the Ford: how they had made up their differences when the snow came, how the accident had happened to Coo-Coo. He realized too late that he had said nothing about a firefight, which would become obvious when they looked at Poulsen's bullet-riddled truck. They hadn't thought of that when they were making up the story in the Ford. Coulter was set back by this and hesitated, wondering if he should change his story, sure his audience must have detected something wrong. Then he found himself taking a second tack that he knew could be very dangerous, particularly if Poulsen showed up alive: he told the sheriff it was Arizo who accidentally shot Coo-Coo. In one instant he had thought that with Arizo dead it would make no difference what he said. In the next he felt himself awash with lies, becoming heavy and increasingly difficult to navigate.

But he went on. He told them how they had lived after the accident, about the snowmobiles and the plane, about attempting to walk out and about Arizo's feet. He told them of Poulsen's leaving and his own journey. He saw the reels revolving on the tape recorder and Goebbels' face above it, watching him and listening. He was aware of Sue-Ellen and Kilpatrick to his right. He was also aware of how little of the story he really could tell, and how exhausted he became in the process of deciding what to tell and what not. When he came to the Wild Horse Ranger Station, he became aware of a gap, and in it something even he did not know, and he felt himself faltering, as though he were reading a letter aloud and midway through a sentence came upon something he didn't wish the audience to hear.

Still the sheriff showed no emotion. He sat on the left side of the bed, opposite the others, slowly chewing gum, elbows on his knees, watching Coulter for the most part, occasionally feeling the stubble on his chin with thumb and forefinger, occasionally asking a question or for something to be repeated. His apparent indifference caused Coulter to search for signs, find none, and fall under further pressure.

A couple of times Kilpatrick intervened, with trivial remarks, to justify his existence.

When Coulter finished, the sheriff stood up, stretched, and asked Goebbels to pack the tape recorder.

"Sounds like you had a rough time," he said, looking down at the patient, unsmiling.

"It wasn't a whole lotta fun." Coulter looked for some sign of encouragement but saw none. When they left, he lay back, suddenly bone-weary. His life, he realized, was even less in his control now than it had been in the mountains.

The telephone rang. He was startled by it. It had been silent until now.

"Yeah," he said.

"Hi, this is Nat Hendricks from *Field and Stream*," the voice said cheerfully. "Am I speaking to Rick Coulter?"

"Yeah."

The man wanted to buy first North American rights to his story.

Coulter didn't know what to say. "I think *Life* already bought them," he said.

"Oh." The man was disappointed. "How about seconds?"

"I don't know nothin' about this," Coulter said. "You best talk to my agent."

Coulter felt very strange saying it, but the man didn't seem surprised.

"What's his number?"

"I don't know."

"Please have him call me collect."

"Yeah."

True magazine called.

"We'd like to send a writer out to see you," the editor said.

"I read *True*," Coulter said. He was excited about the magazine being interested. It was hard to believe. He had read *True* for years, ever since his father won a subscription in a fishing contest. *Life* was a family magazine, but they didn't screw around at *True*. They only ran real adventure, and they had Pete Barrett for a hunting editor, and he had hunted all over the world—with Hemingway, even. Coulter hadn't read Hemingway, but he knew of him from the days when he lived in Ketchum.

"Will that be okay?" the man from *True* was asking.

Dr. Hardy, the psychiatrist, came in and Coulter glanced up and lifted his hand for silence. "You'll have to talk with my agent," he said into the phone. Then he covered the mouthpiece and said to the psychiatrist, "I'll be right with you. It's *True* magazine."

The psychiatrist nodded, impressed.

Coulter got the man's number and hung up. He was feeling good.

"If you've got a moment," Dr. Hardy said, smiling.

"Sure."

But the phone rang again.

"Rick Coulter?"

"Yeah."

"This is Sally Tipp of TV's 'To Tell the Truth,' calling from New York. We'd like you to be on our game show."

The door opened and Kilpatrick came in, frowning. Coulter waved at him and said into the phone, "Can you hold on?"

"Those nurses didn't want to let me in." Kilpatrick was a little peeved.

Coulter shrugged. "You know Dr. Handy here?"

"Dr. Hardy," the doctor corrected.

"No," said Kilpatrick.

"I got some TV people on from New York. From 'To Tell the Truth.' They want me to be on their show. You wanna talk to them?"

"Sure." Kilpatrick took the phone.

"What did you want to talk about?" Coulter asked the psychiatrist.

"Oh, just about your experiences," Dr. Hardy said. "What it was like out there."

"Well, we've already sold first North American," Kilpatrick was saying to Sally Tipp.

"It wasn't too swift," said Coulter.

"Well, tell me this . . ."

"He won't be able to talk about it," Kilpatrick said loudly into the phone. "You realize that, of course. He's under contract to *Life* already."

Dr. Hardy glanced at Kilpatrick, who was standing with his back to them. "Tell me this," he began again. "Was some part of it—some aspect—particularly disturbing?"

"Yeah," Coulter replied. "Definitely."

"Air fare plus hotel and living expenses and what?" Kilpatrick sounded disgusted.

"What was that?" Dr. Hardy asked patiently.

Coulter frowned. "My buddy dyin' like that."

"A *hundred dollars!*" Kilpatrick sounded incredulous.

"Of course," Dr. Hardy said. "But what about the things you saw and experienced?"

"Plus winnings?"

"What about them?"

"There must be a guarantee? I mean . . ."

"Well . . ."

"Well, the whole fuckin' thing was a bummer. I mean, whatta you think?"

"What I'm getting at—" Dr. Hardy began.

"Next week? Wait. I'll ask his doctor. Kilpatrick covered the receiver mouth and looked at Dr. Hardy. "I hate to disturb you," he said, "but will Rick be okay to travel the end of next week? They want to tape this show while he's hot."

Dr. Hardy threw up his hands. "I'm a psychiatrist, not a lousy foot doctor!" he yelled. "How the hell should I know? I'm trying to talk to the man. I'm trying to determine if he's suffered some serious, deep psychological trauma as a result of this extraordinary experience, and you're asking me about some two-bit TV show!"

Kilpatrick withered. "Sorry," he said. "But we're talkin' about money for the young man here."

"I'm talking about his entire future!" Dr. Hardy exploded.

"Hold up, Sal," Kilpatrick said into the phone. "I'm gonna have to call you right back on this. We gotta little problem here."

Dr. Hardy was on his feet. "I'll be back later," he said disgustedly, and left.

Kilpatrick hung up the phone and turned around. "What was eatin' him?"

Coulter shrugged.

The phone rang again.

"Can you get that?" Coulter asked, feeling his newfound power. Kilpatrick answered it. The nurse with the beauty mark looked around the door. "Rick," she said, "if you're through with Dr.

Hardy, would you like to see your father now? He's waiting here."

"Yeah," said Coulter. "An' could you get me a color TV, too? An' another one of those pills. You know?"

"You gonna be on?" the nurse asked. "The TV, I mean."

Coulter nodded. He could see his father standing behind her. "I'll see the head nurse," the nurse said, and disappeared.

Dan Coulter came through the door, smiling uncertainly at his son, holding his hat. He looked worn out, Coulter thought.

"Rick," Kilpatrick said, holding the phone, "it's CBS. They want you for '60 Minutes.'"

Coulter popped his eyes. "CBS, huh? You meet my pa, Dan," he said, pointing.

Kilpatrick smiled and made a little bow. Dan Coulter wasn't paying much attention; his focus was on his son.

Coulter held out his arms.

"Rick!" Dan said.

"Papa," Coulter called softly and sat up more in bed.

They embraced, slapping each other's backs.

"His father's just come in," Kilpatrick commented into the phone. "They're hugging each other." In New York, on Sixth Avenue, he heard the man say, "His father just came in. Hang on. They're hugging each other. In the hospital. We beat the father to it. Not bad, eh?"

Kilpatrick was gesticulating to Coulter. Coulter let his father go.

"Aren't we already sold out?" he asked.

"We could change if they'll offer more."

"I don't give a shit."

"I'll see what they'll go."

Coulter sat back on the bed, and, as his father looked proudly, saw a camera pointed at him through the window in the door to his room. The light was such that he could actually see the shutter blinking in the iris. He tugged at Kilpatrick's coat.

"Jesus," he said, pointing. "Look there!"

"Stop!" Kilpatrick dropped the phone and started for the door. "He can't do that. He hasn't got any photo rights. Nobody has."

THE SURVIVOR   301

The camera disappeared and as Kilpatrick reached the door it opened and the nurse with the beauty mark appeared.

"What'n the hell was that photographer doing here?" Kilpatrick demanded.

"How should I know?" She stepped around him. "I had to go to the bathroom."

"The bathroom?" Coulter grinned at her, wide-eyed. "I didn't know nurses went to the bathroom."

"Oh shit," Kilpatrick swore.

"What's the matter?" the nurse said.

"I forgot CBS is on the line." He ran back to the phone.

Dan Coulter stood by the end of the bed, holding his hat, looking from one to another.

"How come the phone didn't start ringing till now?" Coulter asked the nurse. She was making a note on his chart.

"Because this man said not to put any calls through till he'd seen you." She nodded her head towards Kilpatrick without taking her eyes off the chart. "He said he was your attorney."

"No shit? He said that?"

"When you comin' home to get some rest, son?" Dan inquired abruptly.

Coulter looked at him and grinned. "You must be crazy. You think I'll get any rest when I get home?"

"You ain't gettin' much here, by the look of it."

"When you're a celebrity, you got to give somethin' up, Pa."

His father looked hurt. "You a celebrity now? For survivin'?"

"Well, hell yes, Pa," Coulter said emphatically. "What's wrong with that?"

The old man was uneasy. "I ain't sure," he said.

The phone rang.

"See what I mean?" Coulter looked brightly at him. "It never stops."

Kilpatrick answered it. He turned to Coulter. "It's a woman. Says she's a friend but won't give her name."

Coulter looked at his father again and raised his eyebrows significantly as he took the phone.

"Hey," he said into it.

"Rick. It's Marlene." Her voice came from afar, it seemed. It was soft and uncertain. Coulter was caught. Not knowing what to do. Aware of them watching him.

"Hey," he repeated weakly. "How are you?"

"I think I would like to see you," she said. "I thought a lot about it, an' I think we should talk."

"Yeah . . . yeah, but in a bit. I got a whole lotta people here just now. Can I call you back?"

"You got the number."

The others were looking at him when he hung up.

"Just a friend," Coulter said.

"It was Marlene, wasn't it?" his father said.

Coulter nodded.

Kilpatrick excused himself. "Here's my number, Rick. See you tomorrow. We're gonna go all the way with this. You're big news."

"You gonna see her?" his father persisted.

Coulter looked serious. "I said I'd call her back. Whatta you think?"

"I think you'd better be careful if you wanna go on bein' a hero."

"Jesus!" Coulter blew out his cheeks sharply. "I thought the difficult part was gonna be the mountains." His father gave him a wrinkled grin, reminding Coulter a little of Popeye.

"People's the most difficult part of nature," the old man said. "'Cause mostly they don't see where they got anythin' to do with it."

The nurse with the beauty mark came in, followed by an orderly carrying a television set. He put the set down on the table by the far wall and plugged it in.

"You'll be on in five minutes," the nurse said. "And I've got another pill to give you."

Coulter, high on Quaalude, his father sitting beside the bed, watched himself on TV and, wonder of wonders, heard his name on the lips of Walter Cronkite:

"Tonight in the mountain town of Cope, Idaho, they're celebrating the return of one of the community, mourning the loss of two others and still wondering about a fourth. Hero of the most remarkable survival story of the decade is twenty-nine-year-old Rick Coulter, who went hunting in the Sawtooth Mountains with three friends last December first and vanished. Rescue teams went into those thirteen-thousand-foot mountains to battle the worst blizzards in years and temperatures as low as minus fifty. After three weeks all hope for the men was abandoned.

"But this morning, a month and a half after the party was lost, Rick Coulter walked out of the mountains to a hero's welcome. CBS in Twin Falls has details."

They found themselves looking at footage of the mountains in winter from a helicopter.

"That ain't Copper Basin, that's up north of Challis," the old man said.

Over this came the excited voice of the local announcer: "Still unfolding this evening is the epic of Rick Coulter, who fought his way seventeen days through these mountains to bring help to his dying friend . . ." The film cut to Coulter being brought out of the ambulance. He saw himself grinning foolishly at the camera and giving a little wave as they whisked him into the emergency entrance.

"Details are still unclear, but what is clear is that more than six weeks ago a hunting party vanished in the mountains here. One member was shot, apparently the victim of a hunting accident. The three survivors then waited for help that never came. How they managed to survive the storms and freezing cold is still a mystery. But they did. Two days before Christmas, Cope rancher Vern Poulsen set off to walk out alone and bring help to Mike Arizo, a thirty-year-old quarry worker who, by now, was suffering severe frostbite and could no longer walk. So far there is no trace of Poulsen. He simply walked away from the car where the three men had been huddled for almost a month and disappeared.

"Four days later, Coulter followed. It took him seventeen days to cross this brutal terrain, considered by experts to allow an unprepared individual three days of life at the most. He himself suffered frostbitten feet. But Coulter made it and is tonight resting in a hospital here in Twin Falls. Doctors have described his condition as 'remarkable considering his ordeal.' Sadly, Coulter's heroic march to save his friend was to no avail, for on Friday night or Saturday morning, only hours before Coulter reached safety, Mike Arizo died of cold and starvation.

"Tonight the search is continuing for the fourth man, although Sheriff Burt Meyers"—there was now a close-up of the old sheriff—"is not optimistic."

"One man beat the odds," the sheriff said. "Whether two can or not isn't for me to say. We sure hope so, an' we're still lookin'."

Coulter leaned forward and said, in awe, to his father, "Can you believe that?"

"It's a pity you couldn't make the news for somethin' better," his father said.

"It makes me feel real weird to see it," Coulter said. "You can't imagine. It makes me kinda dizzy an' my mouth all dry. It's real weird. It's not like I'm watchin' anythin' to do with me."

"You weren't," his father said.

"Whatta you mean?"

"Television ain't real," the old man said. "You know that."

Dr. Hardy came in. "Could I see you now?" he asked Coulter.

The elder Coulter got up. "I was just goin'," he said. "See you, Rick."

By now Coulter was very stoned. He thought he should tell Dr. Hardy, but then decided not to. A doctor ought to know. And anyway, Coulter didn't care. He felt like he was floating downriver in a rubber boat on a summer afternoon.

Dr. Hardy sat in the chair Dan Coulter had just left. Coulter could see the TV screen over the psychiatrist's shoulder.

"So how do you feel within yourself?" Hardy began.

Black men were rioting on the screen. "Oh," said Coulter, without taking his eyes from it. "I feel okay. Just bad about Mike is all."

Police had turned fire hoses on the protesting black men, and a helicopter was spraying them with something.

"Mind if I shut that off?"

"Let's watch the news anyway," Coulter said. "Cronkite's my main man."

After the news, Dr. Hardy said, "You really like television."

"It helps keep your mind off things," Coulter said.

"What's your mind on right now?"

"Mike."

"What about him?"

"The thing really is," said Coulter after a moment's thought, "that Mike was the only buddy I had. You know. Most of the guys don't like me so much."

"How come?"

"How come?"

"Yeah."

"Oh, I dunno." Coulter hesitated.

"It's because of sex, isn't it?"

Coulter avoided Dr. Hardy's eyes. "Well," he said, "that, an' I got a loud mouth."

"Are you horny now?"

"What the fuck is this?" Coulter said. "You think I'm a sex offender or somethin'?"

"No."

"I never screwed anyone that was under age, if that's what you mean. I'm no short-eyes."

"Do you feel bad about Coo-Coo?"

"Yeah, I feel bad about him."

"You didn't say anything about him."

"That's because my mind is taken up with Mike."

"You didn't say anything about Poulsen either."

"What's there to say? I hope he makes it. Whatta you hope?"

"Well, naturally . . ."

Coulter was getting up out of bed. "You don't mind," he said. "But this talk we're havin' is bullshit. I mean if I got trouble, it's not helping me." He was standing by the TV and switched it on.

"Ford wants to be your car company," Bill Cosby said.

Coulter walked back to bed. "One thing I learned when I was in the mountains," he said, "is what's trouble and what's bullshit. An' if you don't mind me saying so, Doctor, this is bullshit."

"Well, I don't think so."

"Well, I do. I was just up in them mountains, an' we had a real bad time. I mean worse than anythin' you can imagine. An' you wanna talk to me about sex. It ain't got nothin' to do with sex, Doctor. Nothin'." Coulter was standing by the window in his pajamas thinking he felt a whole lot better. He didn't feel angry, really. At least not specifically with Dr. Hardy. He wasn't a kid anymore.

"Ahhh," he said and went back to sit on the bed.

"Hollywood Squares" was just beginning.

"You seem pretty angry."

"Oh, I'm not angry." Coulter watched the TV show half-heartedly. "I just wanna start runnin' my own life again."

"Isn't there something you'd like to talk about?"

Coulter stretched out on the bed and put his hands behind his head. "There's lots," he said. "It's just that I think I killed the only man I could talk to." He got off the bed and went to the window.

"You do, don't you?" Dr. Hardy said patiently.

Coulter turned around. "Oh, you guys!" he said and waved his hand dismissively. "You take everything a man says so goddamn serious."

That night he had the same dream he had dreamed at Wild Horse: the grotesque figure limping after him through the snow, bound in rags, carrying a staff, slowly catching him, until he fell before it and heard its wheezing, rasping breath as it came on, growing as it did so quite disproportionately to its surroundings until its bulk filled the world and he woke sitting upright in bed, soaked in sweat and more terrified than he had ever been.

He turned on the light and then sat on the edge of the bed, hands covering his face. The night nurse appeared. "Goodness!" she said. "What is it?" She came to stand beside him. "Look at this." She touched his forehead. "You're soaked."

But he didn't tell anyone about the dream. He knew, or at least he felt strongly, that it held the key to something, that it was somehow responsible for the way he felt. Thus he still saw it as an appendage to, rather than an expression of, him. That is, he saw

himself as the cause of the dream; not, as he was, the effect of it.
The dream was something that troubled him, and he no more understood why than he understood why God allowed wars or
plagues or personal tragedy. He no more understood it than he or
anyone around understood that the assault of the mountains had
inevitably been as much against mind as body.

Dr. Hardy came to see him twice more, but Coulter didn't open
up to him, and the dislike was mutual. Coulter was desperate to
talk with someone, but since Dr. Hardy's reference to sex, he not
only mistrusted the man, he regarded him with contempt. As he
told Sue-Ellen when she came to see him the next day, "I'm tryin'
to keep my act together, an' this guy wants to talk sex."

But Sue-Ellen didn't hear him. "You don't worry your pretty
little head about a thing," she said. "We're goin' to New York
soon as you get outta here. New York!" She gave a little squeal
and pinched his cheeks. "Can you imagine that? I can't believe
it!"

They let him go home on Thursday afternoon. Sue-Ellen came
with the pickup. Photographers, reporters, and a local TV video
crew were waiting in the foyer. Kilpatrick warned him as they
came down in the elevator:

"Don't talk to them. Be nice but clam up."

"It'll make me look like a criminal or somethin'."

Kilpatrick shook his head. "Let me handle it."

The newsmen crowded around as the three of them came out
of the elevator and followed them across the lobby. Coulter was
limping, perhaps more noticeably than before.

"What are your plans now?" they asked.

"How was Catlin killed?"

"Is Poulsen still alive, d'you think?"

"Was Catlin's death an accident?"

"What did you tell the sheriff?"

"Talk to Mr. Kilpatrick here," Coulter kept saying. "Please."

"We're not at liberty to talk until the sheriff has issued a state-
ment," Kilpatrick kept saying.

"Does that mean the matter is *sub judice?*" someone asked.

"No," Kilpatrick replied.

"It means," said another reporter, "that he's sold an exclusive someplace else."

Sue-Ellen talked nonstop all the way home. She was full of plans for the trip.

"This is your big break," she kept saying. "We're gonna get outta this place finally. You know that, babe?" She was driving because his feet were still wrapped up. She smiled across at him. "You realize? You're gonna be a star when they see you out there. Like Burt Reynolds. Just like you always said. Remember? Burt Reynolds was just as unknown as you are once."

Coulter sat back in his seat, feeling the warmth in the cab, seeing the snow glide by on either side as they crossed the high Snake plain. He looked out and remembered saying to Arizo, "We should keep a log. They'll pay us a million bucks for our story. That's what some people get."

He remembered how Arizo had peered at him doubtfully. He had thought then that Mike *didn't* understand the way things worked. Now, looking out of the window of the pickup, he gave a short laugh.

"You're not listening to me!" Sue-Ellen was protesting. "Whatta you thinkin' about all the time, hon?"

He grunted but didn't answer.

"You look pretty tired," she said. "You know that?"

"I feel it. I had this weird dream the other night. Shook the hell outta me."

"It'll be a whole lot different when we get to New York," she said, "so don't worry 'bout no silly ol' dream."

Coulter watched the road markers flick by and the black ribbon of frozen snowcrust piled on either shoulder of the road by the plough. If he never told anyone the real story, if no one knew and he always told the same story, maybe in time the made-up story would become fact to him in the same way stories parents tell about you as a child eventually become inseparable from the memory of real experience. That's what he hoped would happen. Unless Poulsen came out of the mountains now and told a different story. Coulter looked up at the distant peaks through the windshield and wondered about Poulsen. The man was a one-eyed jack. Always had been. With Poulsen maybe around, he wouldn't have sold anyone a story if Sue-Ellen and Kilpatrick hadn't dragged him into it. It was one more thing to feel bad about, one more reason to sometimes catch himself hoping that Poulsen wouldn't walk out of the mountains. Jesus, he thought, what have I done to myself?

"They're sending us the tickets," Sue-Ellen was saying. "And they made reservations for us at some big hotel on Broadway. Can you imagine it, hon?"

He looked across at her and saw her as though through water. Even her voice came vaguely to him.

"Jesus, Rick," she said. "There you go again."

Jason was at school when they got home. "I thought we should have it private. To ourselves," Sue-Ellen said pointedly.

They went to bed, but for once Coulter couldn't make love. He was appalled. He punched a hole in the plywood closet beside the bed, then lay with his back to her. She came up on one elbow and leaned over him. "Rick, it's okay, hon. It happens to every man sometime."

"Nothin' works for me anymore," he said, and she realized he was crying.

The phone rang.

"It's Sergeant Goebbels for you," Sue-Ellen said.

Coulter waved negatively.

"He's indisposed right now," he heard her say.

There was a pause before she hung up. Then she was leaning over him again. "I'm sorry," she said, "but the sheriff wants to come over in half an hour."

Sheriff Meyers sat at the dining table by the window waiting for Coulter to finish showering.

"What happened to the goldfish?" he called to Sue-Ellen in the kitchen.

"What always happens to goldfish?" she called back without looking. "They die."

She came in carrying coffee. Her hair was wet. The sheriff looked for some small sign of friendly recognition, but there was none. "I got to get this thing cleared up," he said.

"Not this afternoon you didn't have to," she retorted.

The sheriff sighed. His face sagged a little further.

Coulter came in and the sheriff saw that he had had his hair cut and his beard shaved. "Looks better," he said.

"Feels better," Coulter replied.

Sue-Ellen came in with another coffee.

"What's up?" Coulter asked and sat on the sofa.

"You make your own ammunition?" The sheriff looked at him around Sue-Ellen, who was sugaring his coffee.

Coulter blinked in surprise. "Sure," he said. "Is this an official visit? I mean, should I call Kilpatrick or something?"

"I don't mind," the sheriff said. "I just had a coupla things on my mind I wanted to talk about. If you have anything to worry about . . ." He waved a hand.

"Not me," Coulter said.

"Shit, Burt," Sue-Ellen snapped. "You think he's criminal?"

The sheriff ignored her, then wished he hadn't. But it was too late. "You shoot that three-o-three we found?"

"Uh-huh. My Pa give it me years back."

"How'd you make up the load?"

"Depends. 'Fore me an' Mike went out last time, I made up a hot load. Fifty grains. Normally I shoot substandard, forty-four—that'd be six inches under at a hundred. But I told Mike we mightn't be able to get that close with the snow, and we didn't have that much time, so I made up a hot load. I used a one-fifty gram bullet an' forty-three fifty common powder, an' I went up to the maximum load, which, like I said, is fifty grains. That'll put you two inches high at a hundred, dead on at two, and fallin' off ten-an'-a-half at three." Coulter nodded as he said this, and the sheriff found himself nodding in unison.

"You made these up right 'fore you left?"

"Yeah."

"How many d'you make up?"

Coulter shrugged. "Maybe fifty."

"That you took along?"

"Yeah. No sense leavin' them home."

"An' when you left the car to walk out, you took the .30-30?"

"Sure. It's a whole lot lighter."

"So you didn't take none of them bullets you made up?"

Coulter was beginning to feel uncomfortable. "Whatta you really wanna know?" he asked, eyes locked on the sheriff.

The old man took a sip of coffee, hand shaking slightly, making a considerable noise and it occurred to Coulter that he was nervous.

"Well, we never found any shells in the car when we went in there to fetch back your friend." He put the cup back on the table. "An' I was wonderin' if I missed them or somethin'."

"We used them up."

"The whole bunch?"

Now Sue-Ellen was watching closely, too.

"Sure. We had them guys come by on snowmobiles, and there was the airplane. You think we just stood there an' whistled, or somethin'?"

The sheriff grinned slightly at this, and Coulter relaxed into the sofa. "Get me some more coffee, hon," he told Sue-Ellen.

"You took a full clip when you left the car?" The sheriff looked up with uncharacteristic suddenness.

Coulter hesitated. "I guess," he said. "No sense carryin' a empty gun."

"You shoot at anythin' when you was walkin' out?"

Coulter shook his head. "No."

"You must have."

Coulter took the coffee from Sue-Ellen. The uneasiness was back in him, like a vague nausea. He was beginning to sweat.

"Why's that?" he said.

"That gun you was carryin', it was empty."

Coulter sipped his coffee. Time to think. He was taken by surprise.

"It wasn't empty," he said.

The sheriff stared at him impassively.

"It couldn't've been."

"It was when we checked it."

"You mean I was carryin' that thing all around for nothin'?"

The sheriff shook his head. "You shot the lock off at Wild Horse and the other cabin. Don't you recall?"

"Yeah," Coulter lied. "Now you mention it, I recall."

"You must've been pretty tired when you got there," Sue-Ellen said. And then to the sheriff: "We'll pay for the locks, you know."

"That's nothin'," he said. "But I was wonderin' what happened to the rest of the rounds in that clip."

Coulter thought awhile before he said, "I don't recall firin' it again."

The sheriff put down his coffee and slowly stood up. "If you recollect anythin' more, lemme know. I don't mean to rush, but I gotta get goin'."

"You should come around again sometime," Sue-Ellen said to him, extending a hand. "Anytime there's anythin' you need." A saucy glint in her eye, she turned to Rick. "Sheriff Meyers was *so* good to me while you was gone. He was a real comfort, I can tell you. He took care of me real good, hon."

"I'm glad to hear it," Coulter said offhandedly, while Sheriff Meyers, in total confusion, looked from one to the other.

As often as he had dreamed of the warmth and company of the bar while he was in the mountains, Coulter found going there that evening, after the sheriff's visit and a strained reunion with his son, to be an act of courage. The reporters had asked strong questions; the sheriff seemed to have some doubt. Coulter was uneasy and confused. "Do they all figure it's my fault?" he asked Sue-Ellen. "Did they forget about Vern an' all?"

Word went out immediately that he was in the bar. The place filled so full that Sanders had to call McGarth to help him pour.

The place was very noisy. Coulter felt the weight of many eyes on him and was coming to anticipate the congratulatory smacks on the back.

Leonard was there, grinning out of his good eye, and Rich

Spangler and Jim Rose, nose still redder, and on the end stool, sucking his pipe and leaning against the wall was Epke, talking to Don Puccinelli. Coulter found it strange to see them all standing about, in the flesh, like nothing had ever happened. Early on, Buddy Lane, cheeks pockmarked, rubbing his hands obsequiously, came to buy him a drink.

"I should buy you guys one," Coulter said.

"Hell no," Lane said. "I owe it you. Standin' right here one night, I bet Fred Meyers a yard one of you guys would make it out at least. An' that was Christmas. You shoulda seen it around here Christmas."

"That old boy bet against us, uh?" Coulter said, thinking of Fred Meyers here in the warm bar while they lay freezing in the Ford. For a moment, he heard the wind and he shuddered.

"You can't blame 'im," Red Lewis was saying.

"It was a fair bet," someone added.

"What I wanna know," Bud Lewis pressed in, "is how come you guys took the Burma road? How come if you was goin' to the Big Lost, like you said, did you take the Burma road?"

"We got lost," Coulter replied coolly.

Lewis scratched the back of his neck and raised a red eyebrow. "I can see the Injun gettin' lost," Lewis said. "He just arrived . . ." Suddenly it was tense and all around they were watching Coulter closely, half-fearful cattle, large-eyed and blowing with curiosity. Coulter was groping for an answer when Josie Seiler suddenly burst through and kissed him on the cheek. "Jesus, but it's good to see you again!" she cried.

Coulter grinned wide with relief and his eyes shone. He reached out a hand and shook Lewis by the shoulder in a close way. "Let's drink to Vern," he shouted. "Let's pray he makes it." There was a solid chorus of agreement. They did. And after that they all drank to the men who didn't.

But Coulter did go back. He went back the day after this, which was on Friday. He was flown back in a six-place Bell helicopter chartered by *Life* magazine, with pilot, photographer and assistant, writer, and art director.

The writer was a tall, fair-haired young man with a soft upper lip and sincere eyes. He had been in Vietnam, he said, and he was writing a book on the war. The impression Coulter got of him was that he was a man who didn't need to be doing what he was doing but was doing it because it was the thing to do. Coulter found he couldn't reach bottom with the writer, who asked a lot of detailed questions and kept telling Coulter he knew what it must have been like and comparing it with Vietnam until Coulter wanted to tell the guy he couldn't have any idea what it had been like. But he remembered Kilpatrick's words about the money, held his tongue, and to that degree, answered the guy.

They flew in low over the Burma road, skimming the ridges he and Arizo had so laboriously climbed in the Ford that night. He saw the ground reach up and as they cleared each spine, fall away with breathtaking suddenness. Coulter watched in silence. The latent violence of the mountains was most apparent seen this way: walls, pinnacles, jagged teeth, slopes, ice faces plunging into shadowed crevasses. It was a wild, wild sea, frozen in mid-moment, spume clouds streaming, whitecaps caught tumbling from a razor crest.

And dead. Dead he realized, because he was looking at it through a glass that took away the wind. Wind was the living breath of winter mountains, Arizo said once in the Ford. And their anger, too. With their breath they destroyed you. He would never know another Arizo, Coulter realized. Looking out at the mountains that had killed him, he felt the greatest sadness he had yet felt.

"This the road?" the writer yelled.

Coulter nodded.

"God!"

"Yep."

They had decided to follow the Burma road in and fly out over the route he had walked.

"This is the only way I'd ever go in here," the pilot called back to Coulter. Coulter didn't respond. The pilot had short gray hair and wore slacks and a short-sleeved black turtleneck and a red sweatband around his head. He never took his hands off the controls.

Coulter was sweating. He felt hot and cramped and claustrophobic, with no connection whatever to these people. They were so slick and tight. They had their own language. Their talk spanned the world with familiarity. They spoke of life in terms of newsworthy quotes, of getting things out of people and getting into places he had never heard of, of black and white versus color, of spreads and layouts, of light and shots and words and angles. They were a team that liked to blitz and, he realized with a sense of powerlessness, they were blitzing him.

He heard the strop of the blades: whop, whop, whop, whop. The *real* story, the writer kept saying. What's the real story on this? What then was he to tell them? That he'd been desperate and shit-scared? That he'd blown up and lied and killed the only guy that could help him and the only halfway decent buddy he'd ever had? Should he tell them how much he loved Mike and yet how scared he was of him? Especially now that he was dead. Would they figure that out? Should he tell about the dream? About the black feeling? About how they were making him feel worse all the time, like Dr. Hardy and Kilpatrick and the sheriff and his goddamn greedy wife and his gloomy father and all the rest of them who thought it was over? He'd thought it was over, too—at the cabin where the red-haired girl was washing dishes. He'd thought he was safe then. What bullshit! He looked around the cockpit at the writer, the photographer, the art director, tall and bearded, all peering intently down at the mountains that he knew; with which only he had a covenant. They had come to get the story and they were part of it and didn't know it. Like all the others.

It had something to do with what Mike had said to him just before he left the car. It was maybe the last thing he really said: "Don't go tryin' to figure things out all the while. Sometimes you can't ever see the answer if you're always tryin' to figure it out. Gets your brain all full of stuff an' keeps you too busy. . . ."

"Are we close?" the writer yelled at him.

Coulter instantly lost the thread, and he was upset because he had felt close to understanding something. It had been right there. Right there. Jesus.

"Are we close?" the writer called again.

The photographer was busily shooting from the far window. The short whine of the motor drive cut through even the engine noise.

"Yeah," Coulter yelled. "See that?" He pointed to the mountain coming at them fast. "That's Big Black Dome. It's right below there."

The pilot banked slightly to the left as they came over the ridge of firs into Muldoon Canyon; the way the plane had been banked when they first saw it from the roof of the car, Coulter thought. The Ford was right below them in an instant, a fly caught in a swirl of icing. The pilot straightened up. The sun was dazzling on the surface of the snow. They circled around and came floating in, tail down a little, to alight on the snow twenty yards above the car.

As he got out, Coulter realized that they had landed almost exactly on the spot where he had turned back as he was leaving, at Mike's call. He stepped around the nose of the helicopter and stood looking down the slope at the car. Next to the elegance and mechanical sophistication of the helicopter the old half-buried Ford looked slovenly and ashamed. He felt a sense of betrayal when looking at it. He heard the men talking, calling to one another, complaining about the cold, getting their gear together, and once again he saw Arizo sitting on the hood as he had done, bare feet in the snow.

Coulter turned away in dread, only to see the pilot, still in his seat, staring at him through the bubble. The others were clustered busily about the hatch. What scared him about these people, he realized, was that they were too busy figuring and planning. They couldn't hear. It was *their* story they were going to get. Not his. He looked away, back down to the car, and beyond it he saw the crows sitting in the top of the tallest willow along the creek, watching. A gust of wind came up and briefly stirred the powder. He squinted in the sunshine and he heard the voice again. Even now, in remembrance, it was robust, the phrases kept short, the timbre strong and thick with rough humor. Even when he had been slowly dying: "Hey, Rick. Come here a minute, will you?"

He had known it then, Coulter realized. Known there would be no reunion. Guilt rose up into his throat. He turned away from the car and found the writer standing there beside him, shoulders hunched, hands in the pockets of his fancy parka, face pinched and red, looking at him from the corner of his eye.

"Are you all set?" the writer asked.

Coulter hesitated, not wanting to engage himself in this other world. He shook his head. "I'm not goin' down there," he said.

"Hey, let's go," the photographer yelled. "This light's terrific."

The writer watched him questioningly. "I don't wanna ever go back there," Coulter explained. "I can't." The writer looked pained.

The photographer was coming towards them around the nose of the helicopter, walking with great difficulty, sinking to his knees in the snow, a large aluminum camera box over his shoulder.

"Jesus Christ!" he said as he got to them. "I don't know how you walked a hundred yards in this shit. Honest to God!"

The two men shifted and said nothing.

"What's up?" the photographer asked. He was short and dark-haired, with very energetic eyes and a face always in motion.

"He's not coming down to the car," the writer told him.

The photographer looked at Coulter with keen disappointment. "How can I get a good shot if you don't come?" he asked.

"I'm sorry." Coulter dug his hands deeper into the pockets of his parka.

"I just want to get *one* picture," the photographer pleaded. "All you gotta do is take maybe thirty steps down that hill, sit on the floor at the back of the car when I get the door open, an' that's it. You don't have to go in the car or anything."

"I'm not going back," Coulter insisted. "I'm real sorry."

"You *are* back," the photographer reminded him. "You already *are* back, an' everything's okay. Right?"

"I'm not back—not down there."

318

The Noble Enemy

They looked at him. "Come on, Bob," the writer said, inclining his head. "It's really a heavy number for the guy."

"I can dig it," the photographer said.

The writer took Coulter and Sue-Ellen to dinner at the Bluebird that night. Coulter felt even less like talking and, although the writer didn't push anything and seemed happy to talk about things that had nothing to do with the mountains, Sue-Ellen was determined.

"Tell him about how the accident happened, hon," she prompted.

Coulter demurred. "I already did."

"Did you tell him how you was the one that got them to go back to the car when otherwise you all would've froze?"

Coulter shook his head. "It wasn't me," he said. "It was Mike that done it."

"That's not what he told me." Sue-Ellen turned to the writer. "You wanna hear what he said to me?"

The writer glanced at Coulter and shrugged. "Sure," he said. "I *hope* he tells you things he won't tell me."

Sue-Ellen then went into a long recounting, and whenever Coulter interrupted to correct her, she told him to hush up. "He's just too damned modest," she told the writer. She was also interrupted by several people who came over to shake Coulter's hand and pat his shoulder.

They had taken a booth in the farthest corner from the door, and Coulter had asked Chloe Tippet to keep people away. But Chloe's idea of keeping people away was to tell them that "the missing hunter" was eating at the back with the man from *Life* magazine and didn't want to be disturbed.

"Well, it won't disturb him if I just go over for a second an' say 'Hi!' I got to shake his hand," Bob Fraser, for one, said when he came back from bowling in Twin Falls.

"Well, I guess it won't hurt none," Chloe Tippet said. "Was you his friend?"

"Why, sure. We always know'd Rick."

"I guess it wouldn't hurt then," Chloe said, brushing back an imaginary strand of blond lacquered hair.

Buddy Lane came in and Josie Seiler said "Hi," too. Sue-Ellen greeted them all with a good deal of warmth and familiarity.

"Rick's got a mess of friends in this town," she boasted.

"I can see that," said the writer.

"Everyone loves him. Look at him. He's so cute."

Coulter got up from the table.

"Where you goin', hon?"

"I gotta pee," Coulter said. "You wanna come hold it for me, huh?" He turned and walked away before she could reply.

The john seemed like a sanctuary. He belched as he stood at the urinal, took a couple of deep breaths and blew the air out sharply. He thought of leaving, going to the bar. What did they need with him? he thought. They were doing fine together. Shit. He went out through the kitchen. Sue-Ellen and the writer never saw him.

He didn't go to the bar. Instead, he drove across town to see Pops Bivaletz. When he was home, the old man never locked the door. He was sitting at the table in the kitchen, a cigarette hanging from his mouth, squinting through the smoke, listening to the news. He waved Coulter to a seat, smiling as he did, but saying nothing. Coulter sat and waited for the news to end.

"President Sadat has told an American correspondent for the Washington *Post* in Cairo that unless Iraeli Premier Begin is prepared to concede on all points made in his plan, peace in the Middle East would remain a dream. At the top of his list, President Sadat placed immediate and total withdrawal from Arab-occupied territory in the Sinai," the newscaster said. Pops Bivaletz hunched his shoulders, turned down the volume, and stubbed his cigarette out in the skull ashtray before him.

"Oi, yoi, yoi," he groused. "Regard zis Sadat. You know 'im yes? In ze war 'e was soldier for Hitler. For ze Nazis."

Coulter looked blank.

"Absolutely. 'E was fighting for Rommel. An' ze British zey 'ave put 'im in prison. An' zey want us to trust zis man. I ask. Is impossible, no?"

"I guess," Coulter said.

"Regard," Pops said and there was mischief in his eye. "'Ow many years ze American vant to leave Panama? Twenty-three. Yes? Because it ees in ze national interest." He grinned and stopped to light another cigarette. Coulter sat, watching. Pops suddenly stuck his neck forward, like a heron, and Coulter knew he was at his point.

"So," he said. "Regard. 'Ow can zey sink it ees too much time if ze Israelis want ten years to leave Sinai? No?"

Coulter had little idea what he was talking about. He didn't know where Israel was, or Egypt. But when the old man talked like this, his own problems dissolved considerably. "So," Pops shook his head as if to shake off the thought and surveyed Coulter's considerable bulk, obviously delighted. "Shalom, shalom," he said. "I did not expect to see you again. Yes? But perhaps I am seeing a ghost, yes? Wait." He drew back his head and looked serious. "'Ow can zis be? A ghost zat walks? A ghost zat talks? A ghost right 'ere in my kitchen? I sink zis is a miracle. No?"

Coulter laughed. "Regard," he aped, beating his considerable chest. "A solid ghost."

The old man laughed, rubbed his head, squeezed his eyes, and put a hand upon Coulter's arm.

"Please," he said, "sit down an' I make us some tea. Yes? One minute. Also I 'ave some special cakes for you."

He went to the sink. "Ah," he shook his head and, as the kettle filled, smiled at Coulter. "You cannot know 'ow pleased I am to see you once more. I 'ad sink to myself . . ." He raised his free hand in a flat-palmed gesture of finality. He turned off the tap. "But Mike. I 'ear 'e is dead. An' ze ozer boy . . ."

"Coo-Coo." Coulter was suddenly somber.

"An' zis ozer man, Poulsen. 'E?"

"It doesn't look good," Coulter said.

Pops nodded and set the kettle on the stove. He turned the stove on and came back to the table and slowly sat.

"Regard," he said, looking at him earnestly, "zis is a terrible sing, but now eet is finish and you must go on." He sat back in his chair and put his hands on the table. "Now I sink it ees finish for you 'ere."

Coulter looked surprised. "You mean I should leave town?"

Pops shrugged and raised his hands. "Ees not an easy sing. Zis I know, but regard. Zere ees too much trouble 'ere for you now in zis town."

"You're serious?" Coulter said.

Pops nodded. "You didn't ask me, but I am your friend an' so I say."

"But I'm a hero here. You know that?"

Pops shrugged and said nothing.

"So why should I leave?"

"It will be much trouble for you if you stay."

The old man rose, took the kettle off the stove, and poured out the tea into the glasses with the silver stands. He carried them slowly back to the table and then took a small carton of milk from the refrigerator. He poured a little in both glasses and sat down. Then he spoke.

"Regard," he said, waving his cigarette between his fingers, "a lot of sings 'ave 'appen zat are not so good. Yes? An' oo' is remaining? Only you. So zey will blame you for all zese sings. For all zere trouble. You do not sink zey blame ze dead men? Zere 'usbands, zere friends, zere sons?"

He peered at Coulter. "You do not sink zey blame zemselves? Eh? No. Zey blame you. First one. Zen two. Zen a hundred. Zen all of zem. Zen zere is a pogrom, an' you are finish 'ere. I 'ave seen it." He bent forward, handing a cup to Coulter. "You will stay? Regard. I 'ave seen it. Not once but many, many times. I 'ave seen it in Russia. I 'ave seen it in Poland. I 'ave seen it when ze Germans come to my village, when ze Russians come, ze Bolsheviks . . . You must go."

Coulter gaped in silence, as the old man's words struggled to pierce the membrane of his conditioning and ignorance. The old man looked appraisingly, knowing he had done his best.

"Can I use the phone?" Coulter asked.

He waited for twenty minutes, standing in the snow outside Pops' house, shifting his weight from one foot to another, keeping back in the shadow, filled with conflict about Pops, about Marlene.

She came, wheeling the pickup around the turn with authority. He opened the door and slid onto the passenger seat, catching a brief look at her in the interior light before he slammed the door, her eyes wide, lips pressed together. In the darkness again she reached out and touched his sleeve. "God," she said. "You really are alive."

"Drive up the end," he told her. "There's not gonna be anyone there."

She started off. "I can't believe you came back," she said.

"Whatta you mean?"

"That any of you lived. That I can touch one of you. We talked about you all so long, we prayed, we dreamed, we wished. You can't imagine. And now to have one of you *here*. You can't imagine."

He didn't know what to say.

"Are you all right?" she asked.

"Yeah," he said automatically. And then, letting go a little and even in that small degree finding enormous release: "No, not really."

The trunks of the poplar trees blinked white as they popped into the headlights.

"I don't know what to tell you. I don't *feel* right. I feel tensed up and weird about the whole thing."

She was silent a moment. "Maybe that's just because it isn't over. It'll pass. You'll be fine. You'll see."

"Pops Bivaletz says I should leave town."

"Why?" she was surprised.

A hundred yards off in the headlights he saw the rocks where the road gave out and joined a dirt path that led up the canyon.

"He says people will get down on me."

"Bullshit," she said, slowing the truck. "You're a hero. Everyone thinks so."

She pulled over, turned off the engine and the lights and they leaned against their doors and looked across at each other in the darkness.

"How was it?" she asked.

He stared at where the voice came from, but saw only darkness.

"I was the kid, I guess." He spoke softly. "I got scared, and they kept me goin'."

"I'm glad you said that."

"Yeah?"

"That's what I figured."

"And . . ." he began.

"And you blew out on them."

"No." His voice was hurt and a little angry. "Is that what you think?"

"I dunno," she said. "I was just ending up what it seemed like you were saying."

"I didn't blow up."

"How was Vern?"

"When?"

"When you last saw him. Anytime. I dunno."

"He was real angry at the start. But then the snow came. I guess it was a good thing it did come, in a way."

"Oh?"

"Yeah." He tried to make out her face, but he could only see the silhouette of her head, and that faintly. He was wondering whether to tell her. "It cooled us out, all of us," he said.

"Did you fight?" He felt her eagerness.

He made up his mind. "We didn't have a chance," he said. "The snow caught us goin' in." He told her the agreed story. He told of seeing Vern off on the ridge and of how brave he thought Vern had been. He told her of things Vern had said about her and their children.

"I didn't blow out on Vern," he said. "Vern left the car first. We agreed if he didn't get help in a certain time, I'd go."

"Vern's dead," she said flatly.

Too many things went through Coulter's mind for him to answer.

"It's been a month. You can't last a month up there. Not in the open."

"Maybe he found a cabin."

"You found the cabins. That's all there is up there."

"He coulda got hurt and . . ."

"Oh shit. He didn't make it. He wasn't that tough anyway."

"It seemed like it."

"Yeah?" She seemed pleasantly surprised. She lit a cigarette. He watched her face in the light of the match until she shook it out.

"I don't wanna talk about it," she said.

"Can I have a cigarette?"

She passed him one and their hands touched.

"How d'you feel about me?" she asked.

"Right now?"

"Yeah. Right now."

"I dunno," he said and swallowed. "It's like there's you an' me an' you an' Vern, and I feel bad when we talk about Vern."

He heard her sigh. "Well, I feel real good with you," she said. "You're the only person in my life I can relax with. You know?"

"Yeah," he said. "It's the same for me. That's why I called you." But as he said it he knew it wasn't so. The black feeling was there again. "Something's really wrong," he said. "Something."

"Wrong about what?"

"I dunno." For an instant again he was going to tell her the truth about Vern. How crazy he had been. About the fight and all the rest. For an instant he thought she might be with him enough to handle what he wanted to say. Jesus, he wanted to get it out of him. That and the truth about Coo-Coo. He'd never kept a big secret before. Never seen how close you could walk to the edge. It fascinated him to know he could open his mouth and in an instant change his life completely and forever and to see how tempted he was to do it. There must be a lot of people walking around like that. He wondered how long he was going to be able to keep it up. Or if he could. He saw how the secret was changing him.

"I thought when you came out you'd be angry with me like everyone else," she said. "Or ashamed or somethin'."

He said nothing. He was a long way from her. It was very still.
"Are you gonna leave town?" She seemed hesitant.
"You think I should?"
She thought. "Yeah. An' I'll come with you. I'm a fresh widow
an' a whore in this town. I'm through here."
He was confused.
"Whatta you think?"
"We could," he speculated.
"We should," she said with enthusiasm. "We could start over."
"Yeah, I suppose."
She reached over and pulled out the ashtray to stub her ciga-
rette. She was halfway across the cab. He saw her face in the dark-
ness now, shining slightly, the shadow of her eyes and mouth, the
line of her jaw. It held there an instant, alive, a shadow of consciousness; seen but mostly not, motionless, suspended, com-
pelling. He reached and touched it. He was moving towards it.
"Hold me, cowboy," she whispered. "Just hold me." She said it
softly, as if to herself. "I been so alone you can't believe it. Hold
me."
They didn't kiss. They clung to one another.
"I'm real messed up right now," he said and, thinking about it,
he began to sob. "God, we made such a *mess!*"
She pressed him more tightly. "Come back," she said. "Don't
think about it. It's not just you or me. It's all of us. It's the way
we are that's a mess."
Then he exclaimed, "God! What about Mike? We took him
out, and he wasn't a mess. He was truly somethin'. He's all I think
about."
She said nothing for a while and then, suddenly, "I should get
back. The kids are waitin'."
"I'm sorry to talk like that. Hey . . . I wanna be together like
him y'know, but sometimes . . ."
"I know what you're saying. I cried about it a hundred nights. I
can't cry any more. Not for Vern or Mike or anybody. Not even
for myself."

In the next morning's mail Coulter received a pair of TWA round-trip tickets to New York. He stood by the window in the living room, fingering them. They were in a sleek white folder printed in red and blue: Trans World Airlines, he read, and at the bottom in blue was printed "Present Boarding Pass and Coupon on Departure". Sue-Ellen got off the sofa and came to stand beside him. She took them from him.

"Ooh!" she squealed. "Let me see! New York. Baby, we're really goin'. We're really gettin' outta this town. I can't believe it."

By the same mail, Sandy got a letter from Bell Helicopter Service in Twin Falls addressed to Mrs. Mike Arizo. She opened it with considerable curiosity: "For removal by helicopter of remains of Mr. Mike Arizo (deceased) from Copper Basin, 95 minutes @ $1 per, $95.00. plus tax $9.44 Total: $104.44. With thanks."

Sandy gave a funny little laugh when she read it. She put her hand to her mouth. Then she sat by the telephone stand in the hallway outside the kitchen and cried. When she felt better, she called the helicopter people and told them to bill the county. Then she called Sue-Ellen Coulter.

"Listen," she said. "I want Mike's log."

Sue-Ellen gave her Kilpatrick's number.

"Mr. Kilpatrick's out of the office and the log is in New York with *Life* magazine," his secretary said.

Life said the writer was now on assignment in Lagos.

"I want to get hold of my husband's log," Sandy said.

Life put her on hold and then said, "Our records show that we've already paid Mr. Coulter's agent for all this material. I'm afraid you'll have to get in touch with him."

"But they're not the same person," Sandy argued confusingly.

"No," said *Life*, "but presumably Mr. Kilpatrick was the agent for both parties."

"But he *wasn't*."

"Well, that wasn't made clear to us," came the counter. "I'm afraid you'll have to take it up with Mr. Kilpatrick. Sorry."

Sandy called Sue-Ellen again.

"Rick's out right now," Sue-Ellen said. "I'll tell him to call you when he gets home. Okay?"

"I want Mike's log," Sandy said emphatically. "I never saw it."

"Well, you'll get it. If you're entitled to it, you'll get it. No one's gonna screw you."

Sandy hung up. "No one's gonna screw you," her mind echoed. She looked at herself in the hall mirror. Her olive skin had gone pale and slightly green. She stretched the skin down over one cheekbone and held it there and looked at the dark circle beneath the eye. She would go to Florida, she thought. He said they would go somewhere warm when he came back from the mountains. Fort Myers came to her, for no particular reason. She'd get a job there as a waitress. She'd pretend they were on the beach together, lie in the sun and talk to him, take a double room with a kitchenette and dream of him beside her. She wouldn't talk to anyone but him. Maybe she'd get pregnant with his kid, and when the summer weather came and the season ended, they'd go to New Mexico, to Taos. She'd introduce him to her friends there. The man she'd found. And they'd admire him and her and envy her and the child to be born in the fall. She got up slowly, as if not to disturb the thought, and went to tell Gladys she was leaving.

They buried Coo-Coo's body up in Kellogg, next to his mother's. Coulter didn't go because Rail Catlin told his father, "It won't be necessary." Coulter was relieved. When they went to dig for Coo-Coo's body, he'd felt they might discover Poulsen's pickup all shot full of holes. He thought up several stories to tell: the best was that Poulsen had gone crazy when he realized they were caught in the snow that first morning and shot the hell out of his own truck. It wasn't too great, but still he'd say he forgot to mention it.

But when they came out with the body, no one spoke about the pickup. He wondered whether they hadn't found it or weren't saying anything to him. And then he ran into Epke in the hardware store and Epke said they had a hard time even finding the truck because it was completely buried. Fred Meyers, the sheriff's brother, stood behind the counter in the hardware store looking fresh-scrubbed as a new potato. "I think it's amazin' you guys went back in there right now," he said to Epke. It was something a girl might say, Coulter thought.

Epke looked at him, pipe firmly in his mouth. "We took the chopper," he said. "It was no big thing." Arizo's funeral was the following day, at a parlor in Twin Falls. It wasn't actually a funeral, it was a cremation service. Arizo had no money for a funeral, and anyway the ground would be too hard for burying till spring. Coulter went with Sue-Ellen and his father. The whole town turned out, and people from Challis and Arco came, too. Red Lewis, Seiler, Joey Leonard, Epke, Rose and Len Longren each came with their wives and each caught Coulter's eye and exchanged nods of recognition with him and Sue-Ellen.

Sandy sat in the front row next to Pops. She had persuaded the old man to say a eulogy. Pops stood before them on a carpeted dais in a baggy blue serge suit with wide lapels and pleats, an old gray fedora in his hands. He looked at them, and when they were silent, he cleared his throat, raised his head, and said: "None of us 'as been Mike Arizo's friend for very long. But," he paused, "zis man, oo' vas a stranger to us four months ago when 'e come, 'as 'ad a great effect on all of us. 'E vas a private man. A quiet man. A sinking man. 'E vas a man of peace, an', as ve 'ave seen, a man of great courage." He looked around. "I sink 'e 'as forgiven many sings in 'ees life, an' since I know 'im, I see zat 'e 'as ze two most important quvalities: 'E ees a simple man an' 'e is a *honest* man." He put a very considerable emphasis on this next-to-last word and his sincerity gave him great dignity and strength.

"Regard," he said, looking at them all a little sideways. "I suppose you 'ave come 'ere zis afternoon since you are Mike's friends. Zo. If you 'ave come for zis reason, you will go from zis place an' you will try to be like 'im. You vill know you are afraid, an' zen you will 'ave courage. You vill 'ave compassion, my friends. You vill know you may not judge a man. You vill forgive even yourselves." He bowed slightly to them all. "Shalom," he said. "Peace."

Dan Coulter felt obliged to throw a farewell party the night before his son left for his TV appearance in New York. Cars and pickups blocked the road clear down to Main. It was the biggest party in town since the Fourth of July. A lot of people got drunk and sentimental. It was half a thanksgiving, half a wake. The sheriff came, and Coulter caught him as he arrived, figuring that to be the best move.

"Anythin' goin' on up there?" he asked.

"In the mountains?"

"Yeah."

The sheriff tilted his head. "Looks like you was the lucky one," he said.

Coulter should have been relieved, but the words made him puzzled and uneasy.

"I just hope your luck holds," the sheriff added. " 'Scuse me."

The sheriff's words stayed with Coulter until the plane came in over Queens, dropping a wing through shreds of cloud and driving rain to show him acres of gray concrete, brick, bare trees, and cars edging through wet streets of New York City.

Looking down, he thought, "God. Why did we come here? What sort of people choose to live here?"

"There'll be one of them limousines to meet us," Sue-Ellen said. "They said they'd send someone. We're celebrities here. You act right, hon, and we're gonna be rich. You won't ever have to drive a lousy truck for that two-bit Pops again."

Coulter smiled doubtfully.

"Well," she said. "It's true."

But there was no limousine. Just a junior secretary from the show to meet them and put them in a cab, and a small room in the Americana on Sixth Avenue.

Sue-Ellen chewed her gum more voraciously than usual while she was in New York. And as they were being interviewed in their room by a writer from *True* magazine, she belched loudly and directly into Coulter's face when he disagreed with something she said. The writer was amazed, but Coulter scarcely seemed to notice.

"To Tell the Truth" was taped at a studio on Sixth Avenue on Sunday afternoon. Coulter left the hotel while Sue-Ellen was still in the bath. He had to be at the studio three hours before show-time. Outside it was gray and cold and raining. He took a cab.

He felt very awkward in the studio. None of his clothes seemed to fit. All around him people moved decisively. He thought about leaving, but as he did, a studio assistant grabbed him and led him around like a handler leading a prize bull from show ring to hamburger.

She took him first to the briefing room where he met the "two impostors," as they called them: one a poultry farmer from Ithaca, the other a Brooklyn bookkeeper dressed like a lumberjack. The bookkeeper leaned over to him and said confidentially, "When I go to work, I don't use the elevator. I run up sixteen flights of stairs every morning. How'd you like that, huh?"

Coulter had to spend two hours telling the impostors enough about his experience for them to assume his identity.

"It's terribly important you do this thoroughly," the director told them. "It's not just the panel you're out to stump, it's millions of viewers all across America. Do a good job here," she told Coulter in a confidential whisper, "and you could be noticed."

Sitting in a windowless, air-conditioned room with white styrofoam walls and fluorescent lights, talking to urbane strangers about what had happened in the mountains, he came to loathe himself. He was a whore, he thought. And the spirit of the men he had been with crowded in on him and dried him up and he became immensely depressed.

The panel picked him out with no difficulty while Sue-Ellen sat in the front row waving to the cameras until they stayed away from her entirely. They gave him $50 afterwards. In cash. In the cab on the way back downtown, Sue-Ellen shrieked at him.

"You blew it!" she said. "You know that? You blew the whole fuckin' thing!"

Coulter looked out of the window. It was drizzling. The cab stopped at a light. The man in the car next to them wound down his window and asked for directions. Coulter tapped on the grille. "He wants directions," he said to the driver.

"Are you listenin' to me?" Sue-Ellen screeched.

The cabbie looked at the man in the Mercedes and said to

Coulter, "So whattamy? The fuckin' tourist board or somethin'?" He flipped the man in the Mercedes the finger.

"Rick," Sue-Ellen yelled. "I'm talkin' to you about your god-damned future an' mine an' Jason's, an' you're talkin' to a fuckin' cabdriver!" There was an explosion of horns behind them. The light had turned green. The man in the Mercedes was shouting and giving them the finger. The cabdriver started off with a jolt and a yell to the people behind. Coulter was thrown back in his seat. At the same instant, the cab went into a bad pothole and his head hit the roof.

Coulter did not have a good time in New York City. On Thursday afternoon they flew to L.A. because Sue-Ellen wanted to see Hollywood; in particular, where they had shot the "Beverly Hillbillies" TV series. At L.A. International, Coulter bought a copy of *Life*. He thought for some reason the story would be on the cover. Instead it was buried on page 50, after a piece on antique musical boxes. There was a black-and-white spread of the car on the slope of Muldoon Canyon that transfixed him. He stared at it and heard the wind again and saw the driving snow and black shapes moving in it, and he began to sweat.

"Oh, look!" Sue-Ellen was peering over his shoulder. "Where'd they get that photo of Mike?"

There were pictures of each of them inset at the foot of the spread. The picture of Arizo looked as if it were taken when he was sixteen or so. Coulter stared at it and then closed the magazine. "Let's get a cab," Sue-Ellen said.

Coulter read the story as they drove along the San Diego freeway to the downtown area, with Sue-Ellen crowding his shoulder and the meter clacking furiously. He struggled to identify with the story as being about himself, about the time and people he remembered. But there was not enough there and the meter distracted him.

"See," Sue-Ellen poked him. "You're a hero. I told you."

They spent five days in L.A., during which Coulter was heavy, tired, and clouded in blackness. Sue-Ellen goaded him to get a job so they could settle there. She said he should apply to the studios for a job as an extra in westerns. "Anything to begin with," she said. He left the hotel before she got up and went out into the streets and walked. He didn't try to think of anything, to reason anything. He just walked and looked without curiosity, like an amnesiac: without a reason, without a core. He stayed out until it got dark, sometimes taking a bus to rest his legs. He would come home when it got dark to find her in the hotel's beauty salon having her hair fixed or her nails done. He would go up to the room and lie with the TV on, looking at the ceiling. It was like this every day. When she came up, they would go out to dinner and see a movie. She didn't seem to worry about his silence. She did ask him what he thought about all the time. He said nothing much. He hardly touched her, but she didn't mind that either. They even slept in separate beds.

On the fourth day they were there, a Monday, they got back to the room around midnight and he told her he was going downstairs for cigarettes. He walked down Wilshire to Westlake and turned left on Westlake. Near the end of the block, he found a bar and went in. It was low and dark. He heard Elton John singing "Tiny Dancer." He sat at the bar and ordered a draft. He wasn't interested in getting drunk. He sat for half an hour watching people dance. There was a thin girl with short brunette hair who danced all the time. She seemed boneless. Her hair stuck to her skull and glistened with sweat and her face shone with sweat too. She sometimes danced with a Chicano, but mostly she was too much for anyone to keep up with and she danced alone. She wasn't interested in who she was dancing with anyway. She smiled to herself as she danced, satisfied by what she was doing.

A little after 1:00 A.M. five Samoans came in. Coulter didn't see their entrance. The first he was aware of them they were standing in front of him blocking his view of the girl dancing. They were big, broad men, the collars of their coats turned up. He tapped one of them on the shoulder. The man half-turned. "Hey, man," Coulter said. "You wanna step aside so I can see?" One by one, the other four turned to look at him also. Their faces were round and full and their eyes were dark. They looked at him with contempt and turned their backs again without moving.

"Hey!" Coulter got off his stool and, putting a hand on the

shoulder of each man directly in front of him, he separated them
powerfully, cannoning them one into another. "I said move,
motherfuckers," he yelled. The two men he had touched turned
and grabbed him, but the bartender was already among them.

"Out," he said. "You're eighty-sixed. All of you. Right now."

"Hey, Lou," a man called from the rail. "You can't eighty-six
the solo dude. They'll kill him."

Coulter came out onto the empty street ahead of the Samoans.
He had enough lead to reach a car parked at the curb and turn
and lean against it opposite the door, waiting. They came out
looking at him sullenly and they stood in a knot and spoke for a
moment and then turned and started up the street. "Hey, slopes,"
Coulter shouted after them. "Hey!" They ignored him and the
man who had spoken for him in the bar came out as the Samoans
were getting into a car.

"Look at them chickenshits," Coulter shouted.

The man was pulling on his coat. "They think you gotta gun,"
he said. "So do I. Else you're crazy." He went to his car.

Coulter crossed Westlake, went up to Wilshire and turned left.
He had seen a park a block or so down. He felt depressed again. It
was drizzling now. Wilshire was wet and deserted. He went down
to the park and started across it on a path, walking slowly. The
drizzle drifted into his face, the street lights were spaced far apart
and he threw a long shadow on the asphalt. Somewhere towards
the middle the five Samoans came out at him from behind. He
didn't see them. He fought back with fury but they enjoyed this.
They beat him unconscious, took his billfold, and left him lying
in the shadow of some bushes.

Coulter was released from the hospital two days later and flew
home that evening. They were about broke, although Coulter
hadn't been robbed of much, since Sue-Ellen kept the money. He
had badly bruised ribs, a broken nose, cut eyes, and needed thirty-
four stitches in his head.

On the descent into Twin Falls Sue-Ellen leaned across and
said confidentially, "There'll be a crowd waitin' when we get off.
Go fix your hair, hon. You're gonna be a hero again."

Dan Coulter waited at the gate—more stooped than usual, his
son thought. He stood round-shouldered, hands in the pockets of
his gray windbreaker, hat set forward to where it threw a shadow
across his old face. He was chewing a toothpick.

Coulter pumped his arm and slapped his shoulder. "You sono-
vagun," he said. "I thought it were Gene Autry standin' there."

"Where is the press?" Sue-Ellen demanded.

The old man looked around perplexedly. "I thought there
might be some," he said.

"They couldn't've know'd we was comin'," Sue-Ellen decided.

Pa Coulter shrugged. He turned and walked with them, the
rolled-over heels of his boots sloughing on the tile floor of the cor-
ridor.

"Rick got in a fight." Sue-Ellen proudly cracked her gum.

The elder Coulter nodded without looking up.

"How's everythin', Pa?" Coulter asked.

The old man paused. "Well, it's been snowin' off-an'-on."

They walked in silence a little way more. People hurried towards them, faces gray, lips blue in the fluorescent light.

"What's eatin' you, Pa?" Coulter inquired, eyes narrowing.

"Let's git the bags," Pa Coulter said.

It was snowing as they came out of the terminal. They threw
the cases in the back of the pickup and sat three across on the
front seat, Sue-Ellen pushing either man against the door. The
snow hurried at them through the headlights and splattered on
the windshield. The wipers clicked and one of them scraped
softly. At the airport entrance, Pa Coulter slowed and turned right
onto the highway. He settled behind the wheel, chewing his
toothpick, then leaned forward a little and looked across at his
son. "After you left, they begun talkin' in the town. About how
come it took you all that time to walk out."

"Whatta they know?" Sue-Ellen scoffed. "Rick's a hero all over
the country."

"They isn't mountain people all over the country," Pa Coulter
replied.

"Then what? Tell me, Pa," Coulter said.

The old man took out his toothpick and waved it for emphasis.

"Then there was that TV show an' that article come out in *Life* magazine.

"Yeah?"

"You'da done better not to have spoke to them," his father said. "I'm afraid that's the truth. You'd have done better not tellin' 'bout how you watched TV in the cabins an' all." Pa Coulter put the toothpick back in his mouth while he made a right turn at a red light, then continued: "I'll tell you. They say you is responsible for two men dyin'." He let it fall flat. There was silence in the car except for the squeak of the wiper blade on the wet glass and the muted sound of the engine.

"They say you shot Coo-Coo an' then let Mike die by takin' so long to walk them few miles an' stayin' in them cabins watchin' TV when there weren't nothin' wrong with you."

"I couldn't get my boots on," Coulter said quickly. "I couldn't hardly walk."

"You don't need to tell me, son," his father said, looking around Sue-Ellen. "I'm just tellin' you straight, like you asked. That's all."

"Well, you believe me, don't you?"

"I know what it's like up there in winter. But if you ain't been there, there's no way to tell how it is, son. That's why you'd have been better off not talkin' to the man from the magazine and doin' that TV show an' everythin'. You shoulda stayed quiet. You got problems in this town now, an' to tell you truthful, I don't know they can be put right just now."

Coulter sat back in the seat. "Jesus," he sighed. Many things were tangled inside him, and they left him numb.

While they were away, Coulter had not dreamed the dream, but the first night back, it came again. He woke sweating and trembling, got up without waking Sue-Ellen, and sat in the living room. It was a little after four. He felt beaten. He was, he realized, beginning to dread and hate Arizo. He lay back on the sofa. "I wish to God I'd never met you," he said. "I wish to God." And then, "No. I don't mean that . . ."

He lay on the sofa the rest of the night. He thought a lot about Arizo. He had to make something of the guy's dying. That was for

him, he saw that. There was no point to it unless he could show
something. If he dropped the ball . . . It gave him new impetus
when he thought like this. Jason woke early and came in and
talked to him. Coulter lay still, only half watching and listening
to the boy. His son showed him an earth mover his grandparents
had bought him. He showed how the blade moved up and down
and he pushed the toy model on the carpet in front of him.
Coulter smiled. "That's real nice, Jason," he said.

When Sue-Ellen got up, the three of them dressed and went
out to buy breakfast at the Speedy Mart. As they walked down
Main together, people welcomed Sue-Ellen back and spoke to
Jason, but no one spoke to Coulter. They didn't even look at him.
It was as if he were invisible. Coulter didn't say anything, but
soon he was walking a step or so behind the boy and his mother.
He wasn't insulted; in some odd way he felt initially relieved.
Coming home, Sue-Ellen stopped suddenly and, waiting until he
caught up, she muttered to him, trying to keep it from the boy:
"What's the matter? Why don't you keep up and talk to these
people? They're your friends—you know?"

"They're glad to see *you* back," he replied offhandedly. "You
heard what Pa said last night."

"Well," she said, exasperated. "You ain't gonna make them feel
any better about you skulkin' like that."

Coulter said grimly, "I couldn't care less."

The sheriff called after breakfast. He told Coulter to come
around to the office.

When Coulter walked in, Sergeant Goebbels looked at him
agape. "What happened to you?" he asked while showing Rick
into the sheriff's office.

"There were some people standin' in front of me," Coulter said.
Sergeant Goebbels rolled his eyes and whistled.

The sheriff was reading the sports section. He put the paper
down, took off his glasses and sized up Coulter. "What the hell
happened to you?" he asked.

"I got in a fight in L.A. with these Samoans."

"They'll kill you, Samoans," the sheriff said.

Coulter sat down and the sheriff motioned Goebbels to leave.
"Whatta you tryin' to do?" Burt Meyers asked when they were alone.
"What are *they* tryin'?"
"Who?"
"People in town."
The sheriff got up stiffly and went to the window.
"You got trouble," he said eventually.
"I guess."
Meyers turned around. "They don't want you here."
"How come?"
The sheriff raised his brows. "They say they gotta be able to count on the people they live with, an' they can't count on you."
There was silence.
"You should know how mountain people are," the sheriff went on. "A man that's afraid ain't a man. That's what Rose said to me yesterday."
Coulter sat staring at the corner of the desk in front of him. The sheriff came back and sat down and faced him, deadly serious.
"Why was Poulsen's pickup all shot up?" he asked.
Coulter sat back and picked at a stain on his Levi's. Then he looked directly at the sheriff and told him the truth about the firefight. When he'd finished the sheriff said, "I figured as much."
"The three of us decided to say it was an accident to cover Vern's ass," Coulter said. "But now, what's the difference?" He turned his hands upwards. "Whatta you gonna do?"
"I dunno," the sheriff said. "Right now I'm gonna have Sergeant Goebbels drive you home, an' I want you to stay put. I don't want you on the street. Not till I tell you." He stood up, and from the far side of the desk looked down at Coulter, slouched in his chair. "An' I ain't foolin', Rick. You come out an' I'm gonna have you committed for thirty days psychiatric observation right off."
Coulter nodded. "Don't go tellin' everyone about Vern," he said.
"You're eighty-sixed at the bar, and they won't serve you in the

town, an' there's no law says they gotta. I'm not sayin' it's right or fair or anythin'. I'm just tellin' you that's the way it is, an' I don't want trouble. If I don't do somethin', they're gonna be after you. That's for sure."

Coulter nodded and the sheriff called for Sergeant Goebbels.

It was Thursday when Coulter was put under house arrest. Sue-Ellen was outraged but glad to be still in the limelight. The town was caught in the last grip of winter, awaiting release. It was too cold to snow. The slush in the streets was frozen hard. The bare trees nodded with ice. A cold wind blew incessantly down from the mountains, biting deeply into those hurrying abroad.

Cold compounded the malevolence the townspeople felt. Malevolence not truly in themselves but in the air, so that they become attached to the body of it for fear of it. Most people, when they looked within themselves, felt apprehension and a sense of loss over this business. They felt hope for the man whose fate was unknown and glad for him who had survived. Glad that one among them at least had beaten the mountains. For most of them, Coulter's survival was some small triumph, achieved by whatever means, in the face of massive odds. They spoke of how they would have pressed on, bad feet and all, but they were not unreasonable people and privately they doubted they would have survived. There were exceptions: the strongest were Gould and Lewis and to a lesser extent Boyer, Spangler, Rose, and Leonard. All of these men attempted to recruit people for their side and they were the source of the hostility that the body felt.

Dan Coulter urged his son to leave town, and Sue-Ellen pointed out how right she had been to argue that he take a job in L.A. But Rick noticed she didn't suggest they leave now. It seemed that she was as interested in the outcome of this thing as anyone. Coulter felt he had no option but to stay. It wasn't just Arizo's due. He had to prove his courage to them, for courage is the premium quality among mountain people, besides virility, and these people were his people. Still the old Jew's warning came to him, as did the thought of Marlene and her promise. And they were powerful forces against him.

He stayed at home all Thursday and Friday and only his father called, late Friday afternoon to say, "You can go to work Monday with the phone company if you like."

Coulter drew on a cigarette. "Yeah," he said. "Thanks."

Pa Coulter paused. "Pops'd take you on. You know that. You're crazy to go work for these other people, Rick. Crazy."

"Pops hired someone already."

"So he'd lay him off. You got seniority."

"That'd be worse for me if I got someone laid off."

"That ain't why. It don't make sense," his father said. And it didn't and Coulter knew it.

"Workin' for Pops you'd be outta the way at the quarry. They'd forget about you pretty quick. You go to work for Ma Bell Monday, and you got Lewis for a gaffer. That sonovabitch'd like to kill you, an' you know it."

"I can handle him, Pa."

"Him an' his buddies there? Rose an' Leonard an' them?"

"I can handle them."

"In a pig's eye."

"If I can't handle them Pa, I gotta leave here. If I just go to work for Pops an' get some guy laid off an' play it safe an' duck 'em, who's to say they ain't right?"

His father said, "They gotta lot of years on you, boy, an' that can work both ways."

Sue-Ellen took Jason to her parents for the weekend shortly after this conversation. She left him a TV dinner in the oven, eggs, frozen steak, venison and canned vegetables for the weekend.

"P'r'aps you'll be feeling more sociable when we get back," she said and left without kissing him good-bye.

Coulter locked the door, opened a beer and lay down on the sofa in front of the television set. It was a relief to hear the truck go on up the road. He watched TV through the evening and into the night. He dreaded sleep. He heated his dinner and ate from the tray while watching "M*A*S*H." He didn't laugh, he simply watched. He watched the late movie and then the late, late movie and around 3:30 A.M. he fell asleep on the sofa with the set still on. And he had the dream again; the tall figure in rags coming slowly after him through the snow.

He woke with a sense of real desperation. The TV was still on, showing a man and woman, singing a duet in a convertible. Coulter flung a beer can at the screen, but the empty can bounced off. Coulter yelled and fell back on the couch holding his head.

He was awakened the next time by the telephone ringing. It was broad daylight. He reached out and found the receiver and picked it up clumsily.

"Hi." It was a soft voice.

Marlene. "Jesus," he said, waking up. "Whatta you doin' callin' here?" He looked frantically around and even as he did, remembered that Sue-Ellen and Jason had gone.

"I heard they left you for the weekend," she said. "I thought at least I should call an' find out what's goin' on with you. I was hopin' to hear from you. I been waitin'. Remember?"

He sighed. "Burt's confined me to the house, an' Monday I start work at the phone company. At the yard with Lewis."

"You're crazy."

"I ain't gonna run."

There was silence. Then she said quietly, "I thought we were goin' away."

He shifted the receiver to his other ear.

"I hear you were in a fight in L.A.," she went on.

"Yeah."

"They hurt you?"

"You still wanna go?"

"Yeah," she said. "I do."

"Whatta 'bout your kids?"

"Tissa's in college and Vickissa would come along. She's fourteen next month. She's no sweat."

There was silence.

"Did you change your mind?"

"I dunno what to do, Marlene. What about Vern? Supposin' he shows?"

"Oh come on," she scoffed.

"I dunno. I dunno what's best to do. I gotta get my whole life pulled together. I'm comin' apart, Marlene, I swear to God. An' I can't let those sonsofbitches run me out. At least I gotta show them."

"You don't have to show them anything," she said. "All they are is peckawood, an' if you hang out with them, then that's what you are too, Rick."

"Everyone keeps tellin' me things."

"Don't take the job Monday," she said. "Come away with me."

"I gotta have the money."

"I got lotsa that. An' in a year or so, when Vern's declared legally dead, I can sell the ranch an' we could buy our own someplace where they didn't know who we are an' we could start again."

Coulter thought this over.

"You'd be crazy not to," she said.

"*You're* the one who's crazy."

"You're crazy an' I love you, Rick."

"Jesus," he said. "Can you . . ."

"Can I come 'round late tonight an' see you?"

"Wait," he said. "Call me this afternoon, will you?"

"Yeah."

"Promise?"

"I promise."

On Sunday night at six, Eleanor Holmes called from the hardware store for an ambulance. She might have done a number of things, it was pointed out afterwards, any of which would have left Fred Meyers, in particular, and his brother Burt, the prohibitionist sheriff of Cope County, who remained on earth, with some vestige of dignity. However, Eleanor Holmes clearly wanted it known that she had harbored a secret all these years for a man who would not marry her. So she did nothing to clean up or alter things before she called the ambulance. And when Joey Leonard and Gus Harper, who manned the ambulance Sunday afternoons, arrived, together with the sheriff, whose wife had monitored the call, they found Fred Meyers lying in a child's high-sided cot, dressed in blue cotton pajamas printed with red fire trucks and airplanes, surrounded by baby bottles of bourbon. He was half-stiff; that is, rigor mortis had set in, which was the reason Eleanor Holmes gave afterwards to the sheriff for not having moved him before calling for help. The sheriff's brother's liver had failed, and he had bled to death.

The Monday morning Twin Falls *Gazette* was headlined:

DRINK SLAYS DRY SHERIFF KIN

Coulter didn't go to work. He called the sheriff's office at 7:00 A.M. on Monday, and Goebbels told him to stay home. "I'll come for you this afternoon," he said. It sounded ominous to Coulter. He went to the window. Outside it was snowing lightly. He walked into the kitchen, where his hand shook as he measured out coffee from the jar. His lips felt thick, and his mouth was furry. He took his coffee and went into the garage and made ammunition. Although the sheriff had his .303, he still had a .45 Magnum Ruger pistol. At three-thirty Sergeant Goebbels came for him in the patrol car. Coulter sat next to him in front.

"You gotta job," Goebbels said as they drove.

Coulter was looking away, out of his window. "Yeah," he said without turning his head.

"I thought you were gonna leave town."

"Who said?"

"Just what I heard."

"I'm not."

"Oh no?" Goebbels said and burped slightly. "Hell!" he said and rubbed his belly. "Acid indigestion." He took a roll of Tums from the pocket of his shirt. "You ever get it?"

Coulter shook his head. "I don't get nervous."

Goebbels looked at him as they drove down Main and his eyes bulged. "You're a lucky man," he said. "You don't know how lucky you are."

"I guess I don't," Coulter said. Then, after a moment, he asked, "How's Burt?"

Goebbels looked at him. "I guess you an' he finally got somethin' in common," he said.

"Yeah?" said Coulter casually. "What's that?"

"Well," said Goebbels hesitantly. "You're both in it now."

"In what?"

Goebbels looked at him to see if he were being serious. "In the shit," he said. "Didn't you hear 'bout Fred dyin' of drink? You know how Burt goes on about liquor."

Coulter looked wide-eyed and shook his head. "You could be the next sheriff then," he said pointedly.

"Aww," Goebbels brushed it aside. "It's not that bad. You think?"

"How the hell would I know?" Coulter looked out of his window at Len Longren sweeping outside the Speedy Mart as they passed. "I been locked in my house all week."

The sheriff showed his age today, and Coulter saw the man's hands tremble as he sifted through papers on his desk. He waited for the sheriff to speak.

"I know'd your pa since him and me was kids," Burt Meyers said at last. "I know'd you since your ma was carryin' you. I wasn't the sheriff then. I was like your pa, tryin' to make a livin' farmin'. I didn't know about this law business till after I come back from the war." He looked up and Coulter saw how tired he was.

"I always been square in this job," the sheriff continued. "It ain't an easy job keepin' these people up here goin' straight. They're some pretty wild ol' boys around, an' not much schoolin' for most of 'em. That's how you was brought up, too. I don't hold it 'gainst you. You always been this way." He stopped. Coulter was watching him.

"You give any thought to what I say?"

"What's that?" Coulter asked, though knowing what he meant.

"I heard you took a job with the phone company."

"I did."

The sheriff leaned forward. "I don't know how to put this more plain, but once more: you gotta get outta this town. Least for now."

Coulter shook his head. "I can't run away, Burt."

"An' I can't sit on these boys forever," the sheriff said and gave

a great sigh, like an elephant lying down. They got one on me
now. You can't count on me forever, if that's what you think."

Sandy opened the door to him herself. She was smaller than he
remembered her. This was the first time he had seen her since the
night of the Pejasky party. He remembered her from then, standing by the table in the cabin looking at Arizo as he was making up
his mind whether to stay with her or go with him into the mountains. Now she stood on the step above him, regarding him
evenly, her mouth open slightly as if she were about to speak. But
she said nothing.

Looking down at the envelope in his hands, Coulter broke the
silence. "I've brought Mike's log," he said. "I'm sorry I didn't
bring it before. I'm sorry I didn't come see you before."

She hesitated, holding the front door half open with her hand.

"Could we talk a minute, maybe?" he asked.

She nodded. "We can't talk here," she said. "I'll fetch a coat."

They drove in his truck out over the Snake road across the plain
towards the quarry. It was getting dark. The snow was graying and
sage stuck through the covering here and there in little clumps.
He thought of them gathering the tops beside the Ford to make a
fire. He reached for the pack of cigarettes on the dash and pushed
the lighter in, steering with one hand.

"I was wantin' to come see you before," he said.

"But?" She turned to him.

"I didn't know what to say."

"What's to say?"

"I'm sorry?"

"It was him that decided to go."

"I coulda got out sooner. If I'd been him . . ."

"You aren't him, Rick. You never will be."

He saw her lower her head, shaking it softly, hopelessly.

"I'm in a real mess about it," he said.

"Yes," she sighed. "Me too."

"You seem like you're pretty well together."

She laughed derisively.

"You mind if I talk to you about it?"

They were coming up on the quarry. He saw Pops' light on in the office.

Painfully, in the beginning, he told her about the dream which had first come to him at Wild Horse and which had plagued him since. "It's like Mike's chasin' me," he said. "It's like he's never gonna let me forget. But I don't need remindin', Sandy. I mean . . . I ain't ever gonna live without this thing. Not ever."

She was silent.

"I won't ever have a friend the same as him." He paused. "Did he ever tell you 'bout him an' that dog?"

"Sort of," she said.

"Well the way I feel it's like that all over. You know?"

She shook her head, sucking her lips.

"I mean he screwed up on the dog an' that's how come he came here an' now it seems like I screwed up on him. You see?"

She slowly nodded head and shoulders and then said suddenly, as though she'd been building up the effort, "But he wasn't chasin' you though. He couldn't. He couldn't even stand up."

"I see him comin' through the woods after me with that stiff-legged walk," Coulter said and he saw the grim figure again in his mind as he spoke. "An' I can't ever get away. You ever have a dream like that?"

"Do you see his face?"

"It's just a black thing," he said. "All black. Nothin' ever scared me so bad."

"You don't see his face?"

"No. But I know it's him."

"How do you know it's him?"

"He's comin' after me 'cause I left him."

"He wasn't that kinda guy," she said. "It was Poulsen that was chasin' you in the pickup earlier. Remember?"

Coulter heard her and felt something in him move. His mouth suddenly dried and the hair on his neck began to crawl.

"Poulsen wanted to kill you," she said.

Coulter saw Arizo pushing his hat up on the end of the rifle and he heard the shot and saw the look on Arizo's face as he turned to him. He licked his lips now and looked at Sandy. She saw how tense his face had grown and for a minute she was afraid. Then she heard the engine die and felt the truck slowing. He pulled up, two wheels breaking through the crust of snow beside the road in the near darkness.

"You'd better keep your lights on," she said.

He looked at her as if he had forgotten himself. "But Poulsen was three days ahead of me."

"How'd you know where he was? Anyway, what difference would it make? We're only talkin' about a dream."

Another part of it was coming to him: "I got up from the bed at Wild Horse," he said aloud, though perhaps not to her. "I got up with the gun an' I ran like a shadow an' there it was . . . I think I shot, an' something fell in the doorway, an' . . ."

"You shot—who?"

He stared at her, then looked away again. "I don't recall," he said slowly. "It keeps goin' . . ."

"It was Mike you figured you shot." She gripped her hands between her knees, hunched her shoulders and took a deep breath. "So afterwards you didn't *need* to hurry, did you?"

"No," he said emphatically. "No. I knew I had to get him out. I never forgot that. Never."

"But it wasn't Mike," she said. "Was it?"

He put his fingers to his mouth. "No," he said. "It wasn't Mike."

"It was Poulsen you dreamed about."

"Christ, now I don't know, I don't know . . ."

After he dropped her off at the Hermans, he drove slowly down Main. He felt very nervous, but clear in his mind, poised. It would mean he would do some time, he realized and that thought hit him hard. But at least he would be clean. He'd never be able to come back to town. But he'd been planning to leave anyway. Still, his mouth was dry, and it didn't feel entirely as if it were he that was doing this. The sheriff's car was in the lot. Inside, the lights were all on. The waiting room was empty, but the door to the sheriff's office stood open.

They sat facing each other once again across the big desk.

"What's on your mind now, Rick?" The sheriff carefully arranged a pant leg over his boot.

Coulter looked for a place to begin. At length he said, "I figured out how come Vern didn't make it."

"Yeah?"

"Yeah. I shot him," Coulter said quickly, relieved to get it out. The sheriff regarded him. "You did?"

A little exasperated, Coulter said, "Yeah. I had this dream. I just figured it out."

"You had a dream?"

Coulter told him about the dream in detail.

"So whatta you think happened?" the sheriff asked.

"Well, it was only half a dream." Coulter was surprised it needed explanation. "I musta shot Vern comin' out of the dream." He was leaning forward, tapping the desk with the back of his hand, and the sheriff saw that he was sweating.

The sheriff sat back. "You're tellin' me you shot Vern for real, not just in a dream?"

Coulter swallowed and nodded. "I didn't mean to," Coulter started. "I mean we saved him before. I told you. Remember?"

The sheriff scratched an eyelash with the tip of his little finger and nodded.

"You don't believe me?" Coulter looked wild.

The sheriff held up his hands. "We went to Wild Horse already," he said. "I was there myself. An' we none of us saw anythin' suggestin' anyone was shot. I mean, it's usually a messy thing when someone gets shot to death."

"It doesn't have to be. Does it?"

"I guess not. But there's always a body."

"It's up there," Coulter said quickly. "I think it's behind the station."

"Well, if it is, it'll still be there, 'cause nothin' will have took it yet."

"Let's go see." Coulter was childish in his eagerness.

The sheriff didn't move. "How come you told me this?"

Coulter rubbed his forehead, feeling a dull ache. "I gotta get this whole thing cleaned up."

The sheriff tilted forward in his chair without taking his eyes off Coulter. "I'm glad you come to me. I'm gonna go up to Wild Horse first thing in the mornin'. Meanwhile, you don't tell Sue-Ellen or anyone you figured anythin' out. You just get up an' go to work tomorrow mornin' like nothin' happened. Okay?"

"Okay," Coulter agreed.

The sheriff unloaded his sled in darkness in the yard at the Devil's Bedstead Guest Ranch. Above the hills he saw dawn coming. A dog was barking but no lights came on in the ranch house. The sheriff had a custom Arctic Cat snowmobile with a long wheelbase. Against the side of the machine were strapped two eight-foot aluminum wands and a shovel. When the machine was off the truck, he pulled on a face mask and goggles, started up the engine and moved off as quietly as he could.

But as he passed under a window at the house, he heard a voice and saw a man with a rifle leaning out.

"It's okay, Gary," he called above the engine noise. "It's just me—Burt. I'm goin' out to Wild Horse. I'll be back around lunchtime." He didn't wait for an answer but moved on.

He followed the road along beside the north fork first through the gorge, then past the Felton and Johnson ranches, seeing the light creeping down the opposite wall of the valley two hundred yards across the stream bed, seeing that wall fall away as the valley broadened out until it finally disgorged him into the vastness of the Basin itself. The snow in the Basin was lightly touched with pink, and to the east, above the White Knob Mountains, the clouds were too. Without pause, the sheriff struck out across this vast, fleshlike ocean towards the point in it where Wild Horse lay.

Cruising at 35 mph, he was no more than a black dot crawling across waves of snow, breasting one rise and sliding down the far side into the trough, out of sight. As he climbed towards the growing light, he took his gloved hands off the steering grips and flexed each in turn to restore circulation. Altogether, it took him half an hour to reach Wild Horse.

The face of the cabin was in shadow. The sheriff left his machine outside the front, killing the engine gratefully. Wild Horse

Station stared at him in bleak silence. He left his goggles and mask on the seat of the machine and looked around inside the place but found no marks or evidence of anything. If Coulter had shot the man as he came in, perhaps he had fallen out of the door and never made it into the place at all. The sheriff went slowly down the steps, fetched an aluminum wand, and began probing the snow about the door. Finally the pole stopped short. Eight inches down he came up with what looked like a large piece of tree fungus—thick and black, an irregular oblong tapering bole-like to a point. He knelt down and brushed the snow from it, looking at it closely. It was frozen blood.

The sheriff rode his machine slowly around the back of the trailer.

He defined a long rectangle with the first series of probes he made and each time around he came closer to the center. On the fourth ring, he found the body, a foot or so down. He stopped, took his shovel off the Cat and dug carefully. The body was on its back. The details were a little indistinct. It was like a frozen fish lost in the ice of the freezer, but instantly recognizable from the crude splint lashed to the leg and the torn strips of blanket wrapped about the head. The sheriff sat down sidesaddle on his machine and contemplated the figure.

"Jesus, Vern," he said to it, "no wonder you scared the shit outta the boy." He shook his head, got slowly up, opened a saddlebag and took out a length of rope. He made a running noose and tied this about the body's ankles. Then he maneuvered his machine until it was alongside and ran the line through a chromed handle beside the saddle and, using a foot to brace himself, cinched the line until the feet were pulled up tight against the handle and only the head and shoulders were resting on the snow. He tied off the line and, standing back, looked at what he had rigged. Satisfied, he put on his mask and goggles, started the machine again, and moved off.

He didn't go back around the trailer, but on out, directly behind it, running close through a clump of bare trees. The ground dropped away to his right quite steeply into a stream bed, in summer a deep, leafy gully with rocky sides and a spring at the bottom.

He turned and looked at the body as he went.

"You tried awful hard, Vern," he called out to it. "I can see that. An' I'm sorry for what came of it. But there's no sense wastin' two lives over this thing. An' especially him bein' so young." He turned back to see where he was going. He was running along the edge of the gully at perhaps five miles an hour. He turned back to the body. "In Okinawa I saw this before. An' Iwo Jima. When the boys got real tired, Vern, then went spare. Plain crazy. I seen them machine gun their own men an' not know they ever did it. But if you ain't seen it, there's no way you can believe it. You gotta take my word for it. You got no choice. They ain't ever gonna believe this stuff about Coulter's dream in town, Vern. You know that."

At the bottom of the gully there was a narrow V. He didn't go all the way down, afraid he wouldn't be able to get back out. He unroped the body three-quarters of the way, and it rolled over a couple of times and then stopped. The sheriff turned his machine around and started back up, accelerating, struggling to keep the nose of the snowmobile from slipping sideways on the slope. The belt track thrashed on the snow, the engine crackled and whined loudly. The sheriff bit his lip and concentrated hard, head down, so that he didn't notice the watching figure, motionless against the dark firs at the top of the slope. Nor did he hear the sound of the engine as the man rode away.

At the top, the sheriff went back along the ridge, riding beside the track he had made coming in, filling in the drag marks left by Vern's head and shoulders as best he could.

Rounding the trailer he picked up the bole of frozen blood without stopping, dropped it in the open saddlebag beside the rope and struck out across the Basin.

He took a slightly different route going home. It began snowing heavily before he was halfway across. He raised a gloved hand and waved gratefully, then emptied the saddlebag of its bulging load. By the time he reached the mouth of the canyon that carried the east fork of the Big Lost through to the Devil's Bedstead Guest

Ranch, there was enough fresh powder on the ground to hide not only his original outgoing track, but also a second track that had run over and beside it.

Coulter spent another silent day shoveling snow in the phone company's yard, waiting for word. Scenarios sweeping through his mind like windmill sails. He saw himself in prison denims shoveling snow. What difference would it make? It wouldn't be for so long. At least he was alive. Every day he got was a day on Mike and Coo-Coo. Not to gloat, but that's what it came down to. And they'd have felt the same about it too. It was just like keeping score.

By late afternoon, when he still hadn't heard from Meyers, he figured something had definitely gone wrong. But then Red Lewis came out across the yard and told him the sheriff wanted to see him *rightaway*. Coulter gratefully set down his shovel.

"I guess you're in a mess of trouble, boy," Lewis grinned.

Coulter shrugged and looked at Lewis, wondering what he knew. He didn't say anything. He'd grown used to being silent and he liked it.

The sheriff had his boots up on a stool beside the desk. It seemed he was being casual, but in truth it was to relieve the pain from the varicose veins in his calves. He looked at Coulter across his shoulder as he came in.

"Have a seat," he gestured.

Coulter sat.

"I spent the whole mornin' up there," he said. "There wasn't a body. I guarantee it."

Coulter was shocked.

"It was only a dream you had." The sheriff took his feet off the stool and came around to look at him squarely from behind his desk.

"It can't have been," Coulter said.

"Whatta ya mean, 'It can't have been'? I just spent the whole goddamn mornin' goin' through that whole trailer an' all around it, an' I been trained at the FBI academy to detect murdered bodies, an' there weren't no such thing at Wild Horse, Rick. I tell you that it can't be . . ." His voice stopped a moment. "It can't be anythin' else but a dream."

Coulter sat dumbly, mystified.

The sheriff wrinkled his big nose and got up. As he went to the window, he said, "You can leave town now an' feel good about it, boy. You did the right thing by me an' yourself. I can tell your pa an' I can tell everyone that argues different that you ain't chicken. I don't have to tell 'em why. I can just tell 'em, is all." He turned. "I couldn't tell 'em that before. Will you git now? I ain't askin' just for you."

"Suppose they find Poulsen where you didn't look," Coulter conjectured. "It'll sure look like I was runnin'."

"Hell, we won't ever find Vern. Come spring an' the bears'll find him first an' then there won't be nothin' left for anybody to get too excited about, will there?"

Coulter came away from the sheriff's office with a sense of disbelief. If he had felt uncertain, disconnected, or perhaps disembodied before, he now felt doubly removed from reality. He examined his circumstances, fingered them tentatively, as one awakening from a nightmare, still uncertain of the boundary between fiction and fact, consciousness and subconsciousness, and as yet unwilling to put weight on any feeling of relief.

He did not wish to speak. He was very quiet at home that night, watching his household with what seemed to Sue-Ellen like suspicion.

The following morning, Wednesday, he went to work before the house stirred. When Red Lewis saw him, he said, "You got it worked out with the sheriff?" Again Coulter felt misgiving. But he saw nothing more in Lewis' rough, red-stubbled face and he merely sniffed. It was cold and not yet sunup. They stood in the yard in front of the office, which Coulter could see was warmly lit. "Whatta you want me to do?" he asked.

"I'm afraid you get the shit work till you get some seniority," Lewis said and set Coulter to unsnarling a large roll of rusty barbed-wire fence still on its wooden posts. Coulter worked all day without looking up and only took a half-hour lunch, though Lewis wasn't going to pay him overtime and said so.

Wednesday night he went around to the Hermans' place. He knew Sandy would be gone, but he went anyway, aimlessly, wanting to talk with someone. She had left no forwarding address. After Gladys Herman closed the door, he stood staring about and he came away feeling profoundly lonely. There was no neutral place in town, nowhere that didn't ring with memories. He drove out beyond the Snake Valley trailer park to think. What would Mike do now? He would leave, just as he said he'd done after that business with the dog, Baby Zeus. Coulter remembered that when Arizo had told him the story, he'd thought what an odd name it was. He felt the sadness again, like the sun shining through a fine rain and he yelled out their cry: "We don't have much money, but we sure have fun." It rang emptily and only made him feel worse.

Thursday night, after he got off, he stopped at the pay phone in the Standard station on the way home and, fumbling with cold fingers, dialed Marlene.

"Tomorrow night," he said.

There was a hesitation. "Rick?" she said.

He knew it wasn't the name she was unsure of.

"Of course," he said. "You wanna back out?"

"Oh no," she said. "No."

"Texas."

"I can't believe it, Rick."

"I'll cash my check at the bar and meet you outside at six. We'll take your truck. Okay?"

She hesitated again.

"That isn't too obvious?" she asked.

"Who gives a shit anymore?" Coulter said. "We'll be gone."

"You're right," she said. "Can you imagine it?"

He kissed into the phone and hung up. As he turned around, he saw a grotesque face with distorted nose and lips pressed hard against the glass. He swore aloud in fright and the face pulled away and popped back into the shape of Buck Meyers. Meyers

354   *The Noble Enemy*

grinned. Coulter swore again as he opened the door, wondering
how much Meyers had heard.

"Hey, piss on you, huh?"

Meyers was still grinning. He exuded obscene rawness. "Hell,
Rick," he said. "I didn't know there was anyone in this town
that'd talk with you."

Coulter said nothing to Sue-Ellen. He went home that night
knowing it would be the last he would spend with her. It was
strange how little he felt about either her or Jason. While she was
making supper, he sat on the sofa and took the child on his knees.
Jason had a small piece of wood that he pretended was a gun. He
sat on his father's knees shooting at everything he saw, making a
"tsh, tsh" sound. He didn't pay direct attention to his father until
his father turned him upside-down. He was his mother's son,
Coulter thought. He put Jason back on his knees. The boy struck
his father on the head with his piece of stick and Coulter then
put him down.

Getting up, he went to the window and pulled back the curtain
to stare out into the darkness. The look was wistful, as if he already missed the scene outside. In the light close to the window,
he saw the snow falling softly. It would be thicker in the mountains. Probably there'd be a wind up there. Again he heard the
wind pouring down the canyon, tearing at the walls of the mouth,
then sliding easily across the snow until it struck the empty form
he knew to be still there. It would be blasting, shaking that form
in a fury. Only now that the car was empty, the wind was harm-
less. There was no one to resist, so the mountains had no power.
It was odd, he thought, the mountains being powerless without
them. Shit, maybe they didn't even exist.

He watched Sue-Ellen that night, the way she ate, sucked her
fingers before she turned the pages of the *TV Guide*, smiled to
herself. The way she called to Jason without looking up. Her life
was one automatic action following another. She thought about
nothing that she did. When she saw him watching her, she smiled
automatically. It did not occur to her, he thought, to pause first
and consider why he was watching her. He saw her as one stand-

ing outside, watching dancers dance while unable to hear the
music.

When he left the house next morning, he took nothing but his
lunch, $750 of the *Life* money (leaving her $1,000), and his Ruger
Magnum.

The phone company depot was next to Seiler's tractor dealership, by the Ho-Hum Motel on the main road out at the west end
of town. Coulter drove past the motel and thought of the girl
with the moustache. What was her name? He looked out as he
went past. A man and woman were coming out of a room on the
balcony carrying their suitcases. Snow lay around the swimming
pool. He pulled into the depot yard. Red Lewis was helping
Buddy Lane load a roll of line onto the bed of a pickup. They
looked over as he came in. It was ten to eight on a flat gray Friday
morning. The piles of snow Coulter had made about the yard
were already growing dirty, and there was snow on the cable
drums, the forklift and the rolls of cyclone fencing piled beside
the perimeter wire.

Coulter nosed his pickup to the fence, killed the engine, and
switched the key to accessory to listen to Hank Williams singing
the final verse of "Am I That Easy to Forget," enjoying the
warmth and privacy of the cab a moment more.

The new White stood outside the office, five snowmobiles
loaded on the back. The cab was tipped up, and the mechanic was
working on the engine. Lewis had gone into the office by the time
Coulter reached the truck. The mechanic looked at him over the
engine. Coulter nodded towards the snowmobiles tied down on
the back.

"What's that?" he asked.

"Ask Lewis," was all the mechanic said.

It was warm in the office. There was a propane heater and the
plywood walls were covered with *Playboy* centerfolds. The centerfolds had a warm color to them, too; you could almost feel the
heat of the flesh.

Lewis was sitting behind the desk, his feet up. He held his head
back and looked at Coulter with distaste. There was a cup of

coffee by his boots. He reached for it, held it in both hands, and said to Coulter, "You wait for us in your truck. Power line's down above the quarry. We gotta fix it. When we pull out, follow us."

"Yes *sir*," Coulter said sarcastically and turned away.

"If you want your check tonight, boy, don't give me any more of that shit!" The door banged on Lewis in mid-sentence, and Coulter was gone.

He followed them down through town: Lewis and Buddy Lane, the banty rooster, in the White, two other men from the Arco substation in a company pickup and then him. He looked at the bar as they waited at the Main Street light. It was deserted. There was nothing more deserted, he decided, than a shuttered bar in the morning. They turned right at the light and went down the short grade past the Bluebird Diner, out beyond the turn to the Hermans' place by the river and onto the tableland where the sage was covered with a topping of snow.

They approached the quarry and, to Coulter's surprise, Lewis pulled the White over to the side and stopped about a hundred yards beyond the quarry entrance. Coulter looked into the yard as he passed and through the tall deer-fence saw Pops' green Rambler wagon parked outside the office and smoke coming from the black stovepipe chimney. He thought of the old man rubbing his hands over the fire, waiting for the teakettle to boil, and he felt a sharp regret at not being there with him. You always knew exactly what Pops was doing, and you never knew how much you came to rely on that until the old boy wasn't where you knew he'd be. Coulter had gone to his house once to talk with him and the house had been dark and locked. It had shocked him. He had felt alarmed and anxious. Not, he realized, because he was concerned that something had happened to Pops, but just because there'd been a change in something he counted on to be the same.

They unloaded the snowmobiles and started uphill to where the line was down. It was well up on the foot of the mountain above the quarry, maybe a mile from—and fifteen hundred feet above— the road. The mountain wall rose almost vertically about another mile beyond the line. The cracks and ledges on the wall were dusted in powder, but the footings were buried under one broad, deep blanket. About a mile or so of telephone poles were sagging badly downhill under the weight of snow and wind. After they had made their inspection, Lane took a man and went back down to fetch a winch and more gear and the Sno-Cat and trailer. The rest of them began clearing snow. They were going to winch the poles back upright and set guy wires to hold them.

They broke at noon and ate. All but Coulter pulled their snowmobiles into a circle in the lee of the tall Sno-Cat, which broke the wind. Coulter was thankful to be excluded. He sat twenty feet away with his back to them, lying along the saddle of his machine, his back resting against the control console and handlebars, watching the quarry and the gray line of road below, looking out across the Snake. The breeze blew his breath away, and he uncovered only the hand he ate with.

Now he saw two pickup trucks, one hauling a trailer, coming from town. He picked them up about a mile beyond the quarry. They were hauling snowmobiles, too. They came slowly but gathering speed and then, like curious ants, slowed and pulled over behind his own pickup. He stopped chewing. Several men got out. They began unloading their snowmobiles. Coulter got the same feeling he had had the night Pops wasn't home.

"Hey!" The others had spotted them. They stared down, Lewis looking through glasses. "Hey!" he shouted unnecessarily. "It's Gould an' them guys. Far out."

Red Lewis sat high up in the cab of the Sno-Cat with the door open. Coulter was watching. Lewis turned, saw Coulter's face and pulled at his beard, looking down his nose at him and laughing.

Coulter's gaze went back down the slope. Two men were walking away from the front of his pickup. "Hey," he called under his breath. "You get the hell away from there, assholes." He had locked the Ruger pistol inside the glove compartment and locked the cab. He wished now he had the Ruger with him.

Then a thought struck: "Jesus!" he said aloud. "They've found Vern!" He stared in bewilderment. He knew it. They *had* found Vern. They were coming for him.

A two-stroke engine coughed and started below. He watched in panic. He counted five machines starting up the mountain. He looked back towards the men eating lunch. Some of them were watching him. He sat up and turned sideways on the saddle of his machine so he could more easily watch both groups. The one from below was coming up faster than he expected. He thought to start his machine and run for it. But he had no proof of anything. Maybe he was being paranoid. He stuffed a last bite of sandwich into his mouth and hastily put the lunch pail back into a saddlebag.

His mouth was dry. He was confused, tense, and cold. He felt as he had for one moment in the truck with Sandy, talking of the dream. He swallowed and swallowed again, cowered as prey by the predator's first roar.

Up they came, fanned out to avoid each other's tracks, squat, dark shapes on the spread of snow, engines working noisily against the slope. The air was clear, the light soft, without glare. It had an unusual grain to it. The scene was like a handprinted matte photograph in black and white.

As they came closer, he saw their masks—gleaming silver, black with eyes and mouth grotesquely outlined in red, yellow, and blue Day-Glo colors. The masks had sharp, pointed noses, like beaks, like the tin masks of medieval torturers, hangmen, and inquisitors. It was, he knew, not only that they were warmer behind them and more frightening, not only that they were anonymous from without, but that they were also anonymous from within.

This made him afraid, and so did their silence. No one was yelling. That was it, he realized suddenly. On they came in earnestness, purposefully. There was a ring in Coulter's ears, the elephant was kneeling on his chest, the blood roared, and the seconds registered one by one.

The new riders came up one after another, nosing their machines into a semicircle about the Sno-Cat, raising their masks as they came to rest and glancing over at him, meeting his eye with no sign of recognition, grim-faced, tight-mouthed. With Gould were walleyed Joey Leonard; Len Longren, the Swede; Bill Spangler, the carpenter; Epke, sticking his pipe into his mouth as he looked across; and Gary, from the Devil's Bedstead Guest

Ranch. Gary didn't belong with these others. Coulter didn't even know the man's last name. What was he doing here?

Coulter couldn't hear what they were saying. Not a word of it. They spoke in lowered voices and gathered close to one another. There was no laughter. Coulter began fiddling with the carburetor on his machine as though there was something wrong. In fact he was priming it, and wondering, as he did, if the engine was now too cold to start at first pull. The five new arrivals would restart instantly, and all of them could outrun him. They were riding 650s and 750s and his machine was probably a 300 or 350 and for sure the oldest and slowest thing in the yard that still worked at all. He'd have to bulldog the mountain to beat them to the road. Make a *banzai* run straight down. It was going to be something, he thought, and felt better. He was just two miles of downhill from being gone forever from this place. Gas was squirting from the carb . . .

"Hey, boy," he heard Lewis call. He didn't respond, but kept his eyes lowered, striving still to remain separated from what was going on. "You thinkin' 'bout goin' someplace? 'Cause we got some business with you."

Suddenly a desperado, Coulter turned on them. "Lewis," he called sharply and derisively, "you hear me good?"

Lewis looked at him slowly and long.

"You wanna know what your ol' lady told me, Lewis?"

"You wanna know what Gary here told us?" Lewis countered.

But Coulter, charging, too full of his own momentum to hear anything, blurted out, "She told me she never knew when you had it in her, you know that?" It was pathetic. Absurd as fancy boots and spangles on an aging cowboy. It was all he had left.

Lewis slowly pulled a handgun from his parka and checked the cylinder.

"Yeah. Come on," Coulter's yell was shrill, trying to put life into his insult. "Come on, Lewis. You wanna do it with your gun? A man that has a little prick, he usually carries a big gun. That's what I see, Lewis."

Lewis aimed and fired a round idly into the snow around

Coulter. The rest of them stiffened, and Coulter flinched despite himself.

"We got no hurry. Gary's told us about you," Lewis called slowly. "He found Vern up there at Wild Horse with three holes in him." He paused, watching. Coulter shook his head. His mouth came open and his breathing stopped. Lewis saw and pressed home.

"A man don't shoot hisself to death in the chest," he said. "A man don't shoot hisself at all that wants to live bad as Vern did." This set off a shaking of heads among the rest of them, gathered around, watching intently.

Coulter found himself staring at the handlebars of his machine, aware he should be defending himself but unable to overcome his astonishment that this indeed was happening to him.

"Three men you killed," Lewis shouted. "Three men, boy. An' no doubt about any of it." He paused. Coulter looked up at him and only shook his head.

"I don't know what you did for Burt Meyers to get him covering you. Maybe you gave him some of all that money the TV people give you for gettin' up there an' tellin' all that bullshit. I dunno. But whatever you did, it wasn't enough."

"I didn't give him anythin'," Coulter said at last.

"That's your story," Lewis called, "an' you understand, son, we don't set a whole lot by what you say. Right now," he paused, "we're gonna hunt some. Right now we're gonna give this ol' rabbit a ride and we're gonna consider it a little finger-fuckin' till we get to the real thing. You understand? 'Cause the rest of us, we don't feel so good 'bout shootin' a man down cold."

There was an explosion of laughter, too hard and too long.

"You get my drift?" Lewis asked. "We're givin' you a chance like you didn't give the others."

"*Let's go!*" someone yelled. An engine fired. Lewis stepped down from the Sno-Cat and mounted his own machine. As he did, the others began starting. In a moment the sound was cacophonous. Blue clouds of two-stroke smoke billowed around them.

Coulter sat still a moment longer. Starting would signal his agreement. And yet he must start. Like a child he realized this and set the choke and pulled the cord three times before it caught, behaving, to his own amazement, just as he would do on any occasion. The others were going downhill to a spot twenty or thirty yards below, where there was a slight terrace on the slope. Rose, who wore a silver mask and carried a box, led the way. Coulter saw him take the box off his saddle and set it on the snow in the center of the terrace and look around at the others, waiting for them to assemble.

Lewis and Gould were the last. Lewis was having trouble starting his machine and Gould waited beside him, watching him pull on the starter cord furiously, one hand on the throttle of his own machine, twisting it occasionally. When Lewis got started, he looked up and saw Coulter watching. He gunned his machine and shouted, signaling to Coulter with his arm. "Come on!" he yelled.

Coulter watched him impassively.

"We don't want you stayin' up here. You might get lost." Lewis looked at Gould and the two laughed.

There was a shout below. Coulter looked and saw Rose bent over the box, pulling up a slotted cover at one end. Suddenly there was a jackrabbit, large and gray, running for its life and the rest of them surging across the snow on their machines after it. Lewis and Gould plunged down the slope, eager to catch up, but Coulter lingered. He could maybe make it now, he thought. They might not notice him until it was too late. He looked down at his pickup parked by the quarry far away and slowly began side-hilling across the slope.

The jackrabbit ran in sweeping circles, leading the pack first up the slope and then down. They ran on either side of it, whooping and shrieking and heading it off and changing its direction. All of them behind their masks again and now with handguns taken from the big outside pockets of their parkas. Every so often one of them would get off a shot, but the rabbit was still too fresh and running too fast for them to get close to it. Slowly the pack drifted away from him and slowly Coulter dropped down, crossing their tracks. He was about to break for it altogether when the rabbit turned and headed back down and across the slope diagonally so that he saw it would cross his path about fifty yards below.

"Run straight down," he called to it. "They don't have the balls to follow you straight down." Suddenly he shouted, "Look!" then opened the throttle on his machine until it was hard against the stop, and pulled his goggles down.

He stood as he gathered speed, leaning forward, his feet on the runners, knees half-bent to absorb the shock, and he let out a whoop and aimed himself so that he would turn the jackrabbit downhill.

He was only feet from the rabbit when he cut across its path and it turned with him in a flurry of snow. He saw its ears laid back and how peculiarly intent it was upon its running. He saw its eyes, the strain and fear in them. He saw with extraordinary clarity, as if the rabbit were still a moment and held up in front of him. The roar of the pursuing engines was gone, the shrieks and yells, the shots. He heard only the brush of its white belly fur against the snow and the gasp of its winded lungs. And as he looked, it exploded. It wavered sideways, leaped up, turned to a fireball, and was gone. Then he heard the shot.

There were more shots now. He was past where the animal lay by a good bit and the others were almost on it. He glanced back. They were screaming and shooting at it still, blood loose and reason gone. Coulter's machine bounced badly, almost twisting itself loose from him. He heard more shooting and yelling, and then a clang and felt his machine twist strangely under him as though it were alive. They were shooting at him now. They were coming, as they had said they would.

He danced the machine over a dip and plunged into a gully. The thing flew. The gully was steeper than he had realized. He stood erect and leaned back, pulling on the bars to keep the front end up and stop the metal skis from plowing into the snow when he landed. He landed on the tail and rolled out of the jump forty yards below with a yell, holding one fist triumphantly aloft, shaking it.

All but two of his pursuers refused the gully and went around. The first of the two who attempted it rolled in front of the second as he landed. The machines collided and the second rider was thrown.

Now Coulter had the lead he needed. Pressed down flat, he raced across the last level ground and pulled up beside the pickup truck, throwing off his right glove and reaching for his keys while he was still moving.

He was in the cab as they started across the flat. He put the key into the ignition and turned it. Nothing happened. He swore and turned it again. Still nothing. He looked down to see if it was in gear. It wasn't. He looked at the ammeter to see if there was current. There wasn't. Someone was pulling across the nose of the truck. He heard their whoops and felt their wild presence all around. Frantic, he looked up. Three of them stood at the end of the hood in masks, peering in at him banging on the hood with their handguns. As he looked, more arrived. He had no idea who they were. They had guns drawn. They were crowding the doors.

"Come on out, asshole!" someone called.

Coulter heard Gould shout, "Fuck off, old man. Mind your own business an' you won't get hurt."

There was a chorus of "Yeah" and someone else yelled out, "Go home, you goddamn Hebe. This ain't nothin' to do with you."

It was Pops they were reviling.

From inside the cab, Coulter yelled out, "Go call the sheriff, Pops. Quick!"

"I 'ave," Pops yelled back. And then, "Lewis? Who is Red Lewis 'ere?" He looked around. "Lewis and Chuck Gould?"

The sound of their names awoke them: the agitation began subsiding as soon as the old man's voice rang out. Lewis pushed up his mask and Gould followed suit, revealing creased and sweating faces, the sight of which deflated the mob into an angry, begrudging silence. One or two of the others removed their masks, too.

"I sink ve must go to ze office," Pops said.

"I don't have to go no fuckin' place with you, old man," Lewis sneered.

Pops ignored him and opened the driver's door to Coulter's pickup and Coulter got out slowly, looking warily about.

"Come!" Pops commanded and they walked together through the angered crowd, which turned and followed on their heels.

When they were at the head, Coulter said, "They just tried to shoot me."

"Bullshit," roared Lewis, walking at Pops' shoulder. Others joined in the shouting—inanely, it seemed—and somebody spat on Coulter.

The sheriff arrived as quickly as if he had been expecting trouble. Through the office window they watched the car pull into the yard, roof light flashing, sliding on the snow. Burt Meyers was out before the car had stopped and striding towards the knot of men gathered about the water trough outside the office. Coulter saw him say something and then they were all of them yelling, waving their arms.

Beside him, Pops, Lewis, and Gould were watching the sheriff's arrival, too. Pops had allowed only the three of them into the office. "What a jerk," Lewis said to no one in particular. And then, turning to Gould, "Watch the sonovabitch try gettin' outta this one!"

Gould, still looking out of the window at the sheriff engaging the angry group around the trough, nodded towards Coulter and said, "An' this asshole here is gonna hang." Coulter glanced at him. "Yeah, you," Gould looked disgustedly at him. "You buddy-fucker."

As the anger rose in Coulter, the office door opened and the sheriff came in, his crumpled face red with anger. He looked straight at Lewis. Before the door was closed behind him, he demanded, "What'd you do?"

Lewis was taken aback. Coulter felt like cheering.

Then Lewis rebounded: "What the fucka you talkin' about, Meyers? You covered up a murder."

"You three are under arrest," the sheriff said.

"Hey, man," Gould was red-faced, too. "You're crazy. We got this guy"—he waved at Coulter—"for shootin' Vern Poulsen, an' you know it, man. You know it, 'cause Gary there saw you dumpin' the body out behind Wild Horse. Now, you don't go arrestin' us, man. It's *us* that's gonna make a citizen's arrest outta *you*."

"You're a horse's ass, Gould," the sheriff said slowly, looking down at the man from under his hat. "I been the law in Cope County since you was in grade school. I don't do nothin' without a reason, an' I do things in my own time. You don't know what went on up in them mountains, Gould. You an' all them other self-righteous assholes reckon you know it all, but you don't know shit." His voice had an almost sweet quality to it now. "You don't go tellin' me my business, or I'm gonna have you for assault with intent to kill. The both of you and all them other lunatics out there. You guys wanna be the law. There's no judge that's gonna be sympathetic to that. This ain't the Wild West no more. This is the United States of America." He looked at the three of them with contempt. Coulter was speechless with admiration. Since Mike died, it was, he thought, the first time he'd seen a *man* in operation.

"You tried to hide that body," Lewis said, hesitantly now.

"You get your ass to that car," the sheriff said. "The whole three of you. We'll work this thing out when we get down to the office." He cuffed the three of them together and led them out of the office, Coulter first. A step beyond the door he stopped: "Can you come with me, Pops?" he called back. Coulter stood on the step looking at the men waiting about the trough. Leonard looked at him with his good eye and said to the others, "Will you look at this little psycho? The only mass murderer that likes Jews, faggots, Injuns, an' po-lice."

Coulter sniffed. "Pops!" the sheriff called again. Pops appeared at the door, ushering Lewis and Gould out ahead of him, and they started across the yard towards the waiting car.

It seemed like a long way to the car. Coulter, between Lewis and the sheriff on the outside, said nothing. He was confused. He felt the elation of a man reprieved, on the one hand, and a peculiar anxiety on the other. Beside him, Lewis was grumbling: "You fucked up this time," he said to Meyers.

"Less you say, the better it'll be," Meyers said.

"For you."

"For you, boy. Believe me."

Coulter said nothing. He bent a little to look into the patrol car, met the bulging eyes of Goebbels, straightened up, and suddenly lurched forward. As he did, the others heard a shot. Coulter was falling, struck in the back, and Lewis, manacled to him, fought for balance. The sheriff went to save them both, and Goebbels started scrambling across to open the door. "Jesus, I been hit!" Coulter yelled. "I been hit!"

"Get the radio," the sheriff ordered, but Goebbels froze.

Dropping to one knee, the sheriff swiveled to look back at the crowd clustered about the trough. Coulter was on the ground, crying out. The men by the trough were still, their masks pulled down again. As the sheriff stared at them, there was no movement. Not a face was showing.

They delivered Coulter to Dr. Hardcastle's office on Main. The digital clock on the doctor's desk said three-thirty. Coulter had been shot through the trapezius of the left shoulder, close to the neck, by a .38 caliber bullet which had passed cleanly through the muscle without touching bone. Two or three inches higher, and it would have missed altogether; an inch or two to the right, and it would likely have killed or paralyzed him.

Dr. Hardcastle prepared to give him a tetanus shot. "God, Rick," he said, "how'd you do this?"

"I didn't," Coulter said. In the aftermath of the shock he felt warm and sleepy.

"I mean, what happened?"

Taking his cue from the sheriff, Coulter said unhesitatingly, "It was an accident. We were huntin' jackrabbits."

"How come there's a deputy waiting for you outside?"

Coulter stumbled on his lie: "Oh! Well, I guess these things have to be checked out," he said.

When he had dressed the wound, Dr. Hardcastle put Coulter's arm in a sling and led him into the recovery room. "Take a nap," he said. "I'll check on you."

When he had gone, Coulter lay back. He did feel weak now. He stared at the gray styrofoam tiles on the ceiling and wondered if he had really shot Vern. It was the first time he'd thought about it since they confronted him with it on the mountain and as the thought settled on him he felt sick and angry and incredulous that the issue had returned. He had believed it settled, believed his life back on line and now he was in chaos again. Now, this moment, they were talking it over in the sheriff's office, the jury sequestered before he had been permitted to testify, steamy and leaning at each other in earnestness, fingers jabbing the air, deciding his future, while he lay alone in a sickroom, not knowing what was happening, what would, or even half of what had. It was crazy, he thought, how you lost control of your life whenever it got important. Or maybe you never did have control and it just became obvious when things went wrong.

Marlene must have heard. She must. Gould would have told her. Unless maybe the sheriff was still holding him. Hope rose and as abruptly sank: anyone would tell her, the way people love passing bad news. And she would believe the worst. Maybe. Or maybe . . . he dismissed the thought but it returned. Or maybe she would know and go with him anyway.

When he woke his shoulder was aching sharply and outside it was dark. Feeling panic he went to the door in pants and socks. The surgery was empty, but the lights were on. He looked about the office, blinking, hearing the hum of the fluorescent tubes. The digital clock beside the name plate on Dr. Hardcastle's desk read six-thirty.

"Jesus!" He whistled and ran back to dress clumsily with one arm, and then emerged into the waiting room.

An out-of-town deputy sat reading a magazine, one boot resting on the other knee. He looked up. "I was gonna wake you," the deputy said. He wore square glasses with thick rims.

Coulter nodded, openmouthed. "I gotta piss," he said and closed the door.

He put his coat on over one arm, climbed out of the surgery window, dropped a few feet to the ground and rolled over on his back, cursing with pain. This and the bitter cold quickly alerted him. A car went by on Main. He crouched against the wall until it had passed, then ran to the rear of the house and down the service road that paralleled Main, to the parking lot behind the Two Ball Inn. He crossed the lot, twisting between parked cars and pickups, to the end of the high wall on the west side, beside which she would be waiting, in the shadow, if she had come. He realized how much he had banked on her being there when he saw the space empty. He paused, half-out from behind the wall, the suddenly felt doubt, the cold, the disappointment freezing him, undecided, half-safe in shadow, half-emerging. A siren shrieked and died, and a moment later a sheriff's car raced down Main in the direction he had come, roof light flashing red and orange.

He huddled back in the shadow, shoulder aching, pulling his coat around him, watching the roadway for her truck. The minutes dragged. A pickup went past and then another. He heard the drumming of knobby tires on pavement, saw their shapes glimmer briefly in the street light that hung above the intersection just beyond his sight around the far end of the wall. Another sheriff's car passed, no light flashing this time, cruising, headed west.

Standing up to stretch he looked over the vehicles in the lot behind him and saw a patrol car pulling in on the far side, its spotlight on. He ducked in panic into the cluster of cars, squatting between two of them, listening tensely to the idling sound of the patrol car's engine, and the popping crunch of its tires on the graveled snow-surface of the parking lot, hardly breathing, seeing the spotlight flicker tonguelike over the stand of cars that hid him.

The patrol car was close to pulling out of the lot on the far side when Coulter heard King McGarth's voice call, "Hey, Russ." And Sergeant Goebbels answer, "King." Coulter straightened up slowly until he could see the dark bulk of McGarth standing beside the stationary patrol car only a few feet away.

"What's up?" McGarth asked. It was Friday, Coulter remembered; McGarth worked the bar on Fridays.

"We're lookin' for Coulter," Goebbels said.

"That's what I heard."

"Lewis an' them near killed him up on the mountain."

"Someone told me they found Vern."

"S'what Gary says."

McGarth squatted beside the driver's window and the rest of the conversation was lost to Coulter over the rumble of the idling engine. He strained but it was useless. Finally McGarth stood and said, "Good luck," and moved off, and as the patrol car started forward, Goebbels waved casually to him. Coulter watched them go and then, alone again, returned to his station at the end of the wall to wait for the wife of the man he'd killed to come and save him.

When the absurdity of this penetrated even his desperation, he left, and, feeling dignified rather than abandoned, holding his left arm up with his right to keep the weight of it from pulling on his shoulder, he went down the frontage road behind Main, by the tarpaper shacks and garbage cans silhouetted in the dark, pausing every so often to listen, stepping carefully, tense and ready to duck, watching for the glow of headlights. Beyond Stein and Parker, he crossed the field by the path that came out on the road by his father's house, the path he had taken all his life. When still a few yards from the road he saw the shape of a car and in it the glowing tip of a cigarette. He sank down slowly, his arm hurting, and, on his belly, felt the hard granules of icy snow that lay in frozen clumps among the spiny grass. He hadn't thought they'd be watching this place. And he could make out no roof light on the car, and that puzzled and alarmed him more.

He let his face drop to the snow. He was hungry, he realized. His stomach ached; his arm ached; he felt dizzy and cold and weak. The logical thing to do was give it up. Go to the sheriff's office, be warm, fed, looked after. He pushed up and walked, crouching till he felt safe, back across the field. He must phone his father. Tell him to leave the keys in the Dodge, get out of town and think it over. He needed a phone. From the back shadow of the vacant lot opposite the Standard station, he watched the pay phone outside the garage. Inside, Buck Meyers sat reading a comic book. Len Longren's pickup went by, followed by the old green-and-white two-ton Epke drove. He'd bet they were headed for the bar. It'd be all over town by now, that he was out.

He went down beyond the last street lights, crossed Main in the dark, hurrying, and came back up on the far side. The Standard station was the first thing in town, the fo'c's'le. He made a broad

sweep to avoid the pool of light over the apron and came up to
hide among the litter of highway wrecks behind the forecourt, a
few feet from the pay phone. He could see Buck Meyers in the
office, or at least his boots up on the desk and hear the sound of
country music.

In a while, Longren's kid drove into the station in a '55 Bel Air
coupe with reversed rims. The kid stopped the car by the pumps
and Buck came out. The two of them stood talking. They were
there quite a while. Coulter couldn't catch what they were saying,
but as the Longren kid was getting ready to pull out and Buck
Meyers was walking back to the office, the kid called out to Buck,
"What time you through?"

Buck turned and continued walking backwards, shoulders
hunched against the cold, as he shouted back, "My pa's told me
to stay on late, keep this end of town lit up, an' keep Rick away
from usin' the pay phone."

"Yeah?" the Longren kid was puzzled. "Whatta they think he's
gonna do?"

Buck shrugged. "They think he's dangerous. I give a shit. I got
my piece."

"You an' me both," the kid said and drove off.

Coulter got into one of the cars and lay with his head back on
the seat, staring out through a shattered windshield. "You're all
assholes," he said aloud. "Every one of you." And then he thought
of Fred Meyers' place over the hardware store. There wasn't anyone there since Fred died. If he could get in there, maybe the
phone would still be hooked up, even. Maybe there was some
food.

He had to break the bottom pane in the window beside the
back door to get in. Inside he found the top of a carton and tore
it off and fitted it over the broken pane, trying to make it look like
something old and attended to. There was a connecting door to
the stockroom and hardware store, but it was double-locked, so he
went up the narrow stairs in the dark to the apartment, which already smelled damp and empty. He drew the blinds in the little
kitchen and turned on the gas stove for heat and light. In the liv-

ing room beside the kitchen he found a phone. It was still hooked up.

He smiled and shook his head and, sitting on the arm of the sofa, dialed his father's number. His father answered immediately.

"Pa," Coulter said. "It's me, Pa. I'm okay."

"That's th'only news interests me." His father sounded bone tired.

"They with you?"

"Uhuh."

"Sheriff?"

"The FBI from Boise."

"FBI?" As Coulter groped, his father said, "That's federal land up there."

"Copper Basin?"

"Challis. All that up there."

"Jesus!" Coulter said.

"You never did listen to me, son, else you wouldn't be in this mess now—but if you'll bear that in mind, you'll go down to the sheriff's office right now an' let him put you someplace safe." He paused, but Coulter, alone in the dark living room where the sheriff's dead brother had often sat, said nothing. He wanted his father to say more, wanted to hear the sound of his father's voice.

"Yeah?" he said eventually, to cue his father.

"This town's real jittery, son. They got all worked up, they been drinkin', they got their guns, an' they're half-crazy anyway this time of year, with winter bein' so long. You're best off to find your friends 'fore someone else finds you. You're like to get your head blowed off out there."

How many times his father had said that about women.

"Leave the keys in the Dodge, Pa," Coulter said softly. "I'll be 'round in a bit, after they're gone."

There was a long silence, and in it he heard his father sigh.

"I gotta think about this whole thing," Coulter said. "I gotta be free to think, Pa."

Still there was silence. "Pa?" Coulter said.

"Call me 'fore you make a move," his father said.

"I will. I gotta go, Pa."

"You mind yourself, son."

Coulter hung up. He sat in the darkness hearing his father's voice, thinking about his father—that he had been right; that if there was anyone left in his life who was straight with him, now that Arizo had gone, it was his father—and wishing he had been small enough and straight enough to have listened. He thought of calling Sue-Ellen, but after some argument dismissed the idea as going against himself, and went through the dark into the kitchen in search of food. There was none. He drank a glass of water and as he stood at the sink it came to him that he wanted to speak to Jason before he left. He returned to the living room and, peering closely at the phone, dialed his home. A man answered. "Who's this?" Coulter demanded.

"That you, Rick? This is George." It was Sue-Ellen's father.

"Jesus!" Coulter said. "Whatta you doin' there?"

"I come to be with Sue-Ellen." And then: "I think it'd be best if you stayed away from her, Rick."

"Let me speak to her."

"She doesn't want to speak to you right now, Rick," George spoke slowly.

"How come?"

"She's too upset."

Coulter considered this. "Lemme talk with Jason, then."

"Jason's asleep."

"Wake him up."

"I can't do that."

Coulter's shoulder was suddenly hurting him a lot. "Whatta you mean, George? I wanna speak with my kid."

"Rick." It was Burt Meyers. "It's Burt." The voice was very deep and gentle. After the immediate shock, Coulter found himself staring vacantly into the darkness about his feet.

"Where are you, Rick?"

"How come you lied to me about Vern?" Coulter sounded hurt, and his voice was tired and grave.

There was a pause. "I can't explain it to you on the phone like this."

"I wanted to be clean," Coulter said weakly. "An' now look how fucked up it all is."

"There's a bunch of people in the room here, Rick," the sheriff said. "Let me come to you an' we'll talk."

"I'm done with this town," Coulter said. "I'm through here. I'm gettin' out. You wanna do me a favor, Burt, then don't come lookin' for me."

"Tell me where you are, Rick."

Coulter turned and looked out of the window, down on the lights of his street through the glass. He knew roughly where his house was, and he stared at the spot.

"I wanna talk to Jason," Coulter said. There was muffled talk, and then the sheriff came back on. "Sue-Ellen says he'll get scared, Rick."

"I'm his father, Burt. He's my son. I speak to him when I want."

"Come on in, Rick. You can speak to him all you want then."

"Lemme speak to Sue-Ellen."

"She's too shook up."

Coulter hung up the phone, putting the receiver down slowly, hearing the sheriff's voice calling his name as he did.

He dialed Marlene's number, tension confused with pain and fatigue in his shoulders, thinking of what to say, half-hoping, half-expecting there would be no answer. When the fourth ring was interrupted, he started.

"Are you okay?" She sounded oddly calm.

"I got shot."

"I know. Are you okay?"

"Well, yeah. I'm okay." He meant to sound strong, and he was immediately annoyed with himself for being unable to.

"Where are you now?"

"I'm safe."

"Are you in town?"

"Yeah." That much wouldn't hurt.

"I'll come right over."

"They'll follow you."

"There's nobody here."

"Where's Vickissa?"

"At my sister's in Salt Lake till we get settled."

Coulter was boxed.

"Are you ready to go?" she persisted. "We can get out okay."

He took breath, hesitated. "You hear 'bout Vern?"

"Uh-huh." He sensed no disturbance and in the darkness he frowned. "Well I just thought . . ." He was digging himself in.

"I talked to Burt," she said coolly. "He told me it was an accident. An' I knew it anyway . . ." She trailed off.

Coulter stumbled, as a man who has leaned his shoulder on an open door. "Still, I've gotta have time to think," he said again.

"So I'll come in a little while." She didn't hesitate.

Coulter said he would call and give instructions when it was time to go. Then he stretched out on the sofa, boots hanging uncomfortably over the end, pain in his shoulder nagging, and still fighting to stay awake lest they come to search the house or dawn should catch him sleeping. He must be well clear by dawn, crossing the high desert, the shadow on the land softening, the roadside sage and the low hills beyond emerging as the pale light behind the mountains grew into the sky. The image calmed him. Everything would be different when the light came. If it did not catch him in this place.

When Marlene showed, he would explain it to her: his need to be alone. It would be a lot easier done face to face, he told himself, wishing he'd done it on the phone. He'd tell her and get her to ride over to his father's place. He was pleased with this idea. She could check and see if there was anyone waiting for him at his father's house. It would be a good way to do it, he thought.

Then he'd go to California. He sighed and settled lower. He'd see the places Mike had talked of: Bakersfield, Sacramento, Winters, Fresno and the town he couldn't remember the name of where they grew artichokes. They sounded like interesting places the way Mike had talked about them. There was work and the winters were easy. And what was left of Mike was there. This last was a feeling that strongly drew Coulter to these places. It was not anything that he articulated. The sound of these towns gave him a feeling of companionship. Just the sound of their names.

He would start again when he got there. Change his name and begin over. With what he knew now he felt confident he would do all right. He thought of names for himself, trying them out aloud. And as he did he drifted off.

When he woke, it was still dark. His neck was sore and stiff, he was cold and he felt lousy, but it was still dark. He sat up and dialed a number. The metallic female voice said, "The time is four-seventeen. Exactly." Coulter worked some saliva into his dry mouth and swallowed. It was time to go. He called Marlene. The phone woke her.

He finished his instructions to her, disconnected, and called his father. "I'll be over in fifteen," he said.

"Okay," the old man said. That was all. Coulter hung up the phone and felt such dizziness that he closed his eyes and held on to the arm of the sofa. When the feeling passed, he dragged a chair to the window that overlooked the empty lot and, obliquely, Main Street, and sat in darkness looking out. After fifteen minutes he saw her truck go by, heading east on Main, out of town. As soon as he was sure there was no one following her, he went down the stairs and let himself out. The air was freezing. He stood in the shadow on the back step listening. There was no sound. He went to the corner of the building and peered around. Seeing it was clear he moved quickly along the wall towards the street. He was halfway along when a sheriff's car came slowly down Main driving west. Coulter froze to the wall and turned his face away. It was difficult not watching but his face would be the one light patch. He held his breath waiting for a shout or the sound of a car approaching, or for headlights to pin him in place. When none came, he looked and the car had passed and he went on to the end, to the empty street, where the wind from the mountains played unobstructed, whistling about the light that swung on its moorings above the intersection. Satisfied, Coulter ran directly across, naked for an instant, a frantic figure, one arm working, one held across his chest.

Safely in the dark once more, he cut through between the dark houses to Parker Street. He had gone only a short way down when headlights appeared on the service road that paralleled Main.

Coulter stepped back behind the trunk of a poplar tree and watched. The lights turned up Parker a few feet from him and passed. It was Marlene. He watched the pickup truck as it went away from him down to the end of Parker, growing smaller. At the end it turned, as he had instructed, and came back.

Coulter felt satisfaction. There was no one following. As the truck came on, he went quickly down to the end tree by the stop and waited in the shadow. The vehicle came to a halt not six feet from him. He moved, slipping from his cover before it could start again, opening the passenger door and calling as he did so, "All right, hon. You made it!"

The interior light came on as the door opened, and he looked to see her face. Instead he saw Chuck Gould grinning at him over a gun.

"Marlene and Sue-Ellen asked me to give you this!" he yelled.

The gun exploded as Coulter swung the door closed. It was a .38 with a hollow-nose bullet that shattered when it hit the door. Fragments took Coulter's bad arm, slung across his body, and spun him around and dropped him with a cry. He lay a moment in a frenzy of shock and pain, even now struggling to stifle his cries and then he was up, in a running stagger that carried him crashing beyond the poplars as Gould peered from the cab of the pickup and belatedly fired after him, shouting into the night:

"There's one for Vern, too!"

Coulter ran into a bush against a yard fence behind the trees and turned to face the road again, cornered, breathing heavily in shock, assessing his situation, checking himself for damage, licking his lips, wiping the sweat off his face with the back of his good arm. The pickup started forward again, headlights swinging to the right, and he saw that Gould was turning it around to face the place he hid. In the moment's darkness that he had, Coulter broke through the trees and crossed Parker behind the turning pickup, heading in the opposite direction, cutting along the shoulder of the service road towards his father's house.

Twice as he ran, cars pulled onto the road towards him and twice, before the headlights straightened up and would have caught him, he dropped into the hollow beside the road and lay pressed against the snow till they had passed. Now he felt wetness on his left arm as the blood cooled against his skin and the sharp sting of the pellets lodged in his shoulder, arm, and belly. He stood, ducked out of the sling, and pulled off his coat, muttering at the pain as he slid it over the injured arm. Then he took the sling, opened it out, and used it to make a tourniquet about his left arm, high up at the shoulder, pulling it tight with his right hand and the other end clasped in his teeth. Gingerly he put on his coat once more and continued.

It was difficult to run working one arm only. Behind him he heard their shouts. Once he looked back and saw the lights about the intersection under the trees as they searched for him among houses on foot. The houses ended close to the end of the service road, and he cut a little deeper into the woods. Two cars met close by him as he did so and he stopped as side by side in the road they stopped. One was a sheriff's car. He saw the silhouette of the roof bar and the lights as he looked on, panting, standing among the willow poles, staring out with the full desperation of a fugitive.

One man shouted, "He won't go far. He's hit real bad." Coulter turned and stumbled on heedlessly, clumsily pushing at the thin willow branches that sprang back and whipped his face. He had only one thing in mind: the front seat of the pickup parked waiting beside his father's house. The image of it hung before him as he went. Achieve this place and he would be secure and comfortable, his pain would cease. He would have power, mobility. He would assume the dimension and swiftness of it. He would be free.

His feet found the path that led to his father's house and he struck out across the field. The world about him faltered, moving uncertainly, but he breathed more deeply now that he was on home ground. On this path in his youth he had gone to play. This had been the path to school, to the rituals of manhood and the mysteries of town, from childhood and the place he lived into the world. He had always regarded it as the road to freedom. And now the paradox escaped him, for he could see his father's house standing out as if there were no darkness, and before it his father, waiting. He could see them so close now—Arizo, Poulsen, even Coo-Coo—and all of them from the mountain suddenly were with him. He stood for them all. The enmity that had been between them was forgotten; only the experience remained. The sharing of it. He was the veteran returning. He drove each leg forward with a conscious effort.

So what if the women got together and turned against him? So what if they were all against him. Fuck 'em. Let 'em come. He'd show them all down here how they had been in the mountains. He'd show them. Give 'em a taste they weren't going to believe. Blow 'em off. Motherfuckin' lightweights. He was close now. Real close. So close that if he lay down here to sleep at last, his father would know where to find him in the morning. He would know. . . .

The old man didn't sleep that night. When they came back empty-handed from the river, neither he nor the sheriff said a word. The sheriff had come over from Sue-Ellen's place. Now he lay down on the sofa in his clothes and slept, while the old man sat at the kitchen table under the light and stared ahead, waiting.

Motionless he watched the stars over the field beyond the window fade and the light bloom. He stared, black-eyed, round-shouldered, as the snow on the front yard emerged, and beyond it the broken gate, and he thought about his life. When the first rooster crowed, he stood stiffly, put the coffee on to heat, and went outside into the cold, shrugging a little and drawing breath as he closed the door softly behind him. The sheriff opened his eyes and silently watched him go.

The garage doors were open. The old man walked around the end and looked in. The truck was gone, the empty shed smelled sharply of old oil and a dark oil-stain was revealed on the packed dirt floor by the truck's absence.

The sheriff sat up on the sofa and put his big, stockinged feet to the floor as the old man returned. The old man nodded and with his bowlegged gait crossed to the stove and turned off the burner under the coffee as the sheriff watched and swallowed several times.

"Has it gone?" the sheriff asked.

The old man turned about and questioned with raised eye-brows.

The sheriff shook his head wearily. "Shit," he said. "The truck."

"He must've took it in the night."

"He wasn't ever going to meet us by the river," the sheriff said. "That was to get me away from here. You think I didn't know that?" He reached for his boots.

The old man took down two mugs. "You want coffee?"

The sheriff growled and rubbed his face and yawned hugely, so that for a moment, his face seemed impossibly long. "Which way'd he go?"

The old cowboy, pouring out coffee with his back to the sheriff, shrugged. "Who knows?"

"Well whattya think?"

The old man silently handed the sheriff his coffee.

"He'll be headed west," said the sheriff, staring out of the window.

"You gonna go after him still?"

"Hell, I never went after the sonovabitch. But someone's gonna. He shoulda gone when I told him. Now . . . ?" The sheriff shrugged hopelessly.

Dan Coulter shook his head. "They'll never catch him now," he said with determination. "Not with all he's learned."

"They ain't gonna be lookin' for him in the mountains," the sheriff said wearily. "It's the FBI that's gonna be lookin'. He's gonna go to Los Angeles or Bakersfield or someplace, Dan. An' he doesn't know shit about cities."

There was a knock at the door. The two men looked at one another and then the old man went to answer.

"I 'ope I am not coming too early, but I sink you don't sleep zo good eizer." "I'm pleased to see you," the sheriff heard. The two friends came in side by side and the sheriff nodded to Pops Biva-letz.

"You 'ave 'im?" Pops looked from one to the other.

"He took off," Dan said and poured a third cup.

Pops grimaced and nodded and sat down at the table. The sheriff pulled out a chair and sat, with his coffee before him, gazing out of the window, seeing an old truck rolling across the high desert in the dawn, the tinny radio playing country music, Rick Coulter, wide-eyed and unshaven at the wheel. Somewhere right now that was happening. The sheriff thought of all the fugitives haunting America at that moment and sighed.

"You want anythin' in that coffee?" Dan Coulter asked Pops. Pops shook his head. The old man closed the refrigerator door and, carrying his coffee, came to join them at the table, and in silence the three men watched the new day come across the snow.